21世纪高等学校
英语课程改革规划教材

U0133014

Xintansuo Daxue Yingyu Zonghe Jiaocheng 1&2 Jiaoshi Yongshu　（教师用书）

新探索 大学英语综合教程
New Exploration College English

1&2

主　编	刘　兵	主　审	蔡基刚
副主编	段荣娟		
编　者	郭梅蕊	李慧艳	颜　斌

高等教育出版社·北京
HIGHER EDUCATION PRESS　BEIJING

图书在版编目（CIP）数据

新探索大学英语综合教程.1、2/刘兵主编.—北京：高等教育出
版社，2011.8

教师用书

ISBN 978-7-04-033724-2

Ⅰ.①新… Ⅱ.①刘… Ⅲ.①英语-高等学校-教学参考资料

Ⅳ.① H31

中国版本图书馆 CIP 数据核字（2011）第 163406 号

策划编辑 周继铭 周传红　　责任编辑 周继铭　　封面设计 顾凌芝　　责任印制 朱学忠

出版发行	高等教育出版社	咨询电话	400 - 810 - 0598
社　　址	北京市西城区德外大街 4 号	网　　址	http://www.hep.edu.cn
邮政编码	100120		http://www.hep.com.cn
印　　刷	河北鹏盛贤印刷有限公司	网上订购	http://www.landraco.com
开　　本	787×1092　1/16		http://www.landraco.com.cn
印　　张	24.25	版　　次	2011 年 8 月第 1 版
字　　数	610 千字	印　　次	2011 年 8 月第 1 次印刷
购书热线	010-58581118	定　　价	48.00 元

本书如有缺页、倒页、脱页等质量问题，请到所购图书销售部门联系调换

版权所有　侵权必究

物 料 号　33724-00

前　言

　　教育部颁布的《大学英语课程要求》中指出,大学英语的教学目标是培养学生英语综合应用能力,使大学生在今后的工作和社会交往中能够用英语有效地进行信息交流,同时增强其自主学习能力,提高综合文化素养,以适应我国经济发展和国际交流的需要。当今经济全球化深入发展,科技进步日新月异,人才竞争日趋激烈。作为国家"高等学校教学质量与教学改革工程"重要内容之一,大力提高大学英语教学质量,对于培养新一代高素质创新性人才,加快我国的现代化建设进程有着重要的意义。

　　《新探索大学英语综合教程》(1~4)正是在这一时代背景下,为提高大学英语教学质量,培养学生良好的英语综合能力而编写的。本教程的编写吸收借鉴了近年来国内外英语教学理论与实践的研究成果,在选材和编写过程中强调通过英语学习了解西方的社会风俗及风土人情,以提高学生的跨文化交际能力和英语实际应用能力。

　　《新探索大学英语综合教程》(1~4)每册分10个单元。每一个单元以一个主题为中心,每个主题中安排了不同的场景对话,使学生充分领悟每个话题中的交际策略,另外还设计了学生感兴趣的话题进行课后讨论,以有效地培养学生的英语口语交际能力。阅读部分设计了精读和泛读两部分,强调阅读技能的培养。阅读内容的选择注重西方文化的知识性、趣味性和实用性。文章中的选词提高了大纲词汇的覆盖率和常用词汇的重现率。课后筛选出每课的重点词汇和词组,加以反复操练。每个单元课文中所涉及到的主要语法以练习的形式呈现,内容精练,例句生动,并附有精心编写的语法练习,使学生能够将所学内容加以巩固和提高。

　　本书为教师提供了与教材课文有关的背景知识、例句解释、补充材料以及课文参考译文和课后练习答案。

编　者

2011 年 8 月

Contents

新探索大学英语综合教程1(教师用书)

新探索大学英语综合教程2（教师用书）

New Exploration College English

新探索大学英语综合教程1

（教师用书）

Unit 1

Manners

Part I Teaching Objectives

* Listening & Speaking

Help the students to be familiar with the topic — *how to express yourself politely on some social occasions* and memorize useful expressions.

* Words & Expressions

Study some new words and expressions, such as *particular*, *strive*, *positive*, *genuine*, *overjoyed*, *stick*, *essential*, *interrupt*, *come across*, *take over*, *every once in a while*, *speak highly of*, *out of style*, *in the long run* and so on.

* Grammar

Learn to use the structure of *so that*.

* Writing

Understand and write *a letter of thanks*.

Part II Listening——Manners

New Words

admit /ədˈmɪt/ *v.* 容许,承认,接纳

    e. g.   He never admits that he is wrong.
                他从不承认自己错了。

available /əˈveɪləbl/ *adj.* 有空的,可用到的,可利用的

    e. g.   The lawyer is not available now.   律师现在没空。
               This book is not available here.   这里没有这本书。

communication /kəˌmjuːnɪˈkeɪʃən/ *n.* 交流,信息,通讯

    e. g.   All communication with the East has been stopped by the earthquake.

与东部的一切交通均因地震而断绝。

compliment /'kɒmplɪmənt/ *n.* 称赞,恭维,问候

 e. g. She received many compliments on the design of her new dress.
    她那件新裙子的设计,受到许多人称赞。

congratulation /kən'grætjʊ'leɪʃən/ *n.* 祝贺,贺辞

 e. g. It's your birthday today. Congratulations!
    今天是你的生日。恭喜!

delicious /dɪ'lɪʃəs/ *adj.* 美味的

 e. g. The soup is delicious. 汤的味道美极了。

logical /'lɒdʒɪkəl/ *adj.* 合乎逻辑的,合理的

 e. g. Rain was a logical expectation, given the time of year.
    按时节来看,这时下雨是必然的。

marvelous /'mɑːvələs/ *adj.* 惊异的,不可思议的,非凡的

 e. g. Henry has a marvelous collection of books.
    亨利的藏书令人称奇。

saltshaker /'sɔːlt,ʃeɪkə/ *n.* (调味品)盐瓶

 e. g. Pass me the saltshaker, please.
    请递给我盐瓶。

separate /'sepərɪt/ *v.* 分开,隔离,分散

 e. g. Separate this one from the others.
    不要把这一个与其它的混放在一起。
    A fence separated the cows from the pigs.
    围栏把奶牛和猪分开了。

sneeze /sniːz/ *v.* 打喷嚏

 e. g. When you have a cold, you sneeze a lot.
    感冒时会打很多喷嚏。

tolerant /'tɒlərənt/ *adj.* 容忍的,宽恕的,有耐药力的

 e. g. You should be tolerant of others!
    你应该对人宽容点!

Phrases and Expressions

dining room 餐厅

 e. g. Dinner is ready! Come to the dining room, children.
    饭好了! 孩子们,来餐厅吃饭!

have trouble in doing sth. 在……有困难

 e. g. College students usually have trouble in dealing with realities.
    大学生通常在如何应付现实生活上都存在困难。

help yourself to... (进餐时)请自己取用……

e. g.   Help yourself to some fish.   请自己动手吃点儿鱼吧。

medical history   病历, 病史

e. g.   Don't talk about your medical history when somebody asks you "*How are you*".
当有人问你"你好吗?",不要向别人讲述你的病史。

Dialogue One

Listen to the CD and mark T for True or F for False according to the dialogue.

1. F 2. F 3. T 4. F 5. T

Script

Mr. Huang: Hello, Mr. Smith.

Mr. Smith: Hello, Mr. Huang. Come in.

Mr. Huang: What a lovely house!

Mr. Smith: I'm glad you like it.

Mr. Huang: Where is Mrs. Smith?

Mr. Smith: Oh, she's in the kitchen. She'll be here in a minute. Just go into the dining room. How about a drink before dinner?

Mr. Huang: Okay.

Mrs. Smith: Here we are. Dinner is ready.

Mr. Huang: Thank you very much, Mrs. Smith. Everything looks wonderful and it smells delicious, too.

Mrs. Smith: Help yourself to the salad!

Mr. Huang: Thanks. . . It tastes good!

Mr. Smith: Would you like some vegetables?

Mr. Huang: No, thanks. I have had enough. It has been a marvelous evening. It was very kind of you to invite me.

Mr. Smith: We're so glad to see you. You must come again.

Mr. Huang: Good night and thanks again.

Mrs. Smith: Good night and drive carefully.

Dialogue Two

Listen to the CD and answer the following questions with the information you hear.

1. Who got married a few days ago according to the dialogue?
   Mary got married a few days ago.

2. Where did Tom go several days ago?
   Tom went to Hebei Province several days ago.

3. What did Tom bring as a gift for Mary?
   Tom brought a box of pears for Mary.

4. Was Mary happy to receive Tom's gift?

No, she wasn't.

5. What does it mean sending pears to a newly-wed couple?

Sending pears to a newly-wed couple means that you want the newly-wed couple to separate.

Script

Tom: Hello, Mary.

Mary: Hello, Tom.

Tom: Henry told me that you got married a few days ago. Congratulations!

Mary: Thank you. Where have you been? I called you, but you were not available.

Tom: I'm sorry that I was not able to attend your wedding. I am just back from Hebei Province. I brought a box of pears for you. They taste good.

Mary: Pears? Why did you bring me pears?

Tom: I remembered that you like pears.

Mary: Oh, no. What do you mean by sending me pears on my wedding day? That's terrible!

Tom: Why? What's wrong with that? Don't you like them?

Mary: Yes, I like them, but do you know what sending pears to a newly-wed couple means?

Tom: I don't know.

Mary: It means that you want the newly-wed couple to separate.

Tom: I'm terribly sorry. I didn't know it.

Mary: It's Okay.

Tom: May you live happily ever after!

Mary: Thank you!

Spot Dictation

1. who have some trouble understanding English
2. because of misunderstanding what was said
3. admit it and politely ask the person to repeat or explain
4. A smile and a nod are not enough
5. the correct response is "*God bless you*"

Part III Speaking——*Table Manners*

Useful Expressions About Manners

We would be pleased if you could attend our party.

Would you do the pleasure of attending my birthday party?

Could we have the honor of your presence at the meeting?

That's very kind of you.

That would give me great pleasure.

With pleasure.

We'd be glad to have lunch with you.

Thank you. I'd love to.

Sounds great.

No, thanks.

I'm sorry, I can't.

Oh, what a pity! I'm going to have an exam tomorrow.

I'm afraid I can't. But thank you all the same.

Merry Christmas!

Please send my best wishes for the New Year to Mr. Smith.

Pair Work

Sample

Miss Lee: Mr. Green, I've stayed here for a couple of days. But I must leave now.

Mr. Green: Please feel free to stay as long as you like.

Miss Lee: Thank you. You have been so nice to me.

Mr. Green: I'm glad you are enjoying it.

Miss Lee: Thanks again for your invitation.

Mr. Green: It's my pleasure. Is there anything else I can do for you?

Miss Lee: No, thanks. You've done a lot for me. I really appreciate everything.

Mr. Green: You're always welcome!

Role-play

Sample

Sonia Wang: I heard that you are going to marry next week. I congratulate you with all my heart.

Tom Black: Thank you. Getting married is an important step, and I'm very excited about it.

Sonia Wang: It seems that you have something to tell me.

Tom Black: The wedding will be on Saturday. I'd be very glad if you could come.

Sonia Wang: Thank you very much, but I'm afraid I'm booked up for Saturday.

Tom Black: It would mean so much to me if you could come.

Sonia Wang: All right. I will change my plans. It would be an honor for me to attend.

Tom Black: Thank you, you're welcome.

Part IV Reading

Text A   **Background**

To leave a good impression, you must have good manners. It is difficult to deal with those having no manners or concern for others. A huge societal issue is a general lack of respect for what has been taught in history regarding human concern and compassion towards acquaintances.

"Good Manners" are an increasingly archaic school of thought that displays respect, care and consideration. Everyone has a basic right to help another and feel positive about themselves and others around them. In our age of self-satisfaction, cell phone technology and instant internet gratification, it is often hypothesized that we care more for our equipment than those they are made for.

If you don't have an etiquette resource, keep reading for more ideas. Consider picking up one of many etiquette books. Some colleges offer weekend etiquette lessons, usually open to all ages. This is a great idea for anyone looking to make a better impression.

Also learn from real-world examples — the positive effects of those displaying good manners and how people react to and around them. It's common sense that people prefer a reasonable amount of respect. If you nurture plants, animals or other humans, not only will they grow and bloom—but you will as well. Outside of material goods—the basic things we all really own are ourselves and our actions.

Useful Tips About Good Manners:

1. "Choose your words wisely" and don't rush to comment on things you don't know much about. Being a good listener is better than speaking. You don't need to have an opinion on everything. Don't start sentences with awkward "ums" and "ers" in between. Practise speaking to a mirror, it works! It increases confidence in speaking and it sounds much clearer; you may find you'll be using fewer "ums" and "ers" next time!

2. "Don't speak loudly". You will quickly lose respect if you do, as this is seen as overbearing and rude. It can also make others angry and upset before you even establish a relationship with them. They will think of you as a "big mouth"! Practise turning your volume down.

3. "Speak with respect" to and of others by avoiding negative or insulting remarks. Avoid expressions or theoretical examples implying disrespect, degradation or that invite people to imagine offensive scenarios, like "What's up your butt?" or "How would you feel if someone...." followed by a description of violent or degrading acts. You may not intend this as offensive, but it is. General rule: if you don't want someone to talk about you in that way, then don't speak in this way to others.

4. "Hold open a door" for anyone, male or female, following you closely. This is a good manner and will never change.

5. "Try showing" you are interested in others by asking questions about them. Don't steal their spotlight by just talking about yourself. Don't come off as selfish. Continually talking of yourself is boring and others will avoid you.

6. "Don't phone before 7:00 am and after 9:00 pm" (unless in an emergency or an important overseas call). Also avoid calling people during mealtimes. People don't expect you to drop in and visit at these times, unless it is arranged. This includes texting, though you would obviously not text for emergencies.

7. "Check your voice!" It carries much more than just a tone, and reflects your character and personality even on the phone! Remember: your listener cannot see you, so your phone-voice becomes your facial expressions, gestures, personality and character. Always check your voice when speaking; speak in a pleasant tone and very clearly. Smile through your voice! What they hear will make a positive or negative impression.

8. "Make meaningful introductions." If someone tells you their name, either by shaking your hand and saying their name or by saying "Hi! I'm John!" etc., do not just say "Okay!" or "Hi!". State your name, too! This may seem obvious, but people overlook this and come across as not wanting to know the other people.

9. "Show gratitude and be thankful". If someone gives you a gift, goes out of their way for you or provides an appreciated service, write a thank-you note. "Not an email" unless you are at work, and you should still write a thank-you note for a gift. Saying "thank you" is just not enough. Always keep thank-you cards in your office and at home. Be thankful for what others do or have done for you.

10. "Treat and speak to others as you would like to be spoken to and be treated." Having manners is like the Golden Rule of social behavior.

New Words

chew /tʃuː/ *v.* 咀嚼(食物等),认真考虑
    e.g. You must chew your food well before you swallow it.
              食物要细嚼慢咽。

contagious /kən'teɪdʒəs/ *adj.* 传染性的,会感染的
    e.g. Her laughter's contagious!   她的笑声富有感染力!

domineering /ˌdɒmɪ'nɪərɪŋ/ *adj.* 专横的,盛气凌人的
    e.g. Don't be too domineering in your daily life!
              日常生活中别太专横!

essential /ɪ'senʃəl/ *n.* 要素,要点,必需品
    e.g. The book deals with the essentials of English grammar.
              这本书论述英语语法的要点。

genuine /ˈdʒenjuɪn/ *adj.* 真实的，真正的，诚恳的

    e. g.   This ring is genuine gold.   这枚戒指是真金的。

interrupt /ˌɪntəˈrʌpt/ *v.* 打断(正在说话或行动的人)，中断，妨碍，插嘴

    e. g.   It is not polite to interrupt when someone is talking.

            在别人讲话时插嘴是不礼貌的。

            Don't interrupt me when I am busy.

            我正忙的时候请不要来打扰我。

overbearing /ˌəʊvəˈbeərɪŋ/ *adj.* 傲慢的，专横的

    e. g.   Don't speak in an overbearing manner!

            讲话时不要太傲慢!

overjoyed /ˌəʊvəˈdʒɔɪd/ *adj.* 喜出往外的，极高兴的

    e. g.   The old man was overjoyed at/with the good news.

            老人听到喜讯非常高兴。

particular /pəˈtɪkjʊlə/ *adj.* 特殊的，特别的，独特的

    e. g.   She has a particular preference for Chinese art.

            她对中国艺术有特别的爱好。

            He is very particular about his food.

            他吃东西很讲究/挑剔。

positive /ˈpɒzətɪv/ *adj.* 有把握的，自信的，肯定的，积极的

    e. g.   I am positive that I gave you his address.

            我肯定把他的地址给你了。

stick /stɪk/ *v.* 放置，塞，卡住，陷在……里

    e. g.   I stuck a needle into the cloth.

            我把一根针扎进布里。

strive /straɪv/ *v.* 努力，奋斗，力争

    e. g.   Strive hard to make greater progress, my children!

            孩子们努力，争取更大的进步!

swallow /ˈswɒləʊ/ *v.* 吞下，咽下

    e. g.   She swallowed some milk.   她咽下几口牛奶。

Phrases and Expressions

come across   偶然遇到或找到

    e. g.   I came across my old college classmate in town today.

            今天我在镇上遇到我大学的老同学。

every once in a while   有时，偶尔

    e. g.   He came to the city to buy some food every once in a while.

            偶尔，他会去市里买些食物。

in the long run   从长远看，从最终结果来看

e. g. Learning a foreign language well will do you good in the long run.
从长远来看,学好一门外语将对你有益。

out of style 过时的,不时髦的

e. g. Manners will never be out of style. 礼貌将永不过时。

speak highly of 称赞,高度评价

e. g. His boss spoke highly of him. 老板对他评价非常高。

take over 接管,接替

e. g. He took over the farm from his father last year.
去年,他从父亲手里接管了农场。

参 考 译 文

礼 貌

1 礼貌能使我们的举止行为展示出对彼此的尊重。如果你不确定在某特定情况下该如何做,请记住,礼貌就是尽力让你周围的人感到舒适,根据这个想法采取行动。

2 微笑并自信地开始你的一天。要尊重你遇到的每一个人,这样,他们的一天可能就是美好的一天,也许他们会将此传递给别人。微笑会感染的。到达办公室后,问候你的同事。当你离开时,请说再见。

3 其他人发言时,即使你觉得你能讲得更好,也不要盛气凌人,咄咄逼人地接过话题,尽量让他们说完。

4 如果你正在打电话,一定要时不时地停下来,以便让对方有时间发言——并对他们与你所分享的事表现出真的很感兴趣。这表明你体谅他人。

5 向父母表现出尊重吧。他们会非常高兴,子女在尊重地与自己说话,因为尊重他们说明你有礼貌。

6 如果你是学生,请确保你表现良好,这样老师会高度评价你,比如,课堂上认真听讲并按时完成作业。尊敬老师,把老师看作是你的朋友而不是你的敌人,他们的目的是教育和培养你,让你能有一个好前途。

7 别让你的手机铃声干扰别人。在电影院里,务必关机,开车时,不要把手机的耳机塞进耳朵(这种行为在一些地方是非法的)。它不仅危险,而且会让人认为你是不礼貌的,特别是当你超车时等。

8 表现礼貌的最简单的方法之一就是保持安静,只在有重要的事情时才发言,这样你的话就更显重要。

9 经常使用最基本的礼貌用语,如"女士"、"先生"、"小姐"、"对不起"、"谢谢"、"请"、"欢迎您"和"很荣幸"等。

10 吃东西时不要讲话。不要讲到一半时停下来去吃、咀嚼、吞咽,然后再继续讲话。懂礼貌的同伴当然不会打断你,但他们也不该等着你,看着你吃。吃东西还是说话,两者不可同时进行。

11 礼貌将永不过时,所以表现出你的礼貌吧。从长远来看,礼貌会助你成功。

Exercises

I. Reading Comprehension
Section A
1. B   2. D   3. C   4. D   5. A

Section B
1. Good manners will help us succeed in the long run.

2. If someone else is speaking, we should try to let them finish what they are saying.

3. We should not talk with our mouth full.

4. If we are talking to someone on the phone, we should pause every once in a while in order to allow the other person time to speak, and take a genuine interest in what they have to share with us in order to show that we care.

5. Be sure to turn it off in movie theaters, and don't drive with a cell phone stuck to your ear (this is illegal in some places anyway).

Section C
1. Yes, of course. Nowadays, manners are very important. If you are polite, you are more likely to be popular with others and you are more likely to succeed.

2. Usually I pay attention to manners, but when I am busy I may pay no attention to manners. I think proficiency is more important than manners.

3. Nowadays, young people are not very polite. They pay no attention to manners. Parents and teachers should teach them more about manners. Otherwise, they will not succeed at all. After all, good manners will never go out of style.

II. Vocabulary and Structure
Section A
1. C   2. A   3. D   4. B   5. C   6. A   7. C   8. B   9. D   10. A

Section B
1. Good <u>manners</u> can help us all act with respect toward one another.
礼貌能使我们的举止行为展示出对彼此的尊重。

2. If you are <u>unsure</u> what to do in a particular situation, remember that manners never go out of style.
如果你不确定在某特定情况下该如何做,请记住,礼貌将永不过时。

3. Always use the <u>essentials</u>—ma'am, sir, miss, pardon, thank you, please, you're welcome, my pleasure, etc.

使用最基本的礼貌用语——女士、先生、小姐、对不起、谢谢、请、欢迎您及很荣幸等。

4. One of the <u>easiest</u> ways to show good manners is to be silent and only talk when you have something important to say.

表现礼貌的最简单方法之一就是保持安静,只在有重要的事情时才发言。

5. Avoid <u>annoying</u> others with your cell phone.

别让你的手机干扰别人。

6. Be sure to turn it off in movie theaters, and don't drive with a cell phone <u>stuck</u> to your ear.

在电影院里务必关机,开车时不要把手机的耳机塞进耳朵。

7. It is not only <u>dangerous</u>, but will cause others to think that you are rude.

它不仅危险,而且会让人认为你不礼貌。

8. Remember that manners strive <u>to make</u> everyone around you feel comfortable.

请记住,礼貌就是尽力使你周围的人感到舒适。

III. Word Building

1. This painting has brought <u>unexpected</u> results to the decoration of the room.

这幅画给房间的装修带来了意想不到的效果。

2. It is <u>incorrect</u> to say there is no life in the desert.

沙漠里没有生命的说法是不正确的。

3. The company accused the American airplane makers of <u>unfair</u> competition.

该公司指控美国飞机制造商不公平竞争。

4. After 1833, slave trade was <u>illegal</u> in the U. S.

1833 年后,在美国买卖奴隶是非法的。

5. Using other people for one's own profit is <u>immoral</u>.

利用别人来谋取私利是不道德的。

6. The way you talked to her was most <u>improper</u> considering you didn't know her.

既然你不了解她,那你和她谈话的方式就很不合适。

7. He said, "It's an <u>illogical</u> conclusion. "

他说道:"这是个不符合逻辑的结论。"

8. I'd rather take the bus. The trains here are <u>irregular</u> and take too long.

我宁愿做公共汽车,这里的火车发车时间不是很准点而且坐车时间太长。

IV. Grammar Focus

1. I'll tell you all about it so that you can judge for yourself.

2. That candidate gave speeches of his political viewpoints so that more people would vote for him.

3. Mary did a lot of homework so that her mother might forgive her.

4. Mr. Green made full preparation for the party so that the party would go on smoothly.

5. The mother closed all the windows and doors so that the baby would not catch cold.

V. Translation

1. Good manners will never go out of style, so practice having good manners.

   礼貌将永不过时，所以表现出你的礼貌吧。

2. Be sure to turn your cell phone off in movie theaters, and don't drive with it stuck to your ear.

   在电影院里务必关机，开车时不要把耳机塞进耳朵。

3. If you are in school, make sure that you behave in good manners so that your teacher can speak highly of you.

   如果你是学生，请确保你表现良好，这样老师会高度评价你。

4. They'll be overjoyed that their children are speaking to them with respect, for respect shows that you have good manners.

   他们会非常高兴子女尊重地与自己谈话，因为尊重他们说明你有礼貌。

5. If someone else is speaking, try hard not to be domineering or overbearing by taking over the story or subject matter at hand.

   当其他人发言时，不要盛气凌人，咄咄逼人地接过话题。

VI. Writing

Sample

A   Letter of Thanks

Mar. 10th, 2010

Dear Mr. Smith,

　　We've just returned home after our wonderful stay in England and we would like to thank you again for your kind hospitality.

　　We spent several marvelous days with you and it gave us a real glimpse of life in England. We do hope you will be able to come and see us if you can come to China.

　　Warmest regards to your family.

Yours sincerely,

Wei Zemin

Notes

　　A thank-you note should be written promptly after you have received a gift or been invited to a party, a dinner or one's home. People are always delighted to know you value their hospitality and good will. The note does not need to be long, but the language must be sincere and naturally intimate.

　　At the end of the note you'd better sign your name. Whether your handwriting is beautiful or not, sign it personally. If the note is typewritten, type your name in parentheses. The signed name could be the first name or pet name, while the typed one is usually in full. For example,

Yours faithfully,

Qinghua

（Guo Qinghua）

Text B   Background

Manners in every country are different. What is polite in China may not be polite in the United States. These basic rules will help you enjoy western food with your American friends.

Always put the napkin on your lap first. Before you leave the table, fold your napkin and put it beside your plate.

As the meal is served, use the silverware farthest from the plate first. When eating something in a bowl, do not leave the spoon in the bowl. Put it on the plate beneath the bowl. Soup, as well as all American food is eaten quietly. Do not slurp the soup. The soup spoon is used by moving the spoon away from you. Do not overfill the spoon. The bowl may be tipped slightly away from you to allow the last bit of soup to be collected on the spoon. Do not pick the bowl up to hold it closer to your mouth. When you have finished your meal, place your knife and fork side by side on the plate. This signals that you have finished eating.

Wait until everyone has been served to begin eating. Everyone begins to eat at the same time. The host or hostess may invite you to start eating before everyone is served. Some food may be cold if you are required to wait until everyone is served. If invited to begin before others are served, wait until three or four people have been served before starting to eat.

During the meal, the host or hostess will offer you a second helping of food. Sometimes they will ask you to help yourself. When they offer you food, give a direct answer. If you refuse the first time, they might not ask you again.

At the table, ask others to pass you dishes that are out of your reach. Good phrases to know are: "Please pass the..." or "Could you hand me the..., please?" If asked to pass the salt to someone, you should pass both the salt and pepper which are placed on the table together. Hand the salt and pepper to the person seated next to you. Do not reach over the person next to you to pass anything to others.

Sit up straight at the table. Bring the food up to your mouth. Do not lean down to your plate.

Cut large pieces of meat, potatoes and vegetables into bite-size pieces. Eat one piece at a time.

When eating spaghetti, wind the noodles up on your fork. You may use your spoon to assist in winding. The spaghetti on your fork should be eaten in one bite. It is very impolite to eat half of your noodles and allow the other half to fall back onto your plate.

Some food may be eaten with your fingers. If you are not sure if it is proper to eat something by picking it up with your fingers, watch what others do before doing so by yourself. Examples of food which can be eaten with your fingers include: bacon which has been cooked until it is very crisp; bread should be broken rather than cut with a knife; cookies; sandwiches; and small fruits and berries on the stem. Most fast food are intended to be eaten with fingers.

Do not lean on your arm or elbow while eating. You may rest your hand and wrist on the edge of the table.

In America, people do not use toothpicks at the table.

The best way to learn good manners is to watch others. Observe the way your western friends eat. This is the best way to avoid making mistakes when you are unsure of what to do.

New Words

adequate /ˈædɪkwɪt/　*adj.* 适当的,足够的

　　e. g.　I hope you will prove adequate to the job.
　　　　　我希望你能胜任这工作。
　　　　　The supply is not adequate to the demand.　供不应求。

admit /ədˈmɪt/　*v.* 承认,容许,接纳

　　e. g.　I admit that she is right.　我承认她是对的。

appropriate /əˈprəuprɪət/　*adj.* 适当的

　　e. g.　His casual clothes were not appropriate for such a formal occasion.
　　　　　他的便装与这样正式的场合不合适。

approximately /əˈprɒksɪmɪtlɪ/　*adv.* 大约,近似地

　　e. g.　His income is ten thousand dollars a year approximately.
　　　　　他的年收入近万美元。

argument /ˈɑːgjumənt/　*n.* 争论,辩论

　　e. g.　The argument among the two parties was blown up by the press.
　　　　　双方的争论被新闻界夸大了。

attractive /əˈtræktɪv/　*adj.* 吸引人的,有魅力的

　　e. g.　She is an attractive girl.　她是个很有魅力的女孩。

behavior /bɪˈheɪvjə/　*n.* 举止,行为

　　e. g.　Everyone praises the children's good behavior.
　　　　　每个人都赞扬孩子们的良好举止。

characteristic /ˌkærɪktəˈrɪstɪk/　*n.* 特性,特征

　　e. g.　What are the characteristics that distinguish the Chinese from the Japanese?
　　　　　中国人区别于日本人的特征是什么?

collar /ˈkɒlə/　*n.* 领口,衣领

　　e. g.　The collar of his shirt was dirty.　他的衬衣领子脏了。

companion /kəmˈpænjən/　*n.* 同伴,同事

　　e. g.　He was my only Chinese companion during my stay in Australia.
　　　　　他是我在澳大利亚期间的唯一的中国伙伴。

compliment /ˈkɒmplɪmənt/　*vt.* 称赞,褒扬,恭维

　　e. g.　David complimented Mary on her new job.
　　　　　大卫祝贺玛丽找到新工作。

cue /kjuː/ *n.* 暗示，提示

    e.g. He missed my cue last time. 上次他没觉察出我的暗示。

customary /ˈkʌstəməri/ *adj.* 习惯的，惯例的

    e.g. It is customary with me to do so. 这样做是我的习惯。

dietary /ˈdaɪətəri/ *adj.* 饮食的，规定食物的

    e.g. We don't know about the dietary restrictions of Americans.
          我们不知道美国人的饮食禁忌。

ethnic /ˈeθnɪk/ *adj.* 种族的，人种的，异教徒的

    e.g. Don't talk about religions when you are in ethnic restaurants.
          在宗教饭店吃饭时不要谈论宗教信仰。

indebted /ɪnˈdetɪd/ *adj.* 负债的，感恩的

    e.g. He was indebted to Tom for a large sum.
          他欠汤姆一大笔钱。

          I am greatly indebted to you for your help.
          我非常感激你的帮助。

invite /ɪnˈvaɪt/ *v.* 邀请，招待

    e.g. She invited us to her party. 她邀请我们参加她的聚会。

          Tom invited us to come here with him. 汤姆邀请我们和他一起来这里。

napkin /ˈnæpkɪn/ *n.* 餐巾，餐巾纸

    e.g. The napkin should be placed across the lap. 餐巾应放在腿上。

oblige /əˈblaɪdʒ/ *vt.* 迫使，被迫

    e.g. Circumstances oblige me to do that.
          情况迫使我不得不那样做。

observation /ˌɒbzəˈveɪʃən/ *n.* 观察，观测

    e.g. Keep him under observation. 监视他！

overstay /ˌəʊvəˈsteɪ/ *v.* 逗留过久，停留超过（时间）

    e.g. The guests overstayed their welcome. 客人逗留过久，使人生厌。

promptness /ˈprɒmptnɪs/ *n.* 敏捷，机敏

    e.g. Promptness is very important in America.
          在美国，办事迅速非常重要。

religious /rɪˈlɪdʒəs/ *adj.* 信奉宗教的，虔诚的，宗教上的

    e.g. Do your work with religious care. 严谨地做事！

reservation /ˌrezəˈveɪʃən/ *n.* （旅馆房间等）预定，预约，保留

    e.g. If you want to go to the concert, you'll have to make a reservation.
          如果你想去听音乐会，你得预定。

restriction /rɪsˈtrɪkʃən/ *n.* 限制，约束

    e.g. The restrictions on the use of the playground are: no damaging property.
          使用这场地的条件是：不准损坏设施。

ruin /ˈru(ː)ɪn/ *v.* 破坏，毁灭

 e. g. The fire ruined the books in the library.
    大火毁坏了图书馆的书。

silverware /ˈsɪlvəweə/ *n.* 银器

 e. g. The silverware placement here is quite different from the European style.
    此地餐具的摆法与欧式摆法大不相同。

Phrases and Expressions

find out 查明（真相等），找出，发现

 e. g. I've found you out at last. 我终于识破了你。
    Please find out when the ship sails for New York.
    请打听一下那艘船何时开往纽约。

insist on 坚持，坚决要求

 e. g. I insisted on his coming with us.
    我坚持要求他和我们一起来。

keep in mind 谨记，牢记

 e. g. Keep in mind these general rules for polite behaviors.
    牢记以下这些礼貌行事的常规。

make a fuss about 大惊小怪，小题大做，无事自扰

 e. g. Don't make a fuss about it. 不要大惊小怪！

reach for 伸手拿

 e. g. Don't reach for the dishes that are out of your reach.
    不要伸手去取你够不到的饭菜。

tuck into 塞进，藏进

 e. g. Tuck your shirt into your trousers.
    把你的衬衫塞进裤子里。

参 考 译 文

餐 桌 礼 仪

 1 如果你应邀去一位美国朋友家里共进晚餐，请记住以下这些礼貌行事的规矩。首先，按时到达（但不要早到）。美国人希望守时。晚 10 分钟或 15 分钟并不成问题，但不应迟到 45 分钟。因为到那时菜肴或许会因烹饪时间过长而失去应有的美味。你应约去人家吃饭时，不妨带件小礼物以示礼貌。鲜花或糖果总是很相宜的。如果你带上件自己国家的特产，主人肯定会高兴地收下这一礼物。

 2 有些美国人并不知道来自不同种族或有不同宗教信仰的人的饮食禁忌。如果你的盘中有你不喜欢吃或不能吃的东西，你该怎么办？可别大惊小怪。如果主人没对你不吃的

食物说些什么,那你也不要提起。只管吃你能吃的,但愿人家没有注意你没吃东西。如果被问起,你不妨承认自己不吃肉(或别的什么),但你也可以说你吃了许多其它的饭菜,已经饱得不能再吃了。不应让厨师觉得他还应给你做些别的,一定要夸奖厨师所做的那些可口菜肴。

3 不要吃完就走,但也不宜逗留过长。如果你的朋友看上去已有些疲倦,你们似乎也没什么可聊的了,这时,不妨起身告别。第二天,给朋友打个电话或写张感谢卡,表示自己昨晚过得很愉快。

4 如果你请别人去餐馆吃饭,应先给餐馆打个电话询问是否需要预定,以防到时为了桌位而等候半天。预定时,只需说出你的名字、进餐人数和时间即可。你要是请人家吃饭,就应准备付账单,账单递上时应立即接过来。但如果你的同伴坚持各付各的,你也不必跟他/她争执不休。有些人愿意分摊,这样就不会感到欠人情,应该尊重这种心理。在大多数美国餐馆里,侍者的小费并不算在账单内。如果服务令你满意,依照惯例你应留下约为账单的15%做小费。在较高级的餐馆进餐后,应留下更多的小费。

5 美国人餐桌上的礼节经观察后还是容易掌握的。请注意如下一些特点:餐巾不应塞进衣领或背心内,而应放在腿上;餐具的摆法与欧式摆法大不相同,但只要你先从离餐盘最远的餐具开始,然后随着每道菜上桌依次使用越来越靠近餐盘的餐具就不会出错。在切食物之前,有些美国人会把刀叉换个手,但此举并不是必须的。

Exercises

I. Reading Comprehension

1. B 2. D 3. A 4. C 5. A

II. Vocabulary and Structure

1. C 2. B 3. D 4. A 5. B 6. C 7. A 8. D 9. A 10. B

III. Translation

1. If you have an attractive item made in your native country, your host and/or hostess would certainly enjoy receiving that as a gift.
   如果你带上件自己国家的特产,男主人或女主人肯定会高兴地收下这一礼物。

2. Don't make the cook feel obliged to prepare something else for you. Be sure to compliment the cook on the food that you enjoyed.
   不应让厨师觉得还应给你做些别的。一定要向厨师表示你对喜欢的菜肴的赞赏。

3. Don't leave immediately after dinner, but don't overstay your welcome, either.
   不要吃完就走,但也不应逗留过长。

4. If your companion insists on paying his or her share, don't get into an argument about it.
   如果你的同伴坚持各付各的,你也不必跟他/她争执不休。

5. If the service was adequate, it's customary to leave a tip equal to about 15% of the bill.
   如果服务令你满意,依照惯例你应留下约为账单的15%作小费。

Part V Time for Fun

参 考 译 文

跳 飞 机

一个英国人、一个法国人、一个墨西哥人和一个美国德克萨斯人乘一架小飞机，突然飞行员用扩音器说："飞机出了点故障，要想飞到最近的机场你们中的三个人得打开门跳下去，只有一个可以活下来。"

四个人打开舱门向下看，英国人深吸一口气，大喊一声"上帝保佑女王"，便跳了下去。

法国人深受鼓舞，也大喊一声"法国万岁"跳了下去。

这一举动激发了那个德克萨斯人，于是他大喊了一声"记住阿拉莫之役"，一把抓起墨西哥人，把他扔下了飞机。

Unit ② Psychology

Part I Teaching Objectives

* **Listening & Speaking**

Help the students to be familiar with the topic — *how to mend your mood in order to succeed* and memorize useful expressions.

* **Words & Expressions**

Study some new words and expressions, such as *confidence*, *current*, *consciously*, *fail*, *estimate*, *internal*, *harsh*, *psychologist*, *criticism*, *automatic*, *negative*, *critic*, *whisper*, *affirm*, *qualify*, *motivate*, *memorize*, *be capable of*, *engage in*, *mess up*, *drown out*, *refer to as* and so on.

* **Grammar**

Learn to use the structure of *whatever*, *whoever*, *whenever*. . . .

* **Writing**

Understand and write *a letter of applying for a loan*.

Part II Listening——*Mood Mending*

New Words

attitude /ˈætɪtjuːd/ *n.* 态度,看法

    e. g. What is your attitude towards this question?

           你对这个问题的态度如何?

distressed /dɪˈstrest/ *adj.* 痛苦的,悲伤的

    e. g. He was distressed about the final exam.

           他因为期末考试而苦恼。

influence　/ˈɪnfluəns/　*v.* 影响

　　e. g.　　My teacher influenced my decision to study science.

　　　　　　我的老师对我学理科的决定起了影响作用。

nasty　/ˈnɑːstɪ/　*adj.* 生气的,脾气坏的,恶意的

　　e. g.　　Don't be nasty to others!

　　　　　　不要跟别人闹别扭!

tolerate　/ˈtɒləreɪt/　*v.* 容忍,忍受,容许

　　e. g.　　I can't tolerate your bad manners any longer.

　　　　　　我再也不能容忍你无礼的行为。

Phrases and Expressions

adapt oneself to...　　使自己适应或习惯于某事

　　e. g.　　He adapted himself to the cold weather.

　　　　　　他适应了寒冷的天气。

all day long　整天,终日,一天到晚

　　e. g.　　Don't play computer games all day long!

　　　　　　不要整天都玩电脑游戏!

do sb. a favor　帮某人的忙,答应某人的请求

　　e. g.　　Will you do me a favor and phone for me?

　　　　　　你能否帮个忙,给我打个电话?

 Dialogue **One**

　　Listen to the CD and mark T for True or F for False according to the dialogue.

1. F　2. F　3. T　4. T　5. F

Script

Miss Huang：Do you believe some people are happy in nature?

Mr. Smith：No, of course not. Where do you get that strange idea?

Miss Huang：Don't you find that some people are happy all the time even if they are facing troubles?

Mr. Smith：Yes. It's true. I am just that kind of happy person. I always take a cheerful attitude towards everything.

Miss Huang：Are you happy in nature?

Mr. Smith：No. Actually when I was in my middle school, I was always in a bad mood all day long. But later I learn to reconsider my problems and find that other people may have the same problem but they can tolerate it. Then I ask myself "Why can't I".

Miss Huang：Does it work?

Mrs. Smith: Yeah! I learn to adapt myself to many different situations and I learn to tolerate.

Miss Huang: But I still insist that people are happy because they have more happy genes.

Mrs. Smith: Genes don't have perfect control over everything! Psychologists tell us that we can influence our mood.

Miss Huang: Is it?

Mr. Smith: Of course, even in one family, not everyone develops to be a happy person.

Miss Huang: Hmm, I see what you mean.

Two

Listen to the CD and answer the following questions with the information you hear.

1. Why does Tom look so distressed?

   Because Tom just lost his bicycle again.

2. Is bicycle theft common on campus nowadays?

   Yes, bicycle theft is very common on campus nowadays.

3. What does Tom mean by saying "I want to get a bike for free tonight"?

   To steal one.

4. Will John help Tom to get a bike for free tonight?

   No, John will not do so.

5. What is Tom more likely to tonight?

   Tom is more likely to try to have a good sleep tonight.

Script

John: Hello, Tom. Why do you look so distressed?

Tom: Well, I just lost my bicycle, again! It's the third one that I have lost in this year!

John: My goodness! That's something to let one down. Bicycle theft is so common on campus nowadays.

Tom: You're telling me. I just can't bear it anymore. Can you do me a favor?

John: Sure.

Tom: I want to get a bike for free tonight. I'd like you to give me a hand.

John: Oh, no. You mean to steal one? That's terrible!

Tom: Shh... calm down. I don't think it's fair for me to keep buying one bike after another while someone else gets them free from me. Now it's my turn for a free lunch.

John: But it's wrong!

Tom: Come on. Be a friend.

John: A friend would keep you on the right path. I won't do it, and neither will you.

Tom: But I...

John: Calm down! It may happen to everyone. Have a good sleep, then you will be better tomorrow.

Tom: Ok, I will have a try. Good night!

John: Good night!

Listen to the CD three times and fill in the blanks with the information you hear.

1. he often shakes his head
2. but on the contrary he is expressing agreement
3. when they talk to somebody
4. The driver shook his head
5. "Yes, sir." smiling and shaking his head again at the same time

Part III   Speaking——*Never in a Bad Mood*

Useful Expressions About Mood Mending

I just couldn't help it.

Don't take it to heart.

Let's face it/the music.

I've done my best.

Take care!

Better safe than sorry.

Cheer up!

I'm in a good mood.

I'm easy to please.

I'm lost.

I'm not myself today.

I'm under a lot of pressure.

It may happen to everyone.

It doesn't matter to me.

It will do you good.

Pair Work

Sample

Susan: I have such a bad memory! I must be getting old!

Steve: Oh, don't be silly. Your memory is just fine.

Susan: But I can never remember the English vocabulary I study. I forget the words the very next day.

Steve: That's no big deal. You probably just need a better study method.

Susan: What do you suggest?

Steve: You can write the words on note cards and carry them with you all the time. Look at them whenever you have a chance.

Susan: That's a good idea. There's just one problem.

Steve: What's that?

Susan: I'll probably forget to bring the cards with me. I told you I have a bad memory!

Steve: Don't worry! It may happen to everyone. Let's face it!

Role-play

Sample

Truman: I'm really tired of being a teacher.

Finn: Why? What happened?

Truman: I went to class this morning and found that so many students were late for class.

Finn: It's Monday morning, you know. It may be difficult for the students to get up on Monday mornings.

Truman: That's not the excuse.

Finn: So what did you do? Did you scold them?

Truman: Sure. I told them if they were late next time, they wouldn't be allowed to enter the classroom.

Finn: Do you think there should be some other ways to deal with the students?

Truman: What way?

Finn: Try to find something good in them. Encourage them to be better.

Truman: I just couldn't help it.

Finn: Good teachers can always find something good in their students. And they believe that students can make big progress out of encouragement.

Truman: So?

Finn: So, you see, if you always take a negative view on your students, you will not get along well with your students. But if you try to find good qualities in them, you will find it easy to encourage and inspire them to do well.

Truman: All right. I'll try, although it's not easy.

Finn: It will do you good!

Part IV Reading

Text A   **Background**

Your perception of yourself has an enormous impact on how others perceive you. Perception is reality — the more self-confidence you have, the more likely it is that you'll succeed.

Confidence is generally described as a state of being certain. Self-confidence means having confidence in oneself.

Self-confidence does not necessarily imply "self-belief" or a belief in one's ability to succeed. The key element to self-confidence is an acceptance of the myriad consequences of a particular situation, be they good or bad. When one does not dwell on negative consequences, one can be more "self-confident" because one is worrying far less about failure or (more accurately) the disapproval of others following potential failure. One is then more likely to focus on the actual situation, which means enjoyment and success in that situation is also more probable. Belief in one's abilities to perform an activity comes through successful experience and may add to a general sense of self-confidence.

Although many of the factors affecting self-confidence are beyond your control, there are a number of things you can consciously do to build self-confidence. By using the following 10 strategies you can get the mental edge you need to reach your potential.

1. Dress Sharp

Although clothes don't make the man, they certainly affect the way he feels about himself. No one is more conscious of your physical appearance than you are. In most cases, significant improvements can be made by bathing and shaving, wearing clean clothes, and being cognizant of the latest styles.

2. Walk Faster

One of the easiest ways to tell how a person feels about himself is to examine his walk. People with confidence walk quickly. They have places to go, people to see, and important work to do. Walking 25% faster will make you look and feel more important.

3. Good Posture

Similarly, the way a person carries himself tells a story. By practicing good posture, you'll automatically feel more confident. Stand up straight, keep your head up, and make eye contact. You'll make a positive impression on others and instantly feel more alert and empowered.

4. Personal Commercial

One of the best ways to build confidence is listening to a motivational speech. Unfortunately, opportunities to listen to a great speaker are few and far between. You can write a 30 ~ 60 second speech that highlights your strengths and goals. Then recite it in front of the mirror aloud (or inside your head if you prefer) whenever you need a confidence boost.

5. Gratitude

Set aside time each day to mentally list everything you have to be grateful for. Recall your past successes, unique skills, loving relationships, and positive momentum. You'll be amazed how much you have gone for you and motivated to take the next step towards success.

6. Compliment Other People

Get in the habit of praising other people. Refuse to engage in backstabbing gossip and make an effort to compliment those around you. In the process, you'll become well liked and build self-confidence. By looking for the best in others, you indirectly bring out the best in yourself.

7. Sit in the Front Row

In schools, offices and public assemblies around the world, most people prefer the back of the room because they're afraid of being noticed. This reflects a lack of self-confidence. By deciding to sit in the front row, you can get over this irrational fear and build your self-confidence. You'll also be more visible to the important people talking from the front of the room.

8. Speak Up

During group discussions many people never speak up because they're afraid that people will judge them for saying something stupid. Generally, people are much more accepting than we imagine. By making an effort to speak up at least once in every group discussion, you'll become a better public speaker, more confident in your own thoughts, and recognized as a leader by your peers.

9. Work Out

Physical fitness also has a huge effect on self-confidence. If you're out of shape, you'll feel insecure, unattractive and less energetic. By working out, you improve your physical appearance, energize yourself and accomplish something positive. Having the discipline to work out not only makes you feel better, it creates positive momentum that you can build on the rest of the day.

10. Focus on Contribution

Stop thinking about yourself and concentrate on the contribution you're making to the rest of the world, you won't worry as much about you own flaws. This will increase self-confidence and allow you to contribute with maximum efficiency. The more you contribute to the world, the more you'll be rewarded with personal success and recognition.

Self-confidence is extremely important in almost every aspect of our lives, yet so many people struggle to find it. People who lack self-confidence can find it difficult to become successful. The good news is that self-confidence can really be learned and built on. And, whether you're working on your own self-confidence or building the confidence of people around you, it's well worth the effort!

New Words

affirm /ə'fɜːm/ *vt. /vi.* 断言,肯定;证明,证实(事实等);明确表示(to)

    e. g.   He affirmed his love for her.   他肯定他爱她。

             The witness affirmed to the facts.   证人证明这些确是事实。

automatic /ˌɔːtə'mætɪk/ *adj.* 自动的,习惯性的

    e. g.   The heating system in the hotel has an automatic temperature control.

             旅馆里的取暖系统是自动调温的。

banter /'bæntə/ *n.* (善意的)玩笑,逗乐

    e. g.   This is only internal banter.

             这只不过是一种内在的戏谑。

confidence /'kɒnfɪdəns/ *n.* 自信,信心,把握

    e. g.   She lacks confidence in herself.   她缺乏自信心。

             We have full confidence that we shall succeed.

             我们完全有把握取得成功。

consciously /'kɒnʃəslɪ/ *adv.* 有意识地,自觉地

    e. g.   Most people cannot consciously remember much before the age of 3.

             多数人不能清楚地记得 3 岁之前的事情。

critic /'krɪtɪk/ *n.* 批评家,评论家;吹毛求疵的人,爱挑剔的人

    e. g.   He is a famous film critic.   他是一位著名的电影评论家。

             I'm my own most severe critic.   我对自己要求非常严格。

criticism /'krɪtɪsɪzəm/ *n.* 批评,评论,意见

    e. g.   These two criticisms provide a good starting point.

             这两条批评意见开创了良好的开端。

current /'kʌrənt/ *adj.* 当今的,时下的,流通的,流行的

    e. g.   You have to overcome the current difficulties.

             你必须克服当前的困难。

estimate /'estɪmeɪt/ *vt.* 估计,判断,估价

    e. g.   I estimate her age at 35.   我估计她有 35 岁。

             It is difficult to estimate the possible results in advance.

             很难估计正在发生事物的结果。

fail /feɪl/ *vi. /vt.* 失败,不及格,不足,无法做到

    e. g.   He failed in his English examination.   他的英语考试不及格。

             They fail to recognize that our population is increasing faster than the supply of

             food.   他们没有认识到我们人口的增长超过了粮食的供给。

gymnast /'dʒɪmnæst/ *n.* 体操运动员,体育家

    e. g.   Li Xiaoshuang is a famous gymnast.   李小双是一个著名的体操运动员。

harsh /hɑːʃ/ *adj.* 刺耳的,刺眼的,严厉的,残酷的,无情的

e.g. He heard a harsh voice. 他听到一个刺耳的声音。

He deserves a harsh punishment. 受到严厉的惩罚，他罪有应得。

internal /ɪnˈtɜːnəl/ *adj.* 内部的,在内部的,国内的,本国的

e.g. She enjoys the present internal peace.

她享受着此时此刻的内心平静。

He is in charge of internal affairs. 他负责国内事物。

memorize /ˈmeməraɪz/ *vt.* 记住

e.g. He tried his best to memorize the list of dates.

他尽力记住那一系列日期。

motivate /ˈməʊtɪveɪt/ *vt.* 推动,促起,激发

e.g. Reading will motivate children to learn new words.

阅读会激励孩子们学习生词。

Examinations do not motivate a student to seek more knowledge.

考试不能促使学生去追求更多的知识。

negative /ˈnegətɪv/ *adj.* 消极的,否定的

e.g. You should turn negative factors into positive ones.

你应该把消极因素化为积极因素。

He gave a negative answer to our request for funding.

他对我们的财政要求给予了否定的回答。

psychologist /saɪˈkɒlədʒɪst/ *n.* 心理学家

e.g. Mr. Lee is a psychologist.

李先生是一个心理学家。

qualify /ˈkwɒlɪfaɪ/ *vt./vi.* 使合格,使具有资格

e.g. Do you qualify for the vote? 你有投票资格吗?

I hope to qualify as a doctor. 我希望取得医生资格。

whisper /ˈhwɪspə/ *vi./vt.* 低声说,耳语,私下说,沙沙地响

e.g. He is whispering to his neighbor. 他向邻座的人耳语。

The wind whispered in the pines. 风在松树林中飒飒作响。

wither /ˈwɪðə/ *vt./vi.* 使衰弱,减弱,凋谢

e.g. The flowers withered in the cold. 花在寒冷的天气里凋谢了。

She withered him with a look. 她的一瞥使他无言以对。

Phrases and Expressions

be capable of 有……的能力;可以……

e.g. Are you capable of climbing that tree? 你能爬上那棵树吗?

drown out 赶走,淹没,压过(另一声音)

e.g. You may drown out negative thoughts with exercises.

你可以利用体育锻炼赶走消极思想。

engage in　从事,参加

　　e. g.　He can engage a shy person in conversation.

　　　　　他能使害羞的人加入谈话。

mess up　搞乱,弄脏,弄糟,陷入困境

　　e. g.　Everyone will laugh at you if you mess this up.

　　　　　如果你搞砸了,每个人都会笑话你。

pop into　急急走进……,急急地把(某物)放进……

　　e. g.　A good idea popped into his mind.　她突然想起来一个好主意。

refer to as　称为

　　e. g.　He is referred to as Little Smith.

　　　　　人们称他为小史密斯。

参 考 译 文

倾听你内心的声音

1　自信是一种心灵游戏。自信的人相信自己,因为相信自己,所以他们会获得成功。

2　不管你目前的心境如何,你可以通过有意识地改变考虑自己和世界的方式来迅速提高自己的自信心。如果你认为自己有能力实现更多目标,那么你会感到自信,你也就能做得更多。

3　告诉自己"所有的人都会笑话我"或"我要失败了",你的自信心就会枯萎。如果你认为你能或者你认为你不能——那你想什么就是什么。

4　我们都有一个内在的声音:专家称其为我们的"自我言语"。看到这句话的时候,你也许就听见了这个声音。专家估计,当进入这种内在的游戏时,我们每分钟会说 150 到 300个字——它充当你的鉴定人,比任何其他人都要严厉。

5　心理学家把这种主动跳入我们大脑的批评称作自动消极思想(ANTs)。它们可能有许多种形式,这里举出几个例子:

6　"我做不了——我不够聪明,无法成功。"

7　"别人并不喜欢我。"

8　"我永远无法改变——我太老了,已习惯了自己的方式。"

9　"如果我搞砸了,每个人都会笑话我。"

10　"这件事太难做了。"

11　如何赶走你内心的批评家呢?你内心的批评家可能成为讨厌的家伙。你接受一个新的挑战时,它会低声说:"这将成为严重的错误。"而你利用能力肯定思想(CATs)就能将自动消极思想赶走。

12　心理学家迈克尔·马奥尼在宾夕法尼亚州立大学工作时,研究了一组运动员,他们希望通过选拔进入美国奥运代表队。成功的运动员通过不断地积极的自我言语鼓励自己,告诉自己你能行。要证明自己,你还有很长的路要走。

13　CATs 也被称作积极肯定或有益的自我言语,就像一位教练,激励你不断努力,并

做到最好。

14 实例如下：

15 "我决心要完成这件事。"

16 "加油，你能做到！"

17 "保持微笑。"

18 "我比别人想象得更坚韧。"

19 "想想达到目标后的利益吧。"

20 "保持信心。"

21 "我以前成功过——我能再次成功！"

22 记住你的积极肯定思想，或者记在一个卡片上，放在身边。无论什么时候当你需要鼓励时，就重复一遍。

Exercises

IV. Reading Comprehension

Section A

1. B　2. D　3. C　4. D　5. A

Section B

1. Because confident people believe in themselves, they are more likely to achieve.

2. When I tell myself "Everyone's going to laugh at me" or "I'm going to fail", my self-confidence withers.

3. Psychologists call the unbidden criticisms that pop into our heads automatic negative thoughts (ANTs).

4. You can drown out your inner critic with capability-affirming thoughts (CATs).

5. CATs, also referred to as positive affirmations or helpful self-talk, are like a coach motivating you to keep going, to be the best you can.

Section C

1. No, I am not. Because sometimes I cannot believe in myself, I cannot believe that I can do something better than others. Sometimes I even think that others are better than me in so many aspects.

   or

   Yes, I am. I always think that I can do better than anybody else, because I am clever and capable.

2. When I am in trouble, I tell myself "I cannot do it. Everyone's going to laugh at me", "I'm going to fail", or "It's too difficult."

   or

When I am in trouble, I tell myself "I am better than others, I can do it well", "I'm determined to get this done", "Come on, I can do it!"

3. I will constantly encourage myself by engaging in positive self-talk. Tell myself that I am capable of achieving more. I will try my best to memorize my CATs or write them down on a sheet of card to keep at hand. Repeat them to myself whenever I need a lift.

V. Vocabulary and Structure

Section A

1. A 2. C 3. D 4. B 5. B 6. A 7. B 8. D 9. D 10. C

Section B

1. CATs are like a coach <u>motivating</u> you to keep going, to be the best you can.

   CATs 就像教练一样,激励你不断努力,并做到最好。

2. Because <u>confident</u> people believe in themselves, they achieve.

   因为自信的人相信自己,所以他们会获得成功。

3. If you think that you are <u>capable</u> of achieving more, you become able to do more.

   如果你认为自己有能力实现更多目标,那么你就能做得更多。

4. I <u>estimate</u> that total cost for treatment will be $9,000.

   我估计治疗费总额将有 9 000 美元。

5. Automatic negative thoughts can <u>take</u> many forms.

   自动消极思想有许多种形式。

6. You may <u>drown</u> out ANTs with capability-affirming thoughts.

   你可以利用能力肯定思想将自动消极思想赶走。

7. A psychologist studied a group of gymnasts hoping to <u>qualify</u> for the US Olympic team.

   一位心理学家研究了一组运动员他们希望通过选拔进入美国奥运代表队。

8. Repeat them to yourself <u>whenever</u> you need a lift.

   无论什么时候当你需要鼓励时,就重复一遍。

VI. Word Building

1. The teacher <u>discouraged</u> his students from playing computer games.

   该老师劝阻学生不要玩电脑游戏。

2. The car's clean appearance <u>misled</u> me into thinking it was newer than it really was.

   这辆汽车如此洁净,让我误以为是一辆比较新的车。

3. It was <u>dishonest</u> of you to lie to your employer about your work experience.

   就工作经历对老板撒谎,你这么做不诚实。

4. I think they must have <u>misunderstood</u> me; I meant ten in the morning, not ten at night.

   我想他们误解我的意思了,我指的是上午十点,而不是晚上十点。

5. She writes excellent English essays, except that she sometimes <u>misspells</u> words.

   她的英语散文写得非常棒,但有时候会出现单词拼写错误。

6. I prefer to stay in the quiet and peaceful countryside; I <u>dislike</u> big cities.

   我更喜欢住在安静平和的乡下，我不喜欢大城市。

7. Don't <u>mistake</u> his silence for lack of interest; actually he is very interested in the subject we are discussing now.

   不要误解他的沉默为缺乏兴趣，其实他对我们现在讨论的话题非常感兴趣。

8. Living in a big city has both advantages and <u>disadvantages</u>.

   居住在大城市有利也有弊。

IV. Grammar Focus

1. Whoever you are, you must obey the traffic regulations.

2. I'd like to warn you whatever was said here must be kept secret.

3. The time will come when man can fly wherever he likes in the universe.

4. You can stay at my cottage in the country whenever you like.

5. Learn to relax whichever method suits you best.

V. Translation

1. <u>Whatever your current state of mind</u>, you can quickly improve your confidence in this way.

   不管你目前的心境如何，你可以用此方法来迅速提高自己的自信心。

2. We all have an inner voice: <u>experts call it our self-talk</u>.

   我们都有一个内在的声音：专家称其为我们的"自我言语"。

3. I can't do it—<u>I'm not bright enough to succeed</u>.

   我做不了——我不够聪明，无法成功。

4. The successful athletes constantly <u>encouraged themselves by engaging in positive self-talk</u>.

   成功的运动员不断地通过积极的自我言语鼓励自己。

5. Memorize your CATs <u>or write them down on a sheet of card to keep at hand</u>.

   记住你的积极肯定思想，或者记在一个卡片上，放在身边。

VI. Writing

Sample

A Letter of Applying for a Loan

Nov. 11th, 2010

Dear Sir or Madam,

   I am writing to apply for a loan of $10,000 from your bank to start a small shop.

   I am planning to use the loan in the following ways: I will spend $2,000 to rent a room as the shop; $1,000 to buy some pieces of furniture such as desks, counters and shelves; $7,000 to stock some goods I can sell such as T-shirts, shoes, clothes and blue jeans. I hope to get the loan by the end of next month this year.

   Thank you very much for your help in advance and I am looking forward to hearing from

you soon.

Faithfully yours,

Marry

Notes

A loan is a type of debt. Like all debt instruments, a loan entails the redistribution of financial assets over time, between the lender and the borrower.

To apply for a loan successfully, you must pay attention to the following aspects.

First, you must talk about the amount of the loan you will need to start up your business.

Second, you must talk about the reason for the loan.

Third, you must have a good business plan.

Text B　　　　　　　Background

Six Steps to Make People Like You

Everyone wants to be liked by others and have the ability to make new friends quickly. It seems that the older we get, the harder it gets to make lasting friendship. We lose the magic we had as children that enabled us to confidently walk up to anyone, anywhere and start a conversation. Children find it very easy to make friends because they are confident and they don't label each other as quickly as adults do. Thankfully, you can recapture that magic once again and make almost everyone like you and want to be your friend.

Step 1　Smile! If you want to make people like you, you've got to make a good first impression and a smile makes a great first impression. People who smile seem more friendly and the more genuine the smile, the more friendly you'll seem.

Step 2　Shake hands, introduce yourself first and be sure to make direct eye contact. Direct eye contact conveys that you have nothing to hide and that your motives are genuine. It also shows that you have confidence in yourself that's essential to make others like you.

Step 3　Repeat her name often. Everyone loves to hear her own name because it gives her a sense of importance. Also, repeating her name ensures that you don't forget it. When you're first introduced, say something like, "Kate, it's great to meet you!" Use her name as often as it feels natural to do so.

Step 4　Ask questions. Ask him how he's doing, where he goes to, what he does for a living, or anything that will get him to talk. Everyone loves to talk about himself and if you give him the opportunity to do so and if you show a real interest, he'll open up. He'll come away with a spectacular impression of you and you'll know a bit about him, making the conversation start easier the next time you meet.

Step 5　Flatter her. Comment on her bag, her shoes, her jacket, or whatever you see that you like. Flattery will really get you everywhere as long as it's genuine. Comment only on what you really like and only on one thing. Too much flattery makes you seem artificial and too eager to please. False flattery will get you nowhere when trying to make new friends or encouraging others to like you.

Step 6　Let him do the talking. If you make eye contact, smile, nod and ask questions, you'll rarely have the chance to talk about yourself. As superficial as it sounds, he doesn't want to hear about you, but he wants to hear about himself. When being asked a question, answer it briefly and accurately but immediately draw the conversation back to him. You'll give him a feeling of importance and he'll instantly like you.

New Words

boost /buːst/ *vt.* 增加,提高,增进,改善

e.g.　We need to boost our spirits.　我们需要鼓舞士气。

compel /kəmˈpel/ *vt.* 迫使,强迫

e.g.　The rain compelled us to stay indoors.
　　　　雨迫使我们待在家里。

doormat /ˈdɔːmæt/ *n.* 门前擦鞋的棕垫,[喻]逆来顺受的可怜虫

e.g.　There is no doormat here.　这里没有擦鞋垫。

empathic /emˈpæθɪk/ *adj.* 用心的,移情作用的

e.g.　Real listening should be empathic listening.　真正倾听应该是用心聆听。

fixed /fɪkst/ *adj.* 固定的,不动的,安排好的

e.g.　The date's not fixed yet.　日期尚未确定。

format /ˈfɔːmæt/ *n.* 格式

e.g.　It should be better to parrot back what they said in polite format.
　　　　以礼貌的方式鹦鹉般地重复他们说的话可能会更好。

gauge /geɪdʒ/ *vt.* (用计量器)计量,度量,评价,判断

e.g.　I tried to gauge how many people were there.
　　　　我想估计出那儿有多少人。

hypnotherapist /ˌhɪpnəʊˈθerəpɪst/ *n.* 催眠治疗师

e.g.　Mr. Smith is a hypnotherapist.　史密斯是一个催眠治疗师。

insistent /ɪnˈsɪstənt/ *adj.* 坚持的,紧急的,显著的

e.g.　He set out at once at his wife's insistent request.
　　　　在妻子的一再要求下,他立刻出发。

magnet /ˈmægnɪt/ *n.* 磁铁,有吸引力的人／物

e.g.　Dalian is a magnet for tourists.　大连是个吸引游客的地方。

maintain /menˈteɪn/ *vt.* 保持,维持,保养,维修

e.g.　He failed again and again simply because he had maintained his attitude.
　　　　因为他一直坚持自己的态度,所以失败了一次又一次。

The car has always been properly maintained.
这汽车一直保养得很好。

matchmaking /ˈmætʃmeɪkɪŋ/ *n.* 说媒,做媒,媒介

    e. g.   He works at a matchmaking agency.   他在婚介机构工作。

obvious /ˈɒbvɪəs/ *adj.* 明白的,显然的,显而易见的

    e. g.   It is obvious that she is very clever.   很明显,她挺聪明。

presenter /prɪˈzentə/ *n.* 主持人,推荐者

    e. g.   Ruth Langsford works as This Morning presenter.
           路丝·朗斯佛瑞德是《今天上午》的主持人。

rapport /ræˈpɔː/ *n.* 友好,和睦,友善

    e. g.   He is always in rapport with his neighbor.   他跟邻居一直很和睦。

reciprocal /rɪˈsɪprəkəl/ *adj.* 相互的,交互的,互惠的

    e. g.   Although I gave him many presents, I had no reciprocal gifts from him.
           虽然我送过他很多礼物,但我没有收到过他给我的礼物。

sympathetically /ˌsɪmpəˈθetɪkəlɪ/ *adv.* 同情地,怜悯地

    e. g.   Use facial expressions to show you are sympathetically listening.
           用你的面部表情告诉他你在用心听。

transform /trænsˈfɔːm/ *vt.* 转变,改变,改造

    e. g.   Success and wealth transformed his character.
           成功和财富改变了他的性格。
           A steam engine transforms heat into power.
           蒸汽机将热能转变成动力。

virtuous /ˈvɜːtjuəs/ *adj.* 有德行的,高洁的,纯洁的

    e. g.   He led a virtuous life.   他过着高洁的生活。

wallflower /ˈwɔːlˌflaʊə/ *n.* 局外人

    e. g.   He acted as if he were a wallflower.   他的行为举止就好像他是个局外人。

Phrases and Expressions

embossed with   使凸出,浮雕(图案),装饰

    e. g.   The coins are embossed with letters and figures.
           硬币上铸有浮雕的文字和人像。

keep the spotlight on   注意,关心

    e. g.   Keep the spotlight on people around, and then you will become popular.
           保持对你身边人们的关注,你就会成为受欢迎的人。

pin...to   钉住,固定

    e. g.   In the accident he was pinned to the wall.
           车祸中他被钉在墙上,动弹不得。

slot in   安置,放置,插入

e. g.　Slot in the words "please" and "thank you" in your response.

　　　回应时插入"请"、"谢谢"等字眼。

struggle with　挣扎，搏斗

e. g.　The old man struggled with the heavy load.

　　　老人挣扎地背着沉重的负荷。

参 考 译 文

如何让每个人都喜欢你

1　运用增进信任的小点子吸引人们并让他们支持你。下面简单的五个步骤能将你在几分钟之内从一个局外人改造成局内人……

2　**1. 表达出你喜欢他们**

3　如果别人觉得你喜欢他们，那么他们喜欢你的程度就会增加。"从对方身上能阅读出相互爱慕的信号，当我们收到有人倾慕自己的信号时，自己感觉必须做出回应，"婚介机构的婚姻专家雷切尔·马克林说。因此，如果你对某些人表示出你喜欢他们，他们就更有可能喜欢上你。这样，你们会进入一个"良性循环"，只要双方关系没有中断，你们就会越来越喜欢对方。

4　**2. 用眼神去交流**

5　如果你想立刻变得讨人喜欢，请保持眼神的接触以显示你真的感兴趣。"老向一个人的肩膀上方看是不受欢迎的，"催眠治疗师维多利亚·维尔斯说。"但不要用你逼人的眼神把他们钉在墙上。偶尔看向它处是很自然的。如果你不喜欢直接眼神接触，那就用比较固定的方式看着对方的脸，缓慢而平稳地注视她，从左眼到右眼，再到鼻子，最后再回到左眼，如此循环。""这是很正常的眼球运动，因此没有人会注意。"维多利亚补充道。

6　**3. 对谈话有信心**

7　"你的舌头就像饰有'欢迎'或'消失'字样的门垫，"《如何与人交谈》的作者雷尔·朗兹说。她建议闲聊时要定好调子并选好话题。在你对人或事件发表意见前——查阅当天的报纸头条，在出去前，练习下对你的搭档或伙伴发表你的意见。"要估计下听从的数量，"雷尔说。"当他们发言时，倾听寻找线索，看他们的情绪和活力如何，并考虑他们的兴趣。如果他们说自己喜欢园艺，接话茬！这时只要说，"哦，你是个热心的园丁！"如果没有明显的迹象，像鹦鹉那样重复下他们最后说的问题，并保持对他们的关注。"

8　**4. 配合他们的调子**

9　在交谈中，最重要的不是我们说什么，而是我们怎么说。生活教练和 NLP 专家特鲁迪·希尔建议，模仿身体语言可以帮助交流，同样，你也可以充分使用你的语气。"研究表明，交谈活动中 93% 的谈话与词句及内容无关。关键是我们要融洽，"她解释说。"这让别人觉得我们与他们已有诸多的良好联系。用他们的腔调和语速来说话交流就可以达到效果。"

10　**5. 做一个好的倾听者**

11　"用面部表情和眼神告诉对方，你在用心听，"《今天上午》主持人路丝·朗斯佛瑞

德说。"重复他们的要点表明您知道他们说到哪里了。真正倾听,即用心聆听,而不只是被动的听,这样不用判断就能感觉到他们的内心正在经历着什么。回应时插入'感觉'、'需要'或'想'等字眼,你会因此成为一个更好、更讨人喜欢的人!"

Exercises

I. Reading Comprehension

1. B   2. D   3. A   4. D   5. A

II. Vocabulary and Structure

1. A   2. C   3. B   4. B   5. C   6. A   7. A   8. D   9. B   10. A

III. Translation

1. These five easy steps will transform you from wallflower to people-magnet in minutes.

   这简单的五个步骤在几分钟之内便将你从局外人改造成局内人。

2. Your tongue is like a doormat embossed with either "welcome" or "go away".

   你的舌头就像饰有"欢迎"或"消失"字样的门垫。

3. If the clues aren't obvious, parrot back what they last said in question format and keep the spotlight on them.

   如果没有明显线索,就像鹦鹉那样重复他们最后说的问题,并保持对他们的关注。

4. During conversation, what matters most is not what we say, but how we say it.

   在交谈中,最重要的不是我们说什么,而是我们怎么说。

5. When we receive positive signals, we feel compelled to respond.

   当我们收到有人爱慕自己的信号时,自己感觉必须做出回应。

Part V   Time for Fun

参 考 译 文

发 现

　　德国科学家在地下挖了50米深,发现了一些碎铜片。在研究了很长时间后,德国宣布德国祖先在25 000年前就曾经拥有过一个覆盖全国的电信网络。

　　英国政府自然不会轻易相信这些,就派自己的科学家挖得再深一些。在100米深处,他们发现了碎玻璃片,于是很快传出消息说英国祖先在35 000年前就有覆盖全国的光纤网。

　　以色列人很恼怒,他们在地下分别挖了50米、100米和200米,但是什么也没有发现。最后他们得出结论:古代以色列人早在55 000年前就用手机了。

Unit 3
Green Living

Part I   Teaching Objectives

* **Listening & Speaking**

   Help students to be familiar with the topic—*talking about the weather of green living*, and *memorize useful expressions.*

* **Words & Expressions**

   Grasp some new words and expressions, such as *release*, *volunteer*, *donate*, *special*, *go off*, *make sure*, *have to do with* and *so on*.

* **Grammar**

   How to use the structure of *-ing participle with a conjunction.*

* **Writing**

   Understand and write *a notice.*

Part II   Listening——*Weather of Green Living*

New Words

awful   /ˈɔːfl/   *adj.* 可怕的，极讨厌的

   e. g.   We met with an awful storm during the journey to Tai Mountain.
   我们在去泰山的旅途中遇到了一场可怕的暴风雨。

desertification   /deˌzɜːtɪfɪˈkeɪʃən/   *n.* 沙漠化

   e. g.   We have made achievement in desertification prevention and control.
   我们的防沙治沙工作取得了积极效果。

emission   /ɪˈmɪʃən/   *n.* 排放，发出(气体、光和热)

   e. g.   Most scientists accept that climate change is linked to carbon emissions.

大多数科学家都相信气候变化与排放的含碳气体有关。

fossil /ˈfɒsl/　*n.* 化石

　　e. g.　The fossils may be a million years old.
　　　　这些化石可能有 100 万年了。

immature /ˌɪməˈtjʊə/　*adj.* 未发育完全的；不成熟的

　　e. g.　The immature plants are susceptible to frost.
　　　　幼小的植物易受霜冻的侵袭。

impose /ɪmˈpəʊz/　*v.* 征（税等），处以（罚款、监禁等）；把……强加于

　　e. g.　Don't impose your opinion on others.
　　　　不要把你的观点强加给别人。

meteorologist /ˌmiːtɪəˈrɒlədʒɪst/　*n.* 气象学员，气象学工作者，气象学家

　　e. g.　For a long time, my little brother has wanted to be a meteorologist, and now his
　　　　dream has come true.
　　　　我的小弟弟很早就想当气象员，现在终于如愿以偿了。

potential /pəˈtenʃəl/　*adj.* 潜在的

　　e. g.　It's important to draw out a child's potential capacities.
　　　　发掘孩子的潜在能力是很重要的。

scarcity /ˈskeəsɪtɪ/　*n.* 缺乏，不足

　　e. g.　The scarcity of food was caused by the drought.
　　　　粮食缺乏是由干旱引起的。

storm /stɔːm/　*n.* 暴风雨

　　e. g.　The news reported that a man was struck down by lightning in the storm.
　　　　新闻说有一人在暴雨中被闪电击毙。

toxic /ˈtɒksɪk/　*adj.* 有毒的

　　e. g.　When spilled into the sea, oil can be toxic to marine plants and animals.
　　　　石油溢入海洋可能危害海洋生物。

widespread /ˈwaɪdspred/　*adj.* 分布广的，普遍的，广泛的

　　e. g.　This disease is widespread in tropical areas.
　　　　这种疾病在热带地区蔓延很广。

Phrases and Expressions

at the cost of　以……为代价

　　e. g.　The soldier saved the child at the cost of his own life.
　　　　那个战士救了这个孩子，却牺牲了自己的生命。

call on　号召，呼吁；拜访

　　e. g.　The government called on the workers to oppose waste.
　　　　政府号召工人反对浪费。

speed up　加速

e.g.   We are speeding up the mechanization of our agriculture.

我们正在加快农业机械化的步伐。

take on   呈现;承担

e.g.   The school took on a festival air.

学校呈现出一派节日气氛。

to tell the truth   说实话

e.g.   To tell the truth, I don't agree with your plan.

说实话,我不同意你的计划。

Dialogue One

Listen to the CD and mark T for True or F for False according to the dialogue.

1. F   2. T   3. F   4. T   5. T

Script

Lynch: Oh, today's weather is awful. The wind blows so strongly and dust blows everywhere.

Manning: Yeah, it's terrible. But you know, it's not uncommon to have such dust storms in Beijing.

Lynch: Why do the dust storms come so strongly this year? I've never seen such strong storms before.

Manning: According to the meteorologists' view, the dust weather has much to do with the scarcity of rain, the dry air and exposed soil with immature plants in the area.

Lynch: Right, right. And the worsening desertification is another major reason.

Manning: To tell the truth, I don't like Beijing for two reasons. One is the pollution, and the other is the serious traffic jams.

Lynch: In China, economic development has often been achieved at the cost of the environment.

Manning: But Beijing has tightened its environmental protection measures in the past few years.

Lynch: I hope Beijing starts to take on a new look now.

Manning: I hope so.

Dialogue Two

Listen to the CD and answer the following questions with the information you hear.

1. Why is this year warmer than usual?

It is because of global warming.

2. What are the greenhouse gases?

They are the burning of fossil fuels, such as coals, oil and natural gas.

3. What will global warming affect?

It will affect weather, agriculture, and human health.

4. Are the governments all working to reduce greenhouse emissions?

   Yes, they are.

5. What should we individuals do?

   We should recycle paper, metal and glass, and we also can drive less and take public bus.

Script ---

Tina: This year is warmer than usual, isn't it?

Joe: Yes, it is reported that the rise of the temperature is a result of global warming.

Tina: The chief cause of this warming is thought to be the burning of fossil fuels, such as coals, oil and natural gas, which releases into the atmosphere known as greenhouse gases.

Joe: Right. And the potential results of global warming are great. It will affect weather, agriculture and human health.

Tina: The governments are all working to reduce greenhouse emissions. For example, some countries impose heavy taxes on energy usage.

Joe: It may work. Besides we individuals can take steps, too.

Tina: Yes, so our country is calling on people to have a green life to reduce the pollution.

Joe: Have a green life?

Tina: Yes. It means that we can recycle paper, metal and glass. We can drive less and take public bus.

Joe: We all should have a green life to fight global warming.

Spot Dictation  --

1. Humans are damaging the environment

2. This will lower your water and heating bills too

3. while improving your heart health

4. Reusing bags reduces the amount of waste you produce

5. Keep your electronics out of the rubbish and recycle them

Part III   Speaking——*Weather*

Useful Expressions About Weather

What a glorious day!

It's a nice day, isn't it?

Nice and bright today, isn't it?

What dreadful weather!

What was the weather like yesterday?

I wonder what it's going to be like tomorrow.

The temperature has dropped to the freezing point.

The temperature was up in the thirties yesterday.

It looks as if it's going to rain.

It's clearing up.

The weather is better than yesterday.

It's rather cold and windy today.

It is rather dry in Beijing.

Global warming may raise the temperature.

The weather can't make up its mind what to do.

They said yesterday was the hottest day of the year so far.

Pair Work

Sample

Tom: A lovely day, isn't it?

Kelly: Yes, it's beautiful weather we're having.

Tom: It's quite different from the weather forecast.

Kelly: Don't you think the winter is not as cold as before?

Tom: Yeah. What do you think is the reason?

Tom: It may have something to do with the damage of the ozone layer. Global warming is a serious problem.

Kelly: Yes. Environmental pollution is the key reason.

Tom: I really can't imagine what would happen if we continue to pollute the earth.

Role-play

Sample

Fred: I hear that London is famous for the heavy fog.

Dina: Yes. London is a foggy city.

Fred: Is it really so foggy?

Dina: It used to be foggy, but now it's not so foggy like what we have expected.

Fred: Why is it better?

Dina: You know heavy fog is because of air pollution. The old London fogs were the result of millions of coal fires producing smoke. *The Clean Air Acts* of the 1950s eliminated the domestic coal fires. Nowadays, most people heat their homes with gas and the only fog you're likely to see in London is of the occasional overnight variety.

Fred: So it's not foggy. That's great!

Dina: Yeah, the air pollution in London has decreased. We now have fresh air.

Part IV Reading

Text A   **Background**

1. New Haven

New Haven is the second largest municipality in Connecticut and the sixth largest municipality in New England with a core population of about 124,000 people. New Haven had the first public tree planting program in America, producing a canopy of mature trees (including some large elms) that gave New Haven the nickname "The Elm City". The city is the home of Yale University.

2. Connecticut

Connecticut is a state in the New England region of the northeastern United States. It is bordered by Rhode Island to the east, Massachusetts to the north, and New York to the west and the south (because various islands of New York span Connecticut's entire coast). Connecticut is the 29th most populous state, with 3.4 million residents, and is ranked 48th in size by area, making it the 4th most densely populated state. Being called the Constitution State and the Nutmeg State, Connecticut has a long history, dating from early colonial times, and was influential in the development of the federal government. Connecticut also has temperate climate, due to its long coastline on Long Island Sound. At the same time, the state has a strong maritime tradition.

3. The Connecticut River

The Connecticut River is the largest river in New England, flowing south from the Connecticut Lakes in northern New Hampshire, along the border between New Hampshire and Vermont, through western Massachusetts and central Connecticut discharging into Long Island Sound at Old Saybrook and Old Lyme, Connecticut. It has a total length of 407 miles, and a drainage basin extending over 11,250 square miles.

4. Long Island Sound

Long Island Sound is an estuary of the Atlantic Ocean and the numerous rivers located in the United States between Connecticut to the north and Long Island, New York to the south. The mouth of the Connecticut River at Old Saybrook, Connecticut, empties into the Sound. On its western end, the Sound is bounded to the north by Westchester Country, New York and the Bronx, and connects to the East River. On its eastern end it opens to Block Island Sound.

5. Green Living

Green living is about finding a life style which causes no permanent damage to the planet. It's about finding sustainable answers to people's needs and desires. And it's about living in harmony and balance with other living inhabitants of the world.

6. Low-carbon Life

Low-carbon life refers to a lifestyle with reduced energy consumtion, thereby reducing the carbon, especially carbon dioxide emissions, reducing air pollution, and reducing ecological degradation. The ultimate purpose is measured mainly from energy-saving solar terms and the recovery of ecological links changing the details of life.

New Words

attract /əˈtrækt/ *v.* 吸引

    e. g.   He was deeply attracted by the beauty of the girl.
            他被女孩的美貌深深吸引了。

authentic /ɔːˈθentɪk/   *adj.* 真实的，真正的；可靠的，可信的

    e. g.   This is the authentic signature of the president.
            这是总统的亲笔签名。
            This news must be authentic since it is from CCTV News.
            这是中央电视台的新闻，肯定是可靠的。

biologist /baɪˈɒlədʒɪst/   *n.* 生物学家

    e. g.   The biologist advanced a new theory of life.
            这位生物学家提出一种有关生命的新理论。

donate /dəʊˈneɪt/   *v.* 赠送，捐赠

    e. g.   Local people donate funds to help develop primary education.
            当地人捐赠资金帮助发展基础教育。

eventually /ɪˈventjʊəlɪ/   *adv.* 最后，终于

    e. g.   Eventually, the fire was under control.
            火势最终得到控制。

hatch /hætʃ/   *v.* 孵化

    e. g.   Three eggs have already hatched.
            三只鸡蛋已孵化出小鸡。

injure /ˈɪndʒə/   *vt.* 使受伤，损伤；伤害（感情，自尊，名誉等）

    e. g.   What you said injured my pride.
            你的话伤了我的自尊心。

litter /ˈlɪtə/   *n.* 废弃物，垃圾

    e. g.   There were piles of litter on this street.
            这条街上到处是垃圾。

marine /məˈriːn/   *adj.* 海的，海产的；海军的；海运的

    e. g.   The marine plants are very nutritious.
            海产植物很有营养。

ongoing /ˈɒnˌɡəʊɪŋ/   *adj.* 继续进行的

e. g.　The first ongoing step is to select the team member.
　　　　正在进行的一步是挑选队员。

outgrowth　/ˈaʊtˌɡrəʊθ/　*n.* 自然结果；生长物，副产品

e. g.　Technology is the outgrowth of science.
　　　　技术是科学的副产品。

passive　/ˈpæsɪv/　*adj.* 被动的，消极的

e. g.　Passive acceptation of the teacher's wisdom is not easy to him.
　　　　让他被动地接受老师的智慧不容易。

personal　/ˈpɜːsənl/　*adj.* 个人的，私人的；亲自的

e. g.　This is all a matter of personal taste.
　　　　这完全是个人品味问题。

recyclable　/riːˈsaɪkləbl/　*adj.* 可循环再利用的

e. g.　The material is recyclable and will not pollute the environment.
　　　　这种材料可循环利用，不会对环境有污染。

salmon　/ˈsæmən/　*n.* 大马哈鱼

e. g.　The river is rich in salmon.
　　　　这条河流盛产大马哈鱼。

sneaker　/ˈsniːkə/　*n.* （帆布胶底）运动鞋

e. g.　He wore old jeans and a pair of sneakers.
　　　　他穿着旧牛仔裤和胶底运动鞋。

special　/ˈspeʃəl/　*adj.* 特殊的，特定的；专门的，专业的

e. g.　This is a special day in the history of our Party.
　　　　今天是我党历史上一个特殊的日子。

Phrases and Expressions

along with　除……以外（还）；和……一起

e. g.　Along with the books, a portfolio contained some photographs.
　　　　除了书，还有一个文件夹藏着一些照片。

be filled with　充满

e. g.　He was filled with despair.
　　　　他充满了绝望的情绪。

be interested in　对……感兴趣

e. g.　Neither the father nor the son is interested in the film.
　　　　父子俩对这部电影都不感兴趣。

clean up　收拾，整理，清理；肃清，整顿

e. g.　The mayor is determined to clean up the city.
　　　　市长决心整顿全市。

cut down　减少，削减；砍倒

e. g. If you cannot give up smoking, you should cut it down.
如果你不能戒烟,就应该少抽。

for instance 例如

e. g. A car, for instance, uses a lot of petrol.
比如说汽车要消耗大量汽油。

go off (电灯)熄灭;爆炸;(食物)变坏

e. g. In your area, power will go off at 3 a. m.
你们那个地区下午三点停电。

Meat and fish go off quickly in hot weather.
在热天肉和鱼会很快变坏。

have to do with 与……有关

e. g. What did this have to do with my daughter's wedding?
这与我女儿的婚礼有什么关系?

make sure 确保;确定,查明

e. g. Make sure that you can finish the work before 6 o'clock.
务必在六点之前完成工作。

Have you made sure about the time of the flight?
你有没有弄清楚那趟航班的时间?

turn off 关掉

e. g. Please remember to turn off the lights when you leave the classroom.
离开教室时请记住关灯。

参考译文

绿色校园生活

1　"绿色"学校是什么样子? 对于位于康涅狄格州纽黑文市的巴纳德环境研究学校的学生们来说,"绿色"意味着和大地亲密接触。

2　开设于 2006 年的巴纳德环境研究学校,因"绿色"校园而闻名,它吸引着全国各地有兴趣研究环境的孩子。

3　据学校的老师马乔里介绍:这所学校旨在为孩子们提供"亲身体验"。他说,"我们天天都是'地球日',由于学校特殊的课程设置,这里的 325 名学生整天都在研究环境,绿色意味着建筑中的一切都要考虑到环境"。比方说,人离开房间后,灯就自动熄灭,同时特制的窗户制造出"被动光源"来降低对电的需求。当窗户打开时,空调就关了。

4　保护环境对学生来说不仅仅是节约能源。他们还进行着拯救大西洋大马哈鱼的活动。当得知大西洋的大马哈鱼濒临灭绝时,学生们也开始为此付出——他们抚养大马哈鱼。在教室里,大马哈鱼卵被放置在 2 摄氏度的水中。当鱼卵孵化后,学生观察小马哈鱼的成长。每年学生们孵化约 200 个大马哈鱼卵,然后把幼年马哈鱼放入康乃狄克河里。

5 巴纳德学校还有一个负责废物再循环的小组。小组成员要确保所有能再循环的物品放在正确的回收箱中,然后被运到合适的地方进行再回收利用。

6 在巴纳德学校,几乎所有的事情都与环境有关。学生们唱环境保护的歌,他们的艺术品与环境相关,甚至他们的数学课也是关于保护环境的。

7 对于 12 岁的乔希来说,去伯纳德学校上学是因为他长期以来热爱着大自然。"我一直都想做与环境有关的事。"在农场生活的乔希说。他在当地一家自然保护中心做志愿者,该中心把蛇和受伤的动物捐赠给学校,动物在这里会受到精心照顾,直到它们恢复健康。

8 乔希是伯纳德学校"根与牙"俱乐部的会长。除了种植花草树木外,这个小组还收集了 84 双运动鞋,用来回收制造可以再次穿上篮球场。这位想成为海洋生物学家的 6 年级学生总在担心全球变暖,他同样也痛恨垃圾给环境带来的破坏。今年他将参加清理长岛海峡的活动,那里到处都是垃圾和废弃物。

9 乔希说,"能为地球做出贡献是件很重要的事,我们的最终目标是杜绝污染。"

Exercises

I. Reading Comprehension

Section A

1. C 2. D 3. B 4. A 5. C

Section B

1. Because these kids are interested in environment studies and the Barnard School is an environmental studies school.

2. Being "green" means getting up close and personal with the earth and having a green life.

3. They keep the salmon eggs in water at 2℃, raise the baby salmon after the eggs hatch and release the young fish into the Connecticut River.

4. The members of the recycling team should make sure that all recyclable things are placed in the right boxes and taken to the right place for recycling.

5. Because Josh loves nature, and that he wants to work with the environment, to stop pollution and to save the earth.

Section C

1. Yes, of course. There are lots of trees and greenbelt, and our school calls on our students to attend the tree planting campaign, and...

   or

   No, there are so many teaching buildings, with so few trees and grass around. We cannot have fresh air, and...

2. I will save water and electricity, and won't throw garbage in order to stop pollution and...

3. My ideal green school life is that every thing in the school should be made with the environment in mind. The students in the school should love nature and love the earth.

II. Vocabulary and Structure

Section A

1. B 2. A 3. C 4. C 5. A 6. D 7. B 8. A 9. C 10. D

Section B

1. Many a <u>biologist</u> works in the field.
   许多生物学家在这个领域工作。

2. We take all our bottles and newspapers to be <u>recycled</u>.
   我们把所有我们用过的瓶子和废报纸拿去回收再利用。

3. People <u>have donated</u> a large sum of money to reconstruct the old temple.
   人们捐助了一大笔钱重修这座古寺。

4. The managing director wrote a <u>personal</u> letter to thank what I have done for the company.
   总经理写了封亲笔信,感谢我为公司所做的一切。

5. Mary decided to forget him and begin a new life after being <u>injured</u> by her boyfriend who is ungrateful.
   当被忘恩负义男友伤害之后,玛丽决定忘记他,开始一段新的生活。

6. Foreigners hope we could give something <u>authentic</u> Chinese.
   外国友人希望我们能送他们一些真正有中国特色的东西。

7. His attitude suggests that he is really <u>interested</u> in detective and mystery stories.
   他的态度表明他真的对侦探和神秘故事感兴趣。

8. The bookcase is <u>filled</u> with all kind of books, so you can choose any of them to read.
   书架上放着各种各样的书,你可以选择任何一本来读。

III. Word Building

1. There's been a <u>noticeable</u> improvement in his handwriting after two years' study.
   经过两年的学习,他的字迹有了明显的进步。

2. Do you have a room <u>available</u>?
   你们有空房间吗?

3. I think it is difficult to get along with Paul, because he is so <u>unpredictable</u>.
   我觉得和保罗很不好相处,他这个人深不可测。

4. Will the new plan be any more <u>acceptable</u> than its predecessors?
   新计划比原来的计划更能令人接受么?

5. The strength of the dollar is causing <u>considerable</u> disquiet on the stock exchange.
   美元表现坚挺在证券交易所引起很大的不安。

6. It will not be <u>advisable</u> to pack this course into your already busy schedule.

把这门课硬排进你本来已经很紧的课表是不明智的。

7. She sat up late that night to write a detailed account of the <u>unforgettable</u> moment.

她熬夜写下了那个难忘时刻的详细情景。

8. It is most <u>desirable</u> that they should both come to help me.

他们俩都来帮我是最好不过的了。

IV. Grammar Focus

1. While waiting the teacher in the classroom, I finished my English homework.

2. Before going to see the film, she deliberately didn't learn the story.

3. After reading the book, put it in its proper place.

4. After turning the key twice in the lock, you can open this door.

5. When buying a new car, you'd better get the expert's advice.

V. Translation

1. The boy adores the scientist so much <u>that almost every book of his has to do with the scientist</u>.

这个男孩如此崇拜那个科学家以至于几乎他的每一本书都与这个科学家有关。

2. To the girl, <u>going to the music college is a natural outgrowth of a lifelong study of piano</u>.

对女孩来说,去音乐学院上学是她长期以来学习钢琴的自然结果。

3. <u>Along with the English class I'm interested in</u>, I also study the Chinese classic music and handwriting.

除了我感兴趣的英语课,我还学习中国古典音乐和书法。

4. My mother told me <u>only cutting down the spending we could overcome the crisis</u>.

妈妈告诉我,只有削减开支才能渡过难关。

5. Another way of reducing the amount of rubbish you create is <u>to use recyclable products instead of disposable products</u>.

另一种减少产生垃圾的方法就是使用可循环产品而不是一次性产品。

VI. Writing
Sample

Notice

12 May, 2010

The Student Union has recently agreed to set up an Environment Club. It aims to encourage students to save energy and have an ecology-friendly life to protect our earth. During this term environmental experts will give lectures on environmental protection once a week and students can meet at the Classroom 503. Besides, we will also have some environmental activities.

All the students that are interested are all welcome to join the club. Fill in related forms and provide one photo by the end of this month.

Our first meeting will be held in the school gym at 8:00 am, Saturday, May 20, 2010.

The Student Union

Notes

A notice is an announcement with information about a future event. There are two forms of notice. One form is popularized to such relevant persons as students, andience and so on through public notice. The other is in the form of a letter, whose form is the same as an ordinary letter. A notice should be clear, succinct, felicitous and timely.

In the first form of notice, "Notice" or "NOTICE" is usually written directly on the top. The name of the sender is written at the bottom right-hand corner of the notice. The time of the notice is written at the upper right-hand corner of the body. Sometimes, they could be omitted.

Text B　　　　　　　**Background**

1. Lent

The period preceding Easter in the Christian Church is devoted to fasting, abstinence and penitence in commemoration of Christ's fasting in the wilderness. In the Western Church it runs from Ash Wednesday to Holy Saturday. So it includes forty weekdays.

2. Easter eggs

Easter eggs are a symbol of the new life that returns to nature at Easter Time. The custom of exchanging eggs began long before Easter was celebrated. Easter is a Christian Festival that celebrates the Resurrection of Jesus Christ on the third day after Good Friday, the day of Christ's crucifixion, now called Easter Sunday.

New Words

bakery /ˈbeɪkərɪ/ *n.* 面包房
　　e.g.　The girl works part time in a bakery.
　　　　　女孩在一家面包房作兼职。

balcony /ˈbælkənɪ/ *n.* 阳台, 露台
　　e.g.　You can see the sunrise from our balcony.
　　　　　你从我们的阳台上就能看到日出。

block /blɒk/ *n.* 木头瓶
　　e.g.　I bought a bottle of shampoo in block.
　　　　　我买了一瓶木头瓶装的洗发水。

canteen /kænˈtiːn/ *n.* 食堂, 餐厅, 小卖部
　　e.g.　After work they made a hearty meal in the worker's canteen.

工作完了,他们在工人食堂饱餐了一顿。

colleague /ˈkɒliːg/ *n.* 同事

  e. g. I don't know anything about this, but my colleague can help you.
     我对这事一无所知,但我的同事可以帮你。

cucumber /ˈkjuːkʌmbə/ *n.* 黄瓜

  e. g. Cucumber is rich in vitamin C.
     黄瓜富含维生素 C。

dawn /dɔːn/ *n.* 破晓,黎明
           vi. 破晓,天刚亮
           vt. (开始)被理解,渐渐领悟

  e. g. Did you hear the cock crow at dawn?
     黎明时你听到鸡叫了吗?
     Then the terrible truth dawned on me.
     接着我突然明白了可怕的真相。

embroider /ɪmˈbrɔɪdə/ *v.* 绣花,刺绣

  e. g. She embroidered the dress with flowers.
     她给连衣裙绣上花。

flotilla /fləʊˈtɪlə/ *n.* 小舰队,小型船队

  e. g. I floated almost three days in the sea and was luckily found by a passing flotilla.
     我在海里漂浮了三天最终幸运地被一个小型船队发现。

involve /ɪnˈvɒlv/ *v.* 参与,牵涉

  e. g. The political movement will involve every one at the meeting.
     这场政治运动牵扯到与会的每一个人。

Lent /lent/ *n.* (基督教的)大斋节,禁塑节

  e. g. You must give up chocolates, smoking and meat for Lent.
     在大斋期你必须戒巧克力、烟、肉。

loose /luːs/ *v.* 释放;松开
          adj. 未固定的,零散的,未困在一起的;松散的

  e. g. He loosed the dog.
     他把狗放了出来。
     Do you like loose tea, or teabags?
     您要散装茶还是袋装茶?

non-biodegradable /ˈnɒnˈbaɪəʊdɪˈgreɪdəbl/ *adj.* 生物不可降解的

  e. g. A part of sludge is non-biodegradable.
     一部分污泥是不可生物降解的。

obstacle /ˈɒbstəkl/ *n.* 障碍,妨碍

  e. g. She felt that the easy and comfortable living was an obstacle to her child's study.
     她觉得安逸的生活妨碍了她孩子的学习。

rewarding /rɪˈwɔːdɪŋ/ *adj.* 值得做的,有益的

    e. g.   Teaching can be a very rewarding career.

            教书是一个很有意义的职业。

sacrifice /ˈsækrɪfaɪs/ *n.* 牺牲,舍弃

                        v. 牺牲;献出

    e. g.   He sacrificed his holiday to help his brother's business.

            为了帮助兄弟经商,他放弃休假。

stash /stæʃ/ *v.* 贮藏,隐藏

    e. g.   You can stash your money here.

            你可以把钱存放在这里。

straw /strɔː/ *n.* 稻草,麦秆

    e. g.   There are a lot of straws in the shed.

            棚子里有许多稻草。

supportive /səˈpɔːtɪv/ *adj.* 支持的,给予帮助的

    e. g.   My family are all extremely supportive to my job.

            家人都极为支持我的工作。

toiletries /ˈtɔɪlɪtrɪs/ *n.* (*pl.*) 梳洗用具,卫浴用品

    e. g.   My toiletries are all put in a big bag.

            我的梳妆用品都放在一个大包里。

veg /vedʒ/ *n.* 蔬菜

    e. g.   In the supermarket, you could buy all kinds of veg.

            在这个超市你可以买到各种各样的蔬菜。

versatile /ˈvɜːsətaɪl/ *adj.* 多用途的,用途广泛的;多才多艺的,有多种技能的

    e. g.   Nylon is a versatile material.

            尼龙是一种有多种用途的材料。

wrap /ræp/ *v.* 包裹,包装

    e. g.   You'd better wrap it with a piece of clean paper.

            你最好用一块干净的纸把它包起来。

yeast /jiːst/ *n.* 酵母

    e. g.   Mary gave me some yeast so I can make my cake.

            玛丽给了我些酵母所以我能做面包了。

Phrases and Expressions

account for   占有,占……百分比;解释说明

    e. g.   APEC members account for more than half of the world's economic output.

            亚太经合组织成员的经济总量在世界占一半以上。

            Lack of money accounts for her discontinuing her studies.

缺钱是她辍学的原因。

be involved in 涉及,参与,专心

> **e. g.** More than 30 software firms were involved in the project.
>
> 三十多家软件公司参与了这个项目。

for all the tea in China (口语)不管怎样,无论如何

> **e. g.** You wouldn't get me to wear a mini-skirt for all the tea in China.
>
> 你绝不可能让我穿上超短裙。

give up 放弃,投降

> **e. g.** She has to give up this journey.
>
> 她不得不放弃这次旅行。

rather than 不是……而是

> **e. g.** The parents should be punished rather than the children.
>
> 受惩罚的应该是父母而不是孩子。

run out of 用完

> **e. g.** The truck's run out of gas again.
>
> 卡车的汽油又用完了。

参 考 译 文

我的没有塑料的日子

Anne Watson 今年接受了禁塑期的挑战,坚决不用塑料包装袋。在这里她分享了这段经历,并回忆了其中的感受。

1　在六周的禁塑期里,我不买任何塑料包装的东西。这不像通常意义上的戒巧克力或戒红酒,而是因为太平洋上不可降解塑料垃圾的面积已经有三个英国那么大了,我不想让它再变大。我还想知道离开塑料我是否还能生活,环顾一下自己住的公寓周围,事实上,几乎所有东西都被塑料包装或包裹着。

2　食品包装占塑料污染的一大块,很多时候是完全不必要的。去当地超市买黄瓜,没有不是用塑料包装的,这真令人沮丧。

3　卫浴用品无疑也是很大的挑战,幸运的是我手头上的化妆品够用六周,但洗发水很快就用完了,我居然找不到不用塑料包裹的厕纸。

4　尽管有这么多的障碍,我还是设法坚持不用塑料生活,过正常的日子。我发现在我办公室附近有一家店仍然用纸袋包装的三明治,有一家店卖免包装的果蔬。给家人做复活节蛋我成功地没有用一丁点塑料。这只是需要有个好计划,而不能等到最后,缺什么就冲进商店买。想想我在吃什么,专心地投入做它,这都是很有意义的事。

5　我发现最让人鼓舞的是人们对我所做的很有兴趣并表示支持。朋友、家人、同事都提供支持和建设性意见,塞恩斯伯瑞的面包房老板把他们新鲜的酵母给我,让我做面包,公司员工餐厅的女服务员用纸袋包装我的午餐,朋友用带刺绣的茶杯包装送给我作生日礼物。

6 有些建议作用不大,比如,对于住在伦敦高层公寓里的人来说,自己买头奶牛挤牛奶就不太现实。

7 牛奶和厕纸对我来说是最难克服的困难。在我的住所附近没有送奶工人,我怎么努力找,也找不到一瓶瓶装牛奶!

8 洗发水是另外一个问题,用完塑料包装的洗发水后,我买了些木包装的。我很喜欢卖这些产品的公司。可惜这款产品不适合我,三周后我的头发就像枯草一样干燥,或许那些洗发水广告描述的真的一点都不靠谱!

9 那么在这个过程中我有什么收获呢?我必须承认,塑料无处不在,因为它是非常有用的。它便宜,用途极其广泛,只不过我们使用的太多、太过频繁、回收利用又不够。现在只要能买到非塑料包装的物品我就买,并在口袋里随身携带布制购物袋。现在春天到了,我试着自己种蔬菜,即使在伦敦小公寓的阳台上这也是可行的。

Exercises

I. Reading Comprehension

1. D 2. B 3. C 4. A 5. D

II. Vocabulary and Structure

1. C 2. D 3. A 4. B 5. C 6. A 7. B 8. C 9. C 10. A

III. Translation

1. It was what he said at the meeting that made her angry, so she left indignantly.

正是他会上说的话让她很气愤,因此她气冲冲地离开了。

2. I looked around her study, and the truth dawned that every book in it was connected with English.

环顾她的书房,事实上里面所有的书都与英语有关。

3. Despite the continual warning of his doctor, he still smokes and doesn't quit smoking.

尽管他的医生多次警告,他还是在抽烟。

4. The worst thing I found was that we had used too much of water and we had no water to drink.

我发现最糟糕的是我们用了太多的水,弄的我们已经没有喝的水了。

5. Therefore, we should all do our efforts to stop buying anything plastic and have a cloth shopping bag with us.

因此,我们应该竭尽全力不买塑料包装的东西,并随身携带布制购物袋。

Part V   Time for Fun

参考译文

让我的司机来回答

一个著名科学家起程去作另一个讲座。他的司机出了个主意："老板，您的讲座我已听了这么多次了。我打赌我能作这个讲座，让您休息一个晚上。"

"那太好了。"科学家说。

到了礼堂，科学家戴上了司机的帽子，坐在了后排。而司机走上了讲台，作讲演。讲演结束后，他问听众是否有什么问题。

一个教授说有，并提出了一个高深的学术问题。

司机一时被问懵了，但很快就镇定下来。"这很容易，"他说，"太容易了，我要让我的司机来回答。"

Unit 4

Romantic Love

Part I   Teaching Objectives

* **Listening & Speaking**

Help the students to be familiar with the topic — *romantic love* and memorize useful expressions.

* **Words & Expressions**

Grasp some new words and expressions, such as *recover*, *strike*, *impose*, *out of the question*, *in a great embarrassment*, *make up* and so on.

* **Grammar**

How to use the structure of *not. . . until*.

* **Writing**

Understand and write *a resume*.

Part II   Listening——*He Is the Boy*

New Words

bowling /ˈbəʊlɪŋ/ *n.* 保龄球运动

    e. g.   He takes to bowling with his colleagues.

            他常常和同事打保龄。

common /ˈkɒmən/ *adj.* 共有的;普通的

    e. g.   We are linked together by common interests.

            我们因有共同的利益而结合在一起。

considerate /kənˈsɪdərɪt/ *adj.* 体贴的,考虑周到的

    e. g.   It's considerate of you to give me a birthday cake.

你想得真周到,送我生日蛋糕。

enthusiastic /ɪnˌθjuːzɪˈæstɪk/ *adj.* 满腔热情的,热心的

    e. g. The wonderful speech got enthusiastic applause.

          演讲得到了热烈的掌声。

float /fləʊt/ *v.* 漂浮;漂流

    e. g. Oil will float on water.

          油能浮在水面上。

share /ʃeə/ *v.* 共有,共用

    e. g. Can I share the supper with you?

          我能和你共用晚餐么?

unique /juː(ː)ˈniːk/ *adj.* 独特的,唯一的

    e. g. This is a unique work of art.

          这是独一无二的艺术作品。

Phrases and Expressions

in common 共同的,共有的

    e. g. We've got a lot of interests in common.

          我们有许多共同的爱好。

night and day 夜以继日

    e. g. The girl took care of her sick mother night and day.

          那个女孩夜以继日的照顾她生病的母亲。

on cloud nine 极快乐

    e. g. He was on cloud nine after winning the competition.

          他在比赛胜利后欣喜若狂。

search for 搜寻,搜索

    e. g. They were searching for the missing child.

          他们正在搜找那个失踪的小孩。

 One

Listen to the CD and mark T for True or F for False according to the dialogue.

1. F 2. T 3. F 4. F 5. T

He's just the boy I've been searching for.

Linda: Hello, Jack

Jack: Hello, Linda. You look like you are floating on cloud nine.

Linda: I am.

Jack: What has made you so happy?

Linda: I think I'm in love.

Jack：Are you? Who's the lucky guy?

Linda：His name is Daniel.

Jack：How did you meet him?

Linda：We both study Chinese in the same class. We are sharing the desk.

Jack：Tell me about him.

Linda：He's very an attractive and handsome young boy.

Jack：What do you like best about him?

Linda：He's very funny. And we have so much in common. He makes me laugh all the time.

Jack：What don't you like about him?

Linda：No, none. I love his everything. He is unique. He's just the boy I've been searching for.

Jack：Now, you see him through rose colored glasses.

Dialogue **TWO**

Listen to the CD and answer the following questions with the information you hear.

1. What did the woman do at the weekend?

   She read some magazines, listened to music and did some cleaning.

2. Is this weekend different from the before, according to the woman?

   No, it's just usual.

3. How long have they been together, according to the dialogue?

   It's about four months.

4. What does the woman think about the man?

   The woman thinks the man is enthusiastic and brave.

5. According to the man, what's the meaning of "There will never be another you"?

   It means she is the best love of the man.

Script

Tom：I know it's only been the weekend. But it seems a long time to me. I miss you when we are not together.

Mary：Me too.

Tom：How about your weekend?

Mary：Just the usual. I read some magazines, listened to music, and did some cleaning.

Tom：Sounds great. I was thinking about it this weekend. Do you know how long we've been going together?

Mary：About four months.

Tom：Yeah, four month or so. I want to ask you a question and I hope you'll answer it as honestly as you can, OK?

Mary：Go ahead!

Tom：What do you think of me?

Mary：Great. You're kind and I think you are enthusiastic and brave . . .

Tom：You know I'm happy to have known you and really care about you. You are beautiful, active and considerate. There will never be another you. Wherever you go, whatever you do, I will be right here waiting for you. I can't help falling in love with you.

Mary：I . . .

----

1. they start going on single dates—just one boy and one girl
2. a blind date for you with someone you don't know
3. who your partner will be
4. have romantic interest in mind
5. they don't want to date anyone else

Part III Speaking——*I Love you*

Useful Expressions About Love

Do you have a boyfriend/girlfriend now?

What do you think of me?

I think you're great.

You're the most beautiful woman I've ever seen.

I'm crazy for you.

I'm infatuated with you.

I didn't know you felt that way.

I have strong feelings for Tom.

Are you available tonight?

Are you busy tonight?

If you're free, why don't we go out tonight?

Please keep me company for a while.

May I ask you out?

I want you to meet my parents.

You're my type.

You're my kind of woman/man.

May I hold your hand?

Pair Work

Sample

John: Linda, I need your help. I don't know what to do.

Linda: What's bothering you?

John: I think I've fallen in love with a girl. She's beautiful and clever and her manner is elegant. She's the right girl for me.

Linda: Then ask her out and tell her your thoughts.

John: But she's so excellent. I'm afraid she'll turn me down.

Linda: If you don't try, you'll never know the result. That's my suggestion.

John: Um—yes, you're right. But what should I do, specifically?

Linda: You could do everything like being friendly to her, talking with her and asking her to go with you to the cinema.

John: Not bad. Any other ideas?

Linda: What about going to a picnic? Or you could take her to the art museum to show you have culture.

John: Good idea.

Linda: Certainly I must have come up with something you can use. How do you like the ideas I've given you?

John: They are all good.

Role-play

Sample

Mary: How beautiful they are and they smell delicious! I love them and thank you!

David: Happy Valentine's Day! My sweetheart!

Mary: Happy Valentine's Day to you! Darling!

David: You are more beautiful than these roses.

Mary: I don't know how, but I love you more now than the beginning.

David: Yes, we are a match made in heaven. I still remember that I saw you for the first time and felt like I'd been struck by lightning.

Mary: I want to thank you for your kindness and patience. You've always been there for me.

David: Maybe you didn't realize but you made every day a joyous moment and a happy time.

Mary: I'm happy to have known you.

David: I'm so glad that we met one another, too. I love you.

Mary: I love you, too!

Part IV   Reading

 **Text A**   **Background**

Love is one of the most beautiful emotions you can ever go through. When you are in love, everything looks just perfect. Things move in order and you feel top of the world. You feel that you are lucky to get love. However when you love someone, you have to show it.

One of the best ways to express love is to write a note to your loved one. Write it in a beautiful way with words expressing all your gentle and loving thoughts about your love. No matter how busy you are, it is important that you spend quality time with your love. Take her to a cinema or roam around the town or shop together. Show your care and love. Give gifts to your loved one. It need not to be expensive all the time. Even some simple gifts are good enough to show your love for her.

Loving is good but showing your love is even better.

New Words

durable   /ˈdjʊərəbl/   *adj.* 耐用的,持久的

    e. g.   This pair of shoes is durable.
             这双鞋很耐磨。

embarrassment   /ɪmˈbærəsmənt/   *n.* 尴尬,难堪;令人尴尬的事(人),困境

    e. g.   His financial embarrassment is due to his careless spending.
             他经济上的困境是因为他乱花钱。

gentle   /ˈdʒentl/   *adj.* 和善的,温和的;柔和的,和缓的

    e. g.   I can feel the gentle breeze clearing the mist.
             我能感觉到吹散薄雾的柔风。

glisten   /ˈglɪsən/   *vi.* 闪闪发光,闪闪发亮

    e. g.   Her eyes glistened with tears.
             她闪着泪光。

harmonious   /hɑːˈməʊnɪəs/   *adj.* 和谐的,融洽的

    e. g.   Relations with our neighbors are very harmonious at the moment.
             我们目前同邻居们的关系十分和谐。

immediately   /ɪˈmiːdɪətlɪ/   *adv.* 立即,马上

    e. g.   If you want to catch that train, we'd better set off for the station immediately.
             你要是想赶上那班火车,咱们就最好马上动身去火车站。

luxurious   /lʌgˈzjʊərɪəs/   *adj.* 奢侈的,豪华的

    e. g.   The lady appeared with a luxurious fur coat.

那位夫人穿着华贵的毛皮外套来了。

opinion /əˈpɪnjən/ *n.* 意见,看法,主张

 e. g. What's your opinion on the plan?

   你对此计划是何看法?

recover /rɪˈkʌvə/ *vt.* 恢复,弥补;找回,重新发现

 e. g. He's now fully recovered from his stroke.

   他现已从中风病完全康复了。

romantic /rəʊˈmæntɪk/ *adj.* 富有浪漫色彩的;多情的;空想的,不切实际的

 e. g. I like reading romantic love novels.

   我喜欢读浪漫的爱情小说。

sew /səʊ/ *v.* (sewed, sewn/sewed)

 e. g. My mother is sewing up the hole in my trousers.

   妈妈正在缝我裤子上的洞。

thoughtfully /ˈθɔːtfəlɪ/ *adv.* 沉思地,深思地;体贴地,考虑周到地

 e. g. She looked at him thoughtfully.

   她若有所思地看着他。

tuition /tjuˈɪʃən/ *n.* 学费

 e. g. For a few, scholarship is the source of their tuition.

   对少数人来说,奖学金是他们的学费来源。

valentine /ˈvæləntaɪn/ *n.* 情人,心爱的人;情人节赠送个情人的礼物或卡片

 e. g. Will you be my valentine?

   你愿做我的爱人吗?

Phrases and Expressions

after a while 不久,过一会儿

 e. g. After a while, I fell asleep.

   过了一会儿,我睡着了。

be tired from/of 对……厌倦,厌烦

 e. g. The husband is tired of his wife's never-ending complaints.

   这个丈夫已经厌倦了他妻子没完没了的抱怨。

by oneself 独自地,单独地

 e. g. The student decided to work out the difficult problem by himself.

   这个学生决心独自解决这道难题。

in a great embarrassment 很尴尬

 e. g. She looked away in a great embarrassment.

   她窘得把目光转到别处去了。

in one's opinion 在某人看来

 e. g. In my opinion, the house is not worth the price they are asking.

在我看来,这房子值不了他们要的价钱。

lose one's temper　发脾气

e. g.　You mustn't lose your temper with the child.

　　　　你不应该对孩子发火。

make up　形成,构成;捏造,虚构;化妆

e. g.　The mother made up a story to tell her son.

　　　　妈妈编了个故事讲给儿子听。

out of the question　不可能的,绝对做不到的

e. g.　If you keep on eating like this, losing weight is out of the question.

　　　　如果你照这样吃下去,减肥是不可能的。

参 考 译 文

爱只是一根线

1　有时,我真的怀疑父母之间是否还有爱。他们每天忙着挣钱来支付我和哥哥的高额学费。他们从未像我在书中读到的,或在电视中看到的那样互诉衷肠。在他们眼中,说"我爱你"简直是一种奢侈,更不用说在情人节给彼此送花了。我的父亲脾气不好,经过了一天辛苦的工作,他经常会生气。

2　一天,母亲正在缝被子,而我静静地坐在她的旁边看着她。

3　"妈妈,我问你个问题?"待了一会,我说。

4　"什么?"母亲回答,继续她手头的活。

5　"你和爸爸之间有没有爱啊?"我低声地问。

6　母亲突然停下了手中的活,满眼诧异地抬起头。她没有马上回答,过了一会,她低下头继续缝被子。

7　我很担心我的话伤害了她。我感到很尴尬,不知道该干什么。但是后来母亲还是回答了我。

8　"苏珊",她想了想说:"看看这些线,有的地方,你能看得见,但是大多数的线都隐藏在被子里,这些线让被子长久耐用。如果把生活看成一床被子,那么爱就是其中的线。你不可能随时随地看到它,但是它却实实在在地存在着。爱是内在的。"

9　我认真地听着但却无法明白她的话,直到第二年春天。那次,父亲突然病得很重。母亲在医院陪他呆了一个月。当他们从医院回来时,脸色都很苍白。看上去,两个人都像得了一场大病似的。

10　从医院回来之后,每天早晨和傍晚,母亲都扶着父亲在乡间小路上散步,我的父亲也从来没有这么温柔过,他们看上去是那么和谐的一对。沿着乡间的小路,路旁是许多美丽的鲜花、绿草和树木,太阳透过树叶的缝隙照进温柔的光,所有这一切构成了世间最美的图画。

11　医生说父亲两个月后就会康复。但是,两个月之后,他还是不能自己站起来。我们所有人都很担心他。

12 "爸爸,你感觉怎么样?"一天,我问他。

13 "苏珊,别担心我,"他温柔地说,"说实话,我喜欢和你母亲一起走路。我喜欢这种生活。"透过他的眼睛,我知道他深深地爱着我的母亲。

14 曾经我以为爱就是鲜花、礼物和甜蜜的吻。但是经历这件事之后,我才明白爱就是我们生活这床"被子"里的线。爱是内在的,它让生活坚固而温暖。

Exercises

I. Reading Comprehension

Section A

1. A 2. D 3. C 4. D 5. C

Section B

1. The parents are busy trying to earn money to pay the high tuition for the author and her brother.

2. They never act in the romantic way and never send flowers to each other on Valentine's Day; so to say "I love you" is luxurious.

3. Because mother thinks that life is like a quilt. The thread appears sometimes, but most of it disappears in the quilt. The thread really makes the quilt strong and durable, so love should be a thread. It can hardly be seen anywhere or anytime, but it's really there. Love is inside.

4. The author's mother.

5. The parents' slow walking on the country road, along which were many beautiful flowers, green grass and trees and the sunshine gently glistening through the leaves. All these made up the most beautiful picture in the world.

Section C

1. Love should be romantic and inside. It is not only the sweet kiss and red flowers. It means the two people do through thick and thin together, and share the joy and sorrow.

2. Omitted.

3. Tell your partner you love them. Show appreciation for your partner. Share your likes and dislikes, dreams and fears, achievements and mistakes, or anything else to your partner. Give gifts. Respond gracefully to your partner's demands and shortcomings. Strive for equality.

II. Vocabulary and Structure

Section A

1. D 2. B 3. A 4. C 5. C 6. C 7. C 8. A 9. B 10. D

Section B

1. Mother sewed a patch on my jeans yesterday.
   妈妈昨天给我补了牛仔裤上的一个洞。

2. They increased their income by raising silkworms and so on.
   他们靠养蚕等增加收入。

3. He was so embarrassed when people talked about his privacy.
   当人们谈论他的隐私时他感到很尴尬。

4. You should be gentle when you bath the baby.
   给婴儿洗澡时请轻柔一些。

5. Thank you for introducing me to Dr. Brown. Thanks to him, I have recovered completely.
   谢谢你把我介绍给布朗医生,多谢他的治疗,我已经完全康复了。

6. You can see the beautiful scene of the harmony of rivers and mountains.
   你可以看到山和水的和谐美景。

7. We all like Paul, because he's very thoughtful for all of us.
   我们都喜欢保罗,因为他对我们所有人都很体贴。

8. My doctor says I need an operation, but I think I should ask for a second opinion.
   我的大夫说我需要动一个手术,但是我认为我还应该问一下别人的意见。

III. Word Building

1. The little girl moved his arms upward and downward, calling out her mother.
   小女孩上下舞动着手臂,嘴里喊着妈妈。

2. It is necessary for everybody in the dormitory to live as harmoniously as possible with others.
   宿舍中的每一个人都有必要尽可能地和别人和睦相处。

3. The man pulled thoughtfully at his cigarette before commenting on our suggestion.
   那人若有所思地吸了口烟,然后就我们的建议发表见解。

4. After about a mile, they turned seawards.
   一海里之后,他们掉头驶向大海。

5. She sings beautifully; what's more, she dances well.
   她的歌声优美,此外,舞也跳得不错。

6. If you want to catch the train, we'd better set off for the station immediately.
   你要想赶上那班火车,咱们最好马上动身去火车站。

7. This is a luxuriously appointed bathroom, with gold taps and a thick carpet.
   这是一个陈设豪华的浴室,配有精致的水龙头和厚厚的地毯。

8. The road extends eastward towards the river.
   这条路朝着河流向东延伸。

IV. Grammar Focus

1. They did not stop working until it became completely dark.

2. He didn't go to bed until he had studied deep into night.

3. One does not know the value of health until one loses it.

4. You may not go out until your work is done.

5. The baby did not stop crying until the mother came back.

V. Translation

1. I always think <u>there is a generation gap between the old and the young</u>.

我总认为老人和青年人之间存在代沟。

2. They had no money, so <u>it was out of the question for them to order a pizza</u>.

他们没有钱,因此他们绝对不可能点比萨。

3. <u>Once I thought the idea had changed just as times had changed</u>, but now I see I was wrong.

我以为随着时代的变化这种观念已经改变了,但现在我明白我错了。

4. <u>In my opinion, you have no other choice</u>, so you'd better finish it as early as possible.

在我看来你没有其他的选择余地,因此你最好尽快完成。

5. My parents are busy earning money <u>in order to pay the high tuition for me</u>.

为了支付我的高额学费,父母忙着挣钱。

VI. Writing

Sample

A Resume

Wang Ling

Shanxi University, Taiyuan, Shanxi Province

Telephone Number:13000000000

Email:wangling 0000000@163. com

Employment Objective:a position of teaching

Education

2008/09—2010/06 Shanxi University   English Major M. A

2004/09—2008/06 Shanxi University   English Major B. A.

Work Experience

2008/10—2010/05:as a part-time tourist guide for China Traveling Agency

2006/06—2008/06:as a vice-chairman of the University Student Union

2004/10—2006/05: typing and filling as a part-time job for Stone Company during the vacation

Capabilities and skills

Language skill:excellent English, average Japanese

Certifications:

2008/03 TEM Band 8
2007/04 TEM Band 4
2006/06 CET 6
Computer skill: 2005/12 provincial level computer test band 1 2005111111111

Honors/Awards

The first ranking scholarship
Outstanding student leader
The outstanding prize in the First-Term telecommunications Cup Competition

Personal Information

Gender: female   Date of birth: 1986/02/22
Political background: Probationary Party Member
Leadership position: the chair of League Member
Address: Taiyuan, Shanxi Province

Supervisor

Mr. Zhang
Professor of English Department
Shanxi University
Telephone Number: 13000000123

Notes

Resume, also called curriculum vitae, is important to a job seeker. A resume should include personal information, career objective, education, working experience, capabilities and skills, awards, honors and activities and references.

Personal Information includes full name, gender, date of birth, place of birth, nationality, martial status, religion, and address. Name, address, phone number and email address should be at the top of the first page.

Career Objective is a short sentence describing what type of work you hope to obtain.

Education includes degree or certificates, major and schools. Generally, this section can begin with the most recent education background.

Working Experience consists of paid or unpaid experience, full-time or part-time experience. Begin this section with the most present job.

Capabilities and Skills. List all your relevant abilities in details.

Awards, Honors and Activities. List your awards, honor and activities in chronological order.

In the references Part, give the name, business address, telephone number and the occupation of your supervisor or your teacher.

Text B   **Background**

1. Judaism

Judaism is the religion, philosophy and way of life of the Jewish people. Judaism, originating in the Hebrew Bible and explored in later texts such as the Talmud, is considered by Jews to be the expression of the covenantal relationship that God developed with the Children of Israel. Judaism claims a historical continuity spanning more than 3,000 years. It is one of the oldest monotheistic religions, and the oldest to survive into the present day. Its texts, traditions and values have inspired later Abrahamic religions, including Christianity, Islam and the Baha' Faith.

2. Cathilicism

Catholicism is a general term for the body of the Catholic faith, its theologies and doctrines, its liturgical, ethical, spiritual, and behavioral characteristics, as well as the religious people as a whole. Catholicism is distinguished from other forms of Christianity in its particular understanding and commitment to tradition, the sacraments, the mediation between God, and communion. Catholicism includes a monastic life, religious orders, a religious appreciation of the arts, a communal understanding of sin and redemption, and missionary activity.

Although Christianity and Judaism share historical roots, these two religions diverged in the first century, and continue to diverge in fundamental ways. Judaism places emphasis on actions, focusing primary questions on how to respond to the eternal covenant that God made with Israelites and Proselytes. Christianity places emphasis on correct belief in some Christian denominations going so far as to claim that human actions are irrelevant. Simply put, Christians achieve salvation through accepting Jesus Christ as their Lord and Savior. This is stated clearly as the path and way to heaven for a number of times.

3. Dear John Letter

A "Dear John letter" is a letter written to a husband or boyfriend to inform him their relationship is over, usually because the author has found another lover. Dear John Letters are often written out of an inability or unwillingness to inform the man in person. The reverse situation, in which someone writes to his wife or girlfriend to break off the relationship, is referred to as a "Dear Jane letter".

New Words

affair /əˈfeə/ *n.* 事情,事件
    e. g. The World's Fair is a big affair.
        世界博览会是一个盛举。

catholic /ˈkæθəlɪk/ *adj.* 天主教的;普遍的,广泛的
    e. g. He studied in a Catholic school.
        他在一所天主教学校学习。

commitment /kəˈmɪtmənt/ *n.* 承诺,许诺

e. g. You can offer your lover a commitment that will help stabilize your personal life.
给爱人一个许诺，这将有助于稳固你们之间的关系。

correspond /ˌkɒrɪsˈpɒnd/ *vi.* 通信；相一致，符合

e. g. They often corresponded with each other in the last few years.
他们在过去的几年里经常互相通信。

I promise you that my words should correspond with my action.
我向你许诺我将言行一致。

curious /ˈkjʊərɪəs/ *adj.* 好奇的，好求知的

e. g. Most of little children are curious about what they see.
大部分的小孩子对他们看到的都感到好奇。

discharge /dɪsˈtʃɑːdʒ/ *n.* 退役；释放，解雇

e. g. After his discharge from the army, he went to his hometown.
退役之后，他回到了他的家乡。

fantasy /ˈfæntəsɪ/ *n.* 想象，幻想

e. g. The young people always like living in a world of fantasy.
年青人总喜欢生活在幻想的世界里。

frequent /ˈfriːkwənt/ *adj.* 频繁的，常见的，时常发生的

e. g. Their frequent quarrel made their marriage worse.
他们频繁的吵架使他们的婚姻恶化。

giggle /ˈgɪgl/ *vi.* 咯咯笑，傻笑

　　　　　n. 傻笑

e. g. Hearing the mother's voice, the child couldn't help giggling.
听到妈妈的声音，小孩情不自禁的咯咯笑起来。

grace /greɪs/ *n.* 优雅

e. g. She performed on the stage with an easy grace.
她在舞台上的表演轻松自如。

highlight /ˈhaɪlaɪt/ *n.* 最精彩（或最突出）的部分

　　　　　vt. 使显著；强调

e. g. The highlight of this movie is the last which adds up to a lot of tears.
这部电影最精彩的部分是最后，赚了观众不少眼泪。

interval /ˈɪntəvəl/ *n.* 间隔，间距

e. g. She comes back to see her little daughter at regular intervals.
她每隔一段时间就回来看看她可爱的女儿。

Jewish /ˈdʒuːɪʃ/ *adj.* 犹太人的；犹太教徒的

e. g. He descended from Jewish stock.
他是犹太人的后裔。

mention /ˈmenʃən/ *vt.* 提到，说起；

　　　　　n. 提及，说起

e. g. Did she mention she was married?

她提过她结婚了么？

mermaid /ˈmɜːmeɪd/ *n.* 美人鱼

e. g. Have you heard about the story of mermaids?

你听说过美人鱼的故事吗？

mutual /ˈmjuːtʃʊəl/ *adj.* 互相的，彼此的；共同的，共有的

e. g. The relations between husband and wife are based on the fundaments of mutual respect.

夫妻关系建立在相互的尊敬基础上。

oblique /əˈbliːk/ *adj.* 间接的，拐弯抹角的

e. g. He made oblique references to her lack of experience.

他拐弯抹角地说她缺乏经验。

orthodox /ˈɔːθədɒks/ *adj.* 正统的，正宗的；传统的

e. g. This is an orthodox economic theory.

这是一种正统的经济理论。

prospect /ˈprɒspekt/ *n.* 前景，前途；景象

e. g. I'm sure you'll have a bright prospect.

我确定你会有个光明的前景。

snapshot /ˈsnæpʃɒt/ *n.* 快照，照片

e. g. I'd like to see your girl's snapshots.

我想看看你女朋友的照片。

startle /ˈstɑːtl/ *v.* （使）惊吓，吃惊

e. g. We were all startled when we heard the super star committed suicide.

当我们听说那个超级巨星自杀了都吃了一惊。

strike /straɪk/ *v.* （Struck, struck/stricken）打，击；（钟）敲响报时

e. g. Strike while the iron is hot.

趁热打铁。

tongue-tied /ˈtʌŋˌtaɪd/ *adj.* 结巴；发音不清楚的

e. g. He remained tongue-tied for a long time.

他半天说不出话来。

unrequited /ˌʌnrɪˈkwaɪtɪd/ *adj.* （爱情）没有回报的，单相思的

e. g. Her love for the boy was unrequited.

她对那个男孩的爱情没有得到回报。

upbringing /ˈʌpˌbrɪŋɪŋ/ *n.* 教养；养育，抚育

e. g. He had a normal middle-class upbringing.

他接受的是正规的中产阶级教育。

whereabouts /ˈhweərəˈbaʊts/ *n.* 下落，去向

e. g. He is the only person who knows his boss' whereabouts.

他是唯一知道老板下落的人。

Phrases and Expressions

as though 好像，似乎

    e. g. The teacher treats his students as if they were his children.

    这个老师对待学生像对待自己的孩子一样。

at any rate 无论如何，至少

    e. g. At any rate, you should give me a chance to explain to you.

    无论如何，你应该给我一个向你解释的机会。

at the sight of 看见……时

    e. g. The little girl passed out at the sight of the tiger.

    小女孩一看到老虎就吓得晕过去了。

break out （战争、打斗等不愉快事件）突然发生，爆发

    e. g. Dark clouds were gathering in the skies over Europe. War was soon to break out.

    欧州上空乌云密布，战争即将爆发。

dream away 虚度光阴

    e. g. Life is short. Don't dream away your life.

    生命短暂，切勿虚度人生。

hear from 收到……的来信

    e. g. I look forward to hearing from your letter in the future.

    盼望着不久能收到你的来信。

learn of 听说

    e. g. When did you learn of the death of the film star?

    你什么时候听说那个影星的死讯？

look back on 回忆

    e. g. They like to look back on those unforgettable years in the college.

    他们喜欢回忆在大学的那些难忘的岁月。

参 考 译 文

初 恋

我记得在五年级那喧哗的教室，那一刻柔和的灯光倾泻在她的秀发上，她转过头来，我们四目相对，久久地凝视。刹那间，我的心灵被深深地触动了，这就是我初恋的感觉。

她叫雷切尔，是我整个中学年代魂牵梦绕的名字。只要一看到她的身影，我就会心慌意乱，在她面前说话也变得结结巴巴。她那犹太教正统的教养和自己天主教徒的种种顾虑使我们表现出一种初恋者的羞涩，连亲吻也是可望而不可即的事，尽管我十分渴望。在一次舞会上，我终于拥抱了她。拥抱让她幸福地笑出了声，这信任的笑声让我恨以前的那些犹豫不决的想法。

无论如何我都没想到我对雷切尔的爱会毫无结果。我们中学毕业后,她上了大学,我却应征入伍。二战爆发后,我被派遣到国外。刚开始,我们彼此鸿雁传情,她的信件成了我那段艰苦而又漫长岁月中生命里最精彩的部分。曾有一次,她给我寄来了一张身着泳装的照片,使得我对她的爱痴狂得简直想入非非了。在接下来的那封信中我提出了结婚的请求,她的回信似乎立刻减少,浪漫之情也褪去好多。

我回国后第一件事就是要见见我的雷切尔。她母亲告诉我雷切尔与大学里的一位学医的同学结婚了,早已不在这儿住了。

在我退役前我接到了她的那封"绝交信"。信中她委婉地解释我们之间不能结合的原因,她是爱尔兰人而我是犹太人。回首那段时间,虽然在最初的几个月里我简直不想活在这个世上了,但很快我就恢复过来。以后的生活里,我也像雷切尔那样找到了自己的人生伴侣,我们彼此永久又深深地爱着,同甘共苦直到今天。

然而最近,在相隔四十多年之后,我又收到了她的来信。信中说她的丈夫已经去世。她是在路过我居住的小镇时,从昔日的一位共同好友那里得知我的下落的。我们约好再见一面。

我感到又好奇又激动,因为在过去的这几年里我都没有想起过她,只是一日清晨,她的一个电话又把我带回到尘封的往事中。餐桌前的她令我非常吃惊,这位白发苍苍的家庭主妇难道就是我日思夜想、梦寐以求的雷切尔吗?难道这就是相片上身着泳装,美丽的美人鱼吗?

时间的流逝使我们共同回首往事,探求往日的生活。我们就像老朋友那样愉快地交谈着,发现彼此都是做爷爷奶奶的人了。

我告诉她我对那张照片的感受以及我是如何带着照片渡过那战争的煎熬的。

我们的笑声惊动了邻桌的人,接下来我们的目光躲躲闪闪。那一刻我们彼此凝视对方的那种感觉已经消失了。

在我把她送入出租车之前,她转过身来说,"我想再看你一眼,告诉你一件事。"我们又一次凝视。"谢谢你曾经如此真挚地爱过我。"我们互相吻着,之后,她便消失在我的视野里了。

虽然一切都已经过去了,但我却有一种想高歌、大喊、狂舞的冲动。万事皆有终结,很快这种感觉就过去了。现在,我可以动身回家了。

Exercises

I. Reading Comprehension
1. B 2. D 3. A 4. C 5. D

II. Vocabulary and Structure
1. C 2. D 3. B 4. C 5. B 6. A 7. D 8. A 9. B 10. C

III. Translation
1. <u>The first thing you should notice</u> is that we have divided our search area into a square grid.

你应该注意的第一件事是,我们把搜索区域分割成了方块的格子。

2. She walked along the path, <u>her daughter following close behind</u>.

她沿着小路走,女儿紧跟在后面。

3. <u>Day after day I prayed to hear from him</u>, but nothing happened.

日复一日我祈祷能够收到他的来信,但一封信都没收到。

4. His wife had passed some years ago, now he lived all alone, so now <u>the highlight of this day was waiting by the phone</u>.

几年前他的妻子去世,现在他独自一人生活,所以现在一天的重要事情便是在电话机旁等着。

5. We soon realized <u>the impossibility of reaching the city before midnight</u>.

很快我们便意识到午夜前抵达那个城市是不可能的。

Part V　Time for Fun

参 考 译 文

我晚饭后从不工作

　　一位农场主非常吝啬,不想让他雇佣的帮手停下来休息。一天早上,他对帮手说:"从地里回来,又要洗手吃饭,又花时间,真是太不方便了。我们何不省点时间,现在就吃午饭呢?"

　　雇员同意了。农场主的妻子端进来一些冷肉和油炸土豆。于是,两个人便开始吃起来。

　　吃完后,吝啬鬼说:"既然我们还在桌子边,让我们连晚饭也吃了吧。"这次上桌的有排骨、煮土豆和杂烩青菜。于是两个人又吃起来。

　　"现在三顿饭都吃过了,"农场主宣称道,"我们便可以出去一整天不停地干活了。"

　　"哦,不,"那帮手回答说,"晚饭后我从不工作。"

Unit 5

Happiness

Part I   Teaching Objectives

* Listening & Speaking

Help students to be familiar with the topic — talking about *your feeling of happiness and unhappiness* and memorize useful expressions.

* Words & Expressions

Grasp some new words and expressions, such as *handle*, *joke*, *turn*, *guarantee*, *take on*, *deal with*, *keep in touch with* and so on.

* Grammar

How to use the structure of *no/not +without*, *can not... and not* or *not/not/few/never + negative adv.*

* Writing

Understand and write *a memo*.

Part II   Listening——*I'm Feeling Good*

New Words

dorm   /dɔːm/   *n.* 宿舍
    e.g.   She's not feeling well and is staying in the dorm.
        她感觉不舒服,因此呆在宿舍里。
fault   /fɔːlt/   *n.* 过失,过错
    e.g.   Don't be afraid. We know that it is not your fault.
        别担心,我们知道不是你的错。
mad   /mæd/   *adj.* 恼火的,愤怒的

e. g. His complete lack of responsibility drives me mad.

他的毫不负责使我极为生气。

regret /rɪˈgret/ *v.* 后悔,遗憾

e. g. You'll regret what you have done.

你会为你所做的感到后悔的。

ride /raɪd/ *n.* 骑马(或车)

v. 骑(马或车等),乘坐

e. g. I had a ride on a horse for an hour.

我骑马骑了一个小时。

We ride our horses in the park each morning.

我们每天早晨在公园里骑马。

scream /skriːm/ *v.* 喊叫,尖叫

e. g. She screamed that there was a snake under the bed.

她大声喊叫床下有蛇。

swear /sweə/ *v.* 咒骂,用粗口骂人;发誓

e. g. Her stepmother often swore at him, sometimes for no reason at all.

他的继母经常骂他,有时毫无理由。

trooper /ˈtruːpə/ *n.* 骑兵,骑警

e. g. He hopes to be an excellent trooper.

他希望成为一名优秀的骑兵。

unreasonable /ʌnˈriːzənəbl/ *adj.* 不合理的,不讲道理的

e. g. I know they have made the most unreasonable demands on you.

我知道他们向你提出了最无理的要求。

Phrases and Expressions

as mad as a wet hen 非常生气

e. g. Everybody that was not invited was as mad as a wet hen.

没有收到邀请的人个个都很生气。

in one's shoes 处于某人境地

e. g. If I were in your shoes, I'd tell Jan to get lost.

我要处在你的位置,我会叫简滚开的。

fall asleep 入睡,熟睡

e. g. I always fall asleep when watching TV.

我看电视时总会入睡。

go for a spin 开车兜风

e. g. I have invited them to go for a spin in my new car this Sunday.

我邀请他们星期天坐我的新车去兜风。

pick up　接(某人)上车;拾起,拿起

　　e. g.　My boyfriend will pick me up at the station.

　　　　　我男朋友会到车站接我。

swear like a trooper　满口粗话

　　e. g.　He swore like a trooper when I complained about his work.

　　　　　我对他的工作提出不满意见,他便破口大骂。

Dialogue One

Listen to the CD and mark T for True or F for False according to the dialogue.

1. F　2. T　3. T　4. T　5. F

Script

I'm feeling good.

Mary：It's been a long time. How's everything?

John：I'm feeling good. I feel like a million dollars.

Mary：Is this your new car, so how's it doing these days?

John：Perfect. Couldn't be better!

Mary：You made a good choice, then?

John：Yeah. It's just what I want.

Mary：No regrets?

John：No, no regrets. In fact, I'm very happy with my choices.

Mary：I'm happy that you're happy.

John：Thanks.

Mary：How about giving me a ride in your new car?

John：Sure, anytime. Just say the word, and I'll pick you up, so we can go for a spin. I'm very pleased with my new car.

Mary：Yeah, I agree. It looks great. I wish I could afford to buy one just like it. I love cool cars.

Dialogue Two

Listen to the CD and answer the following questions with the information you hear.

1. Where did Julia go these years?

   She went to China.

2. According to Julia, what are the Chinese people like?

   They are friendly.

3. Who hasn't changed a bit?

   Diana hasn't changed a bit.

4. When will Julia go to China?

   She will go to China next month.

5. Why does Diana congratulate Julia?

Because Julia will be a mother.

I've never been this happy.

James: Is it you, Julia?

Julia: Oh. Diana! How lovely to see you again after so many years!

James: Yes. It's been ages, hasn't it? Where were you these years?

Julia: I went to China and taught American Literature in a university. And I had a wonderful time there.

James: What are the people there like?

Julia: They are extremely friendly. I like them.

James: So you look awfully well!

Julia: So do you! You haven't changed a bit! Were you here these years?

James: I just returned from Canada. I want to stay with my mother for a time. How about you?

Julia: Next month I'll go to China.

James: Why will you go to China?

Julia: My husband is a Chinese professor. I've never been this happy because I'll have a baby.

James: Oh! That's wonderful news! You'll be a mother. Congratulations!

Julia: Thank you!

1. who are as miserable as if they were living in hell
2. money is not the only answer to all problems
3. the secret to happiness lies in your successful work
4. you have earned through your own honest effort
5. by taking advantage of others or by hurting others

Part III Speaking——I'm Unhappy

Useful Expressions About Happiness and Unhappiness

I'm thrilled.

I'm in heaven.

I'm happy you told me.

I feel like a million dollars.

I've never been as happy as I am now.

This is the happiest moment in my life.

This is the best moment of my life.

I'm walking on air.

I jumped for joy.

Nothing could be more wonderful.

It really makes my blood boil when this sort of things happen.

I can't stand your impatience any more.

How irritating!

How infuriating!

Pair Work

Sample

John: Hi, long time no see!

Nancy: Hello, how are you!

John: Not bad. Not as good as you seem, though. You're pretty happy. Why? What's the good news?

Nancy: I can't believe this. I've passed GRE.

John: That's wonderful news. You've been worrying about this for quite some time!

Nancy: Yeah. Thank God! I made it. I'm off to Sydney to study English Literature in Sydney University. I've always wanted to go there. And now I have a big chance.

John: Sounds very exciting! You must be thrilled.

Nancy: I am. I can hardly sleep these days.

John: Hey, I helped you a lot in your preparation for the exam. How could you thank me for that?

Nancy: I'll buy you lunch tomorrow!

Role-play

Sample

Robert: I can't believe this. I spent one year working on my research, and my professor rejected it just in two minutes.

Linda: Oh, he is too mean. Why would he do that?

Robert: He said what I did was useless and unpractical. But I think he just dislikes me.

Linda: Calm down. Why would he dislike you? Maybe your research is indeed too unpractical.

Robert: What? You don't believe me either? I'm so disappointed with you.

Linda: No. What I really mean is that maybe you can change your research a little and your professor will like it.

Robert: I really can't stand his strictness.

Part IV   Reading

Text A   **Background**

Kansas City

Kansas City is the largest city in Missouri, a U. S. state and is the anchor city of the Kansas City Metropolitan Area, the second largest metro area in Missouri. Kansas City was founded in 1838 as the "Town of Kansas" at the confluence of the Missouri and Kansas rivers and was incorporated in its present form in 1850. Situated opposite to Kansas City, Kansas, the whole city was the site to several battles during the Civil War, including the Battle of Westport. The city is well known for its contributions to the musical styles of jazz and blues, as well as to cuisine.

New Words

adventure   /ədˈventʃə/   *n.* 冒险活动;奇遇,历险

    e. g.   She would not allow the marshal to interfere with his adventure.

         她不允许警官干预他的冒险行为。

brace   /breɪs/   *n.* 牙箍

    e. g.   In order to look more beautiful, she had to have braces for a lone time.

         她为了看上去更漂亮,不得不戴好长时间的牙箍。

consequence   /ˈkɒnsɪkwəns/   *n.* 后果,结果;影响

    e. g.   As a consequence of smoking, my father coughs frequently.

         因为吸烟的缘故,我父亲经常咳嗽。

exchange   /ɪksˈtʃeɪndʒ/   *n.* 交流,互换;交谈,对话

    e. g.   He gave me an apple in exchange of an orange.

         他给我一个苹果,交换一个橙子。

furious   /ˈfjʊərɪəs/   *adj.* 暴怒的,狂怒的;强烈的,激烈的

    e. g.   If I am late he is sure to be furious.

         如果我去迟了,他准会大发雷霆。

handle   /ˈhændl/   *v.* 处理,应付;操作,管理

    e. g.   His wise father knows how to handle him.

         聪明的父亲知道如何管教他。

         Oh, this is amazing! How can you people handle so many festivals?

         哇,不是吧! 你们怎么可能应付这么多的节日?

marital   /ˈmærɪtl/   *adj.* 婚姻的,夫妻间的

e. g.　She intimated that she and her husband were having marital problems.

　　　　她含蓄地暗示她和她丈夫的婚姻出现了问题。

negotiation　/nɪˌgəʊʃɪˈeɪʃən/　*n.* 协商，谈判

e. g.　I'm glad our negotiation has come to a successful conclusion.

　　　　我很高兴这次洽谈圆满成功。

orthodontia　/ɔːθəˈdɒnʃə/　*n.* 畸齿矫正术，正牙学

e. g.　He is studying orthodontia.

　　　　他正在学习畸齿矫正术。

orthodontist　/ɔːθəˈdɒntɪst/　*n.* 口腔正畸医师

e. g.　Her boy friend is an orthodontist.

　　　　她的男朋友是个口腔矫正医生。

periodically　/pɪərɪˈɒdɪklɪ/　*adj.* 周期性地；定期地，偶尔

e. g.　These factories are periodically inspected by government officials.

　　　　这些工厂由政府官员定期检查。

resolution　/ˌrezəˈluːʃən/　*n.* 决心，决定；决定要做的事

e. g.　The resolution passed at the last meeting produced a great effect outside.

　　　　上次会议所作出的决定在外界引起了很大的反响。

scare　/skeə/　*v.* 惊恐，恐吓

e. g.　Don't be scared. He's just crying wolf again.

　　　　不要怕，他只不过是在吓人罢了。

schedule　/ˈʃedjuːl, ˈskedʒʊl/　*v.* 安排，调度

e. g.　The secretary is trying to schedule the month's appointments.

　　　　秘书正在设法安排这个月的约会。

stomp　/stɒmp/　*v.* 跺脚，重踏

e. g.　He looked funny stomping round the dance floor.

　　　　他在舞池里跺著舞步，样子很可笑。

volume　/ˈvɒlju(ː)m/　*n.* 容积，体积；总量；音量响度；(书)卷，册

e. g.　The volume of this container is 20 cubic meters.

　　　　这个集装箱的体积是 20 立方米。

　　　　As he stood there, this cataract on a sudden increased in volume.

　　　　他站在那儿，这道瀑布忽然越来越大了。

Phrases and Expressions

at full volume　最大程度，最大量

e. g.　He likes to listen to music with the radio turned on at full volume.

　　　　他听音乐时喜欢将收音机的音量开到最大。

beside oneself　（由于气愤、激动等）失去控制，忘形

e. g.　He was beside himself with joy when his wife gave birth to their first child.

妻子生下第一个孩子时他欣喜若狂。

catch up 赶超,赶上

e.g. After being out of school so long, he had to work hard to catch up with the other students.

缺课这么久,他为了赶上其他同学必须努力学习。

deal with 对付,处理

e.g. We have several important matters to deal with at our next meeting.

下次会议我们有几件重要的事情要处理。

lighten up 放松,别认真

e.g. She is always trying to get her husband to lighten up.

她总是尽力让丈夫心情愉悦。

right now 立刻马上

e.g. We went right now as soon as we received your call.

我们一接到你的电话就出发了。

work on/at 从事于,致力于

e.g. They have been working on a research for new anti-cancer drugs.

他们一直致力于新的抗癌药物的研究。

参 考 译 文

面对烦恼,一笑了之

1 我正在进行"快乐项目",你也应该有一个! 每个人的项目看上去都不同,但是绝大多数人都会从中受益——不需要努力赶超,只要立刻参与。

2 大家都知道,处理消极情绪最有效方式之一是"放轻松"。如果你悲伤,找一个大笑的理由。如果你生气,去开个玩笑。不过,做比说难。

3 昨晚我有机会尝试"一笑了之"。按照去年的家庭协议,我丈夫负责女儿牙齿矫正术的事。牙齿校正医生的办公室就在他的办公室拐角处,丈夫同意由他安排时间带女儿去。这真是太棒了!

4 在我们去堪萨斯度假的飞机上,我女儿把她的"设备"(就是她嘴里戴的新鲜玩意,吃东西时得取下来)弄丢了。我们找遍飞机就是没找到。一周后我们回到家,我丈夫没有打牙医电话预约。时间一天天过去。我隔一段时间就提醒他,但是他无动于衷。

5 一想起他的拖拉,我就十分恼怒。昨晚,我跺着脚进卧室,准备大发雷霆。"这真的很要紧,很重要,她正在发育,而且,那很贵,她还得再等下去,可你答应过会带她去做。"可我想了想,还是给丈夫温柔一刀比较好。

6 于是我走过去,用手臂搂着他,温柔地说:"你知道吗? 如果你明天还不给校正牙医打电话。我会很生气,我会发怒,我不知道会做出什么事情。我可没威胁你,只是给你一个公正的警告"。我边说边笑。

7 他摇了摇头说:"知道,知道啦! 我现在就给自己发一封邮件。"他还真发了。今天

他约好了医生。

　8　我不确定说笑会不会比愤怒更奏效,但是我相信效果不会更差。而且比那些让人不愉快的交流方式要好得多。我对这个方法更满意;我丈夫也一样。

　9　当然,我承认,在遵守"一笑了之"的决议中,我并不觉得有趣。我的笑话一点不好笑,但采用一个幽默的态度能让情况大有改观。

　10　说"一笑了之"容易,但是当你感到愤怒、害怕、无聊或烦心的时候要做到很难。你找到让自己开玩笑的方法了吗?

Exercises

I. Reading Comprehension

Section A

1. C 2. A 3. D 4. B 5. B

Section B

1. To make a joke of it.

2. Because the author thinks that the orthodontist's office is right around the corner from the husband's office and his husband could schedule the appointment with the orthodontist and take their daughter.

3. They went to Kansas City for the holiday.

4. Because she thought of her Happiness Project "make a joke of it".

5. Her husband happily accepted the author's idea and made the appointment. So the author thought the attempt to take a humorous attitude could make a huge difference.

Section C

1. Omitted.

2. No, it is not the best way. But it is the most effective way, because maybe sometimes to lighten up can not solve the problem, however, it could help people feel relaxed, at least it is more effective than getting angry.

3. 1) Go to a new environment, surround yourself with different things, different people and different sensations, and it's easier for you to leave your bad mood behind you.

　2) Watch a funny movie, play your favorite song, go for a walk in your local park, or grab a coffee and a slice of pie in that great coffee shop. Do something that feels good and put a smile on your face, and your bad mood will be history.

　3) Hit the gym. Hitting the gym not only releases those feel-good chemicals, but it's a great distraction, diverting your attention away from your bad mood and giving you something to do that occupies your body and mind.

II. Vocabulary and Structure

Section A

1. B   2. D   3. A   4. C   5. D   6. A   7. B   8. C   9. D   10. B

Section B

1. The new airport is <u>scheduled</u> to open just before Christmas.

   新机场定于圣诞节前开始投入使用。

2. A dog, who was the sole occupant of the vessel, <u>furiously</u> barked and bit the heels of the boarders.

   船上只有一条狗,它疯狂地吠了起来,咬着登船人的脚跟。

3. Physics is an ever-changing <u>adventure</u> with interest first in one direction and then another.

   物理学是一个永远在更新着的冒险科学,它先是在这个方面,接着又在另一个方面吸引着人们。

4. I like to do—to be a sort of cultural—<u>exchange</u> envoy, to do some bridging work.

   我喜欢当一名文化交流的使者,做"搭桥"的工作。

5. Many people regard "<u>periodical</u>" as synonymous with "serial", particularly in the USA, where the term "serial" is preferred.

   很多人用英语的 periodical 和 serial 两个词表示期刊,特别是在美国,更多地是用 serial 一词。

6. I am glad that we have agreed on term of the contract after repeated <u>negotiations</u>.

   我很高兴经过反复磋商我们就合同条款取得一致意见。

7. Alex <u>stomped</u> angrily up the stairs.

   亚历克斯怒气冲冲地重步走上楼梯。

8. Thunder and lightning frighten and <u>scare</u> most children and many adults.

   多数孩子和和许多成人恐惧害怕雷鸣和闪电。

III. Word Building

1. I have an appointment with my <u>dentist</u> this afternoon and ask him to clean my teeth.

   我和牙科医生约好今天下午请他帮我清洁牙齿。

2. Before going traveling, we bought a <u>tourist</u> handbook.

   出去旅游之前,我们买了一本旅游手册。

3. The police are connecting this incident with last week's <u>terrorist</u> bombing.

   警方认为这次事件和上周的恐怖分子爆炸事件有关。

4. He is a famous <u>specialist</u> in English linguistics.

   他是著名的英语语言学专家。

5. A good <u>typist</u> can finish typing the long article in a short while.

   一个好的打字员可在短时间内打完一长篇文章。

6. If you are always ready to accept failure, we have to say you are a <u>defeatist</u>.

   如果你总是能接受失败的话,我们不得不说你是一个失败主义者。

7. The <u>novelist</u> makes his heroine lead a happy life at the end of the book.

这个小说家在书的结尾让他的女主人公过上了幸福的生活。

8. Once a <u>Laborist</u>, he has now reverted to vote Tory like her parents.

他一度是工党党员，但现在已像他父母一样投票支持保守党了。

IV. Grammar Focus

1. It is essential for everyone to get plenty of exercise for a healthy life.

2. Nowadays it is very common for students to work to earn money.

3. It is important for us to have a balanced, healthy diet.

4. It is pleasant for the mother to see her son growing into a man.

5. It is natural for her to refuse to take part in it.

V. Translation

1. Everyone knows that <u>one of the most effective ways to handle negative emotions</u> is to lighten up.

大家都知道处理消极情绪最有效的方式之一是放松。

2. <u>Only on very rare occasions does he give you a word of praise</u>, so it means you did a good job.

他难得称赞你一句，说明你做的很好。

3. He likes to listen to music <u>with the radio turned on at full volume</u>.

他喜欢听音乐时将收音机的音量开到最大。

4. <u>Whether she comes here or we go there</u>, the topic of discussion will remain unchanged.

无论她来这还是我们去那里，论题仍然不变。

5. <u>In order to catch up with and surpass the advanced world levels</u>, we'll have to accelerate our speed.

要赶超世界先进水平，我们还得快马加鞭。

VI. Writing

Sample

TO：The General Manager

FROM：Mr. Wang Ming, the manager of Rong Xin Company

DATE：10：00 am

SUBJECT：Mr. Wang's visit

MESSAGE：Mr. Wang came to visit GM at 10 am.

          He wished to discuss with GM the possibility of opening a food factory in our city.

          GM was having a meeting, so couldn't see him.

          Mr. Wang will leave next Monday.

          He asked GM to call him this afternoon.

Notes

A memo is a hard-copy (sent on paper) document. It is used for internal communicating of an organization. It is usually short, and it contains TO, FROM, DATE, SUBJECT HEADING and MESSAGE SECTIONS. A memo doesn't need to be sighed, but sometimes the sender's name is written at the bottom to be more friendly, or the sender's full name to be more formal.

Sample Memo Format.

A Memo

To: (sender's name and job title)

From: (your name and job title)

Date: (complete and current date)

Subject: (what the memo is about)

Message:

 **Text B**   **Background**

Relax. Don't take yourself too seriously. Happiness is largely a choice. Feel grateful for all of the good in your life.

Smile. Once you have enough to pay for life's basics, think to yourself, "I've won." Happiness is contagious. Find someone who is happy and stand close to him or her.

Success is not the key to happiness; happiness is the key to success. Surround yourself with positive, life-affirming people.

Make others happy, have big dreams, and enjoy the journey. Grab every single morsel of happiness which comes in your way. Look out for moments of pleasure and wonder.

Take care of your body. Be happy right here, right now, while working towards a better tomorrow.

Get sunlight and fresh air. Engage your mind in a puzzle, jigsaw puzzles or crossword puzzles. Listen to music, make music and quiet your mind chatter.

Meditate. practise yoga, tai chi, or Qigong. Get a box of six Guatemalan worry dolls. Before going to bed, tell one worry to each doll and put them under your pillow; while you sleep, the dolls will take your troubles away.

Get involved in a cause that's important to you. Have a cat or a dog; pet them often. Perform random acts of kindness, anonymous or not. Surround yourself with pleasant smells: jasmine, lavender, sandalwood... Put things in perspective. Go for a brisk walk. Stretch. Go to a museum. Find a hobby you love. Engage in pleasurable activities.

Get rid of things that make you unhappy. Make happiness a priority in your life. Do something hedonistic: think afternoon at a spa or go out dancing.

Create a serene environment. Resolve to be a little bit happier today than you were yesterday. Tilt your head back and let out a raucous peal of laughter. . .

New Words

accomplishment /əˈkɒmplɪʃmənt/ *n.* 完成，实现；成绩，成就

   e. g. The first walk on the moon was quite an accomplishment.

         第一次在月球上行走是一项了不起的成就。

achieve /əˈtʃiːv/ *v.* 取得，获得；实现，完成

   e. g. He will grasp at anything that might help him achieve fame.

         他会抢着做任何有助于他成名的事情。

career /kəˈrɪə/ *n.* 事业，职业；经历，生涯

   e. g. He was not interested in her stage career.

         他对她的演戏职业不感兴趣。

create /krɪ(ː)ˈeɪt/ *vt.* 产生，引起；创造，创作

   e. g. His behavior created a good impression.

         他的举止给人留下了很好的印象。

deprive /dɪˈpraɪv/ *v.* 剥夺，使丧失

   e. g. You even want to deprive us of the freedom of our hearts.

         你都要剥夺我们心里的自由。

destination /ˌdestɪˈneɪʃən/ *n.* 目的地，终点；目标，目的

   e. g. If he took the short cut, he would arrive at the destination much earlier.

         如果他走近路，他会更早到达目的地。

disappear /ˌdɪsəˈpɪə/ *vi.* 不见，消失

   e. g. The sun had scarcely risen before the fog began to disappear.

         太阳刚一升起，雾气就开始消散了。

elusive /ɪˈluːsɪv/ *adj.* 难以捉摸的；难以找到的

   e. g. I've been trying all day to reach him on the telephone, but he's very elusive.

         我整天都在打电话找他，但是找不着。

emotion /ɪˈməʊʃən/ *n.* 情感，情绪，激情

   e. g. For the first time there was a hint of emotion in his voice.

         他的声音中第一次露出了少许感情。

guarantee /ˌgærənˈtiː/ *v.* 担保，保证

   e. g. Can you guarantee me a job when I get there?

         你可以确保我到那儿就可以找到一份工作吗？

         We guarantee that the debts will be paid in one month.

         我们保证下个月还清债务。

hesitate /ˈhezɪteɪt/ *vi.* 犹豫，踌躇

   e. g. If you hesitate too long, you will miss the opportunity.

         如果你老是犹豫不决，就会错失良机。

She hesitates about the choice between the two boys.

她在两个男孩之间犹豫。

limit /ˈlɪmɪt/ *v.* 限制,限定

> **e. g.** We must limit the expense to what we can afford.
>
> 我们必须把开销限制在自己经济能力的范围内。

mood /muːd/ *n.* 心情,心境

> **e. g.** She is in a good mood recently.
>
> 她最近心情不错。

pain /peɪn/ *n.* 痛苦,疼痛;辛苦

> **e. g.** His behavior caused his parents a great deal of pain.
>
> 他的所作所为使他的父母极为难过。

permanent /ˈpɜːmənənt/ *adj.* 持久的,恒久的

> **e. g.** Are you looking for a temporary or permanent job?
>
> 你想找一个长期的还是临时的工作?

satisfaction /ˌsætɪsˈfækʃən/ *n.* 满意,满足

> **e. g.** Winning gave us emotional satisfaction.
>
> 获胜给予我们感情上的满足。

spare /speə/ *v.* 省出,抽出

>   *adj.* 备用的;空闲的
>
> **e. g.** Can you spare the time to practice oral English with me?
>
> 你愿意抽出时间和我练口语么?
>
> Every car should carry a spare tire.
>
> 每辆车都应该带有备用轮胎。

undesirable /ˌʌndɪˈzaɪərəbəl/ *adj.* 不受欢迎的,不合意的,讨厌的

> **e. g.** The incident could have undesirable consequences for the government.
>
> 该事件会给政府带来不良后果。

Phrases and Expressions

come true 实现,成真

> **e. g.** Her wish to become a doctor has come true.
>
> 她想当医生的愿望实现了。

keep in touch with 与……保持联络

> **e. g.** I think the best way to keep in touch with my friends is through email.
>
> 我认为和朋友们最好的联系方式是发电子邮件。

share with 与……分享

> **e. g.** I have some good experience to share with the language learners.
>
> 我有一些好的经验与语言学习者分享。

ups and downs 盛衰,沉浮

e. g. The company has undergone many ups and downs.
这家公司历经盛衰浮沉。

参 考 译 文

如果你想快乐

1   快乐不拘泥于形式,每个人总是想拥有更多的快乐。不过除了你竭力保持的美好记忆外,你不可能永远都拥有快乐。快乐在每一分、每一时、每一天都可以被感受。

2   每个人都梦想能一直快快乐乐的,可快乐总是变化着的,让人难以捉摸。此刻你还可能在快乐中,而彼刻就可能感到痛苦。我们总在经历着情绪上的跌宕起伏,没有人知道将来会发生什么。当不幸发生的时候,所有的快乐就会随即消失。然而,什么是快乐呢? 它是指对你的生命价值肯定的一种内心的情感,快乐是你经历收获的喜悦后的满足感。你的情感会按照你的意愿表露出来。

3   你为什么会感到快乐呢? 因为你所做的一切正是你喜欢做的。你会因你的朋友、你的家人、爱人、工作、成功和事业而快乐,任何一种都会让你有快乐的心情。过去那些存在于你内心深处的美好记忆会让你快乐,因为你随时都可以去回忆它们。快乐时你的内心感受不到任何一丝不快,因为它们离你还远。你仍在享受着内心的那份快乐心情。

4   如果你想快乐,就要结识更多的朋友,并和它们保持联系。听听他们的有趣故事,一同分享喜悦。这能让你在生活上保持积极的心态,也能使你因感到满足而获得更好的心情。

5   如果听音乐能使你快乐起来,那就听吧,带上你的 CD 机听你想听的音乐。如果和家人在一起你很开心,那就抽时间和他们呆在一起。和孩子们一起玩耍会让你体验到不曾有过的快乐。如果你很享受旅行,那就买张票,定好目的地,启程吧,美丽的小岛,白茫茫的海滩,你可以感受海风的新鲜气息。

6   如果想提高生活水平,做大事业,你对目前的工作也满意,而且做好了面对压力的准备,那么坚持你的梦想,不要犹豫,奋斗拼搏,努力实现自己的梦想。如果你快乐是因为恋爱了,那就和那个改变了你的女孩子结婚吧。拥有一个自己的家庭,与她共同分担,以你自己的方式应对家庭生活中将会出现的形形色色的难题。如果你喜欢一个人呆着,喜欢看看书籍和杂志,那就以你的方式享受吧。没有人能够剥夺你做能让你快乐的事情的权利,快乐是你自己的。

7   所有能激发你,让你感到很欣慰的都是快乐。趁着还有时间享受快乐吧。将所有你想要的情感都保留在你心间,剔除不想要的。将来你遇到挑战时,至少你还拥有快乐,到那时你可能就会明白快乐对于你及世界的意义。

Exercises

I. Reading Comprehension

1. D   2. B   3. A   4. D   5. C

II. Vocabulary and Structure

1. B 2. C 3. A 4. C 5. D 6. C 7. B 8. B 9. C 10. A

III. Translation

1. Though he has had ups and downs, I believed all along that he would succeed someday.
虽然他历经沉浮,但我始终相信他总有一天会成功的。

2. If you want to improve your living condition, don't hesitate, strive hard and make your dream come true.
如果你想改善你的生活条件,就不要犹豫,奋斗拼搏,努力实现自己的梦想。

3. He loves her, so he'd like to share his joy of success with her.
他爱她,所以他想和她一起分享他成功的快乐。

4. If you have too much time, be a volunteer, which will definitely help you understand that your problems are very small and maybe even funny.
如果你有很多的时间,去做志愿者吧,做志愿者将会帮你认识到自己的问题是多么的渺小甚至是可笑。

5. No matter what happens we'll keep in touch with each other, because I thought you as my best friend.
无论发生什么,我们都要保持联系,因为我把你看成我最好的朋友。

Part V   Time for Fun

参 考 译 文

地　坑

从前,有个农夫住在马路边上。

这不是个繁忙的路段,偶尔有汽车从农场路过。

就在农场大门的旁边,路当中有个大坑。

坑里总是充满了水,汽车司机根本看不出坑有多深。他们以为很浅。

司机们一旦把车开进坑里,就别想再开出来,因为坑太深了。

农夫也不怎么在农场里干活,大部分时间他都在注视着这个坑。

当一个汽车开进坑里,他就用他的拖拉机把它拉上来,然后为此向司机索要很多钱。

一天,一位汽车司机对他说:"你日日夜夜把汽车往外拉,肯定挣了很多钱。"

"哦,不,"农夫说,"我夜里不干这活儿,夜里我得朝这坑里注水。"

Unit 6

Dreams

Part I   Teaching Objectives

* Listening & Speaking

Help the students to be familiar with the topic—*how to express yourself appropriately when talking about dream and success* and memorize useful expressions.

* Words & Expressions

Study some new words and expressions, such as *challenge*, *squeeze*, *retire*, *motivate*, *mesmerize*, *revel*, *bestow*, *frustrated*, *embarrassed*, *optional*, *dream of*, *dress up*, *revel in*, *bestow upon/on*, *give up*, *in tribute to*, *pay (a) tribute to* and so on.

* Grammar

Learn to use the structure of *never too. . . to. . . .*

* Writing

Understand and write *a want ad*.

Part II   Listening——*Dream and Success*

New Words

abject /ˈæbdʒekt /   *adj.* （情况）凄惨的；绝望的

    e. g.   This policy has turned out to be an abject failure.

            这一政策最后以惨败而告终。

adversary /ˈædvəsərɪ/   *n.* 对手，敌手

    e. g.   He saw her as his main adversary within the company.

            他将她视为公司中主要的对手。

bowl /bəʊl/   *v.* 投球；击中三柱门把（击球员）杀出局

e. g.　It is my turn to bowl.　该我投球了。

compromise　/ˈkɒmprəmaɪz/　*v.* 折中解决;妥协,退让

e. g.　They compromised by going to the cinema.

他们采取折中的办法去看电影。

I am prepared to make some concession on minor details, but I cannot compromise on fundamentals.

在一些细节上我可以作些让步,但在基本原则上我是不会妥协的。

debriefing　/ˈdibriːfɪŋ/　*n.* 任务报告,任务报告中提出的情报

e. g.　Put someone through a debriefing and make him report.

让某人作任务汇报或让他作报告。

negotiate　/nɪˈgəʊʃɪeɪt/　*v.* 谈判,磋商,协商,议定

e. g.　We've decided to negotiate a loan with them.

我们决定和他们商定贷款之事。

potential　/pəˈtenʃəl/　*adj.* 潜在的;有可能的

e. g.　It's important to draw out a child's potential capacities.

发掘孩子的潜在能力是很重要的。

profitable　/ˈprɒfɪtəbl/　*adj.* 有利可图的,赢利的;有益的,有好处的

e. g.　That business became profitable last year.

那项生意去年变得很赚钱。

query　/ˈkwɪərɪ/　*n.* 问题,疑问,询问

e. g.　They raised a query on his sincerity.

他们对他是否真诚提出质疑。

ultimately　/ˈʌltɪmɪtlɪ/　*adv.* 最后,最终

e. g.　Ultimately, the war had to end; it cost too much in both lives and dollars.

由于人员伤亡过重和花费过多,战争最终不得不终止。

Phrases and Expressions

be confronted with　面临(危险,困难等),面对

e. g.　I am confronted with a dilemma.　我遇上一个难题。

be in the mood for　有心情

e. g.　I sometimes like listening to blues, but I have to be in the mood for it.

我有时也喜欢听蓝调音乐,但必须是在我有情绪听的时候。

due to　由于,因为

e. g.　Due to the extreme cold, we were unable to plant the trees.

因为天气很冷,所以我们无法去植树。

in the pipeline　在考虑(或规划、准备)中

e. g.　We have an interesting new program in the pipeline. It should be on sale early next year.

我们正在设计一个有趣的新数据库程序,明年年初大概就能上市了。

lose heart 丧失勇气,失去信心

e. g. With all the setbacks, he did not lose heart.

尽管遭受种种挫折,他没有丧失信心。

nothing more than 仅仅,只不过

e. g. They expected nothing more than a new-type machine.

他们期望的只不过是一台新型的机器而已。

pay off 使得益,有报偿

e. g. The investor believes that his investment will pay off handsomely soon.

这个投资者相信他的投资不久会有相当大的收益。

John studied hard before the examination, and it paid off. He made an A.

约翰在考试前努力学习,这没有白费,他得了个 A。

work on 继续工作;致力于……

e. g. They'll work on till sunset. 他们将继续工作,直到日落。

He has been working on a new novel for over a year now.

近一年多来,他一直在写一部新小说。

Dialogue **One**

Listen to the CD and mark T for True or F for False according to the dialogue.

1. F 2. F 3. T 4. T 5. F

Script

Nancy: You'd never guess it, but our meeting has been the most successful ever.

James: Really? How So?

Nancy: All our hard work has finally paid off! We were able to negotiate 3 new highly profitable supply contracts.

James: That's great! How did you manage that?

Nancy: Due to good preparations, we were able to answer every query and compromise on any potential problems.

James: Have you been able to complete your meeting report yet?

Nancy: No, not yet. I'm still putting it together with the rest of the negotiation team.

James: When do you think you'll be able to give the management team a full debriefing?

Nancy: Hopefully, next Tuesday.

James: That'd be great. We have a few more business meetings in the pipeline for you to work on in the future.

Dialogue **Two**

Listen to the CD and answer the following questions with the information you hear.

1. Will the man go to dance with the woman tonight?

No, he won't.

2. Why does the man look so upset?

Because he lost the tennis game yesterday.

3. What was the man wondering?

He was wondering if it's appropriate for him to play tennis.

4. According to the woman, what shouldn't we do when we come across difficulties?

We should never lose heart.

5. What will the man do in the following days?

In the following days he will keep practicing on a regular basis and follow the examples of those who are successful and learn from them.

Failure is the mother of success.

Jane: David, would you like to go to dance with us tonight?

David: Jane, I am just not in the mood for this.

Jane: You look so upset. What's going on?

David: I lost the tennis game yesterday.

Jane: Really? What a pity. Are you OK?

David: Fine. I just don't want to play tennis any more.

Jane: Is it that bad? It's nothing more than a game.

David: My adversary bowled me with the very first ball. I was wondering if it's appropriate for me to play tennis.

Jane: Come on. Failure is the mother of success. I'm sure you'll succeed ultimately.

David: But the worst thing for me now is that I don't know what to do.

Jane: David, you know, we should never lose heart when we come across difficulties or when we are confronted with failure. Instead, we should learn from our experience, build up our confidence and work even harder and smarter towards our purpose.

David: Perhaps you are right. Maybe in the following days I should keep practicing on a regular basis and follow the examples of those who are successful and learn from them.

Jane: Yeah, I think if you can persist in practicing and learning, you will certainly achieve remarkable success in your life.

1. Your habits will determine whether you are successful or not

2. because you are guaranteed to succeed in the long run

3. there is no doubt that you will achieve all your goals and be successful

4. develop positive habits in your life and eliminate your negative habits

5. write down exactly what actions you're going to take every single day

Part III   Speaking——*Succeed in the End*

Useful Expressions About Dream and Success

All our hard work has finally paid off.

Failure is the mother of success.

I am just not in the mood for this.

You look so upset.

What's going on?

What a pity.

Are you OK?

I'm sure you'll succeed ultimately.

We should never lose heart.

We should learn from our experience, and build up our confidence.

If you can persist in practicing and learning you will certainly...

I sincerely think that all you have done deserve it.

It is very necessary for you to build up your self-confidence.

I'll try my best to reach my goal.

Do you plan to be a(n)...?

I am also desirous of becoming...one day.

I cannot agree with you more.

Pair Work

Sample

Michael: Hello, Elizabeth. Why do you look so upset?

Elizabeth: I failed in the English Speech Contest yesterday.

Michael: Oh, I am very sorry to hear that.

Elizabeth: I'm fine, but I just don't know what I should do next to improve myself. What's worse now, I even doubt that what I have done is just a waste of time. Maybe I have no potential to do well in the English speech.

Michael: Oh dear, come on. I sincerely think that all you have done deserve it. Please don't lose heart.

Elizabeth: Can you give me some advice on what I should do next?

Michael: Well, I think, at first, it is very necessary for you to build up your self-confidence. And then maybe it will be helpful for you to imitate some famous speakers and learn from them. Persist in practicing and I'm sure you can be successful finally.

Elizabeth: Yeah, perhaps you're right. Anyway, I'll try my best to reach my goal. Thanks a lot.

Role-play

Sample

Max: Hello, Jenny, what are you doing here?

Jenny: I am reading an article about how to be a good teacher.

Max: Oh, really? Do you plan to be an English teacher after graduation?

Jenny: Yes, of course. How about you?

Max: That's also my dream. I am also desirous of becoming an English teacher one day.

Jenny: Wonderful. And what do you think is the most important thing to be an English teacher?

Max: I think it is significant and basic for us to be professional in the English skills and get familiar with cultures of foreign countries.

Jenny: Yeah, I cannot agree with you more. And I also think the sense of responsibility should be valued, too. As a teacher, apart from being professional, it is very important to be responsible for the students and always remember to set a good example for the students.

Max: So we should always bear in mind to cultivate our sense of responsibility when we are learning professional knowledge.

Jenny: Yes. Let's work together and put our best efforts forth to do good preparations for being a good English teacher after graduation.

Part IV   Reading

Text A   **Background**

Everybody has his or her long-life dream, but not everybody makes a reality of it. You wish to have your own business and to succeed in it. If this is not the case and you are ready to get over a great number of problems to achieve your greatest goal, then go ahead! If you have never faced with time management, you should know the following main rules of successful time management.

Don't ignore setting the goals.

First of all, you have to set your main goal. It has to be clear and reachable in order to map out an effective action plan. If you clearly understand and formulate your goal it will help you to find the ways to achieve it saving your precious time and efforts. Don't try to reach your aim immediately. Break it into short-term goals and go towards it step by step from the simple to the difficult. Make a list of your short-term and long-term goals in order to reach corresponding goals.

If you fail to plan, you plan to fail.

It means that without proper and competent planning you have more chances to meet unexpected problems, poor preparation and to fail your business at all. Good planning forces you to think about your tasks and projects before you start doing them and to put your thoughts in right direction beforehand. Planning your daily, weekly and monthly workflow will help you not to get distracted and to make a full use of the time.

Prioritize to avoid losing time.

You may feel that you have so many things to do that you don't even know where to start. Learn to prioritize your tasks. Make the more important tasks Urgent or High and set Normal or Low priority to the tasks that don't need hurrying up. This will make you more disciplined and productive.

Have dividends of spending time on scheduling.

When you rely on your sense of time and don't estimate it, you shall run risks to spend on particular task more time than it needs in fact. To solve this problem, start scheduling your tasks. Estimate the time you need for each task, its priority, define its deadlines, due dates and in accordance with them schedule the task on required date and time, set the start and the finish date of each task. If you are responsible and organized by yourself, then you can expect your team mates to have these qualities.

Reward yourself with every small triumph.

If you make a habit to track your task list daily, you will be able to watch your progress and enjoy it every day. This feeling will add you extra strength to go further. Let us congratulate you with starting your career. From such small victories your career starts.

New Words

bestow /bɪˈstəʊ/ *v.* 赠给；授予
    e. g.   Many books were bestowed on her.   送给她很多书。

challenge /ˈtʃælɪndʒ/ *v./n.* 要求，需要；挑战；邀请比赛
    e. g.   She challenged the newspaper to prove its story.
                她要求这家报纸证实报道的真实性。
                Mike thought he could play flute better than Apollo and challenged the god to a
                contest.
                迈克觉得他长笛吹得比阿波罗好，便向这位神发出挑战。
                The new government's first challenge is the economy.
                新政府面临的第一项挑战就是经济。

embarrassed /ɪmˈbærəst/ *adj.* 局促不安的，为难的；窘迫的，尴尬的，害羞的
    e. g.   He always mumbles when he's embarrassed.
                他感到难为情时说话就含糊不清了。
                He became embarrassed when a journalist asked him about his finances.

一名记者对他的经济情况接连提出问题,他很是尴尬。

enthusiastically /ɪnˌθjuːzɪˈæstɪkəlɪ/　*adv.* 热心地,满腔热情地

　　e. g.　The audience cheered him enthusiastically.　观众热情地向他欢呼。

frustrated /frʌsˈtreɪtɪd/　*adj.* 挫败的,失意的,泄气的

　　e. g.　He felt extremely frustrated when things went against him.

　　　　　形势对他不利时,他感到非常失望。

　　　　　He was frustrated by deep poverty.　他因赤贫而灰心丧气。

funeral /ˈfjuːnərəl/　*n.* 葬礼,丧礼

　　e. g.　The funeral made its way slowly through the silent streets.

　　　　　送葬的队伍缓缓地穿过肃静的街道。

icon /ˈaɪkɒn/　*n.* 偶像,崇拜对象;东正教圣像

　　e. g.　Only Marilyn has proved as an enduring fashion icon.

　　　　　只有玛丽莲被证明是经久不衰的偶像。

　　　　　They found an icon in the monastery.

　　　　　他们在修道院中发现了一个圣像。

jittery /ˈdʒɪtərɪ/　*adj.* 〈口〉紧张不安的,神经过敏的

　　e. g.　a jittery vigil in the dark　在黑暗中紧张不安的失眠

lyrics /ˈlɪrɪks/　*n.* 歌词

　　e. g.　I prefer music that has great lyrics.　我更喜欢歌词好的音乐。

mandatory /ˈmændətərɪ/　*adj.* 法定的;强制性的

　　e. g.　the mandatory retirement age of 65　65 岁的法定退休年龄

　　　　　Is the appointment of worker-directors to be mandatory?

　　　　　工人董事的任命是不是强制性的?

mesmerize /ˈmesməraɪz/　*v.* (尤用于被动语态)使入迷

　　e. g.　get mesmerized by family computer　为游戏机所迷

　　　　　He could mesmerize an audience by the sheer force of his presence.

　　　　　他只要一出场,观众就为之倾倒。

motivate /ˈməʊtɪveɪt/　*v.* 激发,诱发;作为……的动机

　　e. g.　No one really knows what motivated him to do so.

　　　　　没人确知他那样做的动机。

optional /ˈɒpʃənl/　*adj.* 可选择的,非强制的,选修的

　　e. g.　optional subjects at school　学校的选修课

podium /ˈpəʊdɪəm/　*n.* 表演台;讲台;乐队指挥台

　　e. g.　Unsteadily he mounted the podium, coughed, and went completely blank.

　　　　　他摇摇晃晃地走上讲台,咳嗽了几声,接着脑子就一片空白。

retire /rɪˈtaɪə/　*v.* 退休,退职;退役;退下;退出(比赛等)

　　e. g.　He will retire from the army/his directorship next year.

　　　　　他明年从部队上退役/从主管职位上退休。

The jury will retire to consider its verdict today.

该陪审团今天将退庭来考虑其裁决。

revel /ˈrevl/ *v.* 陶醉于,沉迷于,纵情于;作乐,狂欢

    e. g.   I think he's secretly reveling in all the attention.

          我觉得他对于能够引起广泛的注意心里感到飘飘然。

          She seems to revel in annoying her parents.   她似乎以惹父母生气为乐。

          They were drinking and reveling all night.   他们整夜喝酒作乐。

squeeze /skwiːz/ *n. /v.* 亲切的拥抱或握手;挤,榨,捏

    e. g.   He gave her an affectionate squeeze.   他亲热地拥抱她。

          The room was crowded but I managed to squeeze in.

          房间人很多,不过我还是设法挤了进去。

wrinkled /ˈrɪŋkld/ *adj.* 有皱纹的

    e. g.   A wrinkled purse, a wrinkled face.   手中无钱,愁容满面。

          A little old woman with a wrinkled face told us our fortunes for ten pence.

          一位满脸皱纹的小个儿老妇人向我们收了十便士,替我们算命。

Phrases and Expressions

beam up at sb.   愉快地微笑

    e. g.   The winner beamed (up) at the audiences with satisfaction.

          获胜者冲着观众满意地笑了。

bestow upon/on   赠与;给予

    e. g.   I shall bear witness to the wonder they bring into our lives, and to the beauty they bestow on our souls.

          我证明他们为我们的生活带来的一切美妙,以及赋予我们灵魂的美好。

dream of   梦想,渴望

    e. g.   I never dreamed of such a thing.   我从没梦想过这样的事情。

          I've long dreamed of paying a visit to the Great Wall.   我一直渴望游览长城。

dress up   打扮,梳理,粉饰;装扮

    e. g.   She dressed the children up.   她把孩子们打扮得漂漂亮亮。

          He dressed himself up as Father Christmas.   他打扮成圣诞老人。

give up   放弃;投降;认输

    e. g.   I can' answer that puzzle; I give up.

          我猜不出这个谜语,我认输了。

          After a week on the run he gave himself up (to the police).

          他经过一周的逃亡之后(向警方)投案了。

in tribute to   向……表示敬意;为了悼念

    e. g.   The government built a statue in tribute to the great hero.

          政府建了雕塑以对这个伟大的英雄致敬。

light up   (使)变得喜悦,(使)兴奋起来

e. g.　Her face lit up when she heard the news.

当她听到这个消息时,脸露喜色。

Tom will really light up when he sees his new bike.

汤姆看见他的新脚踏车时,一定十分高兴。

live it up 〈俚〉享受,纵情欢乐;奢侈浪费

e. g.　Let's go to Europe for two weeks and live it up.

咱们到欧洲两个星期,好好享受一番。

After getting a large inheritance, Bob and Alice lived it up for years.

鲍勃和艾丽斯得到一大笔遗产后,过了好几年奢侈生活。

revel in 陶醉于,沉迷于,纵情于

e. g.　The children revel in country life.　孩子们特别喜欢乡村生活。

pay（a）tribute to 对……表示赞赏或敬意

e. g.　His colleagues paid generous tributes to the outgoing president.

同事们纷纷向外向开朗的总裁致敬。

参 考 译 文

永远别放弃梦想

1　开学的第一天教授向我们化学专业学生做了自我介绍,他还要求我们去结识一位我们还不认识的人。就在我站起来四处张望时,一只手轻轻地搭在了我的肩上。我转过身一看,一位满脸皱纹,个子矮小的老太太正冲着我微笑。这微笑让她浑身光彩照人。她说:"嘿,帅小伙儿,我叫罗斯,今年87岁。我可以拥抱你吗?"我笑了起来,热情地答道:"当然可以啦。"她紧紧地拥抱了我。

2　"你为什么在这么'年轻而天真'的年龄上大学?"我问。她开玩笑地回答说:"我要在此遇到一个有钱的丈夫,结婚,生几个孩子,然后退休,去旅游。""真的吗? 不对吧?"我问她。我很想知道,她这么大年纪,是什么促使她接受这样的挑战。

3　她告诉我,"我一直梦想接受大学教育,而现在我如愿以偿了。"课后我们一同走到学生活动楼,共饮了一杯巧克力泡沫牛奶。我们一下子就成了朋友。在此后的三个月中,我们每天都一起离开教室,聊起来没完没了。在她向我传授她的智慧和分享她的经验时,我着迷了,倾听着她这台"时间机器"。

4　在这一年里,罗斯成了校园里的偶像。不管到哪里,她很容易地就交上了朋友。她喜欢精心打扮,陶醉于其他学生对她的注意,尽情地享受着这一切。到学期末,我们请罗斯在我们的足球宴会上讲话。我永远也不会忘记她的教诲。介绍完毕后她就登上讲台。正当她要开始已准备好的演讲时,她那张5寸长3寸宽的卡片掉在了地上。她有些不知所措,还有点尴尬,于是就靠近话筒干脆说了起来:"很抱歉我这么紧张。我为大斋节戒了啤酒,而这威士忌可是毁了我。按原先准备好的讲是不可能了,还是把我所知道的说给你们听吧。"我们都笑了,她则清了清嗓子开始说:"我们并不因为自己老了而不踢球;我们因为停

止追求开心而变老。要想保持年轻,过得幸福并取得成功只有 4 条秘诀。"

　　5　"每天都要笑,每天都要找到幽默。"

　　6　"一定要有梦想。失去了梦想,人就死了。在我们周围有那么多行尸走肉般的人,他们却不自知。"

　　7　"变老和成熟是有巨大区别的。如果你 19 岁,在床上躺一整年,而不做一件有成效的事情,你会到 20 岁。如果我 87 岁,在床上待一年什么也不做,我也会到 88 岁。谁都会老,那不需要天份或能力。我的意思是要通过在变化中不断地寻找机会而达到成熟。"

　　8　"不要后悔。年长的人一般不会为所做的事而后悔,而会为没有做的事遗憾。只有那些人生充满遗憾的人才惧怕死亡。"

　　9　在演讲结尾她勇敢地唱起了《玫瑰之歌》,还要求我们每个人学习歌词,并在日常生活中将词意付诸行动。

　　10　年末,罗斯结束了她多年前就想开始的大学生涯,取得了学位。毕业一周后,罗斯在睡梦中平静地去世了。

　　11　两千多名大学生出席了她的葬礼,对这位了不起的女士表示敬意。她以身示范,教育我们:发挥自己的潜能永不为晚。

　　12　记住,衰老是无法抗拒的,而成熟却是可以选择的。

Exercises

I. Reading Comprehension

Section A

1. B　2. D　3. A　4. D　5. C

Section B

1. The author found a wrinkled, little old lady called Rose who was smiling at him.

2. The dream of having a college education.

3. They would leave the class together and talk nonstop, and Rose shared with the author her wisdom and experience.

4. Yes, she became a campus icon and she easily made friends wherever she went.

5. The four secrets are as follows: you have to laugh and find humor every day; you've got to have a dream; there is a huge difference between growing older and growing up, so grow up by always finding the opportunity in change; have no regrets.

Section C

1. It is impossible for us to avoid becoming old with the flying time. It is definitely a natural rule for one to grow older day by day. However, what's more important for us is to do our utmost to quest for various opportunities in changes to grow up gradually. No one is too old to learn. Although we are becoming older, we can catch every single chance to learn to

become mature in minds and try our best to make our dreams come true. This is what we can do for sure by our efforts.

2. Rose, an eighty-seven-year old lady, finally realized her dream of having a college education. Almost every student who was on the same campus with her would feel great respect for her as well as her wisdom, and would also be very curious about her rich experience. In my eyes, though old, she was still very much alive. She had never given up her dream of pursuing the study in college even advanced in years, which might be the spirit that the youths are lacking in nowadays and also could be the strong willpower that we should certainly learn. I'm sure every student likes to be friend with this beautiful and charming old lady.

3. I have a dream that is to be an English teacher one day after my graduation. To make it come true, I should make a good plan and move forward towards it step by step. The first and the most basic thing for me to do is to improve my English skills such as listening, speaking, reading and writing, which can make me competent in English communication. What's more, it's also significant for me to accumulate the knowledge of western cultures so as to become more familiar with western countries, through which I can broaden my horizon. The last but not least, I should from now on try my best to do good preparations for being an English teacher not only in words but from the bottom of my heart to take actions. Only in that way can I be ready.

II. Vocabulary and Structure
Section A
1. A 2. B 3. C 4. D 5. A 6. C 7. B 8. A 9. C 10. A

Section B

1. He left a note at the scene of the crime, <u>challenging</u> detectives to catch.
他在作案现场留了一张纸条,挑衅侦探们去抓他。

2. Both sides in the dispute appeared very <u>frustrated</u> at the lack of progress.
争执双方因事情毫无进展而显得十分沮丧。

3. The United States <u>bestowed</u> honorary citizenship upon England's World War II Prime Minster, Sir. Winston Churchill.
美国授予了二战期间的英国首相温斯顿·丘吉尔爵士荣誉公民的称号。

4. Annie was smiling and laughing, clearly <u>reveling</u> in the attention.
安妮时而微笑,时而大笑,显然为受到瞩目而陶醉。

5. He was absolutely <u>mesmerized</u> by Pavarotti on television.
他完全被电视上的帕瓦罗蒂迷住了。

6. You have first got to <u>motivate</u> the children and then to teach them.
你首先得激发孩子的学习兴趣,然后再去教他们。

7. I have decided to <u>retire</u> from Formula 1 racing at the end of the first season.

我已经决定这个赛季末退出一级方程式赛车。

8. The goods are <u>optional</u>, but only one.
这些物品是可以任选的,但只能选一个。

III. Word Building

1. The people of Africa have successfully fought against <u>colonial</u> rule.
非洲人民成功地反抗了殖民统治。

2. It is conspicuous that smoking is <u>harmful</u> to health.
很明显,抽烟对健康有害。

3. If the goods prove <u>defective</u>, the customer has the right to get compensation.
如果货品证明有缺陷,顾客有权索赔。

4. Passengers have to pay <u>additional</u> charges for their extra luggage.
旅客们超量携带的行李要额外付费。

5. A diet lacking in <u>nutritional</u> value will not keep a person healthy.
缺乏营养价值的饮食不能维持人的健康。

6. Electric current is often <u>powerful</u> enough to kill a man.   电流常足以致命。

7. Her brother is the king, but she is the <u>effective</u> ruler.
她的兄弟是国王,但她才是实际的主宰者。

8. His refusal was worded in such a <u>graceful</u> way that we could not be offended.
他婉言谢绝,无损于我们的颜面。

IV. Grammar Focus

1. It's never too late (for us) to start the efforts.
2. He is never too old to work to earn his living.
3. It's never too bad (for us) to take measures to solve it.
4. This math problem is never too difficult for me to work out.
5. It's never too late (for us) to rescue the injured.

V. Translation

1. <u>When the government is in a tight squeeze</u>, it usually tries to borrow money from abroad.
每当政府陷入财政困难,总是试图借贷外债。

2. Lots of the citizens attended the funeral <u>in tribute to the great prime minister</u>.
很多市民出席了这场葬礼,对这位伟大的总理表示敬意。

3. Larry said <u>he had no regrets about retiring</u>.
拉里曾说他对于退休没有任何遗憾。

4. Preventing fires is <u>a problem that challenges everyone's attention</u>.
防火是需要大家都注意的一个问题。

5. Released from prison, <u>she was reveling in her new-found freedom</u>.
从监狱放出来之后,她充分享受着新获得的自由。

VI. Writing

Sample

A Want Ad.

Our company is an owned foreign enterprise. Thanks to our steadily growing business in China, we now invite capable person for the following positions:

Quality Engineer/Manufacturing Engineer

- About 30 years old.
- University graduate in Mechanical Engineering or Automation Engineering.
- 1 ~ 3 years' relevant working experience in Quality or Manufacturing environment and experience in joint venture are preferable.
- Knowledge in Quality System.
- Applicants must have good oral and written English, and be willing to travel.
- Skilled at operating Windows and Excel.

Applicants should send full resumes both in Chinese and English, telephone number and address to: the Personnel Department, Guang Ming Co. Ltd, Sichuan Economic & Technical Development District, Chengdu. The postal code is 610000.

Notes

How to Create a Want Ad.

1. Determine the job category that is best suitable for the position. If the position is for a janitor at a school, you might advertise for a "School Custodian". Perhaps the position will be for a person to answer phones at the office. Your advertisement might identify the position as "Receptionist".

2. Briefly describe where the job is located. Such as "XYZ Company in New Haven", or "The Anderson Building, Downtown Smithville". Give an exact address: "123 Main Street, Smithville".

3. Describe the basic duties that are performed at this job. If this position includes a number of chores, mention a few of them; i. e., "Heavy phones, typing, filing", or "sweeping, trash removal, window washing". This information provides the applicant with a general idea of what he/she will be doing at he/her new job.

4. Tell the reader how to apply for the position. If you want the applicant to come to your place of business, you might say "Apply in person at XYZ Company". Or, if you prefer that the applicant submit their qualifications in writing, you might suggest "Please submit resume by mail to XYZ Company", or "Please apply by e-mail, and include the e-mail address".

Above all, a Want Ad. should generally include:

1) The name of the recruiting unit
2) A brief introduction to the recruiting unit
3) Job titles being offered
4) Job responsibilities
5) Qualifications for application
6) The remuneration being offered
7) Way of application

 **Text B** **Background**

Set and Achieve Goals

Dreams come true through actions, and the best action is to set and achieve goals. Realizing your goals is important; as you realize your goals you will find relief from many of the problems that seem to plague you. But first you must set a goal, then plans and actions will follow. With plans and actions come achievement, success and accomplishment.

Self-realization is an understanding of your direction in life. If you understand your direction, you will see what you must do to achieve your goals. When you reach a goal, you get a realization. This act of achievement makes you feel fulfilled and complete even if only for a few hours, but it still feels good.

Goals are an essential part of life. If a person does not have goals, he often feels a lack of purpose. You may wonder what the purpose of life is. The real meaning of life is growth. When something is growing, it is alive. For us humans we stop physically growing around the age of 21, so after that milestone we can only continue to grow mentally, spiritually and psychologically. To keep growing we must have a purpose, whether we invent one or discover one. Having a purpose in life provides principals, ideas, motivation, reason, and a reason to live. If you have a purpose, you feel competent and assured of yourself. This shall take you to your goals since you are focusing on your objectives in life.

The most important way to realize your goals is to set up short-term goals that work toward long-term goals. For instance, a short-term goal is to walk around the block without stopping, then to run around the block without stopping, then increase the distance every time a goal is reached until the ultimate goal of running a marathon is accomplished. If you start by trying to run the marathon, you will fail, but by starting with smaller goals you will succeed. Therefore, you can understand it is important to set small goals you can reach and all the small goals add up to the ultimate goal. Giving up will only cause you stress. If the goal seems unreachable, break it down into smaller goals. If you set goals beyond your reach, it is likely that you will never reach the end of the race. Setting goals out of your reach will also frustrate you, and as you continue to fail, you will loose self-esteem, self-control and confidence.

Self-realization is the ability to recognize your own potentials and abilities. The realization of self will bring you fulfillment. When a person feels fulfilled he often has a life with more success and achievement. The overall point is to set small goals so that you can eventually achieve your ultimate goal.

As for the long-term goals, they are what will determine your life. When one is reached, enjoy the feeling and then set another. You must keep growing to keep living. As you now realize, it takes efforts to reach goals, and it takes work and perseverance to achieve success. However, it is you, and only you, that must take actions to make it happen.

New Words

count /ˈkaʊnt/ *vi.* 有价值,有重要意义

    e. g. Her opinion counts because of her experience.

        因为她有经验,所以她的意见很重要。

        Quality counts above origin. 质量比产地更重要。

        Knowledge without common sense counts for little.

        没有常识的知识没有多大价值。

court /kɔːt/ *n.* 球场;庭院,院子;法庭,法院

    e. g. Are the players on court yet? 球员都上场了吗?

        The court is very dirty. 这个院子非常脏。

        The matter is still pending in court. 这案子还在法院中悬而未决。

cradle /ˈkreɪdl/ *vt.* (小心轻柔地)抱着

    e. g. I cradled him in my arms. 我小心轻柔地拥他入怀。

dribble /ˈdrɪbl/ *v.* 运球,带球;流口水,垂涎;滴下

    e. g. He dribbled the ball towards Ferris. 他运球传向费里斯。

        He dribbled over his food. 他垂涎面前的食物。

        Rain dribbled down the window. 雨打在窗上,一点一滴地流下来。

hesitation /ˌhezɪˈteɪʃən/ *n.* 犹豫,踌躇,不愿;犹豫(之事或行为)

    e. g. She agreed without the slightest hesitation. 她毫不犹豫地同意了。

        His doubts and hesitations were tiresome. 他的疑惑和犹豫令人厌烦。

muscle /ˈmʌsl/ *vt.* 硬挤

    muscle in 强行挤入(以分享利益)

    e. g. Cohen complained that Kravis was muscling in on his deal.

        科恩抱怨克莱维斯正强行插足他的生意。

rank /ræŋk/ *v.* 将……置于行列中,将……分等级;属某等级,居某地位

    e. g. I rank him among the best pupils of his grade.

        我认为他是他们年级最好的学生之一。

        A major ranks above a captain. 少校比上尉军衔高。

recap /riːˈkæp/ *v.* 扼要重述;概括

    e. g. Can you recap the points included in the proposal?

        你能概括一下这个提议中包括的重点吗?

recess /rɪˈses/ *n.* 学校的课间休息;(工作或业务活动的)中止或暂停期间

    e. g. He decides to visit the school library during recess.

        他准备课间休息的时候去学校图书馆。

        Parliament was hastily recalled from recess.

        休会的议员被匆匆召回开会。

recruiter /rɪˈkruːtə/ *n.* 招聘人员;征兵人员

    e. g. The recruiter is prompted by a variety of questions.

这位考官提出了一系列不同的问题。

reply /rɪˈplaɪ/ *n./v.* 回答,答复;作出回应

    e.g.   My reply may not have been polite, but he asked for it.

        我的回答也许不太礼貌,但这是他自找的。

        I replied with a short note.   我回了一封短信。

        Tom replied that he had finished the work.

        汤姆回答说他已完成了那项工作。

routine /ruːˈtiːn/ *n.* 例行公事,惯例,惯常的程序

    e.g.   The security men changed their usual routine.

        保安人员改变了他们通常的做法。

scholarship /ˈskɒləʃɪp/ *n.* 奖学金

    e.g.   She won a scholarship to go to university.   她获得了上大学的奖学金。

shoot /ʃuːt/ *v.* 足球、曲棍球等射门;投篮;开枪,射击

    e.g.   She is looking for an opportunity to shoot (at goal).   她正寻找机会射门。

        He shot(off) several bullets before hitting the target.

        他射出好几发子弹才射中目标。

varsity /ˈvɑːsɪtɪ/ *n.* 大学(尤指牛津或剑桥);(学校的)代表队

    e.g.   varsity football   大学的足球竞赛   a varsity letter   一封大学代表队的信

Phrases and Expressions

a sea of 无限的,很多的

    e.g.   We must face a sea of troubles and bear them.

        我们必须面对无数的困难,慢慢克服。

        You're really asking for a sea of troubles speaking to me like that.

        你这样对我讲话,真是自找麻烦。

at other times 在其他时候,也有时候,平素,往常

    e.g.   He stays late in bed on Sunday and at other times he has to get up at six.

        星期天他起床迟些,平时他六点就得起床。

in wonder 惊奇,惊讶地

    e.g.   The children gazed in wonder when they saw snow for the first time.

        孩子们第一次见到下雪,都惊奇地盯着看。

much less 更不用说

    e.g.   The baby can't even walk, much less run.

        这婴儿连走都不会,更不用说跑了。

        I couldn't assent to, much less participate in such proceeding.

        我对于这种举动并不赞成,更谈不上参与。

muscle one's way through 挤过

    e.g.   He muscled his way through the crowd to see what had happened.

        他挤过人群看发生了什么事情。

stand out from　突出,显眼;远远超过

e. g.　bright lettering that stands out well from a dark background.

由深色背景衬出很显眼的字。

Her work stands out from the rest as easily the best.

她的工作成绩远比其他人都好。

参 考 译 文

如果梦想足够远大

1　我过去常透过自家厨房的窗户看她,看她从操场上一群男孩子中间奋力挤过,那一刻她显得那么矮小。学校在我家对面,中间隔条街,我经常看到孩子们在下课时间打球。尽管有一大群的孩子,但我觉得她跟其他的孩子截然不同。

2　我记得第一次看到她打篮球的样子。看着她在其他孩子旁边兜来转去,我感到十分惊奇。她总是尽全力跳起投篮,就在那些孩子的头顶上投篮,篮球飞入篮筐。那些男孩总是拼命地阻止她,但没有人可以做得到。

3　我开始注意到她有时候一个人打球。她一遍遍地练习运球和投篮,有时直到天黑。有一天我问她为什么这么刻苦地练习。她直视我,不加思索地说:"我想上大学。只有获得奖学金我才能上大学。我喜欢打篮球,我想只要我打得好,我就能获得奖学金。我要到大学去打篮球,我想成为最棒的球员。我爸爸告诉我,如果梦想足够远大,什么也阻止不了你。"说完她笑了笑,跑向篮球场,又开始我之前见过的一遍又一遍的练习。

4　好吧,我服了她——她是下定了决心。我看着她从初中升到高中。每个星期,她带领的学校篮球队都能获胜。

5　高中某一天,我看见她坐在草地上,头埋在臂弯里。我穿过街道,坐到她旁边清凉的草地上,轻轻地问她出什么事了。"哦,没什么,"她轻声回答,"只是我太矮了。"原来篮球教练告诉她,以五英尺五英寸的身高,她几乎没有机会到一流的球队去打球的——更不用说能拿奖学金了——所以她应该放弃上大学的梦想。

6　她很伤心,我也觉得自己的喉咙发紧,因为我感觉到了她的失望。我问她是否和她爸爸谈过这件事。她抬起头,告诉我,她爸爸说那些教练错了,他们根本不懂得梦想的力量。爸爸告诉她,如果真的想到一个好的大学去打篮球,如果她真的想获得奖学金,任何东西也不能阻止她,除非她自己不愿意。他又一次跟她说:"如果梦想足够远大,什么也阻止不了你。"

7　第二年,当她和她的球队去参加北加利福尼亚州冠军赛时,她被一位大学的招生人员看中了。她真的获得了奖学金,一个全面资助的奖学金,并且入选全美国大学体育协会第一区女子篮球队。她将接受她曾梦想并为之奋斗多年的大学教育。

8　是的,如果梦想足够远大,什么也阻止不了你。

Exercises

I. Reading Comprehension

1. D 2. B 3. A 4. C 5. A

II. Vocabulary and Structure

1. A 2. B 3. D 4. B 5. C 6. B 7. B 8. A 9. D 10. C

III. Translation

1. If you had attended to my advice, <u>you would not be in a sea of troubles now</u>.
   要是当时你听了我的劝告,你现在就不至于苦恼了。

2. Happiness is an emotion not often spoken of at the magazine, <u>much less experienced</u>.
   幸福不是经常在杂志上提到的感情,更不用说是能够时常体验得到的。

3. Many parents have moved away from giving their children family or unisex names and <u>want their youngsters to have names that stand out from the crowd</u>.
   如今,很多父母在给孩子取名时不再想用家族成员的名字或男女通用名,而是希望孩子的名字能够与众不同。

4. <u>Had you come earlier</u>, you would have met him.
   你要是来得早一点,就碰到他了。

5. <u>She muscled through the throng of people</u>, frantically searching for David.
   她使劲挤过人群,拼命寻找大卫。

Part V　Time for Fun

参 考 译 文

分享一切

　　有一对老夫妇到速食店去,叫了一罐可乐和一份薯条。然后他们面对面坐下来,那位老先生先把可乐分成两杯,一杯给他自己,另一杯给他太太。接着他又将薯条分成两份,一份给他太太,一份给自己。然后他开始吃薯条、喝可乐,但是他的太太只是喝可乐,不吃薯条。

　　一个年轻人刚好站在旁边,看到老先生把每样食物都分成两半,觉得很奇怪,他想或许他们没有钱,便跟老夫妇说:"我可以再买一份给你们,你们就不用这样分了。"老先生解释说:"不!不!我们结婚四十年了,一直都是分享每件事物,什么东西都是一个人分一半。不用担心我们,不过还是谢谢你的好意。"过了一会儿,他看只有老先生吃着薯条,老太太没吃,便问老太太:"你为什么都不吃呢?"老太太说:"今天轮到他用牙齿。"

Unit 7

Online Shopping

Part I   Teaching Objectives

* **Listening & Speaking**

   Help the students to be familiar with the topic—*how to express yourself appropriately and efficiently in different shopping situations* and memorize useful expressions.

* **Words & Expressions**

   Study some new words and expressions, such as *trade*, *log*, *glimpse*, *budget*, *transmit*, *redeem*, *account*, *offset*, *dedicate... to...* , *check out*, *be here to stay/have come to stay*, *link up*, *account for* and so on.

* **Grammar**

   Learn to use the structure of *rather than*.

* **Writing**

   Understand and write *a letter of complaint*.

Part II   Listening——*At the Supermarket*

New Words

aisle   /aɪl/   *n.* 过道,通道

   e. g.   An aisle ran the length of the house.   过道的长度等于房子的长度。

condiment   /ˈkɒndɪmənt/   *n.* 调味品,佐料

   e. g.   It has long been a precious condiment and food preservative.
   它是一种珍贵的调味料和食物防腐剂。

identify   /aɪˈdentɪfaɪ/   *vt.* 认出;识别

e. g. Would you be able to identify the man who robbed you?

你能够认出那个抢你东西的人吗？

She learned how to identify medicinal herbs from a traditional Chinese doctor.

她向一位中医大夫学习如何识别草药。

ketchup /ˈketʃəp/ *n.* 番茄酱

e. g. There's a spot of ketchup on the tablecloth. 桌布上有一点番茄酱的渍斑。

label /ˈleɪbəl/ *n.* 标签,标记

vt. 贴标签于

e. g. He attached labels to his luggage. 他把标签贴在行李上。

According to the symbol on the label, this sweater should be washed by hand.

根据标签上的符号,这件针织套衫应该用手洗。

The doctor labeled the bottle. 那位医生给瓶子贴上了标签。

liquor /ˈlɪkə/ *n.* 酒,烈性酒;含酒精饮料

e. g. be overcome with liquor 喝醉

He is always in liquor. 他老是喝得醉醺醺的。

organic /ɔːˈɡænɪk/ *adj.* 有机(体)的,有机物的;器官的;器质性的

e. g. Red soil lacks organic matter. 红土缺乏有机物质。

There is nothing organic wrong with you. 你没有器质性病变。

receipt /riˈsiːt/ *n.* 收据,发票

e. g. I asked for a receipt. 我要一张发票。

slack /slæk/ *n.* 宽松裤

e. g. I put on a pair of golfing slacks. 我穿上了一条高尔夫球宽松裤。

sour /ˈsaʊə/ *adj.* 坏脾气的;别扭的;有发酵味道的,酸腐的,馊的

e. g. She really looks sour this morning. 她今天上午脾气的确有些坏。

The soup has gone sour. 这汤发酸了。

soy sauce /sɔɪˈsɔːs/ *n.* 酱,酱油

e. g. Would you mind passing the soy sauce? 把酱油递给我吧?

variety /vəˈraɪətɪ/ *n.* 品种,种类

e. g. There are different varieties of plants in the garden.

花园里有各种各样的植物。

Phrases and Expressions

drive up 驱车来到……;使……上升

e. g. Just then a friend drove up and gave me a ride.

正在那时,一个朋友开车过来,载了我一程。

The shortage of bread will probably drive prices up.

面包短缺很有可能迫使价格上涨。

go with 跟……相配,协调;赶时髦,随大流

> **e. g.** A yellow blouse goes with her blonde hair. 黄色短上衣和她的金发很相称。
>
> We must go with the times. 我们必须跟上时代潮流。

make an exception 例外

> **e. g.** We can make an exception in this case. 此事可以通融。

on sale 有售,上市;廉价出售

> **e. g.** There are some nice apples on sale in that shop.
>
> 那家商店有些很好的苹果出售。
>
> I got this hat on sale; it was very cheap.
>
> 我在大减价时买到这顶帽子,价格很便宜。

try on 试穿;耍花招,哄骗

> **e. g.** I'd like to try on that blue wool coat. 我想试穿那件蓝色的毛外衣。
>
> It's no use of your trying it on with me. 你想骗我是徒劳的。

 One

Listen to the CD and mark T for True or F for False according to the dialogue.

1. F 2. F 3. T 4. F 5. T

Script

Steve: We need to buy some beer, too. Where is the beer?

Daisy: They don't have beer in this supermarket. We have to go to the liquor store.

Steve: Huh? They don't have beer. How can that be?

Daisy: It's a state law. This state doesn't allow supermarkets to sell beer, but only in liquor stores.

Steve: That's too strict.

Daisy: May be. I agree with you.

Daisy: Excuse me. Do you sell organic vegetables here?

Employee: Yes, we do. They're right in front of you. The organic vegetables are marked with the blue label. Here. Do you see?

Daisy: Sure. Thank you. You should have a sign. That way people could identify which are organic and which aren't.

Employee: They're labeled on the packet, man.

Daisy: One more question.

Employee: Yes?

Daisy: We need to buy some soy sauce. Which aisle is the soy sauce in?

Employee: That would be in aisle 7, with the condiments. It is right next to the ketchup.

Daisy: Thank you. Do you want paper or plastic bags?

Steve: Plastic bags.

Daisy: And do you want to drive up?

Steve: What do you mean?

Daisy: We can have someone put the bags in our trunk for us. We just drive up to that door over there.

Steve: Wow! That's convenient. But I think we can take the groceries by ourselves.

Daisy: Yes, our car is not parked far away. I'll tell the cashier we don't want to drive up. It should be about 90 dollars all together.

Steve: Here is 100 dollars. I'll go look the magazine rag, Okay?

Dialogue **Two**

Listen to the CD and answer the following questions with the information you hear.

1. Why is the woman returning those slacks according to the dialogue?

   Because they don't really go with her blouse.

2. What discount did the woman get for these slacks?

   She got thirty percent off for those slacks.

3. Why did the man refuse to return those slacks for the woman in the beginning?

   Because it is the store policy that they don't allow returns on sale items.

4. When did the woman buy those slacks?

   She bought those slacks a week ago.

5. Does the woman succeed in returning those slacks in the end?

   Yes, she does.

Script

Salesperson: May I help you?

Sarah: Yes, I would like to return these slacks.

Salesperson: Alright. Do you have your receipt?

Sarah: Yes. Here it is. I bought them last week.

Salesperson: And why are you returning them?

Sarah: I bought them to go with a blouse of mine. But they don't really match.

Salesperson: I see. Oh, wait. Ma'am, I'm sorry. These slacks were on sale.

Sarah: Yes, they were thirty percent off.

Salesperson: I'm sorry, but we don't allow returns on sale items.

Sarah: I know many stores have that policy. But I have returned sale items here before.

Salesperson: I'm sorry, but we usually don't do it. It is our policy.

Sarah: I just bought these slacks a week ago. And I am a regular customer here. Can you make an exception this time?

Salesperson: Well. Let me talk to the manager for a moment. Ma'am, the manager says I can do it this time.

Sarah: Good. I am glad you can make an exception for me.

Salesperson: Please show me your receipt again.

Sarah: Here it is.

Salesperson: I will have to give you store credit, Ma'am. If you find something else you like in the store, you can use the credit.

Sarah: Store credit is okay with me. I'm sure I will find something I like. I shop here a lot.

Salesperson: We appreciate your business, Ma'am.

1. on the Internet is a little different from checking out items at the mall

2. Confirm the online seller's physical address and phone number

3. Legitimate companies don't ask for this information via email

4. Do not send cash under any circumstances, but pay by credit or charge card

5. check out the terms of the deal, like refund policies and delivery dates

Part III   Speaking——*At the Mall*

Useful Expressions About Shopping

Reception

Do you find anything you like? /Is there anybody waiting on you?

What can I do for you? /Can I help you?

Are you being helped? /Are you being served?

Choosing and buying

I want a pair of shoes/a jacket. /I'd like to see some towels. /Let me have a look at this watch.

Would you show me this cup? /I'm interested in this new type of car.

Show me that one, please. /I'd like to have a look if you don't mind. /I'm just looking, thanks.

Could you try it on please? How is it? /I like this one. May I try it on?

Inquiry

Do you have any on sale? /Do you carry a hundred percent cotton pants?

Can you get me one?

If I order a suit now, how long could it take before I get delivery?

Size and color

The fit isn't good. / It seems to fit well. / Can I have a larger size?

It's too big/too small. / They punch my toes.

How about this blue one? / This color is very popular.

This blue color goes well with the light blue dots on the dress.

Price

How much does it cost? / What's the price for this suit? / How much do I have to pay for it?

How much are these ties?

I'll give it to you for 5250. / Can you make it cheaper?

Check

How can I pay? / May I write a check for you? / Sorry, we don't take checks.

I'll take this.

Pair Work

Sample

Shop-assistant: May I help you?

      Angie: Yes, would you show me some skirts? Do you carry a hundred percent cotton pants?

Shop-assistant: How about this blue one?

      Angie: I like this one. May I try it on?

Shop-assistant: Of course, the fitting room is over there. This way please.

Shop-assistant: Miss, I'm telling you, the skirt will look great on you.

      Angie: It is nice, but I think I'll look around a little first.

Shop-assistant: Well, we only have a few left.

      Angie: It is just too expensive. If you give me a discount, maybe I'll take it.

Shop-assistant: OK, since this skirt looks exactly made for you, I'll give you a ten percent discount.

      Angie: Make it fifteen. I'll take it.

Role-play

Sample

Seller: Hello, may I help you?

Buyer: Hi, I'm looking for a pair of men's shoes for my father.

Seller: What do you think of this pair? I have this in black, too. Would you like to have a look?

Buyer: Are they real cowhide?

Seller: Yes, they are 100% genuine cowhide. They have newly arrived for the coming season.

Buyer: Could you please get me a pair of size 43 in black, please.

Seller: Of course!

Buyer: How much are they?

Seller: Well, we don't usually give discounts on newly arrived shoes. However, you seem to really like these shoes and you really want to buy them for your father, I'll give you 10% off the original price.

Buyer: That's wonderful. Thank you very much!

Part IV Reading

Text A   **Background**

Online shopping is the process whereby consumers directly buy goods or services from a seller over the Internet in real-time, without an intermediary service. If an intermediary service is involved, the process is called electronic commerce. An online shop, e-shop, e-store, internet shop, web-shop, webstore, online store, or virtual store evokes the physical analogy of buying products or services at a bricks-and-mortar retailer or in a shopping mall. The process is called Business-to-Consumer (B2C) online shopping. When a business buys from another business, it is called Business-to-Business (B2B) online shopping. Both B2C and B2B online shopping are forms of e-commerce.

Online stores are usually available all day, and many consumers have Internet access both at work and at home. Other establishments such as internet cafes and schools provide access as well. Searching or browsing an online catalog can be faster than browsing the aisles of a physical store. One can avoid those crowded malls, long lines and the trouble in finding a parking place.

In most cases, merchandise must be delivered to the consumer, introducing a significant delay and some potential uncertainty about whether or not the item was actually in stock at the very time of purchase. Most successful sites will tell the consumer whether a product is in supply or not.

One advantage of shopping online is one can quickly make deals for items or services with many different vendors at one time and then make the best choice. Search engines, online price comparison services and discovery shopping engines are helpful for identifying the proper sellers of a particular product or service.

Being unable to check merchandise before purchase, consumers are at higher risk of fraud on the part of the merchant than in a physical store. Sellers also risk fraudulent purchases, for the buyer may use stolen credit cards or fraudulent repudiation to do online purchase.

Phishing is another danger, where consumers are fooled into thinking that they are dealing with a reputable retailer, when they have actually been manipulated into feeding private information to a system operated by a malicious party. Denial of service attacks are a minor risk for the seller, as are server and network outages.

Privacy of personal information is a significant issue for some consumers. Different legal jurisdictions have different laws concerning consumer privacy and different levels of enforcement. Many consumers wish to avoid spam and telemarketing which could result from supplying contact information to an online merchant. In response, many merchants promise not to use consumers' information for these purposes, or provide a mechanism to opt out such contacts.

New Words

alphabetically /ˌælfəˈbetɪkəlɪ/ *ad.* 按字母顺序地

  e. g. I've arranged the books alphabetically, so don't muddle them up.
    我已按字母顺序把这些书整理了,千万不要再弄乱。

budget /ˈbʌdʒɪt/ *n. /v.* 预算;将(款项)编入预算;(为某目的)存钱

  e. g. a weekly budget 周预算
    The government has budgeted 1,000,000 dollars for education spending.
    政府将 100 万美元编入教育预算。

coupon /ˈkuːpɒn/ *n.* 优待券;票证

  e. g. Tear off this coupon and use it to get 25p off your next jar of coffee.
    撕下这张优惠券,用它再买一瓶咖啡可省 25 便士。

deli /ˈdelɪ/ *n.* 熟食

  e. g. deli food 熟食   a deli restaurant 熟食餐馆

fraction /ˈfrækʃən/ *n.* 小部分

  e. g. The cost is only a fraction of his salary. 那项费用只不过是他薪水的一小部分。

glimpse /glɪmps/ *n.* 一瞥,一看;大致了解,粗略的了解

  e. g. She catches a glimpse of a car in the distance. 她一眼就瞥见了远处的汽车。
    Do you want a glimpse of the future of our education?
    你想大致了解下我们的教育前景/未来吗?

grocery store /ˈgrəʊsərɪsˈtɔː/ *n.* 小卖部;(食品)杂货店

  e. g. The hippies ripped off the grocery store. 嬉皮士抢劫了杂货店。

hassle /ˈhæsl/ *n.* 麻烦,打扰

  e. g. I have decided what to do, so please do not give me any hassle about it.
    我已经决定怎么做,你用不着跟我唠叨。

interactive /ˌɪntə(r)ˈæktɪv/ *adj.* 一起活动或互相合作的;交互的,人机对话的

  e. g. This is valid for interactive as well as batch translation.
    这对于交互式或成批翻译都是有效的。
    The psychotherapy is carried out in small interactive groups.

这种心理治疗是在互动的小组之间进行。

log /lɒg/ *vi.*

1. log on/into/in 登入

　　e. g. Customers pay to log on and gossip with others.
　　　　顾客们花钱登录与其他用户们闲聊。

2. log out/off 退出

　　e. g. If a computer fails to log off, the system is accessible to all.
　　　　如果一位电脑用户没有退出，所有人都可以进入该系统。

minivan /ˈmɪnɪvæn/ *n.* 小型货车

　　e. g. Their minivan was in collision with an Army lorry.
　　　　他们的小货车和军用卡车相撞了。

nutritional /njuːˈtrɪʃənəl/ *a.* 营养的，滋养的

　　e. g. A diet lacking in nutritional value will not keep a person healthy.
　　　　缺乏营养价值的饮食不能维持人的健康。

offset /ˈɒfset/ *vt.* 弥补，抵消

　　e. g. The gains offset the losses.　得失相当。
　　　　Their wage increases would be offset by higher prices.
　　　　他们增加的工资会被物价上涨所抵消。

peruse /pəˈruːz/ *vt.* 细读

　　e. g. to peruse a newspaper　仔细读报

produce /prəˈdjuːs/ *n.* （尤指新鲜水果和蔬菜等）农产品

　　e. g. This is all locally grown produce.　这都是本地农产品。
　　　　The company markets its new produce.　该公司出售它的新产品。

redeem /rɪˈdiːm/ *v.* （债券、股票等）兑换为现金或货物；补救或弥补，补偿

　　e. g. This coupon can be redeemed at any of our branches.
　　　　这种息票可在我们的任何分行兑现。
　　　　The sole redeeming feature of this job is the salary.
　　　　这份工作唯其薪水尚可弥补一切之不足。

retailing /ˈriːteɪlɪŋ/ *n.* 零售业

　　e. g. Retailing in the future will emphasize more and more on added value and convenience.　未来的零售业将越来越强调购物方便和物超所值的服务。

shopping cart /ˈʃɒpɪŋkɑːt/ *n.* 购物车

　　e. g. Once you have filled your shopping cart, it is time to proceed to check out.
　　　　一旦你已经装满你的购物车，就该前去结账了。

subscriber /səbˈskraɪbə/ *n.* 消费者，用户；（报刊的）订阅人，订购者，订户

　　e. g. Subscriber Access Network　用户接入网络
　　　　telephone subscriber　电话用户
　　　　Subscribers to the magazine can take advantage of this special offer.

杂志订户可享有此项特惠。

trade /treɪd/ *v.* 用一物交换另一物,以物易物;做生意,做买卖

 e. g. I'll trade you my stamp collection for your model boat.

   我想用我收集的邮票换你的模型船。

   The firm is trading at a profit/loss. 这个公司做买卖赚钱/赔钱。

transmit /trænzˈmɪt/ *v.* 传播;传导

 e. g. Insects can transmit diseases. 昆虫能传播疾病。

   Glass transmits light but not sound. 玻璃传导光,但不传导声音。

Phrases and Expressions

be here to stay/have come to stay 扎下根来;成为时尚;受到普遍接受

 e. g. I hope that equality of opportunity for men and women has come to/is here to stay.

   我希望男女机会平等能形成风气。

check out 检查,核对,核实;付账后离开

 e. g. Does his story check out? 他的叙述查实了吗?

   He couldn't have checked out so early. 他不可能这么早就结账离开。

dedicate. . .to 致力于,献身于

 e. g. He dedicated himself to conserving our natural resources.

   他把毕生精力用于保护我们的自然资源。

link up 连接,会合

 e. g. These pieces of information link up to suggest who the thief was.

   这些点滴的情况联系起来就让人看得出谁是贼。

   Engineers can link up distant countries by radio or telephone.

   工程师们用无线电或电话可把相距遥远的国家联系在一起。

send out 发送,送出,散布;派遣

 e. g. They sent out invitations to many people. 他们向许多人发了请帖。

   They were sent out as our representatives. 他们是作为我们的代表被派出去的。

set foot in 进入,踏进

 e. g. The rich never set foot in these districts before liberation.

   解放前,有钱人是从不到这个地区来的。

参 考 译 文

食品购物:以手代步

 1 十分钟之内采购完够一星期吃用的东西,你会感觉如何? 在购物的日子,你不是把孩子塞进小面包车里,而是打发他们到外面玩耍,自己却舒舒服服地呆在家中买你想要的东西。成千上万的大忙人已经把购物车换成了键盘。在芝加哥和旧金山地区,人们不愿在人群中挤来挤去,而是登录到彼博得公司(Peapod)的网站,进行网上购物,享受送货上门的服

务。

2　彼博得公司让我们看到了零售业的未来——虚拟商店。彼博得公司是一个正在迅猛发展的产业中的先驱,这个产业致力于让我们能够通过个人电脑买到几乎所有的商品。彼博得公司的用户只要登录到一个系统上就可以在虚拟商店购物,在这里你可以通过人机对话的方式买到包括新鲜的农产品、熟食、烘烤食品、肉类和冷冻食品在内的各种杂货。你不用在商店的过道里转来转去,只要简单地在屏幕上点击你要的商品就行了。一旦上了网,你便可以在20,000多种商品中进行挑选,你也可以迅速地比较一下价格,从而买到价廉物美的商品。为避免超支,你还可随时查看购物费用小计。你可以创建个人购物清单以便节省时间,可以浏览商品图片,可以查看特价商品,可以通过查看营养表来选取你想要的产品,可以按营养成分快速地把货物作一下分类,还可以挑选一个适合你的送货时间。

3　彼博得公司网上购物系统直接与其合作商店的电脑系统联网。当你把购货单发送给彼博得公司时,一份订单就会传送到离你最近的合作商店。受过专门训练的代购员拿着你的订单,推着购物车帮你选购。专业的代购员选购时间很少,只是你购物时间的极小一部分,因为货物是按货架排列,他们很清楚该去哪里找。店主或快递员把食物送到你手上后,你就可以使用现金券了,运送过程中,这些食物会放在温控箱中。

4　虚拟超市肯定会改变我们的购物方式。这种互动式网上购物方式帮我们解除了购买日用杂货的忧虑,购物也不再神秘。我们可以按种类和品牌查看商品,甚至可以查看削价品。我们还可以要求将货物依字母顺序排列,或者按商标、单价、包装尺寸等来分类,甚至还可以要求按营养价值的大小列成一个清单。

5　忙碌的人们选择网购,他们认为网购产生的服务费用可以通过减少其它开销来弥补,如减少旅游的开销。

6　网上购物已成为生活的一部分。各合作商店自从与彼博得公司联合后,销售量增加了8%,网上销量已经占这些合作商店总销售量的15%。

7　彼博得公司网上购物系统使许多人的生活变得更加简单,也为他们省时、省钱。在职的父母们很乐意用购物的时间来换取更多的与孩子相处的时间。有些人很高兴优惠券给他们带来的优惠,而且照顾孩子的花费也节省了不少。由于彼博得公司网上购物系统鼓励人们用最优惠的价格购买产品,每个人都因此节省了钱。已经数月未去逛杂货店的人们说他们的家人现在比以往任何时候都吃得好了。

Exercises

I. Reading Comprehension
Section A
1. C　2. D　3. D　4. C　5. A

Section B
1. They go shopping at the virtual grocery store by logging on to a system that lets them interactively shop for grocery items.

2. When you send your shopping list to Peapod, an order is transmitted to the nearest partner store. A professionally trained shopper takes your order, grabs a shopping cart and does your shopping for you.

3. We can view items by category or brand. We can even peruse the items on sale. We can request the items be arranged alphabetically, by brand, by piece per unit, by package size, or, we can request a listing by nutritional value.

4. Since linking up with Peapod, the grocery store partners have experienced an 8% increase in sales, and online shopping accounts for over 15% of the sales volume at the partner stores.

5. The peapod system has made life easier for a great many people. It has also saved them time and money.

Section C

1. Identity theft is one of the most important concerns of online shopping. If the shoppers are not certain about the security, they could call the customer service to place an order. What's more, the very big disadvantage an online website may have is the credit card security. No matter how secure the website claims to be, you can not always trust them. And although online shopping is 24 hours available, you cannot feel or touch items. You can just see what is present on a webpage, whereas in brick-and-mortar stores you can see many things at a glance and buy after you feel or touch the product. One more problem of online shopping is that the shoppers may buy a wrong item just because of misinterpretation or misunderstanding.

2. I have ever bought a dress online, which was totally a failure. Once I browsed through the clothes in an online shop and found a dress that looked nice. The pictures of the dress were good-looking and it was not expensive, therefore, I decided to buy it, after careful viewing and thinking. About 5 days later, it arrived. Getting the parcel from the courier, I opened the package to find that not only was there a big hole in the dress but there was a big discrepancy between the dress I saw at the moment and the picture online. It was much out of my expectation, so I decided to return it. Finally, I returned it with 15 *yuan* delivery cost on my part.

3. I prefer online shopping. It is very convenient for us to only sit in front of the computer and click the mouse to browse through the detailed information about the items that we want to buy and at the same time we can compare the similar items in different stores through some certain tools, which otherwise may take much time to do in the malls or it is even unavailable sometimes. Moreover, online goods are always cheaper than those displayed in the malls.

(Or I prefer shopping in the malls. On the one hand, we can see, touch and even try on the clothes to see if it fits us or not. And we can also sometimes taste the candies to see whether it is sweet or not. They are the authentic things in front of us that we can feel and we can buy and pay for them right away to walk away with them without waiting for delivery. On another hand, it is safer for us to do shopping in the malls rather than worry about receiving

nothing after payment online. Meanwhile, return the item is also more convenient for us if the item has quality problems.）

II. Vocabulary and Structure
Section A
1. A 2. C 3. B 4. A 5. D 6. D 7. C 8. A 9. B 10. C

Section B

1. Mr. Andrews asked me to <u>log</u> on to the telecommunications network and see if any electronic mail from Japan is waiting for him.
   安德鲁斯先生要我打开电传视讯网路,看看他是否有从日本发来的电子邮件。

2. Our deputy manager is the <u>virtual</u> head of the business.
   我们的副经理是公司的实际负责人。

3. Customers are allowed to <u>redeem</u> their trading stamps for certain items in the shop.
   客户可以拿商品券在商店里兑换特定物品。

4. Can I <u>trade</u> my tobacco for your matches?
   我能用自己的香烟换你的火柴么?

5. Please <u>account</u> for your disgraceful conduct.
   对你的可耻行为请作解释。

6. Ten million francs has been <u>budgeted</u> for the project.
   已有一千万法郎编入此项目预算。

7. I <u>dedicated</u> this volume to my wife in token of affection and gratitude.
   谨以本书献给我的妻子以表示爱意与感谢。

8. They <u>checked</u> out all the goods in the store before they left.
   他们清点了仓库里的货物后才离开。

III. Word Building

1. The search of eternal beauty and wisdom is the <u>ever-lasting</u> endeavor of human kind.
   美和智慧是人类永恒的追求。

2. He favored the efforts to improve relations with all <u>peace-loving</u> countries.
   他赞成为了同所有爱好和平的国家改善关系而进行的努力。

3. He is very <u>well-informed</u>; that's why he won the general knowledge competition.
   他见识非常广博,所以他在常识竞赛中获胜。

4. Though he was born poor, he still had a blissfully <u>carefree</u> childhood.
   尽管他出身贫寒,他的童年还是无忧无虑的。

5. The farmer's <u>weather-beaten</u> face bore witness to his years spent outdoors.
   农夫那张饱经风霜的脸是他在野外生活了数年之久的证明。

6. There is a <u>widespread</u> dissatisfaction among the students with the food on campus.
   学生们普遍对学校的饭菜不太满意。

7. She's very <u>well-meaning</u>, but she only makes the situation worse.

她虽然出于好心,但是却帮了倒忙。

8. They were careful to keep their distance from the <u>ill-tempered</u> professor.

他们都谨慎地避开这位坏脾气的教授。

IV. Grammar Focus

1. Rather than risked breaking up his marriage he told his wife everything.

2. It's management rather than the work-force that's at fault.

3. We will have meeting in the classroom, rather than in the auditorium.

4. His action aggravated the situation, rather than relieved it.

5. She was guided by feeling, rather than by thought.

V. Translation

1. He said <u>he would never set foot in that house again.</u>

他说他永远不再踏进那座房子。

2. They thus increased their annual grain production <u>rather than diminished</u> it.

他们这样增加了而不是减少了粮食年产量。

3. <u>The team sent some people out hunting</u>, and they bagged a wild boar.

那支队伍派了一些人去打猎,他们打了一头野猪。

4. Find what thrills you and <u>dedicate your time to going for it.</u>

找到令你兴奋的事情,然后全身心地投入去做。

5. Engineers can <u>link up romote villages via radio or telephone.</u>

工程师用无线电或电话把遥远的乡村连接起来。

VI. Writing

Sample

A Letter of Complaint

1234 Tianhe Road

Tianhe District

Guangzhou 510620

Guangdong Province

P. R. C

24 August, 2010

33 Kadoorie Avenue

Kowloon

The Administrative Officer

Dear Sir/Madam,

    I attended your exhibition Sound Systems 2010 at the Fortune Hotel from 13—17 August and found it informative and interesting. Unfortunately, my enjoyment of the event was spoiled by a number of organizational problems. I explain each of the problems below.

Firstly, I had difficulty in registering to attend the event. You set up an online registration facility, but I found the facility totally unworkable. Even after spending several wasted hours trying to register in this way, the computer would not accept my application. I eventually succeeded in registering by faxing you.

Secondly, the exhibition was held at one of Hong Kong's most prestigious hotels, but frankly the venue was better suited to a medium-sized business conference than to a large exhibition open by registration to the public. The lack of space led to serious overcrowding in the venue, particularly at peak visiting times (i.e. lunch times and early evening). On one or two occasions I was also seriously concerned about the physical safety of attendees.

The final point I want to make concerns product information. It is very enjoyable to see and test a range of excellent sound systems, but it is also important to be able to take away leaflets on interesting products, so that more research can be done before deciding which system to buy. However, by the time I attended the exhibition all the leaflets had been taken.

Could I please ask you to look into these matters not only on my behalf but also on behalf of other attendees, and in fact on behalf of your company, too.

I look forward to hearing from you.

Yours faithfully,

Beck Lee (signature)

Notes

How to Write a Complaint Letter

Letters of complaint usually include the following sections:
1. Background; 2. Problem-cause and effect; 3. Solution; 4. Warning (optional); 5. closing

Background

This section describes the situation. For example, I am writing to inform you that the goods we ordered from your company have not been supplied correctly. I am a shareholder of Sunshine Bank and I am very concerned regarding recent newspaper reports on the financial situation of the bank. Your company is listed as the auditor in the latest annual report of the bank, so I am writing to you to ask for an explanation of the following issues.

Problem

Cause: You sent us an invoice for $10,532, but did not deduct our usual 10% discount. We have found 16 spelling errors and 2 mis-labeled diagrams in the sample book.

Effect: This error has put our firm in a difficult position, as we had to make some emergency purchases to fulfill our commitments to all our customers. This caused us considerable inconvenience. I am therefore returning the invoice to you for correction.

Solution

I am writing to ask you to make up the shortfall immediately and to ensure that such errors do not happen again. Please send us a corrected invoice for $9,479.

I enclose a copy of the book with the errors highlighted. Please re-print the book and send it to us by next Friday.

Warning（optional）

Otherwise, we may have to look elsewhere for our supplies. I'm afraid that if these conditions are not met, we may be forced to take legal actions.

Closing

I look forward to receiving your explanation of these matters. I look forward to receiving your payment./hearing from you shortly.

 **Text B**   **Background**

Online shopping offers lots of benefits that you won't find when doing shopping in a store or by mail. The Internet is always open—seven days a week, 24 hours a day—and bargains can be numerous online. With a click of the mouse, you can buy an airline ticket, book a hotel, send flowers to a friend, or purchase your favorite fashions. But sizing up your finds on the Internet is a little different from checking out items in a mall.

Know who you're dealing with. Anyone can set up an online shop under almost any name. Confirm the online seller's physical address and phone number in case you have questions or problems. If you get an email or pop-up message while you're browsing that asks for financial information, don't reply or click on the link in the message. Legitimate companies don't ask for this information via email.

Know exactly what you're buying. Read the seller's description of the product closely, especially the fine print. Words like "refurbished," "vintage," or "close-out" may indicate that the product is in less-than-mint condition, while name-brand items with "too-good-to-be-true" prices could be counterfeits.

Know what it will cost. Check out websites that offer price comparisons and then compare "apples to apples." Factor shipping and handling—along with your needs and budget—into the total cost of the order. Do not send cash under any circumstances.

Pay by credit or charge card. If you pay by credit or charge card online, your transaction will be protected by the Fair Credit Billing Act. Under this law, you have the right to dispute charges under certain circumstances and temporarily withhold payment while the creditor is investigating them. In the event of unauthorized use of your credit or charge card, you generally would be held liable only for the first $50 in charges. Some companies offer an online shopping guarantee that ensures you will not be held responsible for any unauthorized charges made online, and some cards may provide additional warranty, return, and/or purchase protection benefits.

Don't e-mail your financial information. Email is not a secure method of transmitting financial information like your credit card, checking account, or Social Security number. If you initiate a

transaction and want to provide your financial information through an organization's website, look for indicators that the site is secure, like a lock icon on the browser's status bar or a URL for a website that begins with "https:" (the "s" stands for "secure"). Unfortunately, no indicator is foolproof; some fraudulent sites have forged security icons.

New Words

accelerate /æk'seləreɪt/ v. 加速;(使)加快,(使)增速;增长,增加

  e.g. The car suddenly accelerated. 汽车突然加速。

       Our country should accelerate the economic growth. 我国应加快经济增长。

attribute /ə'trɪbjuːt/ n. 属性,特性

               vt. 归因于……,把……归咎于

  e.g. Kindness is one of his best attributes. 仁慈是他的好品性之一。

       They attributed Edison's success to intelligence and hard work.

       他们把爱迪生的成功归因于他的智力和刻苦工作。

browse /braʊz/ vt. & vi. 随便看看;(在计算机上)浏览信息

  e.g. Have you come to browse my wares? 你是来看我的商品吗?

       I used to browse my website at the weekend. 我周末时浏览网站。

click /klɪk/ vt. 点击

  e.g. Click here for detailed instructions. 单击这里查看详细说明。

console /kən'səʊl/ n. [计]控制台

  e.g. railway signal control console 铁路信号控制台

corduroy /'kɔːdərɔɪ/ n. 灯芯绒

  e.g. Do you like these corduroy pants? 你喜欢这些灯芯绒做的长裤吗?

cursor /'kɜːsə/ n. [计]光标

  e.g. You can move the cursor by using the mouse. 你可以使用鼠标器来移动光标。

dominate /'dɒmɪneɪt/ v. 在……中占首要地位;控制,支配,统治,左右,影响

  e.g. Sports, and not learning, seem to dominate in the school.

       在那所学校似乎是运动而不是学习占重要地位。

       The stronger man dominates the weaker. 强者支配弱者。

embed /ɪm'bed/ vt. 插入,使嵌入

  e.g. They embedded the pilings deep into the subsoil.

       他们把桩深深打进地基下的土中。

imaginable /ɪ'mædʒɪnəbl/ adj. 可想像的,想像得到的

  e.g. We have been inundated with every bit of information imaginable.

       凡是想得到的各种各样的信息如潮水般地向我们涌来。

joystick /'dʒɔɪˌstɪk/ n. 操纵杆

  e.g. A joystick allows the safe room occupant to lock and unlock doors throughout the house to trap an intruder.

控制杆可让安全密室里的人锁上或打开房子里的任何门,以便捕捉入侵者。

motorise /ˈməʊtəraɪz/ *vt.* 给……装上发动机

    e. g.   motorised vehicles   机动车辆

pad /pæd/ *n.* 垫子,衬垫

    e. g.   a shoulder pad   垫肩

priority /praɪˈɒrɪtɪ/ *n.* 优先考虑的事;优先权,重点

    e. g.   The development of the national economy is a top priority.

        发展国民经济应予以最优先考虑。

sensation /senˈseɪʃən/ *n.* 感觉,感受

    e. g.   Seeing him again after so many years was a strange sensation.

        那么多年以后又见到他,是一种不可思议的感觉。

        He lost all sensation in his legs through cramp.

        他的腿部因抽筋而失去知觉。

simulate /ˈsɪmjʊleɪt/ *vt.* 模拟

    e. g.   A sheet of metal was shaken to simulate the noise of thunder.

        猛力抖动金属片以模仿雷声。

surfer /ˈsɜːfə/ *n.* 冲浪运动员

    e. g.   The wave curled over the surfer.

        波浪从冲浪运动员头上盘旋而过。

tactile /ˈtæktaɪl/ *adj.* 触觉的,可触知的

    e. g.   a tactile organ   触觉器官

        an instrument used to measure tactile sensitivity   一种用来测量触觉的装置

tautness /ˈtɔːtnɪs/ *n.* 紧绷

    e. g.   droop, sink or settle from pressure or loss of tautness

        因为压力或失去拉紧的力而低垂、下沉或下陷

texture /ˈtekstʃə/ *n.* 质地,纹理

    e. g.   We could feel the smooth texture of silk.   我们能感觉出丝绸的光滑质地。

Phrases and Expressions

attach to   (使)贴(系,粘)在……上

    e. g.   respect teachers and attach importance to education   尊师重教

        We used paste to attach our designs to the poster.

        我们用浆糊把我们设计的图案贴在招贴牌上。

compare with   (把……)与……相比

    e. g.   How does your new house compare with your old one?

        你的新房子和你的旧房子比起来怎样?

expect to do sth.   预计将……;期望

e. g.　What type of work will you expect to do at first?　你希望起初做什么工作？

queue up　排队等候

e. g.　If you want to see the film, you will have to queue up for tickets.
如果你想去看电影,那得排队买票。

参 考 译 文

网 上 购 物

1　圣诞节来临的前两个星期,买礼物是许多人会优先考虑的事情。然而,今年并没有许多人外出逛商店。现如今,许多人可以舒舒服服地在家通过网络购物。

2　网上购物变得越来越流行有一系列的原因:网上物价一般比较低,你不需要在拥挤的商店排队,而且点击几下鼠标你就可以买到几乎任何自己可以想到的东西。

3　以往电脑多是男性使用,但是今年女性通过网上购物将多于男性。现在似乎女性比以前更受网上购物便利性的吸引。女性今年平均花费在网上购物的花销将增加到 240 英镑,相比较,男性稍微低点儿,平均 233 英镑。而每人通过商业街购物的花销平均只有 197 英镑。70% 的上网者,无论男女,现在都在网上购买圣诞节礼物。

4　然而,网上购物有一个问题,那便是你无法触摸任何东西。幸运的是,这种状况将要有所改变。一种机动电脑鼠标将帮助网购者感知网上所展示商品的质地或商品其它的物理特性。

5　上周在旧金山召开的 99 网络大会让参观者能够试用“触感”鼠标:将光标移到一个网球拍图片上,让使用者感受球拍线的紧绷感。你还可以抚摸一条灯芯绒裤的质地,或者试开一辆车,感受一下车的弯道性能和直道上的加速功能。这种鼠标甚至能模拟在大风中逆风行车的感觉。

6　到目前为止,制造此鼠标的技术仅可用在电脑游戏的控制台和操纵杆中。强迫反馈技术最初由斯坦福大学和美国国家航空航天局开发,起初仅用于模拟飞行。最近,加州圣何塞市的“潜浸公司”(Immersion Corporation)成功地实现了数据高速交换,给网购顾客提供真实的触感。

7　鼠标与一块垫板相连,板的上端有一小盒,里面装有两台电动机,一台驱动光标左右移动,另一台驱动光标上下移动。当你在网络画面上移动光标时,预设的运动指令会被传达到鼠标内的微型处理器上,指挥它运动,产生所想要的感觉。

Exercises

I. Reading Comprehension

1. D　2. D　3. C　4. A　5. C

II. Vocabulary and Structure

1. B 2. D 3. A 4. C 5. B 6. D 7. B 8. C 9. D 10. A

III. Translation

1. We used to use this trick in the Army <u>to simulate illness</u>.

   我们在军队服役时曾用这一伎俩装病。

2. She <u>attached a cheque to</u> the order form.

   她在定货单上附了一张支票。

3. In the car accident, Tom was badly hurt and <u>lost all sensation in his legs</u>.

   在这起交通事故中,汤姆受伤严重,腿部完全失去知觉。

4. <u>She attributes her success to</u> hard work and a bit of luck.

   她认为她的成功是由于她的勤奋努力外加一点点运气。

5. I've learnt from the poem <u>the Victorian values embedded in</u> Tennyson's poetry.

   我从这首诗歌中体会到了深植于丁尼生诗歌中的维多利亚时代价值观。

Part V   Time for Fun

参 考 译 文

拿破仑病了

　　杰克到一所大学去学历史。第一学期结束时,历史课教授没让他及格,学校劝他退学。然而,杰克的父亲决定去见教授,强烈要求让杰克继续来年的学业。

　　"他是个好孩子,"杰克的父亲说,"您要是让他这次及格,我相信他明年会有很大进步,学期结束时,他一定会考好的。"

　　"不,不,那不可能,"教授马上回答,"你知道吗? 上个月我问他拿破仑什么时候死的,他都不知道。"

　　"先生,请再给他一次机会吧。"杰克的父亲说,"你不知道,恐怕是因为我们家没有订报纸,我们全家人连拿破仑病了都不知道。"

8 Unit

Disaster

Part I Teaching Objectives

* **Listening & Speaking**

Help the students to be familiar with the topic — *how to express your idea on the natural disasters* and memorize useful expressions.

* **Words & Expressions**

Study some new words and expressions, such as *survive*, *foreseeable*, *terrorism*, *massive*, *starvation*, *convey*, *overcome*, *medication*, *distribute*, *Richter scale*, *migrate to*, *emerge from*, *pour into*, *deal with*, *provide for* and so on.

* **Grammar**

Learn to use the structure of *If. . . were. . . .*

* **Writing**

Understand and write *a letter of inquiry*.

Part II Listening——Earthquake

New Words

aftershock /ˈɑːftəʃɒk/ *n.* 余震

  e. g. A 6.4-magnitude aftershock happened today and it caused some secondary disaster.
  今天发生了6.4级余震,引起了一些二级灾害。

basement /ˈbeɪsmənt / *n.* 地下室

  e. g. Does the house have a basement?
  这房子有地下室吗?

casualty /ˈkæʒʊəltɪ/ *n.* 伤亡人数

e. g. She read through the casualty list anxiously.
她焦虑地把伤亡人员名单从头到尾看了一遍。

distribute /dɪsˈtrɪbjuːt/ *v.* 分配,分发

e. g. The teacher distributes the relative literature to trainees.
老师把相关的资料分发给学员。

drought /ˈdraʊt/ *n.* 干旱

e. g. Drought and famine stalked the land.
干旱和饥荒在这片土地肆虐。

foreseeable /fɔːˈsiːəbl/ *adj.* 可预见的

e. g. This problem can be solved in the foreseeable future.
这个问题在可预见的将来能得到解决。

massive /ˈmæsɪv/ *adj.* 大规模,大量的

e. g. She drink a massive amount of alcohol.
她喝了大量的烈性酒。

refugee /ˌrefjʊˈdʒiː/ *n.* 逃亡者,避难者

e. g. The refugee was re-admitted into his home country.
难民被他的故国重新接纳。

relief /rɪˈliːf/ *n.* 救援,救助物品

e. g. Many relief supplies were rushed in the area。
大量的救济物资已急速送到该区域。

starvation /staːˈveɪʃən/ *n.* 饥荒,挨饿

e. g. They live at the verge of starvation.
他们生活在饥饿的边缘。

survive /səˈvaɪv/ *v.* 幸存,从……生还

e. g. We can not survive without water.
没有水我们就无法生存。

terrorism /ˈterərɪzəm/ *n.* 恐怖主义

e. g. Terrorism does a great threat to the county.
恐怖主义对这个国家是个巨大的威胁。

tornado /tɔːˈneɪdəʊ/ *n.* 龙卷风

e. g. A tornado destroyed everything in its path.
龙卷风所到之处片甲不留。

tremor /ˈtremə/ *n.* 震动,颤抖

e. g. There was a tremor in her voice.
她的声音有点颤抖。

Phrases and Expressions

make a mountain out of a molehill 小题大做

e. g. You are not hurt badly. Stop trying to make a mountain out of a molehill with crying.

你伤的并不重,不要放声大哭,小题大做。

migrate to 迁徙,移民

e. g. People often migrate to another country to find work.

人们经常迁往另一个国家去找工作。

refugee camp 难民营

e. g. The government has set two refugee camps.

政府已经建了两个难民营。

Richter scale 里氏震级

e. g. The magnitude of this earthquake is 6 on the Richter scale.

这次地震的震级是里氏六级。

rip out 狠狠地拔出

e. g. Many trees are ripped out by the roots after a tornado.

龙卷风过后许多的树木被连根拔起。

Dialogue ▸ **One**

Listen to the CD and mark T for True or F for False according to the dialogue.

1. F 2. F 3. T 4. F 5. F

Script ▸

Marco: Hello.

Dora: Hey, Marco. It's Dora. Are you watching TV now?

Marco: No, why?

Dora: Just turn it on and switch to CCTV Channel 9. There's striking news!

Marco: What is it?

Dora: Earthquake!

Marco: In China?

Dora: No, in Africa. It's such a serious quake, measured 8.2 on the Richter scale. Lots of people died.

Marco: I already knew it. And there're still lots of aftershocks.

Dora: Yes, that's horrible. You know you may survive the quake, but die in the aftershocks.

Marco: No worries, Dora. That's in Africa which is really far from China.

Dora: Are you sure there're no earthquakes in Beijing?

Marco: So far as I know, there're no so-called earthquakes in the foreseeable future in Beijing.

Dora: Are you sure?

Marco: Absolutely. In my 29 years of living in China, I have only experienced one earthquake and that's like 28 years ago, when I was only 1 year old.

Dora: Did anyone die?

Marco: I don't know. I was like a 1-year-old baby, Dora. Don't try to make a mountain out of a molehill.

Dora: I do?

Marco: You do. China, especially Beijing is the safest place. There's no such thing as terrorism or earthquakes here.

Dora: I guess I'm overworried.

Dialogue Two

Listen to the CD and answer the following questions with the information you hear.

1. Who experienced the earthquake?

   Mary experienced one when she was in America.

2. How long did that earthquake last?

   It lasted only a few seconds.

3. Did Mary know the magnitude of the earthquake?

   No, she didn't remember.

4. What did Jim experience when he was younger?

   He was in quite a few tornados when he was younger.

5. What was the most interesting thing in Jim's childhood?

   It was spending time with his family in the basement waiting for the tornados to pass.

Script

Jim: Hi, Mary. How is everything going?

Mary: Hi, Jim. Not bad. And you?

Jim: Fine.

Mary: I just read a report about disasters. It's terrible.

Jim: Yeah. Have you ever been in an earthquake?

Mary: Yes, I experienced one when I was in America once. The tremors only lasted a few seconds though, and then it was over.

Jim: Do you know where it measured on the Richter scale?

Mary: I don't remember, but it wasn't very serious. Have you ever been in an earthquake?

Jim: No, but I was in quite a few tornados when I was younger.

Mary: Really?

Jim: I'm from the plains of the Midwest. It's a prime location for tornadoes.

Mary: Did your house ever get damaged from the winds?

Jim: Most of the time we were lucky, but once a tree from our front yard was ripped out

by its roots and ended up in our living room.

Mary: Wow, that must have really been scary.

Jim: Actually, some of my fondest memories of my childhood were of spending time with my family in the basement waiting for the tornados to pass.

1. dangerous and deadly of all natural events
2. by the shifting of rocks along cracks
3. are pulled in different directions
4. where and when an earthquake will occur
5. so that lives can be saved

Part III Speaking——*Forest Fire*

Useful Expressions About Disasters

The strongest earthquake of the century struck the area on Sep. 11.

The epicenter of the quake was situated at the center of the city.

It cut off the power and the water supply in broad areas.

The last aftershock was terrible.

More than 2,000 are killed and 8,000 injured in this disaster.

There are still hundreds of people buried alive under the rubble.

The rescue team combed through the rubble to save survivors.

Powerful aftershocks still continue shaking the area.

I hope everyone can pray for the helpless victims in the disaster.

It's such a serious quake, measured 8.2 on the Richter scale.

The earthquake causes severe damage to infrastructure in several cities.

Hours after the initial earthquake, a 5.4 magnitude aftershock rocked the area.

Pair Work

Sample

Emily: So Ivan, in California we have earthquakes. Do you have any natural disasters in Houston?

Ivan: Uh, it floods a lot and we get hurricanes.

Emily: Oh, how is that going?

Ivan: Sometimes it rains a lot that the river fills up over, and the next thing you know you get water in your house. Hurricanes are really, really angry typhoons I think.

Emily: Did you get the hurricane before?

Ivan: The first hurricane I experienced was two years ago, named "Hurricane Alice" I believe. Oh, my God, it's raining. Trees are falling down and cars are kind of being pushed away from the water and stuff. I'm scared to death.

Emily: How long does a hurricane usually last?

Ivan: Usually, about two or three days.

Emily: Oh, really?

Ivan: Yeah, they just kind of stay in Houston. They like Houston. Something about the weather pattern. They just float to Houston and stay here.

Emily: Man, that's pretty intense. So afterward everything is just kind of wiped out?

Ivan: Right, but it's fun when it stops because the streets are flooded and you can go swimming.

Emily: You swim in the water?

Ivan: Sure. It's just rain water.

Role-play

Sample

Gary: How do you think of the local climate in recent years?

Belle: I think it changed a lot. It has been getting steadily warmer and warmer in recent years.

Gary: I feel the same way. The summers are much hotter that without air conditioners it's hard to fall asleep at night.

Belle: That's true. Drought lasts longer in some dry areas, while in another floods have been more widespread and more frequent.

Gary: Yeah, we have also experienced several snowfree winters. It's just not cold at all!

Belle: I think they are signs that we have done much damage to the earth.

Gary: You're right. Droughts, severe storms, hurricanes, people suffer a lot from these disasters.

Belle: I hope the situation will change soon.

Part IV   Reading

 **Text A**   **Background**

What is earthquake?

An earthquake is a natural event where the ground shakes and moves in opposite directions. It is a sudden movement of the Earth, caused by the abrupt release of energy that has accumulated underneath for a long time.

For hundreds of millions of years, the forces of plate tectonics have shaped the Earth as the huge plates that form the Earth's surface slowly move over, under or past each other. Sometimes the movement is gradual. At other times, the plates are locked together, unable to release the accumulating energy. When the accumulated energy grows strong enough, the plates break free.

What is the aftershock?

An aftershock is an earthquake that occurs after a previous earthquake, the main shock. An aftershock is in the same region of the main shock but always of a smaller magnitude. Aftershocks are formed as the crust adjusts to the effects of the main shock.

What are the effects of an earthquake?

The effects of earthquakes include, but are not limited to, the following:

1. Shaking and Ground Rupture

Shaking and ground rupture are the main effects caused by earthquakes, principally resulting in more or less severe damage to buildings and other rigid structures.

Ground rupture is a visible breaking and displacement of the Earth's surface along the trace of the fault, which may be of the order of several meters in the case of major earthquakes. Ground rupture is a major risk for large engineering structures such as dams, bridges and nuclear power stations, and requires careful mapping of existing faults to identify any possible breakage of the ground surface within the life of the structure.

2. Landslides

Earthquakes, along with severe storms, volcanic activity, coastal wave attack and wildfires can produce slope instability, which lead to landslides, a major geological hazard. Landslide may endanger emergency personnel when they are attempting rescue work.

3. Fires

Earthquakes can cause fires through damaging electrical power or gas lines. In the event of water mains rupturing and a loss of pressure, it may also become difficult to stop the fire from spreading once it has started.

4. Floods

A flood is an overflow of any amount of water that reaches land. Floods usually occur when the volume of water within a body of water, such as a river or a lake, exceeds the total capacity of the formation, and as a result, some of the water flows or sits outside of the normal perimeter of the body. However, floods may be secondary effect of earthquakes, if dams are damaged. Earthquakes may cause landslips to dam rivers, which then collapse and cause floods.

5. Human Impacts

Earthquakes may lead to disease, lack of basic necessities, loss of life, higher insurance premiums, general property damage, road and bridge damage, and collapse or destabilization (potentially leading to future collapse) of buildings. Earthquakes can also precede volcanic eruptions, which cause further problems.

New Words

aftereffect /ˈɑːftərɪˌfekt/ *n.* 后果,事后影响;(药效)的副作用

> e. g.　She has recovered without any aftereffect.
> 她已经完全病愈,没有任何后遗症。

chaos /ˈkeɪɒs/ *n.* 混乱;紊乱

> e. g.　Your bedroom is in great chaos.
> 你的卧室太乱了。

clutch /klʌtʃ/ *v.* 抓住,因痛苦而紧紧握住

> e. g.　A drowning man will clutch at a straw.
> 即将溺死的人连一根稻草也要去抓。

collapse /kəˈlæps/ *v.* 倒坍,坍塌

> e. g.　The earthquake caused many buildings to collapse.
> 地震使许多建筑物倒坍。

commitment /kəˈmɪtmənt/ *n.* 承诺,保证;奉献,献身

> e. g.　We should make a commitment to peace.
> 我们应该对于和平做出贡献。

devastation /ˈdevəsteɪʃən/ *n.* 毁灭;破坏

> e. g.　Due to ecological devastation, the wilderness is shrinking.
> 由于生态的破坏,野生环境范围正在日益缩小。

endanger /ɪnˈdeɪndʒə/ *v.* 使有危险,危及

> e. g.　You will endanger your health if you smoke.
> 你如果吸烟,就会危及健康。

frightening /ˈfraɪtənɪŋ/ *adj.* 可怕的,令人恐惧的

> e. g.　His face had a frightening aspect.
> 他的脸色很吓人。

handle /ˈhændl/ *v.* 解决,处理

> e. g.　How do you handle frustration?
> 你如何面对挫折?

initial /ɪˈnɪʃəl/ *adj.* 最初的,开始的;第一的

> e. g.　What is her initial reaction to the news?
> 她对这个消息最初是什么反应?

magnitude /ˈmæɡnɪtjuːd/ *n.* 震级

> e. g.　Hours after the earthquake, a 6 magnitude aftershock rocked the area.
> 地震几个小时后,一场6级的余震再次席卷了这个地区。

moan /məʊn/ *v.* 呻吟;悲叹;抱怨

> e. g.　A moan escaped the badly wounded soldier.
> 那个重伤员不禁呻吟了一声。

overwhelm /ˌəʊvəˈhwelm/ *v.* (情感)难以接受;淹没;打倒

e. g.   No difficulty can overwhelm us.
　　　　困难无法压倒我们。

phenomenon　/fɪˈnɒmɪnən/　*n.* 现象；杰出、非凡的人或事情

e. g.   A rainbow is a natural phenomenon.
　　　　彩虹是一种自然现象。
　　　　Beethoven was a phenomenon among many musicians.
　　　　在众多的音乐家中贝多芬是天才。

rubble　/ˈrʌbl/　*n.* 碎石，瓦砾

e. g.   Some people were dug out of the rubble.
　　　　一些人从碎砖烂瓦中被救出。

severe　/sɪˈvɪə/　*adj.* 恶劣的，严重的，艰难的

e. g.   The house suffered severe damage in the earthquake.
　　　　这个房屋在地震中遭受到了严重的损害。

utter　/ˈʌtə/　*adj.* 彻底的，完全的

e. g.   What he said was utter nonsense.
　　　　他刚才说的纯粹是十足的废话。

Phrases and Expressions

break out　（战争、打斗等）突然发生，爆发

e. g.   It appears as if a war will break out.
　　　　看来一场战争即将爆发。

scream out　尖声发出；宣传

e. g.   Don't scream out in the classroom.
　　　　不要在教室里大声喊叫。

show up　出席，露面；炫耀

e. g.   She dressed herself up and found nowhere to show up.
　　　　她打扮得整整齐齐，却无处炫耀。

take place　发生，举行，进行

e. g.   When did the accident take place?
　　　　事故是什么时候发生的？

参 考 译 文

无论发生什么

　　1　大地震及其恐怖的震后影响被人们认为是自然界中最可怕、最具有破坏力的自然灾害之一。30 年前，一场里氏 8.2 级的地震几乎将美国夷为平地。在短短不到 4 分钟的时间里，地震夺去了数以万计人民的生命。在彻底的破坏与混乱之中，有位父亲将他的妻子在家

里安全地安顿好之后,立刻跑到他儿子就读的学校,而触目所见,却是被夷为平地的校园。

2　经过最初的难以置信的震惊之后,他想起了曾经对儿子所作的承诺:"不论发生什么事,我都会在你身边。"当父亲目睹曾经的学校已成为了眼前的一堆瓦砾,感觉非常绝望,非常的无助,泪水早已顺着脸颊流淌而下。但父亲的脑海中仍然牢记着他对儿子所做出的承诺。

3　他开始努力回忆每天早上送儿子上学的必经之路,终于记起儿子的教室应该就在那幢教学楼后部,位于右边的角落里。于是他冲了过去,开始在碎石瓦砾中搜寻儿子的下落。就在这位父亲奋力挖掘时,其他学生的家长也赶到了现场,跪倒在一片废墟旁,手里往外扒拉着石块,揪心地呼唤着孩子的名字。

4　此时,一些好意的家长试图把这位父亲劝离现场,告诉他"一切都太迟了!他们全死了!这样做没用的。"

5　"回去吧……面对现实吧……这样做只会使事情更糟……"

6　面对种种劝告,这位父亲的回答只有一句话:"你们愿意帮我吗?"然后继续进行挖掘,在废墟中不停地寻找他的儿子。

7　消防队员赶到了现场,也试图把这位父亲劝走,对他说:"火灾频现,四处都在发生爆炸,你在这里太危险了,这边的事我们会处理,你回家吧!"

8　对此,这位父亲仍然回答:"你们要帮我吗?"

9　警察随后也赶到了现场,对他说:"我知道,你现在很着急,但是你这样未必能找到你的孩子。回家吧!我们会处理一切的。"

10　这位父亲依旧回答:"你们愿意帮我吗?"

11　然而,人们无动于衷。

12　为了弄清楚儿子是死是活,这位父亲独自一人鼓起勇气,继续在废墟中挖掘。他挖了 8 小时,12 小时,24 小时,36 小时。在 38 个小时后,当父亲推开了一块巨大的石头时,他听到了儿子的声音。

13　父亲大叫着:"阿曼达!"

14　儿子回喊到:"爸爸吗?是我,爸爸,我告诉其他的小朋友不要着急。我告诉他们如果你活着,你会来救我的。如果我获救了,他们也就获救了。你答应过我,不论发生什么,你永远都会在我的身边!你做到了,爸爸!"

15　"你那里的情况怎样?有几个人活着?"父亲问。

16　"我们有 14 个人还活着。爸爸,我们好害怕,又渴又饿,幸亏你来了。教室倒塌时,刚好形成一个三角形的洞,救了我们。"

17　"快出来吧!儿子!"

18　"不,爸爸,让我的同学先出来吧!因为我知道你会和我在一起的!不管发生什么事,我知道你永远都会来到我的身边!"

Exercises

I. Reading Comprehension

Section A

1. D　2. B　3. C　4. C　5. D

Section B

1. The magnitude of the earthquake is 8. 2 on the Richter scale.

2. They kneeled down, clutched the rubbles and cried out their children's name.

3. No one helped the father.

4. There were 33 students in that class.

5. Because the father promised to the son that no matter what happens, he will always be there.

Section C

1. I think the earthquake is the most frightening disaster, since it can cause thousands of deaths in a few seconds, which is so short that most of the people do not have time to take reaction. It's terrible.

2. The most common disaster in my city is the sand storm. In recent years, it seems that the environment becomes worse and worse that every spring we would experience it several times.

3. Up to now, it seems that there is no need to prepare for the sand storm, since it can not do the real damage to our life. However, it is hard to say what would it be like if we just leave it alone and pay no attention.

II. Vocabulary and Structure

Section A

1. B 2. B 3. A 4. C 5. B 6. C 7. A 8. B 9. C 10. D

Section B

1. A manager was appointed to <u>handle</u> the crisis.
   一个经理被任命去处理这次危机。

2. His advice is <u>well-meant,</u> though he is a little cold.
   尽管他有些冷漠,他的建议还是用意良好的。

3. There has not been a man who <u>responds</u> to your plan so far.
   到目前为止,还没有人响应你的计划。

4. <u>Frightened</u> by the explosion, we all rushed out of the hall.
   受到了爆炸的惊吓,我们全都冲出了大厅。

5. We are looking for someone with a real sense of <u>commitment</u> to the job.
   我们正在寻找一个对工作有真正奉献精神的人。

6. The swimmer <u>emerged</u> from the lake.
   那个游泳的人从湖面上探出头来。

7. The village was <u>overwhelmed</u> when the floods came.
   当洪水来临的时候,这个村子被淹没了。

8. The new aircraft has performed very well in its <u>initial</u> trials.
   这款新型飞机在试航中性能表现非常好。

III. Word Building

1. The doctor thinks that coughing is the sign of weakness.

   医生认为咳嗽是身体虚弱的表现。

2. If your son shows any sign of illness, take him to the hospital right away.

   如果你的孩子有任何得病的症状,立刻带他去医院看病。

3. He stands in front of the classmates with such nervousness that he can not stop his hands from trembling.

   站在全班同学面前,他紧张得双手不停地在抖动。

4. We are treated with great kindness by the local people.

   当地人对待我们非常友善。

5. As the sun sets, the house sinks into complete darkness.

   太阳落山后,这个屋子陷入一片漆黑当中。

6. New rules are made in this factory to punish laziness.

   这个工厂制定了新的措施以惩罚懒惰现象。

7. The child broke the mirror and had a feeling of sadness.

   这个小孩打破了镜子,心里非常难过。

8. A smoker's carelessness resulted in a forest fire in this country.

   这个国家的森林大火是由吸烟人的粗心引起的。

IV. Grammar Focus

1. I'll be strict with my students if I were a teacher.

2. I'll buy my parents a lot of things if I were rich.

3. I'll do it in a different way if I were to do the math problem.

4. I'll face the problem bravely if I were in your place.

5. We would lose the way in the forest if it were not for his help.

V. Translation

1. Earthquakes are among the most powerful natural disasters on Earth, and their results can be terrifying.

   地震是地球上最具破坏力的自然灾害之一, 它们造成的影响也是非常可怕的。

2. A severe earthquake may release energy 10,000 times as great as that of the first atomic bomb.

   一场大地震所释放的能量相当于第一颗原子弹爆炸释放能量的 10,000 倍。

3. Rock movements during an earthquake can make rivers change their course.

   地震中的板块运动能使河流改变它们当初的河道。

4. Earthquakes can trigger landslides that cause great damage and loss of life.

   地震能够引发山体滑坡从而造成更大的破坏,并夺取人们的生命。

5. Many deaths and injuries in earthquakes result from falling objects and the collapse of buildings.

地震中的许多伤亡是由坠落的物体和倒塌的建筑造成的。

VI. Writing

Sample

A Letter of Inquiry

Mar. 10th, 2010

Dear Sir or Madam,

I am a Chinese student who wishes to apply for admission into your prestigious university. My plan is to start my course next term and I would be grateful if you would be kind enough to provide me with certain essential information.

First, what qualifications do I need to follow a course of study at your university? I already have a bachelor's degree from Beijing University, but I wonder if there are any further academic requirements. Second, how much are the tuition and fees? Although I intend to be self-supporting, I would be happy to know if there are any scholarships available for international students. Third, what is the situation as regards accommodation?

I look forward to your reply and to attending your esteemed institution. Thanks for your time.

Yours sincerely,

Li Ming

Notes

Begin your letter by stating who you are and what your status or position is (such as student, researcher, interested consumer, etc.), and tell how you find out the individual or entity that you are writing to.

Clearly state what it is that you are inquiring about and what you would like the recipient of your letter to do. Make your inquiry as specific as possible.

You might want to briefly explain the purpose of your letter or what you hope to accomplish. Such an explanation may prompt the recipient of your letter to act more quickly.

Include the date by which you need the information, services that you are requesting, and indicate that you await the reader's response. Thank the person for his/her time.

 **Text B**   **Background**

What to do before an earthquake?

Earthquakes strike suddenly, violently and without warning. Identifying potential hazards ahead of time and planning in advance can reduce the dangers of serious injury or loss of life from an earthquake.

Check potential hazards in your house. You should fasten shelves securely to walls and place large or heavy objects on lower shelves. Store breakable items such as bottled foods, glass and china in low, closed cabinets with latches. Repair defective electrical wiring and leaky gas connections. These are potential fire risks.

Identify safe places and educate yourself and family members. Keep in mind the safe place is under a heavy desk or against an inside wall. Teach children how and when to call police, or fire department and which radio station to listen to for emergency information. Teach all family members how and when to turn off gas, electricity and water.

Have disaster supplies at hand and develop an emergency plan. Always keep first aid kit, emergency food and cash handy. And develop a plan for reuniting after the disaster in case family members are separated from one another during an earthquake.

What to do during an earthquake?

Stay as safely as possible during an earthquake. Be aware that some earthquakes are actually foreshocks and a larger earthquake might occur. Minimize your movements to a few steps to a nearby safe place and stay indoors until the shaking has stopped and you are sure exiting is safe.

If you are indoors, drop to the ground, take cover by getting under a sturdy table or other piece of furniture, and hold it until the shaking stops. If there isn't a table or a desk near you, cover your face and head with your arms and crouch in an inner corner of the building. Stay away from glass, windows, outside doors and walls, and anything that could fall.

If you are outdoors, move away from buildings, streetlights and utility wires. Once in the open, stay there until the shaking stops. Ground movement during an earthquake is seldom the direct cause of death or injury. Most earthquake-related casualties result from collapsing walls, flying glass and falling objects.

If you are in a moving vehicle, stop as quickly as safety permits and stay in the vehicle. Avoid stopping near or under buildings, trees, overpasses and utility wires. Proceed cautiously once the earthquake has stopped. Avoid roads, bridges, or ramps that might have been damaged by the earthquake.

What to do after an earthquake?

Expect aftershocks. These secondary shockwaves are usually less violent than the main quake, but can be strong enough to do additional damage to weakened structures and can occur in the first hours, days, weeks or even months after the quake. Listen to the radio or television for the latest emergency information.

Help injured or trapped persons. Remember to help your neighbors who may require special assistance such as infants, the elderly and people with disabilities. Give first aid wherever it is appropriate. Do not move seriously injured persons unless they are in immediate danger of further injury.

Check for gas leakage. If you smell gas or hear blowing or hissing noise, open a window and quickly leave the building. Turn off the gas at the outside main valve if you can and call the gas company from a neighbor's home.

Look for electrical system damage. If you see sparks or broken wires, turn off the electricity at the main fuse box or circuit breaker. If you have to step in water to get to the fuse box or circuit breaker, call an electrician first for advice.

New Words

allocate /ˈæləkeɪt/   *v.* 分派,分配,划拨

    e. g.   The manager allocates duties to the clerks.
                经理为店员分配工作。

authority /ɔːˈθɒrɪtɪ/   *n.* 政府,权威

    e. g.   My sister is an authority on the history.
                我姐姐是历史方面的权威。

clinical /ˈklɪnɪkəl/   *adj.* 诊所的,医院的;临床的

    e. g.   He practices as a clinical psychologist.
                他是临床心理医生。

convey /kənˈveɪ/   *v.* 传递,传达

    e. g.   I cannot convey my feelings in words.
                我无法以言语表达我的感受。

counsel /ˈkaʊnsəl/   *n.* 劝告,建议

    e. g.   A fool may give a wise man counsel.
                愚者千虑,必有一得。

heroic /hɪˈrəʊɪk/   *adj.* 英雄的,英勇的

    e. g.   The newspapers glorified their heroic deeds.
                报纸称颂了他们的英雄事迹。

insure /ɪnˈʃʊə/   *v.* 保证,确保;为……投保

    e. g.   Their support will insure me success.
                他们的支持将成为我成功的保证。

intervention /ˌɪntɜ(ː)ˈvenʃən/   *n.* 干扰,干预

    e. g.   Her intervention brought the meeting to a close.
                会议因她干预而中断。

medication /ˌmedɪˈkeɪʃən/   *n.* 敷药,施药;药物

    e. g.   The doctor prescribed some medication.
                医生给开了些药。

mounting /ˈmaʊntɪŋ/   *adj.* 上升的;增长的

    e. g.   There is mounting pressure on the Government to resign.
                要求政府辞职的压力正在增长。

overcome /ˌəʊvəˈkʌm/   *v.* 克服;胜过;超越

    e. g.   Can you overcome your shortcomings?
                你可以克服你的缺点吗?

psychologist /saɪˈkɒlədʒɪst/ *n.* 心理医生

    e.g. Freud was a brilliant psychologist.

        弗洛伊德是位杰出的心理学家。

suffer /ˈsʌfə/ *v.* 遭受,蒙受;受苦,受折磨

    e.g. I cannot suffer such rudeness.

        我不能容忍这种粗鲁的举止。

supervise /ˈsjuːpəvaɪz/ *v.* 监督,监管

    e.g. The school staff are expected to supervise school meals.

        学校的教职员应监督学校的膳食。

temporarily /ˈtempərərɪlɪ/ *adv.* 临时的,暂时的

    e.g. The shop has been shut up temporarily.

        这家商店暂时停业了。

Phrases and Expressions

be true to 真实反映;适用于;忠实

    e.g. Will Mary be true to her work or true to her heart?

        玛丽将忠实于她的工作,还是直面自己的心灵?

deal with 解决,处理,打交道

    e.g. He have a great deal of letters to deal with.

        他有大量信件要处理。

emerge from 露出,浮现,出现

    e.g. After the rain, the sun emerged from behind the clouds.

        雨后,太阳从云层后面出来。

pour into 大量投入,涌入,倒入

    e.g. Thousands of farmers pour into big cities every day.

        每天成千上万的农民涌入大城市。

provide for 为……作准备;提供生活费;规定

    e.g. We have to provide for possible accidents.

        我们要为可能发生的意外作些准备。

recover from 恢复,痊愈

    e.g. Many needed a couple of days to recover from the tragedy.

        许多人需要好些天才能从悲剧中恢复过来。

参 考 译 文

我在灾区做心理医生

1   一场里氏8级的大地震,震惊了所有人。听着在这场巨大的灾难中伤亡人数不断攀

升的报告,我和所有人一样伤心落泪,希望自己能帮忙做点什么。

2　因为自己受过临床心理辅导的培训,所以我特别关心这场大灾难给受伤的幸存者和他们的亲人带来什么样的心理和情感创伤。我知道,如果幸存者能够接受一些基本的心理治疗,他们就能更快地恢复,重新回到正常生活也会有保证,并免受长期的心理折磨。

3　地震几天后,我从报道中看到很多外国的心理专家都抵达灾区,提供必要的心理危机干预,我非常激动。政府非常鼓励和支持这方面的工作,让我燃起了去灾区支援的希望。

4　通过相关部门,我提出志愿服务灾区的申请,并受邀请去当地一个医院工作。这家医院正在为所有的病人做灾后心理治疗,他们非常欢迎我去,与那里的心理顾问一起工作。他们希望我在美国作心理顾问的经历能帮助培训一些经验不足的心理治疗师,并指导他们工作。

5　在灾区担任志愿者工作给我留下了三点深刻的印象。一是这次地震带来的巨大灾难。这所医院或许是世界上最大的医院,拥有3 000个床位。尽管这样,所有的病床都挤满了重伤的病人,许多走廊上都设了临时病床以应对不断到来的伤者。

6　悲伤与痛苦充斥在各个角落,承受苦难的人数达到了惊人的数字。我知道,这只是这个国家数百所挤满地震伤员的医院之一。而且,这些受伤人数还不包括那些震后无家可归、住在帐篷里面的灾民。亲身面对这么大的灾难,让我终身难忘。

7　二是政府和各地人民为灾区提供的大量援助。每天,我都能看到数百辆的救护车。其中一些是从远在千里之外的首都日夜兼程开到灾区,然后从灾区救出伤员,再带走治疗。看到这些,我非常感动。全国各地的志愿者来到灾区,提供力所能及的帮助,陪护病人,或者做志愿医生、护士。

8　成千上万的警察和士兵为了把伤者运出灾区和维持治安而竭尽全力,他们都是真正的英雄。我还遇到了几个从海外回来的人,他们都生活在国外。但是地震后,立即离开自己的工作岗位回到了祖国,尽己所能为灾区提供帮助。此外,政府提供的物资数量之大,也令我印象深刻,政府把这些物资都分配给了灾民。每一项能够帮助灾民从灾难中恢复的工作,都正在进行。

9　三是当地人民的坚强。我在医院中看到的所有病人,都从来没有埋怨,没有痛苦的呻吟声,或是要求开药减轻病痛。

10　在这里,人们皆以竹自喻,弯而不折,以我这些天的经历来看,这句话是如此的真实。这就是希望,即使是在这样可怕的灾难面前,坚强的人民也将战胜困难,重建他们的城市,重建他们的心灵与生活。

11　灾难无情,但人人心中有真情。

Exercises

I. Reading Comprehension

1. A　2. B　3. C　4. D　5. D

II. Vocabulary and Structure

1. D 2. D 3. D 4. C 5. A 6. C 7. C 8. B 9. C 10. B

III. Translation

1. It would help them to recover from this suffering more quickly and insure that they could <u>return to a more normal life free of long-term emotional suffering.</u>

   这将帮助他们更快的从悲惨的遭遇中恢复,并保证他们能重新回到正常生活中,免受长期心理折磨。

2. The second impression my time there left me with was <u>the massive amount of aid from both the government and the people had poured into helping the victims.</u>

   那份志愿者工作给我留下第二个深刻印象的是政府和人民为灾区提供的大量援助。

3. It conveyed a message that <u>anything that could be done to help people recover from this disaster was being done.</u>

   它也传递出一个信息:每一项能够帮助灾民从灾难中恢复的工作,都正在进行。

4. In the midst of such a horrible disaster, the people will overcome the difficulties and <u>be able to rebuild their cities, their hearts and their lives.</u>

   在这样可怕的灾难面前,坚强的人民也将战胜困难,有能力重建他们的城市,重建他们的心灵与生活。

5. There is no love in disasters, but <u>we have love in our hearts.</u>

   灾难无情,但人人心中有真情。

Part V   Time for Fun

参 考 译 文

搞 错 了

一位美国人,一位苏格兰人和一位加拿大人在一场车祸中丧生。他们到达天堂的门口后,醉醺醺的圣彼德解释说是搞错了。"每人给我五百美元,"他说,"我将把你们送回人间,就像什么都没有发生过一样。"

"成交!"美国人说。立刻,他发现自己毫发无损地站在现场附近。

"其他人在哪儿?"一名医生问道。

"我离开之前,"那名美国人说,"我看见苏格兰人正在砍价,而加拿大人正在争辩说应该由他的政府来出这笔钱。"

9 Unit

Cyberspace

Part I   Teaching Objectives

* **Listening & Speaking**

  Help the students to be familiar with the topic—*how to meet and communicate with people on the Internet* and memorize useful expressions.

* **Words & Expressions**

  Study some new words and expressions, such as *matchmaking*, *profile*, *personality*, *correspondent*, *withstand*, *anonymous*, *compatible*, *alter*, *register*, *log onto*, *hook up to*, *screen out*, *sign up*, *put up*, *finish with*, *set about* and so on.

* **Grammar**

  Learn to use the structure of *only to discover*.

* **Writing**

  Understand and write *a letter of recommendation*.

Part II   Listening——*Online Dating*

New Words

anonymous   /əˈnɒnəməs, əˈnɒnɪməs/   *adj.* 匿名的,不署名的

  e. g.   The writer wishes to remain anonymous.
          作者希望姓名不公开。

correspondent   /ˌkɒrɪˈspɒndənt/   *n.* 通过信件联系的人;通讯员,(外派)记者

  e. g.   He is a poor correspondent.
          他是个懒于写信的人。

cute   /kjuːt/   *adj.* 漂亮可爱的,聪明伶俐的

148

e. g. What a cute little baby!

多可爱的婴儿!

matchmaking /ˈmætʃmeɪkɪŋ/ *n.* 作媒

e. g. I bet they will not provide us the matchmaking service.

我打赌他们不会帮我们介绍对象。

percentage /pəˈsentɪdʒ/ *n.* 百分比,比例

e. g. What percentage of the students were absent?

旷课的学生占百分之几?

personality /ˌpɜːsəˈnælətɪ/ *n.* 人格,个性;特点,特征

e. g. His personality comes through his writing.

他的性格生动地显现在他的文章中。

personally /ˈpɜːsənəlɪ/ *adv.* 亲自地,本人地

e. g. The owner of the hotel welcomed us personally.

这家旅馆的主人亲自欢迎我们。

playful /ˈpleɪfʊl/ *adj.* 活泼的,快乐的

e. g. The little cat gave me a playful bite.

小猫顽皮地咬了我一下。

profile /ˈprəʊfaɪl/ *n.* 简况,人物简介

e. g. How can I update my profile?

我该如何更新我的个人资料?

pub /pʌb/ *n.* 酒吧,酒馆

e. g. Many young men like to go to pub for relaxation.

许多年轻人喜欢去酒吧放松。

standout /ˈstændaʊt/ *adj.* 出色的,杰出的

e. g. All the cameras we tested were good, but there was no real standout.

测试的所有相机都不错,但没有一个是性能超棒的。

website /ˈwebsaɪt/ *n.* 网站,网址

e. g. I will check his website.

我会上网去浏览一下他的网页。

Phrases and Expressions

cut oneself off from 使……远离

e. g. The leaders should not cut themselves off from the masses.

领导不应该脱离群众。

hook up to 连接到

e. g. All the speakers hook up to a single amplifier.

所有喇叭都接在一个扩音器上。

keep in mind 记住,牢记

e. g. You must constantly keep in mind that haste makes waste.

你必须常记"欲速则不达"。

log onto 进入,注册,登陆

e. g. Log onto the website and vote for your favorite star!

登陆网站,为你喜爱的明星投票吧!

put up 粘贴;容忍;上传

e. g. She put her photos up to her profile yesterday.

她昨天把自己的照片上传到个人资料中了。

One

Listen to the CD and mark T for True or F for False according to the dialogue.

1. T 2. F 3. F 4. T 5. F

Script

Ann: Hey, Tony, did you see that? It is reported that millions of Americans looking for love try Internet dating. That's a quite crowd.

Tony: Yeah, that's sounds no surprise. You know, I'm working as an engineer for a matchmaking website. Thousands of people log onto our site everyday.

Ann: Really? Come on. Tell me something.

Tony: For the millions, their online dating profile is their one and only chance to make the first impression, so the picture is very important.

Ann: What are the main things that you need to know about your profile picture?

Tony: Your main picture needs to be a clear view of your face. You can be smiling. You can be doing whatever. Look at those on the site. That is very cute, but black and white is not very good. This one, I would say, it is really good because it's a very natural looking. It shows personality.

Ann: Is there something you should keep in mind when you build your profile picture?

Tony: Answering these who, what, where, when and why really makes your personality stand out. If you are serious and you want serious correspondents, then write very seriously; if you wanna playful, write playful.

Ann: Wow, so many inside views. Thank you very much.

Tony: You're welcome.

Two

Listen to the CD and answer the following questions with the information you hear.

1. What do they usually do on Saturday?

They usually go to pub on Saturday.

2. Why do they go there?

They go there to meet some women.

3. What is the real reason that they will not go there again?

   If they only go to bars, they're only meeting a small percentage of the population who do like to go out and have fun.

4. What would they try?

   They would try online dating.

5. How does the online dating work?

   One can put up a profile of oneself, and can see a lot of basic information about people even before you're ever in contact with them.

Script

Jonathan: So, Jeff, you know, I don't know if I want to go out to the pub again on Saturday. The music is a little bit too loud. I don't know. I've been thinking we should do some online dating. You know, try to meet some women that way.

Jeff: What do you mean? We just sit at home and... through the computer... Or why do you do that?

Jonathan: You know, in the modern world people are rushed. They always don't have time to go out and meet people. If you only go to bars, you're only meeting a small percentage of the population who do like to go out and have fun. You're cutting yourself off from a lot of people.

Jeff: So how does this work, this online dating?

Jonathan: You can put up a profile of yourself, with a picture if you like, or perhaps you would like to stay more anonymous and not put your picture up. You can see a lot of basic information about people even before you're even in contact with them.

Jeff: That sounds great. I'm gonna give it a go.

Spot Dictation

1. where you can make friends
2. put up a profile of yourself with a picture
3. find love just around the corner
4. that they are comfortable sharing
5. that really matches up with you

Part III　Speaking——*Computer and Website*

Useful Expressions About Cyberspace

Log onto the website for free.

You need a password to log on.

Jane will appear offline whenever Paul is online.

I'm showing offline.

I hook up to the Internet every day.

Check that the computer is hooked up to the printer.

I've just added you to my contacts list.

When I don't feel like talking to certain people online, I block them.

Remember your ID/username and password.

If you forget your password, you should remember your security question at the very least.

It includes provision for the retention of the date and time for "log in" and "log off" a website.

You should set up your profile first at the site.

You could stay anonymous.

Pair Work

Sample

Li Ming: Hi, would you like have a chat?

　　Lily: Hi.

Li Ming: I have just read your profile and find that your description is very funny.

　　Lily: Really? Thank you.

Li Ming: And I find we have a lot in common. I like to go hiking, boating and things like that.

　　Lily: Wow, that's great. I like them, too.

Li Ming: When do you usually go hiking?

　　Lily: Sometimes on weekends, sometimes on vacations. And you?

Li Ming: Mainly on vacations, so I could stay outside a little longer.

　　Lily: Sounds good. How do you think of the friendship in the virtual world?

Li Ming: I think mutual understanding is essential to friendship. True friendship also exists in the virtual world of cyberspace.

　　Lily: I agree whole-heartedly.

Li Ming: Hope to be your friend.

　　Lily: Me too, but I have to be off line now. See you.

Li Ming: See you.

Role-play

Sample

Todd: OK, Jean, you like the computer!

Jean: Yes, I do.

Todd: OK. Talk to me about computers.

Jean: Well, I go on the computer a lot and I talk with friends through AOL instant messenger. And I just moved from my hometown to Sacramento, so it's a good way to keep in touch with old friends.

Todd: Yeah. Do you learn about computers at school or on your own?

Jean: I picked most of what I know. I've picked it up, through, you know, the years, and some at school, like keyboarding and such.

Todd: OK. Do you have a laptop or a PC?

Jean: I have a PC.

Todd: Do you like your computer or do you want a new one?

Jean: I want a new one because I think I screwed mine up and it's a little bit slow now.

Todd: OK. How long have you had your computer?

Jean: I've had it for about 3 or 4 years.

Todd: Oh, yeah, that's pretty old for a computer. Yeah, so do you talk with your friends every night by e-mail?

Jean: Yeah, yes, I do.

Todd: OK.

Jean: See going on and, you know, the gossip.

Todd: So nowadays, do high school kids talk by e-mail more than phone?

Jean: Most people talk by either e-mail or cell phone. You know, a lot of people don't use their house phones as much and a lot of people have cell phones.

Todd: OK. Alright, thanks a lot Jean.

Part IV   Reading

 **Text A**   **Background**

Online dating is the best possible way to meet fantastic people who share your interests and passions. Every year there are tens of thousands of marriages that occur as a result of people meeting each other on an online dating website. In general, online dating is regarded as a safe medium for meeting potential dates. In order to improve your results, it's vital to enhance your presence. There are some tips to help improve your experience and your success. Use these tips to better understand yourself and the one who you are looking for in order to bring about better results.

1. Follow important safety tips. From the time you sign up for a website to the time you meet on a date, it's important to be safe. In a nutshell: never give out too much personal information; never give a home phone number; always meet in a public place for the first date; ask for a recent photo; and trust your gut instinct.

2. Build a winning profile. Your profile is one of the two key elements that will determine if a person emails you on an online dating website, the other being the photo. Thus it's important to make sure that your profile is lively, fun and positive. Examine other profiles and determine which part of it makes you more interested or less interested. If a person finds your profile interesting, then you have increased your chances of winning others' favor. Make yours interesting!

3. Post great recent photos. When doing a search on an online dating website, the first thing that grabs your attention is the photo. This is the most important element to get people to read your profile. These days, generic photos won't make it. You need to determine what colors look best on you, dress nice, be clean cut and have someone take various funny and lively photos of you. The photo can break the ice or become the topic for two of you to start chatting.

4. Learn effective communication techniques. Your first email to someone you're interested in is the most important one you'll ever write, because it will help determine whether or not they write back. It's important to personalize your introductory email and spend more time asking questions (based on the other person's profile) than providing information about yourself. Throwing a compliment doesn't hurt either (i. e. "I love your smile" or "your profile is one of the best I've read").

5. Always be respectful of others. By learning to respect others, you enhance your character. Being respectful means not being rude in communicating with others and not dropping off the face of the earth when you move on. One of the biggest complaints is from people who say the person they were communicating with just "disappeared" and stopped communicating. It's very disrespectful when you don't send a polite message to let other people know you are moving away.

6. Avoid white lies. In the world of online dating, white lies take on many forms. It may include: posting a photo more than nine months old and lying about your age, your income or your job. Since you are looking for soul mate, so those lies will come back to haunt you once you start a dating relationship with the very person. Always be honest and truthful in everything you say and post. By telling the truth, you'll never have to remember what you said!

7. Learn how to better identify and avoid married people. It's a sad fact that nearly one fourth of those people who participate in online dating are married. Whether looking for a way to cheat or trying to see what they "missed out", these people are a threat to those people seeking true relationships. Married people will be extremely secretive and irregular in their communication with you. If you reach the point of talking on the phone, you'll get their cell

phone answering machine a lot and calls will be returned on an irregular basis. They generally won't post a picture or sometimes, they post one dark-and-white photo. After all, they don't want a friend or family member to come across their profile! Avoid married people at all costs. As the saying goes: once a cheater, always a cheater.

8. Avoid becoming a professional online dater. The term "professional online dater" is coined to describe the growing number of people becoming addicted to online dating. The addiction is bad enough to affect potential relationships by hurting others in the process. And hurting others should be the last thing you want to do. A professional online dater is one who is on several dating websites, going out on several dates regularly and always thinking "the next one may be better". If they enter into a relationship, they just hide their profile. Once they have trouble in a relationship, they generally return to the online dating world instead of working out the issues in real world. A professional online dater generally just "drops off the face of the earth", instead of telling you directly he/she is no longer interested in communicating with you.

New Words

adjacent /əˈdʒeɪsənt/ *adj.* 邻近的，与……相连的

　　e.g.　We work in adjacent rooms.
　　　　　我们在毗邻的房间里工作。

attach /əˈtætʃ/ *v.* 附上，贴上；把……固定

　　e.g.　They attach great importance to education.
　　　　　他们十分重视教育

chaste /tʃeɪst/ *adj.* 纯真的；有道德的；忠于配偶的

　　e.g.　Tess is a chaste young girl.
　　　　　苔丝是一个纯真的少女。

compatible /kəmˈpætəbl/ *adj.* 和睦相处的；相容的，协调的

　　e.g.　Health and hard work are compatible.
　　　　　健康与努力工作是一致的。

compulsive /kəmˈpʌlsɪv/ *adj.* 强迫性的

　　e.g.　He went to a psychiatrist about his compulsive gambling.
　　　　　他去看精神科医生治疗不能自拔的赌瘾。

cyber /ˈsaɪbə/ *adj.* 计算机的，网络的；信息技术的

　　e.g.　I'd like to surf the Internet in a cyber bar.
　　　　　我想到网吧上网。

embrace /ɪmˈbreɪs/ *v.* 拥抱；包括；欣然接受

　　e.g.　The hills embrace the village.
　　　　　山丘环绕着村庄。

enthusiasm /ɪnˈθjuːzɪæzəm/ *n.* 热情，热心；极大的或强烈的兴趣

e. g. Their enthusiasm was infectious.

他们的热情非常有感染力。

generosity /ˌdʒenəˈrɒsətɪ/ *n.* 慷慨,大方;宽宏大量

e. g. His generosity gained him popularity.

他的慷慨为他赢得了人气。

glamorous /ˈɡlæmərəs/ *adj.* 富有魅力的;迷人的

e. g. The models in the fashion show are glamorous.

时装秀中的模特们都非常的迷人。

grant /ɡrɑːnt/ *v.* 准许;答应给予,同意

e. g. I can not grant your request.

我不能接受你的请求。

huntress /ˈhʌntrɪs/ *n.* 女猎人

e. g. Wasteland huntress can handle any type of enemy.

荒原女猎手能应付各种类型的敌人。

recommend /ˌrekəˈmend/ *v.* 推荐,介绍

e. g. What restaurant can you recommend?

你能不能介绍一家餐馆?

specify /ˈspesɪfaɪ/ *v.* 详述,具体说明

e. g. Please specify the senders' name!

请指定发信人名字!

vigorous /ˈvɪɡərəs/ *adj.* 精力充沛的,有活力的

e. g. He looked vigorous, tough and lively.

他看起来体格健壮,活力四射。

well-bred /ˈwelˈbred/ *adj.* 有教养的,受过良好教育的

e. g. She was too well-bred to show her disappointment.

她很有涵养,遇到失望的事亦不显露声色。

withstand /wɪðˈstænd/ *v.* 经受,承受

e. g. They can withstand severe tests.

他们能经得起严峻的考验。

Phrases and Expressions

in the first place 首先,从一开始

e. g. How did life arise in the first place?

生命最初是怎样起源的?

put the seal on sth. 在⋯⋯上打上封印

e. g. I put the official seal on document.

我在文件上盖了一个正式的印章。

screen out 筛选出

e. g. The curtains screen out the sunlight.

窗帘遮住了阳光。

set about 开始做(某事)

e. g. I must set about my packing.

我必须得开始收拾行李了。

sign up 签字参与;签订合同

e. g. Can I sign up through Internet?

我能通过网络报名吗?

参 考 译 文

网 上 交 友

1 我的"万人迷"女友在进行网上约会。这很可怕吗?有一天,她将这种体验推荐给另一位单身女士,对方的反应是"我可没那么疯狂。"

2 为什么人们会认为网上约会是疯狂的呢?我觉得,无论你是一家全球大型石油公司的首席执行官,还是像"万人迷"女友这样一位离过两次婚的金发碧眼美女,你都有权在网上寻找配偶,而不必为此感到羞愧。

3 网络空间给我的印象是,它是个寻找志趣相投伴侣的理想场所,这主要是因为你能在最初阶段就把不合适的候选者筛出局,而不用在他们身上浪费巨大的感情精力。我曾经对一些人一见钟情,后来却发现他们要么是强迫症,要么一生中只读过一本书,要么喜欢瓦格纳——如果在与他们见面之前,我和他们在网上聊一会儿,就能发现所有这一切。

4 当然,真正重要的是,你能明确找到你要在某人身上寻找的东西。比如:"某某人必须年轻、漂亮、明智、有教养、正派而又温柔、人品好、非常大度,如此等等。"

5 不,这可不是网络广告,而是美国开国领袖之一的托马斯·汉密尔顿在 1779 年寻觅一位女士做妻子时写的开头,详细说明了他理想中的妻子。想想如果他能上网,那么将会容易多少!

6 但即便是"万人迷"女友最初也很不愿意。于是一天晚上,我硬把她拽到自己的办公室,给她端上饮料,帮她在两个网站上注册,并付费,这样她才同意上网交友。注册交费成功后,她便饶有热情地开始了这种交友生活,找了一张好看的照片,附在个人详细资料上。

7 确切地讲,效果出奇地好。她将交友年龄范围确定在 50 至 60 岁之间,因此拒绝了所有来自年仅 35 岁的男性的求爱信。尽管其中一些人辩称,他们可能比 50 岁以上的人更有活力。随后,她开始从 150 名写信过来要求交往的人员中进行大幅删减,最后列出一份可以私下见面的名单。然后再与一小群人聊天,接连往复,最终定下一位可以相亲的。

8 目前,尽管我还没见过他,但我在网上读过他的个人档案。他似乎做了所有正确的事——在她生日时和她一起共度了一个浪漫周末,听了一场范·莫里森的音乐会,为她做饭,在早晨令人头痛的时间开车送她去机场。我没有询问关于卫生习惯的问题,但如果我知道他会把自己的脏衣服放在篮子里,而不是地板上,那么我无疑是会嫉妒发疯的。

9 20 年前,我遇到了我的白马王子,那个时候人们还不能普遍使用互联网。但我们还是通过电脑结缘的——澳洲航空公司（Qantas）的电脑将我们的飞机座位安排在了一起。事到如今我们一直在一起，尽管卫生习惯不太一样。但如果他将我退回到"二级市场（单身）"上，我将以充分的热情（而不是绝望地）奔向互联网寻找爱情。

Exercises

I. Reading Comprehension

Section A

1. D   2. D   3. C   4. A   5. C

Section B

1. The first reaction of the common people is that they are reluctant to try it.

2. The author sees cyberspace as the perfect place to meet new people.

3. No, she doesn't.

4. The advantage is that you can screen out unsuitable candidates at an early stage without having to waste an enormous amount of emotional energy on them.

5. The author would rush to the Internet if she were put back onto the secondary market.

Section C

1. Yes, it is very popular, since the Internet is very convenient and almost everyone can get access to it. People spend more and more time on the Internet. Therefore, there are more chances to meet new people.

2. No. I tried to communicate with many more strangers in the chat room, but it failed. It is hard for me to show real feelings. It is weird, I think.

3. Cyberspace is a great medium, as more and more things could be done through the Internet. It really offers us a lot of convenience and should have a brighter future.

II. Vocabulary and Structure

Section A

1. C   2. C   3. A   4. A   5. D   6. C   7. B   8. B   9. A   10. B

Section B

1. Cyberspace is the electronic medium of computer networks, in which online communication takes place.

网络空间是由接入网络中电脑构成的一个电子媒介，通过这一媒介人们可以进行在线交流。

2. The glamorous movie stars would always set the trend for the young people.

漂亮迷人的电影明星们总是为年青人引领时尚的潮流。

3. The same commercial is repeated on television to brainwash people into <u>compulsive</u> consumption.

   同一个广告片在电视上反复播放的目的就是为了给你洗脑,强制你去消费。

4. It is <u>recommended</u> that Facebook is the largest website to make new friends.

   Facebook 被认为是最大的交友网站。

5. Tony's children are <u>well-bred</u>, whereas those of his sister are naughty.

   托尼的孩子们都非常有教养,而他妹妹的孩子们则非常淘气。

6. You should read the <u>specification</u> of the microwave oven first before you use it.

   使用微波炉前,你应该阅读它的说明书。

7. Clowns like him will not get anywhere, so we <u>attach</u> no importance to him.

   像他这样的小丑不会有什么出息的,所以我们都对他不抱任何期望。

8. The mother held out her arms to <u>embrace</u> the little boy.

   母亲伸出双臂拥抱住了这个小男孩。

III. Word Building

1. The old lady never has any <u>visitor</u> since she moves to a new place.

   自从这个老妇人搬到新的地方居住后,再没有人拜访过她。

2. The <u>waiters/waitresses</u> are very busy in the dinner time in that famous restaurant.

   晚饭时间那个著名饭店的服务员都非常忙。

3. Many newspaper <u>reporters</u> cannot get access to the building where the accident took place.

   很多新闻记者无法进入到事故发生的那栋大楼。

4. Nowadays every family in the village has a gas <u>cooker</u> in the kitchen.

   如今,村子里的家家户户的厨房里都装有燃气灶。

5. Knowing two foreign languages, Miss Li wants to be a <u>teacher</u> in the school.

   懂得两门外语,李小姐想去学校当一个老师。

6. There are many famous <u>actors/actresses</u> in the evening performance.

   晚会上有很多著名的演员。

7. Miss Lin is an excellent <u>hostess</u> of a television programme.

   林小姐是一名优秀的电视节目主持人。

8. He is a good <u>learner</u>, as he always takes a dictionary with him.

   他是一个非常爱学习的学生,随身总是带一本字典。

IV. Grammar Focus

1. A group of students plan to cook meals over a fire only to discover that the firewood is in short supply.

2. Many people pay for expensive seats at the theatre only to discover that the show is disappointing.

3. Mr. Smith gets up early in the morning only to discover that the bus has gone when he arrives at bus station.

4. Lily is looking for the keys in her room all day along only to discover that the keys are in her hand.

5. Tom works hard on his paper every day only to discover that he can not meet the deadline.

V. Translation

1. Internet dating can be scary, since <u>you will have to post a description and photograph of yourself onto the website</u> for thousands, if not millions, of people to see.

网络约会也让人感到害怕，因为你必须把自己的简介和照片传到网站上让人去浏览，没有上百万人，也有成千上万人。

2. It's a step into the unknown. <u>What happens if no one replies at all</u>?

这一步通向未知的世界，如果没有人回复该怎么办？

3. In my opinion, cyberspace is the perfect place to find someone, because <u>you can screen out unsuitable candidates at an early stage</u>.

在我看来，网络是交友的完美平台，因为你能在最初阶段就把不合适的候选者筛选出局。

4. You can research them on the Internet and even take up references, <u>so it is a far more objective way of finding a mate than a random selection</u>.

你可以上网调查他们，甚至还可以向人问询，所以这种寻找伴侣的方式，可比随便选一个要客观多了。

5. Before you meet someone you will know a lot about them. At least, <u>Internet dating eliminates some uncertainty</u>.

在见面之前，你可以了解他们的许多信息。至少，网上交友可以消除某些不确定性。

VI. Writing
Sample

A Letter of Recommendation

Mar. 10th, 2011

Dear Sir or Madam,

I am writing to you to recommend one of my best friends, Zhou Botong, for this post. With his outstanding leadership and cheerful personality, he was elected chairperson of the Student Union of Fudan University several times.

Busy as he was, he completed his major, Teenage Psychology, with an outstanding school record. Upon graduation he was assigned to be a teacher in Fudan Middle School. What's more, he loves his job and enjoys working with children. This has won him great popularity among his students.

Therefore, I do not hesitate to recommend him as an ideal candidate for the post you advertised. I am sure you will make a wise decision in hiring him.

Yours sincerely,
Li Ming

Notes

If you need to secure a good position in the work force or be admitted to a school of higher learning, you will probably need one or more letters of recommendation. Both employers and admissions boards need to know as much as possible about an applicant to determine his or her ability to perform adequately.

Letters of recommendation provide information given by a former employer or a credible associate who has been personally involved with the candidate. This piece of information provides a valuable record of the candidate's previous experience and can testify to his or her skills and abilities. An effective letter of recommendation verifies experience, confirms competence, builds credibility and strengthens confidence.

The information contained in a letter of recommendation depends on the type of letter and its intended audience. Information is often different between a letter for an academic admissions board and that for a prospective employer.

Text B   **Background**

Facebook is a social network service and website launched in February, 2004, operated and privately owned by Facebook, Inc. Till July, 2010, Facebook has more than 500 million active users, which is about one person for every fourteen in the world. Users may create a personal profile, add other users as friends and exchange messages, including automatic notifications when they update their profile. Additionally, users may join those common interest user groups organized by workplace, school, college or other institutions.

Facebook is founded by Mark Zuckerberg with his college roommates and fellow computer science students. The name of the service stems from the colloquial name for the book given to students at the start of the academic year by university administrations in the US with the intention of helping students to get to know each other better.

Colleges and universities in the United States often publish official or unofficial books listing their students, faculty or staff, together with pictures and limited biographical data. In the early 2000s some facebooks are published online, offering a number of new features, including password protection, more detailed information, more advanced indexing and searching, and the ability for people to upload and enter information and photographs.

In early 2004 Harvard University sophomore Mark E. Zuckerberg creats an unofficial online facebook at the website "thefacebook. com", the forerunner of the Facebook service, out of frustration that the university's official online facebook project is taking too long.

The website's membership is initially limited by the founders to Harvard students, but is expanded to other colleges in the Boston area, the Ivy League and Stanford University. It gradually adds support for students at various other universities before opening to high school students, and, finally, to anyone aged 13 and over.

Facebook has met with some controversies. It has been blocked intermittently in several countries including Pakistan, Syria, the People's Republic of China, Vietnam, Iran, Uzbekistan and North Korea. It has also been banned in many places of work to discourage employees from wasting time using the service. Facebook's privacy has also been an issue, and the safety of their users has been compromised several times.

Facebook's growth as an Internet social networking site has met criticism on a range of issues, especially data mining and the inability to terminate accounts without first manually deleting all the content. Many of these issues have been fully resolved, specifically the ability to delete account.

A January-2009-Compete. com study ranks Facebook as the most used social network by worldwide monthly active users, followed by MySpace. *Entertainment Weekly* says, "How on earth did we stalk our exes, remember our co-workers' birthdays, and bug our friends before Facebook?"

New Words

alter /ˈɔːltə/ *v.* 改变,变更

　　e. g.　Alter the spacing and you alter the colour.
　　　　　　改变其间隔则可以改变颜色。

automatically /ˌɔːtəˈmætɪkəlɪ/ *adv.* 自动地;不自觉地

　　e. g.　The machine is automatically controlled.
　　　　　　这机器是自动控制的。

bridal /ˈbraɪdəl/ *adj.* 新婚的,婚礼的

　　e. g.　They are now making a bridal tour.
　　　　　　他们正在新婚旅行。

gracious /ˈɡreɪʃəs/ *adj.* 高雅的,漂亮的,华美的

　　e. g.　She has always a gracious smile.
　　　　　　她脸上总是带着优雅的微笑。

irritated /ˈɪrɪteɪtɪd/ *adj.* 恼怒的,生气的

　　e. g.　He was irritated with you.
　　　　　　他在生你的气。

nifty /ˈnɪftɪ/ *adj.* 俏皮的,极好的

　　e. g.　That is a nifty suit.
　　　　　　那是一身很漂亮的衣服。

recover /rɪˈkʌvə/ *v.* 重新获得,找回;恢复

　　e. g.　We prayed that she would recover.
　　　　　　我们为她尽快康复而祈祷。

register /ˈredʒɪstə/ *v.* 注册,登记;记录

　　e. g.　You may also register online.
　　　　　　你也可以通过网络注册。

thumping /ˈθʌmpɪŋ/ *adj.* 非常大的

e. g. My heart was thumping with happiness.

我的心兴奋得咚咚直跳。

upmarket /ˈʌpˌmɑːkɪt/ *adj.* 高档的,高级的

e. g. They always go to an upmarket restaurant for lunch.

他们总是去一家高档的饭店吃午饭。

wellbeing /ˈwelˈbiːɪŋ/ *n.* 健康,幸福

e. g. The warm summer weather always gives me a sense of wellbeing.

融融夏日总让我有种幸福感。

Phrases and Expressions

along with 和……一起,随同

e. g. He came along with some friends.

他和几个朋友一道来的。

amount to 发展成,共计

e. g. Your words amount to refusal.

你说的那些话等于是拒绝。

ask after 问候,询问健康状况

e. g. Do not ask me after John Smith—he has joined the angels.

不必问候约翰·史密斯了——他已不在人世了。

bump into 撞上,偶然碰见

e. g. I often bump into him at the supermarket.

我经常在超市同他不期而遇。

finish with 断绝关系,绝交

e. g. She should finish with him for he treats her very badly.

她应该和他断绝关系——他对她太不好了。

go straight to 直奔,径直朝……走去

e. g. They go straight to the point, without preliminaries.

他们开门见山直奔主题,不走过场。

hit on 忽然想到,偶然发现

e. g. Who hit on this brilliant idea?

这个好主意是谁想到的?

pay the bill 付账,买单

e. g. Please pay the bill in cash.

请用现金支付。

参 考 译 文

恋人分手也上网

1   分手从来都不是件开心的事情,即使现在有很多不同的分手方式。以吉米为例,几

周前,他和女友分手了。至少他用的是打电话的方式,而不是发邮件或(更糟糕的)发短信。但挂掉电话后,他就上网,在他的 Facebook 博客上修改了他的爱情状态。

2   显然,这样消息就自动传递给了他的朋友——约有 300 个人。我不得不说,我很庆幸自己青少年时代的约会是在互联网出现之前。分手已经够糟糕了,但更糟的是有 300 个人在半小时内就知道了这件事。

3   但不管怎么说,吉米现在是单身,换言之,正如他在 Facebook 博客上写道的:"目前没有恋爱"。

4   可爱的露辛达现在也没谈恋爱。这可不是因为她辛苦地为我工作,帮我付费,为我找回落在出租车上的笔记本电脑,也不是因为她花了太多个晚上去学习婚礼插花。我真不明白为什么可爱的露辛达还是单身,她非常漂亮、高雅和善良,给人带来快乐。在为我工作期间,她至少有过两段相当认真的恋爱,但都没修成正果。

5   与我许多单身女友一样,如果不是多数,她也尝试过网恋,但成功与否就难说了。最近,因为自己在找结婚对象的事上没有什么进展,她请了一周假,到一家非常高档的婚介所去注册。这需要一周的时间吗?露辛达告诉我,这是个非常漫长而细致的过程,要填很多表格,还有一个综合面试。

6   此外,可爱的露辛达还得给那家婚介所开一张金额庞大的支票。她跟我说,这是一项认真的投资,必须做出牺牲。

7   但后来,露辛达偶然发现了一种为婚介所付钱的新方法。几周前,她在某个聚会或其它什么地方遇到了她的第一任丈夫。是的,露辛达以前结过婚。不过她已经 5 年没见过那个家伙了。他显然仍非常喜欢露辛达,询问她的近况,并问能为她做点儿什么。

8   处于这种尴尬境地的她,脑海中一片空白。但考虑了几天之后,露辛达给她的老相好打了个电话,告诉他有件事他可以为她做——他愿意为她给那家婚介所付钱吗?

9   这没什么不合理的。既然她的第一任丈夫不能成为露辛达孩子们的爹,而且也不能在未来 40 年的时间里照顾她,那他至少可以帮她找到一位能做这些事的人。这种事甚至可以成为一种新的服务。每位离婚的女人都应该得到这种服务——还有那些结束长期恋爱关系的人。

10   这项服务有着巨大的潜在市场。露辛达或许是无意中找到了一种非常实用的方法,既能缓解提出分手或离婚一方的罪恶感,又能帮助重回单身的人找到新的人生伴侣。

11   因此,或许吉米应给他的前任女朋友一笔钱,让她去参加网络相亲,以这种方式帮她找个新男友。不过告诉 Facebook 上的 300 个朋友他们分手了,也相当于起到了同样的效果。

Exercises

I. Reading Comprehension
1. C   2. D   3. D   4. D   5. B

II. Vocabulary and Structure
1. D   2. B   3. B   4. A   5. C   6. A   7. D   8. B   9. A   10. C

III. Translation

1. Having put down the telephone, he went straight on to the Internet, and altered her official status on his Facebook page.

挂掉电话后,他直接上了网,在他的 Facebook 页面上修改了他的官方状态。

2. It is bad enough to end a relationship, but far worse to have 300 people notified of the fact within 30 minutes.

分手已经是一件很糟糕的事情了,但更糟的是有 300 个人在半小时内就知道了这件事。

3. Irritated with her lack of progress in finding someone to marry, Lucinda took a week off work and registered with a very upmarket dating agency.

出于对自己在寻找结婚对象方面的裹足不前的恼怒,露辛达请了一周假,去一家非常高档的婚姻介绍所注册。

4. A few weeks earlier, she had bumped into her first husband at some party or other.

几周之前,她在某个聚会或其它什么地方遇到了她的第一任丈夫。

5. Telling 300 Facebook friends that he has broken up with her amounts to pretty much the same thing.

告诉 Facebook 上的 300 个朋友他们分手了,也相当于起到了同样的效果。

Part V Time for Fun

参 考 译 文

完 美 搭 配

有一天某位女士看到一只老鼠在自家的厨房地板上窜过。她很害怕老鼠,所以她冲出屋子,搭上了公共汽车直奔商店。在那儿,她买了一只老鼠夹。店主告诉她:"放点奶酪在里面,很快你就会逮住那只老鼠的。"

这位女士带着鼠夹回到家里,但她没有在碗橱里找到奶酪。因为已经很晚了,她不想再回到商店里去。于是,她就从一份杂志中剪下一幅奶酪的图片放进了夹子。

令人称奇的是,这画有奶酪的图片竟然奏效了!第二天早上,这位女士下楼到厨房时,发现鼠夹上奶酪图片旁有一张画有老鼠的图片!

Unit 10

Life

Part I   Teaching Objectives

* Listening & Speaking

Help the students to be familiar with the topic — *how to form their own opinions on some certain phenomena and learn the appropriate ways to express worries and reassurances* and memorize useful expressions.

* Words & Expressions

Study some new words and expressions, such as *delay, swallow, affect, recovery, deteriorate, lethal, film, prosecute, confirm, undermine, opt, sensitive, be for/against, in addition to, in that case, opt out* and so on.

* Grammar

Learn to use the structure of *an appositive*.

* Writing

Understand and write *a letter of sympathy*.

Part II   Listening——See a Doctor

New Words

anaesthetic   /ˌænɪsˈθetɪk/   *n.* （使局部或全身失去知觉的）麻醉剂

    e. g. He was given a general anaesthetic. 他被全身麻醉。

            It would have to be done under anaesthetic. 这个只能在麻醉的情况下做。

anaesthetist   /æˈnesθɪtɪst/   *n.* 麻醉师

    e. g. The anaesthetist gave the patient an anaesthetic. 麻醉师给病人施麻醉剂。

capsule   /ˈkæpsjuːl/   *n.* （装药物的）胶囊

    e. g. The doctor advised me to take a capsule this morning.

医生建议我今天早晨服一粒胶囊。

drowsy /ˈdraʊzɪ/ *adj.* 欲睡的,半睡的,使人昏昏欲睡的

  e. g. I feel drowsy after lunch every day. 每天午饭后我就想睡觉。

    It was a warm, quiet, drowsy afternoon.

    那是一个暖和、寂静而令人昏昏欲睡的下午。

flu /fluː/ *n.* 流感

  e. g. Lung fever develops from flu. 肺炎是由流行性感冒引起的。

ointment /ˈɔɪntmənt/ *n.* 药膏

  e. g. The ointment healed his wounds. 这药膏治好了他的伤口。

prescribe /prɪsˈkraɪb/ *v.* 给……开(药),让……采用(疗法),开(处方)

  e. g. The doctor prepared to prescribe a receipt. 医生准备开个药方。

rash /ræʃ/ *n.* 发疹,疹子

        adj. 太急速的;鲁莽的;轻率的

  e. g. The rash soon disappeared. 疹子很快就消了。

    Don't be rash in making your decision. 别轻率做出决定。

surgery /ˈsɜːdʒərɪ/ *n.* 外科手术;外科学

  e. g. Your condition is serious and requires surgery.

    你的情况很严重,需要动外科手术。

symptom /ˈsɪmptəm/ *n.* 症状

  e. g. The doctor told her to watch out for symptoms of measles.

    医生叫她注意麻疹出现的症状。

Phrases and Expressions

clear up 治疗,治愈

  e. g. This herbal medicine will soon clear up your cold. 这种草药能很快治好你的感冒。

combine with 与……结合

  e. g. If your talent combines with diligence, you can excel in your pursuit.

go into detail 详述,逐一细说

  e. g. Could you go into a little more detail about it?

    你能不能稍微再详细一点呢?

 One

Listen to the CD and mark T for True or F for False according to the dialogue.

1. F 2. T 3. T 4. T 5. F

Doctor: Good morning. What seems to be the problem?

Patient: Good morning, doctor. I feel terrible. I've got a cold and I have a rash here on

my neck. I'm not sleeping well either. What do you think the problem could be?

Doctor: I'd say you've been working too hard or are under stress for some reason. Have you been taking anything for your cold?

Patient: Yes, I bought some medicine at the chemist's. I've been taking it for three days.

Doctor: Good. I'm going to prescribe something stronger. It will make you feel drowsy, so you certainly should rest.

Patient: Okay. I can afford to take a few days off work.

Doctor: Have you been working hard recently?

Patient: Yes, I have. I had to get a project finished. It's done now, so I can relax a little.

Doctor: Good. Let's take a look at that rash. . . . It looks worse than it is. I'm going to prescribe some ointment for it. If the rash doesn't clear up in a few days, come back and see me. Do you have any other symptoms?

Patient: I have a bad headache, but. . .

Doctor: Don't worry about that. It's probably the stress you've been under. Just take some aspirin. Combined with the stronger cough medicine, it will make you feel very tired. You shouldn't work or use any equipment which requires concentration. If I were you, I'd just sleep, read a book or watch TV. Here is your prescription.

Patient: Thanks, doctor. I'll get these immediately. Goodbye.

 Two

Listen to the CD and answer the following questions with the information you hear.

1. What happened to Robert a few days ago?

   He went into hospital to undergo surgery because there was something wrong with his stomach.

2. How did Robert feel before his surgery?

   He was very nervous before the operation.

3. According to Robert what was the worse thing after his surgery?

   He wasn't permitted to eat anything for 48 hours.

4. Could Robert eat steak once he went out of the hospital after the operation?

   No, he couldn't. The doctor gave him a list of food he couldn't eat for another 72 hours, and the steak was just on the very list.

5. What did Robert think of the nurses in the hospital?

   He thought them to be very kind and professional, although strict with what he could drink.

Linda: Hello. Nice to see you again. I heard you went into hospital for a few days to undergo surgery. I hope everything will be Okay.

Robert: Yes, fine. I had something wrong with my stomach. I won't go into detail, but it wasn't serious.

Linda: I really dislike going to a doctor or to a hospital.

Robert: I think most people are a little nervous about it. I was really very, very nervous just before I had the operation, but the anaesthetist gave me an anaesthetic and the next thing I remember I was waking up after the operation.

Linda: It must have really hurt afterwards.

Robert: Well, the nurse gave me plenty of painkillers, but it did feel uncomfortable. I wasn't permitted to eat anything for 48 hours. That was the worse thing.

Linda: I bet you were ready for a thick juicy steak when you got out of hospital.

Robert: I certainly was! However, the doctor gave me a list of food I couldn't eat for another 72 hours, and steak was on the list!

Linda: Is there any pain now?

Robert: No, not at all. I stopped taking painkillers after a couple of days.

Linda: Did they take good care of you in the hospital?

Robert: Oh, yes. The nurses were very kind, though they were strict about what I could drink. In the end, I just drank water and nothing else. Everyone was very professional and I actually enjoyed some aspects of my stay.

Spot Dictation

1. Only in good shape can you expect to live comfortably or work effectively

2. he will eventually turn out to be a wreckage of modern life

3. you must give up the habits that damage your health

4. Whenever you are found to have any disease, you should have it timely treated

5. Health is the most important ingredient of your success

Part III Speaking——*Worries and Reassurances*

Useful Expressions About Worries and Reassurances

Worries

Are you all right now? /Are you feeling better today? /Is it serious, doctor?

What do you think the problem could be? /What's wrong? /What's on your mind? /

It worries me. /I can't help worrying. /I'm worried about my health. /I'm afraid. . . /

I feel terrible. /I had something wrong with my. . . .

Reassurance

You have got a touch of flu. /You are a bit down with the flu.

Don't worry. Everything will be OK. / Take it easy. / No need to get so nervous. / Your condition is not so bad. / There's really no reason to be worried. / You'll be fine. You should be back on your feet in a week.

Pair Work
Sample

Doctor: Come in, please.

Carl: I'm Carl Mathews.

Doctor: Have a seat. What seems to be the problem?

Carl: I've lost a little weight recently, and I don't seem to have as much energy. My head and stomach were killing me yesterday. I might have had a fever and I thought I ate something bad because I had the runs.

Doctor: Everything was fine with your last checkup 3 months ago. Are your eating OK? Do you bring anything up?

Carl: I'm eating fine, more or less. Last night, I thought I was going to vomit.

Doctor: Do you sleep well?

Carl: A little fitfully sometimes. This morning, I felt too sick to even get out of bed.

Doctor: Everything seems to be Okay. Any other symptoms?

Carl: No, nothing I can think of. I must say that things have been quite hectic around the office, recently.

Doctor: I think you may have a touch of the flu that's going around. And you do seem a little tired. I'll give you a flu shot and I recommend you take some vitamin supplements. Try to take it easier at work for a while, too.

Carl: Thanks, doctor.

Role-play
Sample

Jessica: Peter, are you feeling any better?

Peter: Thanks for asking, Jessica. I am feeling quite a bit better now.

Jessica: I am glad to hear that.

Peter: But I hate being sick! It was only a cold.

Jessica: How did you get that cold in the first place?

Peter: I normally get a cold when the season changes from winter to summer or from summer to winter.

Jessica: You mean it follows a certain pattern?

Peter: Yes, it always happens. So I am not surprised about getting this cold now.

Jessica: So what do you usually do to fight the cold?

Peter: I normally take cold tablets and rest a lot. Also I drink flat lemonade as well as water.

Jessica: You are experienced. As for me, every time I come down with a cold, I just leave it there.

Peter: That is not the best way to do things. I was lucky though because I still had some medicine.

Jessica: But I do sleep more, as I believe, sleep is the best medicine.

Part IV   Reading

 **Text A**   **Background**

1. Euthanasia

Euthanasia (from the Greek ευθανασία meaning "good death": ευ-, eu-(well or good) + θάνατος, thanatos — death) refers to the practice of ending a life in a painless manner. According to the House of Lords Select Committee on Medical Ethics, the precise definition of euthanasia is "a deliberate intervention undertaken with the express intention of ending a life, to relieve intractable suffering".

Euthanasia conducted with consent is termed voluntary euthanasia, while euthanasia conducted without consent is termed involuntary euthanasia. Involuntary euthanasia is conducted where an individual makes a decision for another person incapable of doing so. Both voluntary and involuntary euthanasia can be conducted passively or actively. A number of authors consider these two terms to be misleading and unhelpful. Passive euthanasia entails the withholding of common treatments (such as antibiotics, chemotheraphy in cancer or surgery) or the distribution of a medication (such as morphine) to relieve pain, knowing that it may also result in death (principle of double effect). Passive euthanasia is the most accepted form and it is a common practice in most hospitals. Passive euthanasia may also entail the withdrawing of life support, which is more controversial. Active euthanasia entails the use of lethal substances or forces to kill, and is the most controversial means. An individual may use a euthanasia machine to perform active voluntary euthanasia on himself/herself.

2. Euthanasia in the Netherlands

In 2002, the Netherlands legalized euthanasia. Euthanasia is still a criminal offence but the law codified a twenty-year old convention of not prosecuting doctors who have committed euthanasia in specific circumstances. *The Dutch Euthanasia Act* states that euthanasia and physician-assisted suicide are not punishable so long as the attending physician acts in accordance with criteria of due care. These criteria concern the patient's request, the patient's suffering (unbearable and hopeless), the information provided to the patient, the presence of reasonable alternatives, consultation of another physician and the applied method of ending life. To demonstrate their compliance, the Act requires physicians to report euthanasia to a review committee.

By far, most reported cases concerned cancer patients. Also, in most cases the procedure was applied at home. A study in 2000 found that Dutch physicians who intend to provide assistance with suicide sometimes end up administering a lethal medication themselves because of the patient's inability to take the medication or because of problems in the completion of physician-assisted suicide.

New Words

affect /əˈfekt/ *vt.* （疼痛，疾病等）侵袭；感染；影响

　　e.g.　Cancer had affected his lungs.　癌已侵及他的肺脏。

　　　　　The tax increases have affected us all.　加税已经影响了我们所有人。

confirm /kənˈfɜːm/ *v.* 证实，证明；肯定，确认；批准；认可

　　e.g.　We have confirmed the report.　我们证实了那则报道。

　　　　　The king confirmed that the election would be held on July 20th.

　　　　　国王批准选举在 7 月 20 日举行。

criteria /kraɪˈtɪərɪə/ *n.* （criterion 的复数）标准

　　e.g.　How do we set hiring criteria?　我们如何设定录取标准？

delay /dɪˈleɪ/ *v.* 耽搁，延迟

　　e.g.　Traffic was delayed by the bad weather.　交通被糟糕的天气延迟了。

　　　　　Don't delay your application or else it won't be considered.

　　　　　别耽搁了你的申请，否则将不予考虑。

deteriorate /dɪˈtɪərɪəreɪt/ *v.* 恶化，变坏；退化

　　e.g.　Leather can deteriorate in damp conditions.　皮革受潮可变质。

　　　　　From week to week we could see his health deteriorate.

　　　　　我们看到他的身体一个星期一个星期地差下去。

Dutch /dʌtʃ/ *adj./n.* 荷兰人的；荷兰的；荷兰语的；荷兰语；荷兰人

　　e.g.　Clogs are part of the Dutch traditional costume.

　　　　　木屐是荷兰传统装束的一部分。

　　　　　The British and the Dutch belong to the same race.　英国人和荷兰人是同一种族。

euthanasia /ˌjuːθəˈneɪzɪə/ *n.* 安乐死

　　e.g.　Euthanasia is illegal in most countries.　安乐死在大多数国家被认为是非法的。

film /fɪlm/ *v.* （把……）拍摄（成）电影（电视等）；（给……）覆上一薄层

　　e.g.　Tom filmed his daughter playing in the garden.

　　　　　汤姆把他的女儿在公园嬉戏的镜头拍摄了下来。

　　　　　Thin ice filmed the lake.　湖上结了一层薄冰。

guideline /ˈɡaɪdlaɪn/ *n.* 指导方针，指导原则，行动纲领，准则

　　e.g.　We laid out the economic guidelines and followed it.

　　　　　我们制定了经济方针并且遵循它。

hospice /ˈhɒspɪs/ *n.* （晚期病人的）安养院

e.g. You are invited to become a Friend of the Bristol Hospice, ie, to contribute money regularly.　邀请您作布里斯托尔末期病人安养所的赞助人。

injection /ɪnˈdʒekʃən/ *n.* 注射；注入

e.g. Those drugs are given by injection as well as through the mouth.
那些药品可以注射，也可以口服。
The firm would be revitalized by an injection of new funds.
该公司重新注入资金即可复苏。

lethal /ˈliːθəl/ *adj.* 致命的，可致死的；破坏性的，有害的

e.g. The closure of the factory dealt a lethal blow to the town.
那座工厂关闭是对该镇的致命打击。

majority /məˈdʒɒrɪtɪ/ *n.* 多数，大多数；半数以上

e.g. A majority vote enabled the passage of the resolution.
多数人投赞成票使议案得以通过。
The majority of his books are kept upstairs.　他的大部分书收藏在楼上。

opt /ɒpt/ *vt.* 选择，挑选

e.g. What courses are most students opting for?　多数学生选什么课程？
I think I'll opt out of the game.　我不想参加这场比赛了。
To opt out at the critical moment would be quite indefensible.
在关键时刻置身事外的做法是决不能原谅的。

parliament /ˈpɑːləmənt/ *n.* 议会，国会

e.g. The British Parliament consists of the House of Lords and the House of Commons.
英国议会由上院和下院组成。

prohibition /ˌprəʊhɪˈbɪʃən/ *n.* 禁令，禁律；禁酒

e.g. The prohibition order meant that the book could not be sold in this country.
这道禁令意味着该书不能在这个国家出售。
Prohibition was abolished in 1933.　禁酒令于 1933 年废除。

prosecute /ˈprɒsɪkjuːt/ *v.* 检举、告发某人；对某人提起公诉

e.g. He was prosecuted for theft.　他因偷窃而被告发。
Trespassers will be prosecuted.　闲人免进，违者必究。

recovery /rɪˈkʌvərɪ/ *n.* 恢复健康；复原

e.g. He made a quick recovery from his illness and was soon back at work.
他生病后康复得很快，不久就去上班了。

sensitive /ˈsensɪtɪv/ *adj.* 易受伤害的，易损坏的；易受影响的；敏感的；过敏的

e.g. A sensitive nerve in a tooth can cause great pain.
牙神经易受损伤，可产生剧痛。
The cost is not sensitive to the batch size.
价格不因整批尺寸的变化而发生波动。

Photographic paper is highly sensitive to light.

感光纸对光十分敏感。

undermine /ˌʌndəˈmaɪn/ *vt.* 逐渐削弱;损坏,暗中破坏

  e. g. Illness undermined his strength.   疾病逐渐削弱了他的力气。

          She tried to undermine our friendship.   她试图破坏我们的友谊。

vulnerable /ˈvʌlnərəbl/ *adj.* 易受伤的,脆弱的;敏感的

  e. g. He volunteered to protect her as she looked so vulnerable.

          她看上去很脆弱,他就主动去保护她。

weaken /ˈwiːkən/ *vt.* (使)削弱,(使)变弱;减弱,动摇,犹豫

  e. g. She weakened as the illness grew worse.   由于病情恶化,她变得更虚弱了。

          They have not yet agreed to our requests but they are clearly weakening.

          他们还没有同意我们的要求,但态度已明显缓和。

Phrases and Expressions

be for/against 支持/反对

  e. g. You must be either for or against the plan.

          你或赞成或反对这个计划,必须二者择其一。

care for 照顾,照料,关心;喜欢

  e. g. care for the younger generation 爱护年轻一代

          Do you care for fruit? 你喜欢吃水果吗?

in addition to 除……之外

  e. g. She gets various perquisites in addition to her wages.

          她工资以外,还有各种津贴。

in that case 那样的话

  e. g. In that case, just tell him that I called.

          这样子的话,就转告他我打过电话就好了。

open up 打开,张开;开发;开辟;揭露;展现

  e. g. open up new market.   打开新的市场

          open up wasteland   垦荒

          open up a magnificent prospect   展现出一幅壮丽的图景

opt out 撤退;退出,不参加

  e. g. Today there is a tendency for people to opt out of social activity.

          今天,越来越多的人倾向于不参加社会活动。

take into account 重视,考虑

  e. g. Take into account the quality and workmanship, you will find the price is justified.

          考虑到质量和做工,你会发现其价格是公道的。

参考译文

安乐死:赞同还是反对

1 "我们再也不能耽误了,……我难以咽下食物……呼吸也有困难……,浑身疲乏无力,……不要再拖了"。

2 荷兰人齐斯·范·温德尔临死前请求医生帮助他一死了之时说了这番话。他因身患重病,说话已经不很清楚,也知道自己毫无康复的希望,而且病情还在迅速恶化。

3 在医生注射那致命的最后一针前,范·温德尔生前的三个月生活被拍成了电影,于去年在荷兰的电视台首次播出。此后,有20个国家先后购买了这个电视节目,每在一国放映,都会在全国引起一场对安乐死的议论。

4 荷兰是欧洲唯一允许安乐死的国家,尽管安乐死在技术上还不具有合法性,但如果医生按照两年前荷兰议会制定的议案的严格指导原则实施安乐死,通常不会受到法律的追究。这些指导原则规定,当病人极度痛苦,没有治愈的可能,而且一再要求的情况下才能实施安乐死。另外,还必须有第二位医生证实已经符合上述条件,并且要向警察机关报告病人的死亡。

5 能允许医生结束他人的生命吗? 齐斯·范·温德尔的私人医生威尔弗雷德·冯·奥依金解释了他对这个问题的看法:

6 "这么说吧,这和我计划用机关枪杀死一大群人完全不一样。若是那样,杀人是我所能想象的最可怕的事。但我作为医生实施安乐死和用枪杀人是绝对不同的。我是关心人,我要尽量保证他们不受更多的痛苦。这和用枪杀人完全是两码事。"

7 然而,仍然有很多人坚决反对使用安乐死。"反安乐死健康医疗"组织的主席安德鲁·福格森说:"在使用安乐死的大多数病例中,患者实际上需要的是其它的东西。他们可能需要在健康专家的指导下,与所爱的人或家人进行交流。在寻求安乐死的背后还有其它问题。"英国有设立晚期病人收容所的优良传统,专门护理垂危病人并满足他们特殊需要。国家收容所委员会主席和收容运动的发起人茜西莉·桑德斯认为,使用安乐死等于把护理垂危病人的其它方式都排除了。她还担心允许使用安乐死会削弱人对于照顾和关心的要求。在今天的社会里,这样很容易让老年人、残疾人和靠他人生活的人们感到自己是社会的负担,应该从生活中消失。我觉得法律上任何允许缩短人们生命的做法都会使那些人变得更容易受伤害。

8 很多人认为禁止一个人选择死亡的权利是没有道理的。尽管他们也认为生命很重要,并且应当尊重生命,但是生活的质量也不容忽视。范·奥依金医生认为如果人们想死,他们应当有选择死亡的权利。"那些反对使用安乐死的人们想告诉我们生命垂危的人没有这种权利。当他们病重时,我们害怕他们会死去。但是有的情况下死亡是不可避免的。在那种情况下,为什么不使用安乐死呢?"

9 但"为什么不呢"是一个会引起强烈情感的问题。那部反映齐斯·范·温德尔死亡情景的电影既感人又发人深醒。很显然,这位医生是他们一家人的朋友;温德尔的妻子也是一心为丈夫好。然而,有些人争论用这种特殊事例来支持安乐死很危险。再说,不是所有的病人都会受到如此周到的个别护理和关注。

Exercises

I. Reading Comprehension

Section A

1. B 2. D 3. A 4. C 5. A

Section B

1. He asked his doctor to help him die.

2. Each time it was shown, it started a nationwide debate on the subject.

3. Doctors who carried out euthanasia under strict guidelines introduced by the Dutch Parliament two years ago were usually not prosecuted.

4. What they were actually asking for is something else that may be a health professional they want to open up communication for them with their loved ones or family.

5. No, she doesn't. Because she argues that euthanasia doesn't take into account that there are ways of caring for the dying, and she is also concerned that allowing euthanasia would undermine the need for care and consideration of a wide range of people.

Section C

1. My belief tells me that human life is given by god, and that anyone other than the god who takes it away is committing a crime. I have lots of friends who do not believe in anything. They just think they have the right to do anything they like, including doing away their only lives. When I got to know this, I was shocked by their views not only towards death, but also towards their own right. If people set their right on themselves and then nothing is done by them, it would be considered by them to be a crime. And the morality would not exist at all. In my opinion, a person should not take away others' lives. His own life is no exception, it's not just a matter of personal willingness or happiness. It's what they are that makes it.

2. I can't decide how long I shall live, but I can choose the way of my living. At that time, I would know the essence of life. I would do what I dream of, and enjoy every minute. For example, I might travel around the world. At the same time I would donate all my belongings and property to the people who are in need, especially organs.

3. I really prefer staying with my parents when my life is coming to the end. After high school, I rarely spent lots of time staying with my mother and father. Especially after I entered into university, there is no more than a week that I could be at home. I love my parents, and they are my beloved people in the world. Now I quite miss them and appreciate the time we stay together.

II. Vocabulary and Structure

Section A

1. D 2. A 3. B 4. C 5. A 6. C 7. C 8. A 9. D 10. B

Section B

1. Do you know the Netherlands is the only country in Europe which permits <u>euthanasia</u>?
   你知不知道荷兰是欧洲唯一允许施行安乐死的国家?

2. Water pollution causes the residents <u>vulnerable</u> to decease.
   水的污染让居民们面临死亡的威胁。

3. The rumors of an attack were later <u>confirmed</u>.
   发动攻击的谣传后来得到了证实。

4. The attorney-general will <u>prosecute</u> in trial for serious crime.
   首席检查官将在严重犯罪案的审判中作公诉人。

5. Tom <u>filmed</u> his daughter playing in the garden.
   汤姆把他女儿在公园嬉戏的镜头拍摄了下来。

6. Many severe colds <u>undermined</u> the old man's health.
   多次严重的感冒损害了老人的健康。

7. His work quality has been <u>deteriorating</u> in recent years.
   最近几年他的健康越来越差。

8. He is well on the way to <u>recovery</u> by the doctors' treatments.
   通过医生的治疗他正在顺利恢复。

III. Word Building

1. Is this not serious enough for us to <u>heighten</u> our vigilance?
   这难道不应该引起我们的警惕吗?

2. Knives can be <u>sharpened</u> by grinding them against a rough stone.
   刀能在一块粗石上磨锋利。

3. Education makes a people easy to lead, but difficult to drive; easy to govern, but impossible to <u>enslave</u>.
   教育使一个民族易于引导,难于驾御;易于管理,但不能奴役。

4. You have no right to play ducks and drakes with money that has been <u>entrusted</u> to you.
   你没权挥霍委托你保管的钱。

5. The new law <u>empowered</u> the police to search private house.
   新法律授予警察搜查私人住宅的权利。

6. The heroic deeds of him <u>embodied</u> the glorious tradition of the troops.
   他的英雄事迹体现了军队的光荣传统。

7. We must broaden and <u>enrich</u> our knowledge with practice.
   我们必须通过实践扩展和丰富我们的知识。

8. Officials have been instructed to <u>loosen</u> up on the rules for admitting people into the country.

官员们已收到命令放宽对入境人员的限制。

IV. Grammar Focus

1. Last week I went climbing, something I hadn't done for a couple of weeks.
2. Mr. Smith, a computer expert, says computers can recognize human voices.
3. Yesterday I talked to Mr. James, my English teacher.
4. This morning I met Tom, a friend of my brother's.
5. Jason, Judy's father, works at a factory in the city.

V. Translation

1. Those doctors who are for the idea never mean they don't care for patients.
   医生们支持这一观点并不意味着他们不关心病人。
2. I really understand what you mean, but we must take everything into account.
   我当然明白你的意思,但我们必须把每件事考虑进去。
3. Either you make a real effort or there's no real chance of your feeling better.
   除非你真正地作出努力,否则你的身体状况不会有很大改观。
4. This is an instrument designed and used to take the life of a criminal.
   这是一种设计用来取走罪犯性命的器械装置。
5. We shall open up the resources of the NW areas of our country.
   我们将开发我国西北地区的资源。

VI. Writing

Sample

A Letter of Sympathy

Dear Xiaoming,

In these days' newspapers, I read about the recent events in your town and I am writing to extend my deepest condolences.

It broke my heart to see all those pictures of those whose homes have been destroyed in the mudslide. I am really worried about you and your family, and all your friends there. I am crossing my fingers for you now in hopes that you are all safe and sound. I can only imagine how difficult this time must be for you, and I want to extend to you my unwavering support. Our government and many nongovernmental organizations are initiating various campaigns to urge people to donate money and necessary things to send to you. I donated all my allowance that I have been saving for years.

I feel extremely sorry for this tragedy, and I will be looking forward to hearing from you. Please pass my concern on to your parents. May God bless you and your family during this time and always.

Yours sincerely,

Li Meng

Notes

A sympathy letter can be a great source of comfort to someone who is grieving the loss. It's a simple way to let that person know they are in your thoughts as they go through the difficult process of grief and mourning.

The best sympathy letters are like conversations you would have with the family, so it should only be in written form. The letters are usually handwritten, under one page in length and are sent promptly. If you want to use a store-bought card, write a personal note on stationery and stuck it inside the card. They can be addressed to the person in the family you feel the closest to, or to the family as a whole. Write the letter in your own voice, meaning the way you would normally speak to the person. There is no reason to get too fancy and to come up with a poem or verse unless that is how you normally speak (which could be weird) or unless you're a writer by profession.

Components of a Sympathy Letter

1. Acknowledge the loss. As a starting point you need to acknowledge the loss. Examples could be: *I wanted to write and tell you how sorry I am for your loss. / I was so sorry to hear about the tragic circumstances. / I am writing on behalf of all of my family to express our sympathy for your sad loss.*

2. Express your sympathy. Examples could be: *I want to express my heartfelt sympathy. / May it comfort you to know that so many people care and are thinking of you and your family at this moment. / While there is nothing I can say that will ease your loss, I wanted you to know that I am grieving and thinking of you all.*

3. Offer help. Instead of "Let me know if I can help with anything at all," make sure it is a specific offer and don't make offers you can't fulfill.

4. End the letter with a thoughtful word, a hope, a wish, or expression of sympathy. e. g. *You are in my thoughts/Wish you God's peace. / Our thoughts are with you at this difficult time. / May the love of family and friends comfort you.*

5. *The ending and sign off*: *With love and sympathy, Sincerely, Your friend, Love, Affectionately yours, Yours, Very sincerely, With my deepest sympathy,* etc.

Text B   Background

Physician-assisted suicide (PAS) generally refers to a practice in which the physician, upon the patient's request, provides a patient with a lethal dose of medication, which the patient intends to use to end his or her own life.

Physician-assisted suicide means the physician provides the means for death, most often with a prescription. The patient, not the physician, will ultimately administer the lethal medication. Euthanasia generally means that the physician would act directly, say, by giving a lethal injection, to end the patient's life.

Is Physician-assisted Suicide Ethical? The ethics of PAS continue to be debated. Some argue that PAS is ethical. Often this is argued on the grounds that PAS may be a rational choice for a person who is choosing to die to escape unbearable suffering. Furthermore, the physician's duty to alleviate suffering may, at times, justify the act of providing assistance with suicide. Those who argue that PAS is ethically justifiable offer the following arguments:

Respect for Autonomy: Death are very personal, and competent person should have the right to choose death.

Justice: Justice requires that we "treat like cases alike." Competent, terminally ill patients are allowed to hasten death by treatment refusal. For some patients, treatment refusal will not suffice to hasten death; only option is suicide. Justice requires that we should allow these patients to have assisted death.

Compassion: Suffering means more than pain; there are other physical and psychological burdens. It is not always possible to relieve suffering. Thus PAS may be a compassionate response to unbearable suffering.

Individual Freedom vs. State Interest: Though society has strong interest in preserving life, this interest lessens when a person is terminally ill and has strong desire to end life. A complete prohibition on assisted death excessively limits personal freedom. Therefore, PAS should be allowed in certain cases.

Is PAS Illegal? In most states, including the state of Washington, aiding a suicide is a crime, while suicide or attempted suicide itself is not illegal. The state of Oregon is the only state that currently has legalized PAS.

However, several major court decisions have been made regarding PAS. In the case of Compassion in Dying v. Washington, the Ninth US Circuit Court of Appeals held that individuals have a right to choose how and when they die. Later, the Second Circuit Court found a New York law on PAS in conflict with the 14th Amendment, which says that no state shall "deny to any person within its jurisdiction the equal protection of the laws." The Court held that competent patients were being treated differently than incompetent patients. The US Supreme Court has ruled that there is no constitutional right to assisted suicide, and made a legal distinction between refusal of treatment and PAS. However, the Court also left the decision of whether to legalize PAS up to each individual state.

New Words

abuse /ə'bjuːz/　*n.* 滥用,妄用,虐待;非法服用,过度服用

　　e. g.　　I'm afraid the position is open to abuse.　恐怕这个职位容易使人滥用职权。

　　　　　　crime related to drug abuse　与滥用麻醉药品有关的罪案

acknowledge /ək'nɒlɪdʒ/　*v.* 承认……属实,供认……

　　e. g.　　He acknowledged it to be true/that it is true.　他供认那是事实。

　　　　　　He was generally acknowledged to be the finest poet in the land.

　　　　　　他是公认的全国最优秀的诗人。

agony /ˈægənɪ/ *n.* 极大的痛苦

 e. g.　He lay in agony until the doctor arrived.
　　　　在医生来到之前,他一直非常痛苦地躺在那里。
　　　　I was in an agony of doubt.　我疑虑不安,十分痛苦。

constitutional /ˌkɒnstɪˈtjuːʃənəl/ *adj.* 宪法的

 e. g.　Parliament was accused of constitutional impropriety.　议会被指控有违宪行为。

contend /kənˈtend/ *v.* 声称,主张;争夺;竞争;争斗

 e. g.　He contended that there must be life on Mars.　他声称火星上面一定有生物。
　　　　The firm is too small to contend against large international companies.
　　　　这家公司太小,无法与国际性的大公司竞争。

despair /dɪˈspeə/ *n. /v.* 失去一切希望,绝望

 e. g.　He gave up the struggle in despair.　他绝望地放弃了斗争。
　　　　Your son is the despair of all his teachers, ie They had no longer expected to be
　　　　able to teach him anything.
　　　　你的儿子在所有的教师的心目中已毫无希望了。
　　　　We have despaired of him; he can't keep a job for more than six months.
　　　　我们对他已经绝望了,他做什么工作都不超过半年。

dosage /ˈdəʊsɪdʒ/ *n.* (按剂量的)给药

 e. g.　The recommended dosage is one tablet every four hours.
　　　　规定剂量为每四小时服一片。

dose /dəʊs/ *n.* (一次)剂量,一剂,一份

 e. g.　He gave me a dose of medicine for my cold.　他给我开了一剂治感冒的药。
　　　　In the accident, the workers received a heavy dose of radiation.
　　　　在那次事故中,工人受到大剂量的辐射。

foresee /fɔːˈsiː/ *v.* 预知,预见,预料

 e. g.　No one can foresee what will happen in the future.
　　　　谁也无法预见将来会发生什么事。

fuel /ˈfjʊəl/ *n.* 燃料
　　　　　　　　v. 给……加燃料

 e. g.　What sort of fuel do these machines need?　这些机器需要哪种燃料?
　　　　All aircraft must be fueled before a long flight.
　　　　所有飞机均需先加油方能做长途飞行。

hasten /ˈheɪsn/ *v.* 加速;催促;赶快

 e. g.　I hasten to add that I knew nothing of the fraud at the time.
　　　　我忙不迭地补充说,当时自己对那个骗局一无所知。
　　　　Her row with the MD probably hastened her departure.
　　　　她与总裁的争吵很可能加速了她的离去。

homicide /ˈhɒmɪsaɪd/ *n.* 〈律〉杀人(行为)

e. g.   The jury returned a verdict of justifiable homicide.

陪审团作出了正当杀人的裁决。

ineffectual   /ˌɪnɪˈfektjʊəl/   *adj.* 效果不佳的，无效果的，不起作用的

e. g.   He won't be able to deal with the situation; he's too ineffectual.

他无法应付局面，他太无能了。

initiative   /ɪˈnɪʃɪətɪv/   *n.* 为解决困难而采取的行动；主动权，主动性

e. g.   It is hoped that the government's initiative will bring the strike to an end.

希望政府采取的行动可以结束罢工。

It's up to this country to take the initiative in banning nuclear weapons.

这个国家应该主动提出禁止核武器。

In the absence of my commanding officer, I acted on my own initiative.

指挥官不在场，我主动见机行事。

legitimate   /lɪˈdʒɪtɪmɪt/   *adj.* 法定的，依法的，合法的

e. g.   the legitimate heir   法定继承人

I am not sure if his business strictly legitimate, ie. is legal.

我说不好他的生意是否绝对合法。

license   /ˈlaɪsəns/   *v. /n.* 批准，许可，颁发执照；执照

e. g.   They have licensed the private hotel.   他们已发了许可证给那家私人旅馆。

mediation   /ˌmiːdɪˈeɪʃən/   *n.* 调解

e. g.   The dispute was settled by mediation.   争端经调解后得以解决。

morphine   /ˈmɔːfiːn/   *n.* 吗啡

e. g.   The morphine was administered by injection.   那吗啡是注射进去的。

permissible   /pə(ː)ˈmɪsəbl/   *adj.* 可允许的，许可的，容许的

e. g.   Is smoking permissible in the theater?   在剧院里允许吸烟吗？

physician   /fɪˈzɪʃən/   *n.* 医师；(尤指)内科医生

e. g.   In case of diabetes, physicians advise against the use of sugar.

对于糖尿病患者，医生告诫他们不要吃糖。

prolong   /prəˈlɒŋ/   *v.* 延长，延伸

e. g.   They prolonged their visit by a few days.   他们把访问时间延长了几天。

Don't prolong the agony — just tell us the result.

别再让我们着急了——快告诉我们结果吧！

relieve   /rɪˈliːv/   *v.* 解除；减轻，缓和(不快或痛苦)

e. g.   The doctors did their best to relieve the patient.   医生们尽力减轻病人的痛苦。

risk   /rɪsk/   *v.* 使……面临危险

e. g.   risk one's health, fortune, neck   冒丧失健康、财富、生命之险

shield   /ʃiːld/   *v. /n.* 保护，掩护，庇护；盾，盾牌，护罩；防护物

e. g.   These trees will shield off arid winds and protect the fields.

这些树能挡住旱风，保护农田。

The sword glanced off the knight's shield.   剑掠过武士的盾。

Dark glasses are an effective shield against the glare.   墨镜能有效地遮挡强光。

sufficient /səˈfɪʃənt/ *adj.* 足够的;充足的

    e. g. We have gained sufficient experience to tackle this problem.

          我们已经有了足够的经验来处理这个问题。

          A word to the wise is sufficient.   有灵犀者一点就通。

suicide /ˈsjʊɪsaɪd/ *n.* 自杀

    e. g. The death was adjudged a suicide by sleeping pills.

          该死亡事件被判定为服用安眠药自杀。

          It will not be suicide to admit your mistake.   承认你的错误并不等于自毁前程。

suspension /səsˈpenʃən/ *n.* 暂停,终止;暂令停职(或停学等)

    e. g. the suspension of business/a meeting   暂时停业/会议的终止

          A four-day suspension was imposed on her.   她被勒令停职 4 天。

          Grima has started to work off his eight-match suspension.

          格里马开始经受被停赛八场的处罚。

therapy /ˈθerəpɪ/ *n.* 疗法

    e. g. The doctor said she should be given a physical therapy.

          医生说她应该进行理疗。

Phrases and Expressions

in effect   实际上,事实上;(法律或规则)在实施中;有效

    e. g. His reply is in effect an apology.   他的答复事实上是一种道歉。

          In effect, the tow systems are identical.   实际上,这两种系统完全一样。

          The rule is still in effect.   本规则仍然有效。

in part   在某种程度上,部分地

    e. g. Tom was only in small part responsible.   汤姆只有一小部分责任。

make it clear that   明确表示

    e. g. I want to make it clear that I have no prejudice against you.

          我要表明我对你没有偏见。

play a key role in   起关键作用

    e. g. Address forms play a key role in social interaction.

          称呼语是社交中的一个重要组成部分。

relieve of   解除(负担、困难等)

    e. g. This relieved us of part of our luggage.   这给我们减去一部分行李的负担。

          It will relieve her of a tremendous burden.   这将给她解决一个巨大的负担。

result in   导致,结果是

    e. g. The flood resulted in a considerable reduction in production.

          这次水灾造成相当大的减产。

seek to　力图,试图,设法

　　e. g.　States seek to become stronger through alliance.

　　　　　各国力求通过结盟而更加强大。

to the extent　在某种程度上

　　e. g.　To the extent, Martin Luther King, like Prometheus, illuminated the road to liberation for the American black people.

　　　　　从某种程度上说,马丁·路德·金就像普罗米修斯,照亮了美国黑人解放的道路。

参 考 译 文

医 助 自 杀

1　最高法庭关于医生协助病人结束生命问题的裁决对于如何用药物减轻病危者的痛苦这个问题来说,具有重要的意义。

2　尽管裁决认为,宪法没有赋予医生帮助病人自杀的权利,然而最高法庭实际上却认可了医疗界的"双重效应"原则,这个存在了好几个世纪的道德准则认为,如果某种行为具有双重效果(希望达到的正面效果和可以预见得到的负面效果),那么,只要行为实施是想要达到正面效果的目的,这个行为就是被允许的。

3　近年来,医生们一直在用这项原则,为自己替病危患者注射大剂量的吗啡镇痛的做法提供正当的理由,尽管他们知道,不断增加的剂量最终会杀死病人。

4　蒙特非奥里医疗中心主任南希·都博勒认为,这项原则将消除部分医生的疑虑,因为这些医生在此之前一直坚持认为,如果加大剂量可能会加速病人的死亡,那么他们就无法给病人足够的用药来控制病人的痛苦。

5　波士顿大学健康法律系主任乔治·安纳斯则声称,只要医生是出于合理的医疗目的开药,那么即使服用此药会加速病人的死亡,医生的行为也没有违法。"这就像做手术,"他说,"我们不能称那些手术死亡为谋杀,因为医生并没有想杀死病人。假如你是一名医生,只要你并没有想让病人自杀,你就可以去冒险给此病人治病。"

6　另一方面,许多医疗界人士承认,致使医助自杀这场争论升温的部分原因是由于病人们的绝望情绪而引起的,对这些病人来说,现代医学延长了临终前肉体上的痛苦。

7　就在最高法庭对医助自杀进行裁决的前三周,全国科学学会公布了一份长达两卷的报告《临近死亡:完善临终护理》。报告指出了医院临终关怀护理中存在的两个问题:对减轻病痛处理不力和大胆使用"无效而强制性的医疗程序,这些程序可能会延长死亡期,甚至会让死亡期难堪"。

8　医疗行业正逐步地让年轻医生去晚期病人休养所参加培训,测试他们有关各种大胆的镇痛疗法方面的知识,健全以医院治疗为基础的医疗保险法规,制定新标准来评估测定和处理病人的临终痛苦。

9　安纳斯说,必须坚持将善意的医疗动机转化为更好的护理。"不少医生对病人所遭受的毫无必要且可预见的痛苦无动于衷",乃至于已构成"蓄意虐待病人"。他说,行医资格理事会"必须明确令人痛苦的死亡可以认定是治疗不当造成的后果,应该吊销行医执照"。

Exercises

I. Reading Comprehension

1. B 2. C 3. B 4. A 5. D

II. Vocabulary and Structure

1. B 2. D 3. C 4. A 5. C 6. B 7. A 8. D 9. C 10. C

III. Translation

1. Woman used to play a passive role in a marriage.

   过去妇女在婚姻中常常扮演顺从被动的角色。

2. The talks resulted in reducing the number of missiles/missile reduction.

   谈判导致了导弹数量的削减。

3. The adoption of this policy would relieve them of a tremendous burden.

   采取这个政策会给他们解除一个巨大的负担。

4. All we are doing now is to seek to halt corruption and increase efficiency.

   我们现在所做的都是为了设法制止腐败行为并提高工作效率。

5. At the risk of offending you, I must refuse the offer.

   即使有可能冒犯你,我也必须谢绝这一提议。

Part V   Time for Fun

参 考 译 文

我把他吊起来好让他晾干

吉姆和玛丽都是精神病院里的病人。一天,他们沿着医院的游泳池散步,吉姆突然跳入泳池的深水区,他沉到了底部。玛丽立刻跳下去救他,她潜到水底,把吉姆拉了上来。

当院长听闻了玛丽的英勇行为后,他立刻翻看了她的病历档案,把她叫进了自己的办公室,"玛丽,我有一个好消息和一个坏消息要告诉你。好消息是你能跳入水中救其他病人,这说明你的意识已经恢复了,你可以出院了。坏消息就是,吉姆,你救的那个病人,他还是用自己的浴袍带子在浴室上吊自杀了。"

玛丽说:"他没有自杀,是我把他吊起来好让他晾干。"

新探索大学英语综合教程 2
（教师用书）

Unit 1

Festival

Part I Teaching Objectives

* **Listening & Speaking:**

    Help the students to be familiar with the topic—*how to express yourself when talking about a party* and memorize useful expressions.

* **Words & Expressions:**

    Study some new words and expressions, such as *abundance*, *anthropological*, *calendar*, *celebrate*, *commemorate*, *declare*, *folklore*, *foolery*, *inversion*, *legend*, *lure*, *observe*, *origin*, *property*, *transition*, *trick*, *trickery*, *fall for*, *play jokes on sb.*, *trace back to* and so on.

* **Grammar:**

    Learn to use the structure *as*....

* **Writing:**

    Understand and write *a letter of invitation*.

Part II Listening——*Holding a Party*

New Words

appreciate /əˈpriːʃɪeɪt/ *v.* 感激,感谢

    e. g.   We greatly appreciate your timely help.

           我们非常感谢你们的及时帮助。

definitely /ˈdefɪnɪtlɪ/ *adv.* 明确地,确切地,无疑地

    e. g.   I can't tell you definitely when I will come.

           我不能肯定地告诉你我什么时候来。

DJ *abbr.* (广播电台)流行音乐播音员;流行音乐节目主持人(disc jockey)

live /laɪv/ *adj.* 现场直播的

    e. g. It wasn't a recorded show; it was live.

           那不是录音节目，是现场直播。

wonder /ˈwʌndə/ *v.* 想要知道

    e. g. I wonder why James is always late for school.

           我想知道为什么詹姆斯上学总是迟到。

Phrases and Expressions

pretty much   几乎

    e. g. Pretty much all her friends came to her birthday party.

           几乎所有的朋友都来参加了她的生日聚会。

Dialogue One

Listen to the CD and mark T for True or F for False according to the dialogue.

1. T 2. F 3. F 4. T 5. T

Script

Student A：Are you going to the party on Saturday?

Student B：I'm not sure yet. Are you going?

Student A：Of course I am, because it's going to be great.

Student B：Is it really? When does it start?

Student A：The party starts at 8 o'clock, and you should really try to go.

Student B：I'm thinking about it. Who is going to the party?

Student A：Pretty much everybody of the school.

Student B：What makes you think it's going to be fun?

Student A：There will be food, drinks, and live music at the party.

Student B：That sounds like great.

Student A：Are you going to go?

Student B：Certainly.

Dialogue Two

Listen to the CD and answer the following questions with the information you hear.

1. Who is going to have a party on Friday night?

   Tom is going to have a party on Friday night.

2. Will Mary be available to go to the party on Friday night?

   Yes, Mary will be available to go to the party.

3. Does Mary know how to get to Tom's house?

   No, she doesn't.

4. Who else will be invited to the party?

John will be invited to the party, too.

5. What will Mary bring to the party?

Mary will bring something special that Mary and John would like to drink.

Script

- -

Mary: Hi, Tom. Is everything going OK with you?

Tom: Things are great. Mary, I am having a party on Friday night and was wondering if you would be available?

Mary: I would love to come to your party!

Tom: I am glad you are free. Do you know how to get to my house?

Mary: Please send me your address by e-mail.

Tom: Sure, no problem. Can you think of anyone else I can invite to the party?

Mary: My friend John is in town, and I would like it if I could bring him.

Tom: Sure, bring John along. The more the merrier!

Mary: Would you like some help with the food?

Tom: If there is something special that you and John would like to drink, bring that along.

Mary: OK, I will. See you on Friday!

Tom: See you on Friday!

Spot Dictation

- -

1. to communicate with others

2. you will make new friends at the party

3. you can collect all kinds of information

4. you can enjoy yourself and have a good rest

5. taking part in a party and holding a party will be wonderful

Part III Speaking——Attending a Party

Useful Expressions About a Party

We will have a party on Friday night.

Can you come to my birthday party?

When will the party start?

What clothes should I wear for a formal party?

I'm going to plan the New Year's party.

Could you recommend a place to go for a party?

It's a surprise party for her, and please don't tell her.

I've been looking forward to your party.

Thank you for inviting us to your birthday party.

Thank you so much for inviting me.

Welcome to our English party!

I don't like to attend dinner parties at all.

I had a good time tonight.

It is really a casual and nice party. I like it very much.

Thank you so much for a wonderful meal and a very enjoyable evening.

Happy thanksgiving!

The same to you!

We had a lot of fun. We talked and sang and drank a lot of beer at the party.

We would party after exams. You know we need to relax. So we hit the bars.

What do you do at parties, drinking?

What's the party like in your country?

Do you like going to parties?

It's a surprise party.

Pair Work

Sample

Linda: Hi, Alex. Welcome to my birthday party!

Alex: Hi, Linda. Happy birthday! Here is a present for you!

Linda: Oh, it's so kind of you! What is it?

Alex: Why don't you open and see?

Linda: Wait. Let me guess. Is it a box of chocolate?

Alex: No. Just open it and you will see.

Linda: OK. It is a big surprise. A dress! Look at this beautiful dress!

Alex: Do you like it?

Linda: Yes, I love it. Thank you so much. Have a good time here.

Alex: I'm glad you like it. Is everybody here now?

Linda: Not yet. Let's wait inside.

Role-play

Sample

Mary: Are you going to the party on Saturday?

Tom: I haven't decided yet. Are you going to go?

Mary: Yeah, I heard it's going to be a lot of fun.

Tom: Really? Well, what time does it start?

Mary: It starts at 8:00 pm, and I hope to see you there.

Tom: Well, who is going to be there?

Mary: Everybody of our class.

Tom: How do you know it's going to be so fun?

Mary: There's going to be a live DJ, food, and drinks at the party.

Tom: Wow. It seems like it will be a very good time.

Mary: So I guess I'll see you there?

Tom: Yeah, I will be there.

Part IV Reading

 **Text A**　　　　**Background**

April fool's day is a day to play jokes on others, no one knows how this holiday began but some people think it first started in France.

In the 16th century, people celebrated new years day from March 25th to April 1st. In the mid of the 1560s king Charles IX changed it from March 25th to January 1st. But some people still celebrated on April 1st, so others called them April fools.

Each country celebrates April fool's day differently. In France, people call the April fools "April fish". They tape a paper fish to their friends' backs to fool them. When he or she finds this, they shout "April fish!"

In England, people play jokes only in the morning. You are a "noodle" if someone fools you. In Scotland, April fool's day is 48 hours long. They call an April fool "April gowk". Gowk is another name for a cuckoo bird.

In America, people play small jokes on their friends and any other people on the first of April. They may point down to your shoe and say, "Your shoelace is untied." If you believe them and look down to see, you are an April fool then.

New Words

abundance /əˈbʌndəns/ n. 丰富，充足，富裕

　　e.g.　The tree yields an abundance of fruit.

　　　　　这树结果甚多。

　　　　　He wished to have money in abundance.

　　　　　他希望富有。

anthropological /ˌænθrəˈpɒlədʒɪkəl/ adj. 人类学的

　　e.g.　Anthropologists provide anthropological explanations for the rise of April Fool's

　　　　　Day.

193

人类学家从人类学的角度对愚人节做出了解释。

calendar /ˈkælɪndə/ *n.* 历法,日历,月历

   e. g. From January 1st to February 1st is one calendar month.

    从一月一日到二月一日是一个公历月。

celebrate /ˈselɪbreɪt/ *v.* 庆祝;祝贺;颂扬

   e. g. We celebrated the New Year with a dance party.

    我们举行跳舞晚会庆祝新年。

    The names of many heroes are celebrated by the poets.

    许多英雄的名字为诗人所歌颂。

commemorate /kəˈmeməreɪt/ *v.* 庆祝;纪念

   e. g. This monument commemorates our victory.

    这座碑是为纪念我们的胜利而建的。

declare /dɪˈkleə/ *v.* 断言,宣称,宣布,宣告,声明

   e. g. She declared that she didn't want to see him again.

    她宣称再也不愿见到他。

    Have you anything to declare?

    你有东西要申报吗?(指应纳税的东西)

folklore /ˈfəʊklɔː/ *n.* 民间传说

   e. g. Rumors of their antics became part of the folklore of Hollywood.

    他们滑稽动作的传闻成了好莱坞民间传说的一部分。

foolery /ˈfuːlərɪ/ *n.* 愚蠢的行为,蠢事

   e. g. The tradition of a day devoted to foolery had ancient roots.

    将一天专门用来捉弄人,这一传统有其古老的渊源。

hoax /həʊks/ *n.* /*v.* 愚弄,恶作剧,骗局,玩笑

   e. g. A telephone caller said there was a bomb in the hotel but it was just a hoax.

    打电话者声称旅馆里有一颗炸弹,但这不过是一场恶作剧而已。

inversion /ɪnˈvɜːʃən/ *n.* 倒置

   e. g. Festivals occurring during the spring often involved temporary inversions of the social order.

    春季的节日期间,社会秩序常被暂时颠倒。

legend /ˈledʒənd/ *n.* 传说

   e. g. According to the legend, Odysseus was a Greek hero.

    奥狄修斯是传说中的希腊英雄。

lunatic /ˈljuːnətɪk/ *n.* /*adj.* 疯子,狂人,大傻瓜

   e. g. He must be a lunatic to drive his car so fast.

    他把车开这么快一定是疯了。

lure /lʊə/ *n.* 诱饵;诱惑;诱惑物

   e. g. These young fish were easy to fool with a hook and lure.

这些小鱼很容易上钩。

observe /əbˈzɜːv/ *v.* 纪念;庆祝(节日、生日等);遵守(法律、习俗、规章等);观察

    e.g. We are planning a surprise party to celebrate her birthday.

        我们正准备一个惊喜的派对来庆祝她的生日。

        I observed him going out.

        我看见他出去了。

origin /ˈɒrɪdʒɪn/ *n.* 起源;出身;血统;来历

    e.g. Many Americans are African by origin.

        许多美国人是非洲血统。

        The lady is of noble/humble origin.

        那位女士出身高贵/微贱。

property /ˈprɒpətɪ/ *n.* 财产,所有物

    e.g. This car is my property.

        这车是我的财产。

transition /trænˈzɪʃən/ *n.* 转变,变化,过渡,变迁

    e.g. Normal behavior no longer governed during April Fool's Day.

        在圣诞节,人们的行为举止不再受规矩的约束。

trick /trɪk/ *n./v.* 诡计,骗局;恶作剧;欺骗;窍门,诀窍

    e.g. I can do magic tricks.

        我会玩魔术。

        He got the money from me by a trick.

        他用诡计骗走了我的钱。

        The children played a trick on their teacher.

        孩子们捉弄了他们的老师。

trickery /ˈtrɪkərɪ/ *n.* 欺骗,诈欺;诡计

    e.g. April Fool's Day has supposedly commemorated their trickery.

        人们便设立愚人节来纪念善耍花招的愚人村村民。

whimsy /ˈhwɪmzɪ/ *n.* 怪念头,奇想

    e.g. He told me a lot of stories full of whimsy.

        他给我讲了很多充满离奇古怪情节的故事。

Phrases and Expressions

fall for 信以为真;被欺骗;爱上,迷恋

    e.g. Don't fall for his tricks.

        别为他的花招所骗。

play jokes on sb. 戏弄,开玩笑

    e.g. We all played jokes on him.

        我们大家都和他开玩笑。

New Exploration College English

trace back to 追溯到,追查到

e. g. The celebration of April Fool's Day traces its roots back to festivals marking the springtime. 圣诞节起源于庆祝春天的到来。

Proper Names

Gotham　　　　　　　哥谭镇,愚人村(英国传说中的愚人村)

Gregorian calendar　　格列高利历,公历(即目前全世界通用的阳历,由教皇格列高利十三世于1582年倡导使用)

Julian calendar　　　　罗马儒略历(十六世纪以前西方采用的一种历法,在公元46年由罗马统治者儒略·凯撒颁行。历年平均长度为365.25日。该历法最后被格列高利历取代)

参 考 译 文

愚人节的起源

1　世界上许多国家都过愚人节,然而这个节日的起源却尚待明确。但有一点是清楚的,那就是将一天专门用来捉弄人,这一传统有其古老的渊源。回顾历史,我们发现愚人节有许多种历史悠久的起源。

2　**法国的传说**

3　最普遍的说法是,愚人节起源于法国的历法改革。

4　1582年,法国率先使用公历而不再使用儒略历,这意味着一年的开始从三月底变到了一月一日。如果有人没有跟上这个变化,仍然在三月二十五日至四月一日庆祝新年,人们就会用各种方式捉弄他。这个说法也许可以解释为什么四月一日成为现今愚人节的日子。

5　**英国的民间传说**

6　英国的民间传说认为愚人节起源于愚人村。传说在13世纪,有一个传统,凡国王走过的路都要成为公共财产。愚人村的人不想失去属于他们自己的主干道,便散布了一个假消息,以阻止国王走那条路。约翰国王得知他们的诡计后,派了一个使者去愚人村。当那位使者到达愚人村时,他发现村子里到处都是忙着干傻事的疯子。他们有的想把鱼淹死;有的想把鸟儿关进无顶的栅栏里。国王信以为真,便宣布说,这个村子里的人太傻了,不值得惩罚。据说自那以后,人们便设立愚人节来纪念善耍花招的愚人村村民。

7　**人类学方面的解释**

8　人类学家和文化历史学家对愚人节的起源有他们自己的解释。他们认为这个节日起源于庆祝春天的到来。

9　春天是一年中天气变得反复无常的季节,好像大自然在与人类开玩笑,所以传统上春天里的节日都反映了这种反复无常和令人惊奇的特征。节日期间,社会秩序常被暂时颠倒。在旧的一切逝去、新一轮的季节循环开始的短暂过渡中,人们的行为举止不再受规矩的约束,大家尽可以开玩笑、耍花招、颠倒社会身份。

10　此外,另一种观点也认为愚人节与春天有关。这种观点认为愚人节的起源是这样的:四月初,法国的溪流里满是刚孵出的小鱼。这些小鱼很容易上钩,因此,法国人便叫它们"四月的鱼"。很快,人们形成了一个习俗,在四月一日这一天捉弄别人,以此庆祝四月里"傻"鱼儿的丰收。

语 法 补 充

As 的各种用法

在英语里,"as"有多种用法,下面便是常用的九种:

一、用作介词。例如:

1. He has worked as a diplomat in the US and Sudan.

2. The scenery here is beautiful as a picture.

二、用作表示"程度"的副词。例如:

3. You have performed well. Other students' performance is as good.

三、用作从属连词,引导"比较"从句。例如:

4. The friendship between us is as strong as a rock.

5. Can our runners run as fast as they used to?

四、用作从属连词,引导"时间"从句。例如:

6. As the new teacher entered the classroom, the pupils clapped their hands.

7. Alex caught sight of Nancy as she was getting on the bus.

五、用作从属连词,引导"方式"从句。例如:

8. You may act as you think fit.

9. It is safer for you to do as you are told.

这些由"as"引导的从句可以节缩,如:

10. It is safer for you to do as told.

11. The meeting will be held as (it has been) scheduled.

12. The weather here is not mild as (it is) in your country.

六、用作从属连词,引导"原因"从句。例如:

13. As the weather is fine, let's go fishing.

14. We helped Tony, as he was a good man.

七、用作从属连词,引导"让步"从句。例如:

15. Improbable as it seems, he is now Managing Director.

16. Young as Sam is, he has performed his task creditably.

八、用作关系代词,引导从句。例如:

17. Is this the same thing as you showed me before?

18. You can visit such places as you want to.

注意,"as"之前有"the same"或"such"和它搭配。

九、组成短语与句型。例如:

19. They departed early so as to reach the airport early.

20. As long as you work hard, you will make it.

21. I'll help you as best as I can.

Exercises

I. Reading Comprehension

Section A

1. D 2. B 3. C 4. A 5. C

Section B

1. No, the origin of April Fool's Day remains unknown.

2. In 1582, France became the first country to switch from the Julian calendar to the Gregorian calendar.

3. The Julian Calendar is the solar calendar introduced by Julius Caesar in Rome in 46B. C. , and has a year of 12 months and 365 days and a leap year of 366 days every fourth year. It was eventually replaced by the Gregorian calendar.

4. People in Gotham were very clever, so they made up a false story to stop the King.

5. Spring is the time of year when the weather becomes uncertain.

Section C

1. April Fool's Day is observed in almost every county around the world, yet the origin of April Fool's Day remains unknown. But I'm sure that the tradition of a day devoted to foolery had ancient roots. And various jokes can be played on April Fool's Day.

2. Because normal behavior no longer governs during April Fool's Day; and that jokes, trickery, and the turning upside down of status expectations are all allowed. We usually play tricks on each other, even on our elders, teachers, leaders and so on.

3. I think the story of "April Fish" is true. Because according to our common sense, the abundance of fish can really be found in streams in early April when the young fish had just hatched. And young fish were really easy to fool with a hook and lure.

II. Vocabulary and Structure

Section A

1. A 2. C 3. A 4. D 5. B 6. C 7. D 8. A 9. B 10. B

Section B

1. April Fool's Day is <u>observed</u> in many countries around the world.
世界上许多国家都过愚人节。

2. Another story traces the origin of April Fool's Day back to the <u>abundance</u> of fish.

另一种看法也认为愚人节与鱼的丰收有关。

3. It became customary to fool people on April 1st, as a way of <u>celebrating</u> the abundance of "foolish" fish.

人们形成了一个习俗，在四月一日这一天捉弄别人，以此庆祝四月里"傻"鱼儿的丰收。

4. If someone failed to <u>keep up with</u> the change, various jokes would be played on him.

如果有人没有跟上这些变化，人们就会用各种方式捉弄他。

5. According to the legend, it was <u>traditional</u> in the 13th century for any road that the King traveled over to become public property.

传说在 13 世纪，有一个传统，凡国王走过的路都要成为公共财产。

6. But when the messenger arrived in Gotham he found the town was full of lunatics who <u>were engaged in</u> foolish activities.

当那位使者到达愚人村时，他发现村子里到处都是忙着干傻事的疯子。

7. The King fell for the hoax and <u>declared</u> the town too foolish to deserve punishment.

国王信以为真，便宣布说，这个村子里的人太傻了，不值得惩罚。

8. During April Fool's Day, jokes and the turning upside down of status <u>expectations</u> were all allowed.

圣诞节期间，大家尽可以开玩笑、颠倒社会身份。

III. Word Building

1. He believes everything with <u>childlike</u> simplicity.

他像孩子一样单纯，对一切都信以为真。

2. It was very <u>foolish</u> of you to park the car near the policeman.

你真愚蠢，竟然把汽车停在警察附近。

3. He declared that dolls were silly <u>babyish</u> things.

他宣称洋娃娃是愚蠢的幼稚之物。

4. She looked <u>boyish</u> and defiant.

她看起来像个大男孩，目中无人。

5. The paper criticized what it described as the <u>animal-like</u> behavior of the football fans.

报纸批评足球迷的行为像动物一样。

6. You would be laughed at with such a <u>childish</u> question.

你提出这样幼稚的问题，会被人嘲笑的！

7. With her was a <u>youngish</u> man in a jacket.

和她在一起的是一个颇年轻的男子，穿一件茄克。

8. There was a large, <u>ball-like</u> structure on the top of the building.

在建筑物的顶部有一个像球一样的巨大结构。

IV. Grammar Focus

1. I saw him as I was coming into the building.

2. Angry as he was, he couldn't help smiling.

3. He got divorced, just as his parents had done years before.

4. As it was getting late, I decided to book into a hotel.

5. I can't run as fast as you.

V. Translation

1. If someone continued to celebrate the New Year between March 25th and April 1st, various jokes would be played on him.
如果有人仍然在三月二十五日至四月一日庆祝新年,人们就会用各种方式捉弄他。

2. The King fell for the hoax and declared the town too foolish to deserve punishment.
国王信以为真,便宣布说,这个村子里的人太傻了,不值得惩罚。

3. Spring is the time of year when the weather becomes uncertain, as if Nature is playing tricks on man.
春天是一年中天气变得反复无常的季节,好像大自然在与人类开玩笑。

4. Soon it became customary to fool people on April 1st, as a way of celebrating the abundance of "foolish" fish.
很快,人们形成了一个习俗,在四月一日这一天捉弄别人,以此庆祝四月里"傻"鱼儿的丰收。

5. April Fool's Day is observed in many countries around the world, yet the origin of April Fool's Day remains unknown.
世界上许多国家都过愚人节,然而这个节日的起源却尚待明确。

VI. Writing
Sample

A Letter of Invitation

Mar. 10th, 2011

Dear Mr. Black,

   To celebrate the 10th anniversary of Shenzhen Trading Co., Ltd, we are holding a dinner party at Hilton Hotel in Shenzhen from 7:00pm to 9:30pm on Saturday, June 8th.

   You are cordially welcome to the party so that we can express our sincere appreciation for your generous support. For your information, the party will be attended by other business elites such as Mr. Zhao Hong and Mr. Li Peng from Beijing International. We believe that this may offer many of us an excellent opportunity to get acquainted with one another.

   We do hope that you will be able to join us on this occasion, and look forward to meeting you at the party.

Yours sincerely,

Wang Hui

Notes

   When we invite a friend to party, or dinner, or merely to have a drink, we all prefer, if possible, to invite someone in person, but sometimes we need to leave a written message or send a letter. The general points in a note/letter of invitation are:

1. Offer an invitation to a friend, describing the kind of the party or the event;

2. Tell in detail when and where the activity is to be held;

3. Ask for a reply if necessary. This request is sometimes called an "R. S. V. P." (Please Reply) in a formal invitation letter/card.

Useful Expressions for Invitations:

Informal: Why don't you come...?

                 How about coming...?

                 We'd think it'd be a good idea if...

                 Can you come for the weekend?

                 We'd really like you to spend a few days with us.

Formal: We would like to invite you to...

                 We wondered if you'd like to come...

More formal or polite:

                 Is there any chance of you/your coming...?

                 We were wondering if you could/wanted to come...

Text B   **Background**

Many Christmas customs are based on the birth of Christ, such as giving presents because of the Wise Men, who brought presents to the baby Jesus. Christmas carols are based on Christ's birth and on scenes of the birth with figures of shepherds, the Wise Men, and animals surrounding the baby Jesus.

But some of the ways that people celebrate Christmas have nothing to do with Christ's birthday. Many bits of older holidays have crept into Christmas!

It wasn't until about 200 years after Christ's death that Christians even thought about celebrating his birth. No one knows the exact date of his birth. It is believed that December 25th was chosen to turn people away from celebrating other holidays at this time of the year.

Saturnalia (农神节,古罗马节日,从 12 月 17 日开始,共 7 天), was the Romans holiday that they celebrated in December. It was a time of feasting and parties. Also, in northern Europe there was a holiday known as Yule (〈古〉耶稣圣诞节). They celebrated this holiday by making great fires. They then would dance around the fires, yelling for the winter to end.

In time, Christmas took the place of these holidays. But people kept some of the old customs—such as burning a Yule log (圣诞柴) and having feasts and parties. The word Yule is still used as a name for the Christmas season.

As time went on, new customs crept into Christmas. One was the Christmas tree, which was started in Germany. As the Germans settled in new lands, they brought with them this tradition.

Last but not least is Saint Nick. A long time ago, a bishop named Nicholas lived in what is now the country of Turkey. No one knows much about him. There are stories that he often helped children in need. Many years after his death, Nicholas was made a saint （圣徒）. In time, he became the patron saint of children.

New Words

blaze /bleɪz/ *v.* 燃烧；照耀；激发

    e. g.   Lights were blazing and men were running here and there.
              灯光明亮，人们忙来忙去。
              Her eyes blazed with anger.
              她眼里闪着怒火。

bonfire /ˈbɒnfaɪə/ *n.* 篝火，营火

    e. g.   The camp bonfire flamed away all the evening.
              整个晚上野营的篝火都在燃烧。

decorate /ˈdekəreɪt/ *v.* 装饰，布置

    e. g.   People usually decorate their houses for New Year.
              人们通常会装饰房子过新年。

firework /ˈfaɪəwɜːk/ *n.* 焰火；烟花；烟火

    e. g.   As the evening was drawing to an end, the firework display took place.
              晚会接近尾声，烟花表演开始了。

glow /ɡləʊ/ *v.* 发光；发热；（常与 with 连用）脸色发红，容光焕发

    e. g.   Maple leaves glowed red in the sunlight.
              枫叶在阳光下红通似火。
              His face glowed with delight.
              他高兴得满面红光。

import /ɪmˈpɔːt/ *n. /v.* 输入，进口

    e. g.   Imports of household appliances rose last month.
              上个月我们的家用电器进口增加了。

lacy /ˈleɪsɪ/ *adj.* 花边的

    e. g.   She wears a lacy skirt.
              她穿了一条带花边的裙子。

lamb /læm/ *n.* 小羊，羔羊

    e. g.   There are several lambs around the sheep.
              这只羊的周围有几只小羊。

loosen /ˈluːsən/ *v.* 解开，放松，松开

    e. g.   My belt is too tight; I must loosen it.
              我的腰带太紧，我必须松开它。

magnificent /mæɡˈnɪfɪsənt/ *adj.* 壮丽的,宽宏的,极好的

    e. g.   The magnificent scene of the waterfall is a perfect delight to the eye.

            瀑布的宏伟景象真是一道视觉盛宴。

ooze /uːz/ *v.* 渗出;(常与 with 连用)使满满流出

    e. g.   The spring oozes out of a rock.

            泉水从岩石中渗出。

pancake /ˈpænkeɪk/ *n.* 薄煎饼,烙饼

    e. g.   His hot pancakes are delicious!

            他做的热煎饼味道真好!

pastry /ˈpeɪstrɪ/ *n.* (用面、牛奶、水、油和成的)油酥皮,酥皮糕点

    e. g.   There was pastry on my fingers, and on the telephone.

            我手指上、电话机上,全粘上了油酥面。

pillow /ˈpɪləʊ/ *n.* 枕头,枕垫

    e. g.   He used his boots for a pillow.

            他用靴子作枕头。

pudding /ˈpʊdɪŋ/ *n.* 布丁(一种以面粉、牛奶、鸡蛋等为基料的糊状甜食)

    e. g.   The proof of the pudding is the eating.

            空谈不如实践。

rigging /ˈrɪɡɪŋ/ *n.* 索具,绳索

    e. g.   During Christmas, the riggings of many fishing boats are strung with lights.

            圣诞节时,渔船的缆绳上也挂起一串串的灯。

scrap /skræp/ *n.* 小片,废料,残余物,废料

    e. g.   I made some notes on a piece of scrap paper.

            我在一张小纸片上记了一些笔记。

Spanish /ˈspænɪʃ/ *adj.* 西班牙的,西班牙人的,西班牙语的

                          n. 西班牙人;西班牙语

    e. g.   French is a sister language of Spanish.

            法语是西班牙语的"姐妹语"。

unwrap /ˌʌnˈræp/ *v.* 打开,解开,展开

    e. g.   He unwrapped a package.

             他打开包裹。

Phrases and Expressions

be strung with 挂起;串起

    e. g.   During Christmas, the streets are strung with lanterns.

            圣诞节时,大街上挂起一串串的灯笼。

play a part in 与……有关;对……有影响

    e. g.   The books you read as a child can play a part in the job you have later in life.

你在童年时读过的书,对你后来的职业会产生一定的影响。

Proper Names

Arctic Circle	北极圈
Christmas Eve	圣诞节前夕(12 月 24 日)
Holland	荷兰
Jolasveinar	圣诞少年
Nicholas	尼古拉斯(男子名),小亚细亚半岛上米拉的主教,他通常与圣诞老人和圣诞节赠送礼物的习俗联系在一起。
Norway	挪威(北欧国家)
Oslo	奥斯陆(挪威的首都)
Pere Noel	圣诞神父
Reykjavik	雷克雅末(冰岛首都)
Santa Claus	圣诞老人(常被描述成为一个快乐的,胖胖的,长着白胡子并穿红衣服的老人,他会在圣诞夜中给表现好的孩子带去礼物)
Yule lads	圣诞少年

参 考 译 文

冰岛的圣诞节

1   无论圣诞节在哪里庆祝,孩子们都期待非常特别的客人——能给这个节日增添趣味和刺激的客人。圣诞老人在圣诞前夕到达美国家庭;圣诞之父来到英国家庭;在法国,孩子们等待圣诞神父的光临;在荷兰,尼古拉斯骑着马;在西班牙,孩子们在 1 月 6 日那天,把鞋子装满稻草,等候三位国王的骆驼。

2   设想一下,有 13 位圣诞客人造访会是什么情况!在冰岛,孩子们知道圣诞少年从12 月 12 日开始到来。他们是一个晚上来一个,带来一些小礼物、糖果和惊喜。这些东西孩子们可以在他们的枕头底下找到。最后一位圣诞少年在圣诞前夕降临。

3   这 13 名圣诞少年并不总是那么友好。他们从前总爱恶作剧、偷食物、吓唬顽皮的孩子。

4   灯光在冰岛的圣诞节里起很重大的作用。冰岛因离北极圈很近,所以在圣诞节里,太阳在上午近 11 点才升起,下午才 3 点就下山。每家每户的窗户上都挂着不同造型、不同图案的灯;商家把日常用灯换成了五颜六色的彩灯;渔船的缆绳上也挂起一串串的灯。北极之夜,圣诞节的冰岛是彩灯的世界。

5   跟其他很多国家一样,冰岛的圣诞树也是一个重要的圣诞装饰。然而,因为冰岛是一个树木非常匮乏的国家,所以树木必须从挪威等国家进口。差不多在圣诞少年开始到达的时候,圣诞树也到了。社区圣诞树由挪威的"姐妹城"送到冰岛城。挪威的首都奥斯陆,是冰岛首都雷克雅末克的姐妹城。每年奥斯陆人都要将一颗壮丽挺拔的圣诞树送给雷克雅末克人。装饰着彩灯的圣诞树,在黑暗的冬日,光彩熠熠。

6   圣诞前夕是幸福欢聚、共享一切的时刻。在冰岛这更是家庭团聚的日子。在早早地做完晚礼拜后,全家人聚在家中共享圣诞晚餐。传统的小羊羔与火鸡或肥鹅同为圣诞佳品。晚餐最后吃圣诞大米布丁和花边薄煎饼,饼上奶油多得都流出来了。当家人很惬意地围坐在圣诞树前,互相递杯咖啡或送盘点心时,大家得松松腰带才吃得下。

7   有人,或许是祖父,边慢慢地读着赠送人的名字边分发礼物。他要等到打开包装,人们都赞赏一番,向赠送人表达谢意,才接着分发下一份礼物。全家人用这种方式享受每一件礼物带来的乐趣。

8   这时孩子们困得打盹了,因为睡觉时间到了。在过去,人们会留下一支点燃的蜡烛,以指引可能经过这里的路人。如今是电蜡烛,但留蜡烛的风俗仍保留着。

9   幸福一天结束了,但圣诞节没结束。在新年除夕,冰岛人点燃篝火,一连数周孩子们收集木料和碎木,让篝火延续。篝火映照着皑皑白雪,周围数英里内都清晰可见。午夜时分,大家在外面燃放花炮,彩色的烟花在冰岛渔村和农场的上空绽放。

10   1月6日标志着冰岛圣诞节的结束。最后一名圣诞少年离开了,圣诞蛋糕也吃完了。

11   冰岛人在圣诞节里用灯光、游戏、礼物和友谊照亮了冬季最黑暗的夜晚,并相互问候:"圣诞节快乐!"

Exercises

I. Reading Comprehension

1. D   2. C   3. A   4. B   5. C

II. Vocabulary and Structure

1. D   2. B   3. A   4. C   5. B   6. D   7. B   8. D   9. C   10. A

III. Translation

1. Christmas Lads used to play tricks, steal food, and scare misbehaving children.
   圣诞少年从前总爱恶作剧、偷食物、吓唬顽皮的孩子。

2. Lights, in different patterns and designs, decorate house windows.
   每家每户都用不同造型、不同图案的灯装饰窗户。

3. After attending early evening church services, families gather in their homes to enjoy Christmas dinner together.
   早早地做完晚礼拜后,全家人聚在家中共享圣诞晚餐。

4. Today the candles are electric, but the custom is still followed.
   如今是电蜡烛,但点蜡烛这一风俗仍被保留着。

5. It is the end of a happy day but not of the Christmas season.
   幸福一天结束了,但圣诞节没结束。

Part V Time for Fun

第一次与最后一次

乔治35岁时买了架小型飞机,并开始学习驾驶。不久,他就能很娴熟地驾机做各种各样的特技飞行了。

乔治有个朋友名叫马克。一天,乔治主动邀请马克乘他的飞机上天兜一圈。马克心想,"我乘大客机飞行过好几次,还从来没有乘过小飞机,不妨试一试。"

升空后,乔治飞了有半个小时,在空中做了各种各样的飞行特技。

后来他们着陆了。马克很高兴能够安全返回地面。他用颤抖的声音对他的朋友说:"乔治,非常感谢你让我乘小飞机做了两次飞行。"

乔治非常吃惊地问:"两次飞行?"

"是的,我的第一次和最后一次。"马克答道。

Unit ② Sleep

Part I Teaching Objectives

* Listening & Speaking:

Help the students to be familiar with the topic—*how to express yourself when talking about sleep and health* and memorize useful expressions.

* Words & Expressions:

Study some new words and expressions, such as *annual*, *consolidation*, *crucial*, *deteriorate*, *devote*, *download*, *encoding*, *initial*, *nap*, *perform*, *present*, *prime*, *retrieval*, *solidify*, *tax*, *whereas*, *clog up*, *get hold of*, *soak in*, *turn out* and so on.

* Grammar:

Learn to use the structure *The more... the more....*

* Writing:

Understand and write *a letter of acceptance or refusal*.

Part II Listening——Sleeping and Health

New Words

alert /əˈlɜːt/ *adj.* 警觉的,警惕的,机灵的

    e. g. You must keep alert in class.

        你们应该在课堂上保持活跃。

multiply /ˈmʌltɪplaɪ/ *v.* 乘;增加

    e. g. 3 multiplied by 5 is 15.

        三乘五等于十五。

relaxation /ˌriːlækˈseɪʃən/ *n.* 放松;松弛

e. g.   He used to play golf for relaxation.

他以前总是打高尔夫球来放松。

subtract   /səb'trækt/   v.（常与 from 连用）减去；扣除

e. g.   If you subtract 3 from 5, you get 2.

五减去三得二。

Phrases and Expressions

in particular   特别地；详细地

e. g.   He doesn't have one time to go to bed in particular.

他没有特定的睡觉时间。

in the black   有盈余

e. g.   Our account is nicely in the black this month.

我们的账上本月颇有盈余。

One

Listen to the CD and mark T for True or F for False according to the dialogue.

1. F   2. F   3. F   4. T   5. T

Huang：Hello, Mr. Smith. How are you feeling today?

Mr. Smith：I'm pretty tired. I haven't been sleeping well.

Huang：Do you have enough time to get the right amount of sleep?

Mr. Smith：I have enough time. I just can't fall asleep and stay asleep.

Huang：What time do you usually go to bed?

Mr. Smith：I don't have one time in particular. I just go to sleep whenever I feel tired.

Huang：Have you been under a lot of stress lately?

Mr. Smith：I just lost my job, and I am unsure about being able to find another one.

Huang：Have you ever tried doing relaxation exercises before you go to bed?

Mr. Smith：I have never tried that, but it sounds like a good idea.

Huang：Just have a try.

Mr. Smith：OK, I will. Thank you.

Two

Listen to the CD and answer the following questions with the information you hear.

1. Is Tom ready to go to bed?

   No, he isn't.

2. Can Tom get up late tomorrow?

   No, he can't. He has an early day tomorrow.

3. Does counting sheep work to Tom?

No. It really doesn't work.

4. Does Tom want to go to bed now?

No, he doesn't.

5. What will Tom do next?

Tom will have to go to bed.

Script

- -

Mother: Tom. It's time for bed!

Tom: I'm not ready to go to sleep. I'm not tired.

Mother: It's quite late, and you have an early day tomorrow.

Tom: I'm not going to be able to fall asleep.

Mother: Why don't you try counting sheep?

Tom: I've tried that before. It really doesn't work.

Mother: You still need to go to bed.

Tom: Why can't I just stay up until I fall asleep?

Mother: If I let you do that, then you're just going to be up all night.

Tom: I promise I'll go to sleep soon.

Mother: No, you're going to sleep now. Good night. Sweet dreams!

Tom: Good night!

Spot Dictation

- -

1. and find out how to recover
2. Don't include the weekend
3. How many hours of sleep did you get the night before
4. The number you are left with is your sleep debt
5. should get you back into balance

Part III   Speaking——*Sleep*

Useful Expressions About Sleep

It's time to get up!

I don't wanna get up.

It's time to wake up!

Are you awake?

Did you sleep well?

Yes, I slept very well.

No, I couldn't fall asleep.

I'm still sleepy.

Did you stay up late last night?

Did you go to bed late last night?

You were snoring last night.

Did I keep you up?

You were sawing logs last night.

I had a nightmare.

I'm still drowsy.

I'm still yawning.

I'm a night person.

Time to go to sleep.

I set the alarm clock for 8:00.

Wake me up at seven tomorrow.

Good night! Sweet dreams!

Have pleasant dreams.

Pair Work

Sample

Mary: Isn't it past your bedtime already?

Tom: I am not sleepy.

Mary: It's getting late, and you have to wake up early tomorrow.

Tom: There is no way that I can fall asleep right now.

Mary: Try listening to some soft music.

Tom: It doesn't work. I'm a night person.

Mary: I really don't care. Just go to sleep.

Tom: What if I stay up and do something, until I get tired?

Mary: You'll be up all night.

Tom: I'm going to go to sleep eventually.

Mary: If you don't go to bed, I can't go to sleep. You need to go to sleep now, so go to sleep.

Tom: Yes, I see. Good night.

Role-play

Sample

Liu: How have you been doing lately?

Tom: Actually, I haven't been sleeping well.

Liu: Is there some reason why you can't get enough sleep?

Tom: I go to bed, but I just can't get comfortable enough to stay asleep.

Liu: When do you go to bed at night?

Tom: I usually try to go to bed around 11:00 or so during the week.

Liu: What do you think about when you try to go to sleep?

Tom: My mother is ill with cancer, and I think about her a lot.

Liu: Did you ever read before bedtime?

Tom: I usually watch a lot of television before I go to bed. Maybe I should try something else to help me quiet down.

Liu: Yes, I think so. Why not have a try?

Tom: Thank you, I will.

Part IV   Reading

 ***Text A***   **Background**

Mad dogs and Englishmen, so the song has it, go out in the midday sun. And the business practices of England's lineal descendant, America, will have you in the office from nine in the morning to five in the evening, if not longer. Much of the world, though, prefers to take a siesta. And research presented to the American Association for the Advancement of Science meeting in San Diego suggests it may be right to do so. It has already been established that those who take a siesta are less likely to die of heart disease. Now, Matthew Walker and his colleagues at the University of California have found that they probably have better memory, too. A post-prandial snooze, Dr. Walker has discovered, sets the brain up for learning.

The role of sleep in consolidating memories that have already been created has been understood for some time. Dr. Walker has been trying to extend this understanding by looking at sleep's role in preparing the brain for the formation of memories in the first place. He was particularly interested in a type of memory called episodic memory, which relates to specific events, places and time. This contrasts with procedural memory of the skills required to perform some sorts of mechanical tasks, such as driving. The theory he and his team wanted to test was that the ability to form new episodic memories deteriorates with accrued wakefulness, and that sleep thus restores the brain's capacity for efficient learning.

The benefits to memory of a nap, says Dr. Walker, are so great that they can equal an entire night's sleep. He warns, however, that napping must not be done too late in the day or it will interfere with night-time sleep.

New Words

annual   /ˈænjʊəl/   *adj.* 每年的，年度的

    e. g.   What about your annual income this year?

            你今年的年收入如何?

consolidation /kənˌsɒlɪˈdeɪʃən/ *n.* 巩固,合并

    e. g.   Sleep can help the memory consolidation process.

            睡眠有助于巩固记忆。

crucial /ˈkruːʃəl/ *adj.* 关系重大的;决定性的

    e. g.   at the crucial moment

            在关键时刻,重要关头

            a crucial decision

            极重要的决定

deteriorate /dɪˈtɪərɪəreɪt/ *v.* 使恶化,变糟

    e. g.   His work has deteriorated last month.

            他的工作在最后一个月变糟了。

devote /dɪˈvəʊt/ *v.* 专心致力于,献(身),贡献

    e. g.   He devoted his life to literature.

            他把一生都献给了文学。

            He has devoted his whole life to benefiting mankind.

            他为全人类的利益献出了自己的一生。

download /ˈdaʊnləʊd/ *v.* 下载

    e. g.   He wanted to download some important information.

            他想下载一些重要信息。

encoding /ɪnˈkəʊdɪŋ/ *n.* 编码法,编码技术

    e. g.   memory encoding 记忆编码

hippocampus /ˌhɪpəˈkæmpəs/ *n.* (脑内的)海马状突起

initial /ɪˈnɪʃəl/ *adj.* 开始的,最初的

    e. g.   The initial talks were the base of the later agreement.

            最初的会谈是后来达成协议的基础。

nap /næp/ *n.* 小睡,午睡

    e. g.   I want to have a nap.

            我想打个盹。

perform /pəˈfɔːm/ *v.* 表演;表现

    e. g.   The singer performed beautifully.

            这个歌手唱得好极了。

Ph. D. *abbr.* 博士学位;获得博士学位者(Doctor of Philosophy)

present /prɪˈzent/ *v.* 提出;呈递

    e. g.   The committee is presenting its investigation report next week.

            委员会将于下星期公布调查报告。

prime /praɪm/ *v.* 事先为……提供消息;使准备好,使完成准备工作

e. g.　They primed the lamp with oil.

　　　　他们给灯加满了油。

retrieval　/rɪ'triːvəl/　*n.* 检索

e. g.　information retrieval

　　　　信息检索

solidify　/sə'lɪdɪfaɪ/　*v.* 使牢固、结实

e. g.　Sleep after learning is crucial to solidify learned information.

　　　　学习后的睡眠非常重要，它可以巩固学到的信息。

tax　/tæks/　*v.* 对……征税；使负重担，使受压力

e. g.　Reading in a poor light taxes the eyes.

　　　　在暗淡的光线下读书伤眼睛。

whereas　/hweər'æz/　*conj.* 但是，相反

e. g.　Some people like fat meat, whereas others hate it.

　　　　有些人喜欢肥肉，相反有些人讨厌肥肉。

Phrases and Expressions

assistant professor　助理教授（级别高于讲师而低于副教授）

clog up　填塞，塞满

e. g.　The machine must have been clogged up with dirt again.

　　　　机器一定又是被脏东西堵住了。

get hold of　抓住，得到

e. g.　Can you get hold of that rope?

　　　　你能抓住那根绳子吗？

prefrontal cortex　前额叶皮层

REM sleep　眼球快速运转睡眠（REM：rapid eye movement）

soak in　吸收；理解

e. g.　The speaker paused to let her words soak in.

　　　　讲话者暂停了一下，以便她的话被人们理解。

turn out　（常与 to, that 连用）结果是……

e. g.　Things turned out to be exactly as the professor had foreseen.

　　　　事情正如教授所预见的那样。

参 考 译 文

午睡能否让你更聪明？

1　研究显示，午睡的成年人会学得更好，工作得更好。如果你在午饭时间睡个午觉，你下午的学习或工作表现可能更好。美国加州大学心理学助理教授马修·沃克博士说："在

测试中,午睡的人比不午睡的人表现要好。"他在本周圣地亚哥举行的美国推进科学协会的年会上宣读了他的研究成果。

2   沃克说:"一天中,大脑学习信息的能力是不稳定的。学习工作一段时间,大脑的记忆存储区域可能会"堵塞"。到中午时大脑的学习能力可能会有所下降,午睡一会儿或能清理大脑的记忆存储区域,为新信息腾出地方。"

3   **午睡或不午睡:这项研究是什么?**

4   沃克和他的同事让 39 位平均年龄为 21 岁的健康成人接受一项艰难的学习任务,旨在让大脑的海马状突起——一个有助于人类根据事实存储记忆的区域——担负很重的责任。这项测试为学习 100 位人名和他们的相貌,然后做匹配练习。测试在中午开始。下午2 点,一组给予 90 分钟午睡时间,另一组则没有午睡,须保持清醒。

5   下午 6 时,沃克对他们再次进行测试。沃克说:"无午睡的一组其学习能力略有下降,降低了约 10% 。而午睡过的人其学习能力提高了 10% 。"

6   沃克发现在 90 分钟的午休中,受试者睡眠的总时间多少在他们后面的表现并不是很重要。但他发现 2 期眼球非快速运转睡眠(比较浅的无梦睡眠)的时间越长,受试者的表现就越好。

7   **小睡和学习:研究的启示**

8   沃克说:"这项研究的结果表明,学习前的睡眠或许也很重要,正如专家已发现的,学习后的睡眠对巩固所学的信息很重要。"沃克发现,以事实为基础的记忆暂时储存在大脑中的海马状突起中,然后被发送到叫做前额叶皮层的区域——他怀疑这个区域有更多的存储空间。沃克说:"海马状突起善于掌握信息,但在某个临界点就需要把信息下载到前额叶皮层之中。在学习前小睡可帮助海马状突起清空记忆内存,并发送数据到前额叶皮层,以便接收新的信息。"

9   **第二种意见**

10   印第安纳州圣母玛利亚大学的心理学助理教授杰西卡·佩恩博士说:"已经证实,睡眠除了帮助巩固记忆外,还让大脑能预先准备,以便学习新信息,这正是该研究新颖且令人振奋的地方。记忆分三个阶段。它们是:初始记忆编码、记忆存储或巩固及记忆检索。

11   佩恩说:"大多有关睡眠的研究都集中在睡眠在巩固记忆过程中的作用,但这项新的研究着眼于研究睡眠如何影响记忆的初始编码,新的研究结果特别有助于解释人衰老,记忆力也减退的现象。简短的午睡可以帮助他们在当天晚些时候学习和记忆。"

12   沃克和佩恩承认,在工作日中,许多人不可能获得 90 分钟的午睡。但佩恩说:"即使是短暂的小睡也能够有相同或类似的作用。"

Exercises

I. Reading Comprehension

Section A

1. B   2. A   3. D   4. B   5. C

Section B

1. Study shows adults who nap learn better, perform better.

2. The area of the brain that stores memories may get "clogged up" as the day goes on, similar to a full email in-box on your computer.

3. A brief midday nap may help people, especially the aging people, learn and remember later in the day.

4. The total time the participants slept during the 90-minute nap didn't matter much in their later performance.

5. The hippocampus is good at getting hold of information, but at some point needs to "download" the information to the pre-frontal cortex.

Section C

1. No, most of the time a 90-minute nap in the middle of a workday isn't possible for me, and of course, it isn't possible for many people. But I usually try my best to have a briefer nap, because I know that a briefer nap could also provide the same, or similar benefits.

2. Usually I can have enough sleep at night, but I do not have enough time to have the midday nap everyday. Because I am very busy with my study or job.

3. Yes, I think sleep is very crucial to our health. Not only sleep at night but also the midday nap is very important. I've heard that lack of sleep is connected with obesity, but I was surprised to hear that it is also linked to smoking, drinking alcohol and not being physically active. In addition, people who have a nap probably have better memory, too. A post-prandial snooze sets the brain up for learning.

II. Vocabulary and Structure
Section A

1. C 2. A 3. D 4. B 5. D 6. B 7. C 8. C 9. A 10. D

Section B

1. Napping at midday may clear the brain's memory storage area and make <u>room</u> for new information.
   午睡一会儿或能清理大脑的记忆存储区域,为新信息腾出地方。

2. Fact-based memories are stored <u>temporarily</u> in the brain's hippocampus.
   以事实为基础的记忆暂时储存在大脑中的海马状突起中。

3. Study shows adults who nap learn better, <u>perform</u> better.
   研究显示,午睡的成年人会学得更好,工作得更好。

4. Walker gave 39 healthy young adults a difficult learning task <u>intended</u> to tax the brain's hippocampus.
   沃克让39位健康成人接受了一项艰难的学习任务,旨在让大脑的海马状突起担负很重的责任。

5. In addition to <u>helping</u> the memory consolidation process, sleep also primes the brain to learn new information.

睡眠除了帮助巩固记忆外，还让大脑能预先准备，以便学习新信息。

6. The new study findings may be of <u>particular</u> help for aging people who feel their memories are failing.

新的研究结果可能对那些觉得自己的记忆力正在衰退的老年人特别有帮助。

7. Walker <u>admits</u> that a 90-minute nap in the middle of a workday isn't possible for many people.

沃克承认，在工作日中，许多人不可能获得 90 分钟的午睡。

8. <u>Devote</u> your lunch hour to a restful nap, and you may perform and learn better in the afternoon.

如果你在午饭时间睡个午觉，你下午的学习或工作表现可能更好。

VI. Word Building

1. He is blacklisted for <u>non-payment</u> of debts.
   因为拖欠债务，他上了黑名单。

2. All <u>non-violent</u> religious and political beliefs should be respected equally.
   对所有非暴力的宗教和政治信仰应予以同等尊重。

3. Gestures are a <u>non-verbal</u> means of expression.
   手势语是一种非言语的表达方式。

4. He was disqualified from the council for <u>non-attendance</u>.
   因为缺席，他失去了理事会委员的资格。

5. Both countries agreed that normal relations would be based on <u>non-interference</u> in each other's internal affairs.
   双方一致同意，两国之间的正常关系建立在互不干涉内政的基础上。

6. Children of smokers are more likely to start smoking than are children of <u>non-smokers</u>.
   吸烟者的孩子比非吸烟者的孩子抽烟的可能性更大。

7. She told me that the moon was made of cheese. What <u>nonsense</u>!
   她告诉我月亮是奶酪做的，真是胡说八道！

8. She took a <u>non-stop</u> flight from Hong Kong to Beijing.
   她乘坐香港至北京的直达航班。

IV. Grammar Focus

1. The sooner you finish it, the better it will be.
   你完成得越快越好。

2. The more exercise you take, the stronger you are.
   锻炼得越多，身体越强壮。

3. The better the food is, the more popular a restaurant gets.
   食物越可口，饭店的生意就越红火。

4. The harder you work, the more progress you will get.

你越努力,进步就越快。

5. The more I read the book, the more I liked it.

这本书我越看越喜欢。

V. Translation

1. Just as experts have known, sleep after learning is crucial to solidify information learned.

正如专家所知道的,学习后的睡眠非常重要,它可以巩固所学的信息。

2. People who had a nap improved their ability to learn by 10%.

午睡过的人其学习能力提高了10%。

3. The new study findings may be of particular help for aging people who feel their memories are failing.

新的研究结果可能对那些觉得自己的记忆力正在衰退的老年人特别有帮助。

4. Sleep, in addition to helping the memory consolidation process, also primes the brain to learn new information.

睡眠除了帮助巩固记忆外,还让大脑能预先准备,以便学习新信息。

5. The greater the amount of non-REM sleep, the better the subject's performance.

眼球非快速运转睡眠的时间越长,受试者的表现就越好。

VI. Writing

Sample

(1) A Letter of Acceptance

Mar. 10th, 2011

Dear David,

Many thanks for your letter dated February 25, 2011, and for inviting me to attend the get-together to be held in Taiyuan, from May 2 to 10, 2011.

Your letter is a lovely surprise. Of course I'll come. Not having seen you and other old classmates for such a long time, I really miss you and others. I can hardly wait! I'll go to your place straight from my office around 5 a. m. , Friday.

Thank you for remembering me. See you then.

Yours ever,

Black

(2) A Letter of Refusal

Mar. 10th, 2011

Dear David,

Many thanks for your letter dated February 25, 2011, and for inviting me to attend the get-together to be held in Taiyuan, from May 2 to 10, 2011.

Much to my regret, I shall not be able to honor the invitation because I have been suffering from a disease this winter. I am firmly advised that it would be unwise to undertake any distant

and long travel in the near future.

I feel very sad to miss this opportunity of meeting you and many others classmates. I wish the get-together a complete success.

Yours ever,

Black

Notes

A letter of invitation usually requires a reply. To accept the invitation, we write a letter of acceptance. To say "no", we write a letter of regret or refusal.

Acceptance: in a letter of acceptance, we ought to express our thanks for being invited, and let our friend know it is a pleasure to get the invitation.

Refusal: In a letter of refusal, before or after we say we cannot accept the invitation, we should express our thanks to the person for inviting us. Then explain why we cannot accept the invitation. The reasons we give should be convincing; otherwise, the letter will sound impolite or insincere.

Useful Expressions for Acceptance:

Informal: Thanks for your...

               Your invitation to... is very welcome/was a delightful/lovely surprise...

Neutral: Thank you for...

Formal: I'd be very pleased to come to...

               I'd be very delighted to accept your...

Useful Expressions for Refusal:

Informal: I'm very sorry, but I have to say "no" to...

               I simply can't make it...

               I can't come...

More formal: Thank you for your..., but unfortunately...

               It's not possible for me to...

               It's (quite) impossible for me to...

               I'm quite unable to...

               I regret that/It's a pity that...

               I have a previous/prior arrangement.

Text B   **Background**

Lack of sleep does appear to be associated with obesity. One theory is that sleep deprivation disrupts production of hormones that regulate appetite. But findings from a door-to-door government survey of 87,000 U. S. adults from 2004 to 2006 suggests that those who get the least sleep are also more likely to put their health at risk by smoking cigarettes, drinking too much alcohol, and not being physically active. In the case of cigarettes and physical inactivity, this was also true for those who slept nine or more hours per night.

The study was conducted by the National Center for Health Statistics, an arm of the Centers for Disease Control and Prevention. It does prove that in some cases, depression or stress could be the underlying reasons for not getting enough sleep and for drinking.

But the findings are striking. Here's a summary：

Smoking：Of those who slept seven to eight hours a night only 18 percent were smokers compared to 31 percent of those who slept less than six hours and 26 percent of those who slept more than nine hours.

Alcohol：Adults who got the least sleep were slightly more likely to have had five or more drinks in one day than those who got seven to eight hours, but here, the difference was only three percent：19 percent of those who had a good night's sleep had five or more drinks a day compared to 22 percent of those who slept six hours or less.

Physical Inactivity：For both men and women regardless of age, those who slept less than six or more than nine hours a night were more likely to be physically inactive than those who slept seven to eight.

Obesity：The rate of obesity was highest (33 percent) among those who slept less than six hours and lowest (22 percent) among those who slept seven to eight hours a night. This held true for both men and women regardless of age.

Adequate sleep is key to a healthy lifestyle, and accumulating research suggests that it plays an even larger role in health than we once thought. There is more to learn about this subject. I'll keep you posted on developments. Meanwhile, if you're not getting seven to eight hours sleep per night, based on what we now know, it might benefit your weight — and your overall health — to strive for more shut-eye.

New Words

applicable /ˈæplɪkəbl/ *adj.* 生效的，适用的

    e. g. The new law on the protection of the environments is applicable to everybody from next year.

        新的环境保护法明年起将生效。

chronic /ˈkrɒnɪk/ *adj.* 慢性的；长期的

    e. g. He suffered from a chronic disease.

        他患有一种慢性疾病。

constant /ˈkɒnstənt/ *adj.* 经常的；稳定的，不变的

    e. g. I'm tired of her constant complaints.

        我厌倦了她没完没了的抱怨。

debilitate /dɪˈbɪlɪteɪt/ *v.* 使衰弱，使虚弱

    e. g. What a debilitating climate！

使人虚弱无力的气候!

deprivation /dɪpraɪˈveɪʃən/ *n.* 剥夺;丧失

    e. g. Staying in bed on the weekends can not make up for a long time of sleep deprivation.

            周末待在床上不能弥补你长时间内所失去的睡眠。

erase /ɪˈreɪz/ *v.* 清除掉,消除;忘掉(from);

    e. g. He tried to erase from his memory the terrible accident.

            他试图忘掉那起可怕的事故。

noticeable /ˈnəʊtɪsəbl/ *adj.* 显而易见的;值得注意的

    e. g. The hole in your trousers is not noticeable.

            你裤子上的洞不明显。

resident /ˈrezɪdənt/ *n.* 住院医生

    e. g. medical resident   住院医生

snooze /snuːz/ *v.* 小睡,打瞌睡,打盹

    e. g. Snoozing in summer does you no harm.

            夏天时打盹对人没坏处。

vulnerable /ˈvʌlnərəbl/ *adj.* 易受攻击的,脆弱的

    e. g. We are vulnerable both by water and land, without either fleet or army.

            由于没有舰队和军队,我们在水路和陆路上都易受攻击。

undo /ˌʌnˈduː/ *v.* 解开;放松;使复原;使失效;破坏

    e. g. Please undo the package.   请解开这包裹。

            His pride will undo him some day.   他的傲慢总有一天会毁了他。

Phrases and Expressions

be equivalent to   相当于,相等于

    e. g. This wish was equivalent to a command.

            这个请求相当于命令。

circadian rhythm   生理节奏

go hand in hand   关系密切;手拉着手地走

    e. g. Dirt and disease go hand in hand.

            脏与疾病是密切相关的。

interfere with   妨碍;干涉,干扰

    e. g. Don't interfere with him. He's preparing for the final exams.

            他在为期末考试做准备,不要打扰他。

on-call shift   值班的,随时待命的

    e. g. The nurse is on-call shift tonight.

            今夜这位护士值班,随时待命。

参 考 译 文

研究表明：失去的睡眠无法弥补

1　如果你认为周末待在床上可以弥补你一周内所失去的睡眠，请三思。一项新研究发现长时间不睡觉能够导致"睡眠负债"，这无法简单地通过短时补觉来解决。

2　这种长期的睡眠缺失可能最终会影响一个人在需要集中精力的任务中的表现，在夜间这种情况特别明显，这时身体的自然睡眠周期不能为你提供更多的动力。

3　任何一个曾经通宵熬夜的人都会知道，睡眠缺失在短时期里会让人多么的虚弱。的确，研究表明一个24小时没有睡觉的人，其表现会降至与一个喝醉酒的人一样低的水平。但那些通宵熬夜的人要是整个星期都这么做，又会怎样呢？本研究将集中研究长期睡眠缺失，研究经常性的睡眠缺失所带来的负面影响能否通过延长休息来减轻。

4　**睡眠研究**

5　研究人员为9名志愿者制订了一种睡眠计划，和医生或住院医生白班连夜班所经历的一样——睡10小时，然后连续工作33小时，这样循环下来相当于每24小时里只睡了5.6小时。参与者按这种计划，坚持三个星期，在此期间，他们长期处于睡眠缺少状态。这项研究还有8位年轻人参加，但他们的睡眠时间没有被剥夺。

6　这些受试者需要周期性地完成一个任务，测试他们能否集中注意力及反应时间。如果测试是在早上9点或10点进行，此时受测试者，已经有了很长的睡眠时间，清醒了没有2个小时，睡眠不足的与睡眠充足的两组受测者，他们的表现基本差不多。这项研究通过三整周的实践，发现闭眼休气养神一段时间能暂时性地弥补慢性睡眠缺失。

7　然而，经过数周的研究，发现如果受测者在30个小时内没有任何睡眠休息，测试又在近中午时分才开始，其测试表现则非常糟糕。受测者看上去已经有睡眠缺失的症状，缺少睡眠已经开始影响到他们的表现。

8　这项研究结果在现实生活或许是这样的：在工作日长期缺乏睡眠的人或许会在周末补觉，他们多睡上一阵，醒来后或许感觉颇好，但研究表明，他们若再次熬夜不睡觉，其表现会开始恶化。研究还表明长期睡眠缺失与短期睡眠缺失对大脑的影响是不一样的。

9　**太阳产生的影响**

10　在夜间接受测试时，受测者的睡眠负债最明显。研究者称这是由于人们睡眠的自然周期循环，"日出而作，日落而息"的生理节奏。我们自然的趋势就是白天不睡觉，因此当光线充足时，我们身上的各种"睡眠负债"迹象就被遮盖了起来。研究者认为当夜晚来临，这些迹象就会消失。

11　这项研究尤其适用于那些长时间连续工作而不睡觉的人，如卫生工作者、卡车司机和急救人员。研究人员说，长期的睡眠缺失能导致这些人在面对"突发事故和错误时容易受伤害"，他们建议人们关注"长期睡眠缺失的潜在影响"。

Exercises

I. Reading Comprehension

1. B 2. C 3. D 4. A 5. D

II. Vocabulary and Structure

1. C 2. D 3. B 4. A 5. C 6. D 7. B 8. C 9. A 10. C

III. Translation

1. Study suggests that lost sleep can't be made up.

   研究表明失去的睡眠无法弥补。

2. A new study finds that going long periods without sleep can lead to a sort of "sleep debt".

   新研究发现长时间不睡觉能够导致"睡眠负债"。

3. The authors of the current study turned their attention to long-term sleep loss.

   本研究将注意力放在了长期睡眠缺失上。

4. The subjects appeared to have developed a sleep debt—all that lost sleep really was catching up with them.

   受测者看上去已经有睡眠缺失的症状,缺少睡眠已经开始影响到他们的表现。

5. Researches suggest that this could be due to the effects of our natural sleep-wake cycle.

   研究表明,这可能是由于人们睡眠的自然周期循环——"日出而作,日落而息"的影响。

Part V   Time for Fun

参 考 译 文

走 私 犯

一个形迹可疑的人开车来到边境,哨兵迎了上去。哨兵在检查汽车行李箱时,惊奇地发现了六个鼓得紧绷绷的大口袋。

"里面装的是什么?"他问道。

"土。"司机回答。

"把袋子拿出来",哨兵命令道:"我要检查。"

那人顺从地把口袋搬了出来。确实,口袋里除了土以外,别无它物。哨兵很不情愿地让他通过了。

一周后,那人又来了,哨兵再次检查汽车上的行李箱。

"这次袋子里装的是什么?"他问道。

"土,又运了一些土。"那人回答。

哨兵不相信,对那些袋子又进行了检查,结果发现,除了土以外,仍旧一无所获。

同样的事情每周重演一次,一共持续了六个月。最后,哨兵被弄得灰心丧气,干脆辞职去酒吧当了侍者。有天夜里,那个形迹可疑的人碰巧途经酒吧,下车喝酒。那位从前的哨兵急忙迎上前去对他说,"我说,老兄,你要是能帮我一个忙,今晚的酒就归我请客。你能不能告诉我,那段时间你到底在走私什么东西?"

那人俯身过来,凑近侍者的耳朵,裂开嘴笑嘻嘻地说:"汽车"。

Unit 3

World Expo

Part I Teaching Objectives

* **Listening & Speaking:**

Help students to be familiar with the topic of talking about World Expo on some social occasions and memorize useful expressions.

* **Words & Expressions:**

Grasp some new words and expressions, such as *address*, *acute*, *professional*, *revive*, *integrate*, *struggle for*, *concentrate on*, *as much as possible*, *as regards*, *as well*, *lay out*, *be engaged in*, *in accord with*... and so on.

* **Grammar:**

How to use *it* as the formal subject.

* **Writing:**

Understand and write *a letter of congratulation*.

Part II Listening——*World Expo*

New Words

architect /ˈɑːkɪtekt/ *n.* 建筑设计师

    e. g. The new building was built from the design of a famous architect.
           这座新楼是根据一位著名建筑师的设计建成的。

atomiun /ˈætəmɪən/ *adj.* 原子形的

    e. g. Do you know the Atomiun Built for World's Fair 1958?
           你知道1958年世界博览会的哪个原子形建筑物么？

domestic /dəˈmestɪk/ *adj.* 本国的,国内的

e. g.　This is domestic news.
　　　　这是国内新闻。

gramophone /ˈɡræməˌfəʊn/ *n.* 留声机

e. g.　The telephone and the gramophone were contemporary.
　　　　电话和留声机是同一时代的产物。

landmark /ˈlændmɑːk/ *n.* 地标；有历史意义的建筑物

e. g.　The church on the hilltop was a well-known landmark.
　　　　山顶上的教堂是一个显著的陆标。

latecomer /ˈleɪtˌkʌmə/ *n.* 迟到者

e. g.　Latecomers might be punished by the teacher.
　　　　迟到者可能会受到老师的惩罚。

memorable /ˈmemərəbl/ *adj.* 值得纪念的，值得记忆

e. g.　That was one particularly memorable evening last year.
　　　　那是去年一个特别难忘的夜晚。

metro /ˈmetrəʊ/ *n.* 地铁

e. g.　There are metros in many big cities.
　　　　许多大城市都有地铁。

slogan /ˈsləʊɡən/ *n.* 标语，口号

e. g.　The crowd chanted slogans and waved banners.
　　　　人群有节奏地呼喊着口号并挥舞着旗帜。

strain /streɪn/ *n.* 压力

e. g.　It was a great strain on my resources.
　　　　这在我财力上是一个很大的负担。

stunning /ˈstʌnɪŋ/ *adj.* 了不起的，出色的

e. g.　The audience was awed into silence by her stunning performance.
　　　　观众席上鸦雀无声，人们对他出色的表演感到惊叹。

suspend /səsˈpend/ *v.* 吊，悬挂

e. g.　A lamp was suspended from the ceiling.
　　　　天花板上吊着一盏灯。

symphony /ˈsɪmfənɪ/ *n.* 交响乐，交响曲

e. g.　They play over the whole symphony.
　　　　他们把整个交响乐重新演奏了一遍。

wizardly /ˈwɪzədlɪ/ *adj.* 神奇的

e. g.　He has wizardly power.
　　　　他有着神奇的力量。

Phrases and Expressions

be supposed to do　应当，应该

225

e. g. Earth Day is supposed to be a day when every person promises to do something to help take care of our world.

在地球日这一天,每个人都应当承诺做点什么来爱护我们这个星球。

remind of 提醒,使(某人)想起

e. g. Thanks for your gift—it will always remind me of you.

谢谢你们的礼物——它将使我经常想到你们。

 One

Listen to the CD and mark T for True or F for False according to the dialogue.

1. T 2. F 3. T 4. F 5. T

Visitor: Hello! Where should I park my car?

Volunteer: To the parking lot, just over there.

Visitor: Thanks!

Visitor: Excuse me. Where is the entrance?

Volunteer: Please go along this way. The Expo Site entrance is ahead, 500 meters away from here.

Visitor: Shall we travel within the Expo Site by walk or by car?

Volunteer: Almost by walk. You may also take a bus. The bus station square is on the west side of the Expo Site; you need to walk another 800 meters to get there. The direction boards will guide your way.

Visitor: OK, thanks. I find the parking here quite under strain. The latecomers might find no parking space available.

Volunteer: Yes, it's true. Therefore, coming by metro is suggested.

Visitor: I see. Thanks!

Volunteer: You're welcome.

 **Two**

Listen to the CD and answer the following questions with the information you hear.

1. Where does the designer of the Eiffel Tower come from?

   The designer of the Eiffel Tower comes from French.

2. Why was the Eiffel Tower built?

   The Eiffel Tower was built for Universal Exhibition 1889 New York.

3. Who invented the gramophones?

   Edison invented the gramophones.

4. When was World Expo hold in Brussels Belgium?

   It was held in 1958.

5. Is the Atomiun called as the most stunning building in the world?

Yes, it is.

- -

Julia: Hi, do you know the "origin" of the Eiffel Tower?

Simon: It's designed by Gustavo Eiffel, a French architect. Is there anything different?

Julia: Something you've never known! The Eiffel Tower was built for Universal Exhibition 1889 Paris, France.

Simon: Did people construct buildings for World Expo?

Julia: Of course! World Expo brings us not only the landmark buildings, but also many great inventions. Have you ever heard the slogan — "Everything starts with World Expo"?

Simon: Are you joking?

Julia: Of course not. Look at the cameras in your hand. Most of cameras today are digital ones; however, the first roll film for domestic use was also launched in World Expo.

Simon: I know, but how is it related to World Expo?

Julia: The gramophones invented by Edison, its voice were first heard by visitors in World Expo, and then introduced into people's life.

Simon: What you said reminds me of the marvelous building in Belgium, which is supposed to be of a blood tie with World Expo, isn't it?

Julia: Bingo! What you mentioned is the Atomiun built for World's Fair 1958 Brussels Belgium. It was called as the most stunning building in the world!

Simon: Right, I saw the model, suspended cable structure, unbelievable!

- -

(1) explore different cultures and landscapes

(2) make this dream come true

(3) there will be 194 countries and 50 international organizations on display

(4) to be much less expensive than a trip around the world

(5) to share their best and latest ideas for the future

Part III Speaking——*Expo Performance*

Useful Expressions About Expo

The World Expo is held every five years.

The Expo emblem looks like three people holding hands to each other.

China will be the first developing country to host the World Expo.

What's the theme of Expo 2010? Better city, Better life.

Shanghai is known as the "Exhibition of the World's Architecture".

Shanghai welcomes friends from all over the world.

The Expo Site is along both sides of the Huangpu River.

Shanghai is most beautiful in autumn.

It's the best time of year for people to visit Shanghai.

Do you want to take the Maglev or the shuttle bus to the airport?

How far is the airport from the Expo Village? About an hour by bus.

Is the Expo Center still far off? You can walk there right down the sightseeing corridor.

Expo economy will be a new growth factor for China's economy.

It will create over 1 million job opportunities.

It is impossible to work out a correct figure of the income that the Expo will bring to China.

The Expo will help to improve Shanghai's environment.

By the mid-21st century, the city will become a first-class modern international metropolis in the world.

Pair Work

Sample

Volunteer: Hello! May I help you?

   Visitor: Hello! I would like to have a brief idea of the pavilion layout and orientation prior to my visiting, or to I would be lost. The one ahead is China Pavilion, isn't it?

Volunteer: Yes, it's the building with a red crown.

   Visitor: Where are the Theme Pavilions?

Volunteer: The Theme Pavilions are located on the left of China Pavilion. The belt amid them is the Expo Axis.

   Visitor: Where is the Expo Axis?

Volunteer: You may walk forward. It's about 500 meters away from here.

   Visitor: Is the Expo Center located on the other end?

Volunteer: Go along the Expo Axis, and you'll find the Expo Center to the end.

   Visitor: How about the Expo Performance Center? I learn that a large amount of performances will be offered there.

Volunteer: Yes, the Expo Performance Center is on the right of the Expo Center, only one step away.

   Visitor: Oh, I see. Thanks!

Volunteer: You're welcome!

Role-play

Sample

David: Look at the square building. It's France Pavilion. Let's go inside.

Lily: Watch, in the court the garden with a pond. It's so beautiful.

David: Look over there, stand an exhibition hall, and two French restaurants also.

Lily: Did you visit the Poland Pavilion?

David: Just came from there. Do you feel its appearance looks like paper cut-outs?

Lily: Yes, it does. In addition, several different traveling routes are available for visitors.

David: Right. What's our next destination?

Lily: It should be the Switzerland Pavilion. I learn that visitors can ride cable-car at the pavilion.

David: It's unbelievable. Let's go.

Part IV   Reading

Text A   **Background**

Shanghai Expo

Expo 2010, officially Expo 2010 Shanghai China was held on both banks of the Huangpu River in the city of Shanghai, China, from May 1 to October 31, 2010. The theme of the exposition is "Better City — Better Life" and it signifies Shanghai's new status in the 21st century as a "next great world city".

New Words

acute /əˈkjuːt/   *adj.* 严重的

    e. g.   There's an acute shortage of water.

          这里严重缺水。

address /əˈdres/   *v.* 设法解决,满足需求

    e. g.   Policymakers are also trying to address the problem.

          决策者也在努力解决这个问题。

architectural /ˌɑːkɪˈtektʃərəl/   *adj.* 建筑的,有关建筑的

    e. g.   Each period had its own particular style of architectural decoration.

          每个时期都有其建筑装饰上的风格。

atmosphere /ˈætməsfɪə/   *n.* 大气,空气;气氛,环境

    e. g.   There were no windows to admit moist atmosphere to enter.

没有窗户使潮湿的空气进入室内。

burgeoning /ˈbɜːdʒənɪŋ/ *adj.* 迅速成长的,迅速发展的

e. g. He enjoyed their burgeoning friendship.

他为他们之间萌生的友谊感到欣慰。

construction /kənsˈtrʌkʃən/ *n.* 建筑业,建筑物

e. g. The building is a peculiarly shaped construction.

这是一栋造形独特的建筑物。

conversion /kənˈvɜːʃən/ *n.* 变化,转换

e. g. He underwent quite a conversion.

他彻底变了。

cosmopolitan /ˌkɒzməˈpɒlɪtən/ *adj.* 世界性的,受世界各国文化影响的

e. g. It is so clever of them, and such a compliment to art. Makes it quite cosmopolitan, doesn't it?

他们真聪明,给艺术增光,使艺术在全世界通行无阻,是不是?

host /həʊst/ *n.* 主人,东道主

e. g. The host team was clobbered in last night's game.

东道主队在昨晚的比赛中惨败。

infrastructure /ˈɪnfrəˌstrʌktʃə/ *n.* 基础设施

e. g. Vast sums are needed to maintain the infrastructure.

保养基础设施需要巨额款项。

integrate /ˈɪntɪɡreɪt/ *v.* 使完整,使成为整体

e. g. We need an enterprising workforce that will integrate skills, funds and human resource to produce high value-added products.

我们需要一支创业家队伍来整合技术、资金和人力资源,产生高附加值。

internal /ɪnˈtɜːnl/ *adj.* 内部的,里面的;国内的,内政的

e. g. It's not difficult to understand this world when you mastered the internal relations of things.

掌握了事物的内部联系你就不难理解这个世界。

legacy /ˈleɡəsɪ/ *n.* 遗产,遗赠物

e. g. The court would not even consider his claim for the old man's legacy.

法庭根本不会考虑他所提出的对老人遗产的要求。

metropolis /mɪˈtrɒpəlɪs/ *n.* 大都会,大城市

e. g. He was dazzled by the gaiety and splendor of the metropolis.

大都市的花花世界使他感到眼花缭乱。

offspring /ˈɒfsprɪŋ/ *n.* 子孙,后代

e. g. John is her only offspring.

约翰是她惟一的孩子。

pavilion /pəˈvɪljən/ *n.* 展馆,文体馆

e. g.　They're looking round the Russian Pavilion.

　　　　他们正在俄罗斯馆那儿参观。

professional　/prəˈfeʃənl/　*adj.* 职业的,专业的;内行的,有经验的

e. g.　She is a professional actress.

　　　　她是职业演员。

prow　/praʊ/　*n.* 船头

e. g.　Jack yelled with open arms on the prow.

　　　　杰克站在船头振臂高呼。

refresh　/rɪˈfreʃ/　*vt.* 使恢复,使振作

e. g.　I think I'll just refresh myself with a cup of tea before I go to meet the children.

　　　　我想在见孩子们之前先喝杯茶来恢复一下精神。

residential　/ˌrezɪˈdenʃəl/　*adj.* 住宅的,适于住宅的

e. g.　This is an exclusive white residential area.

　　　　这是一个纯粹的白人居住区。

revive　/rɪˈvaɪv/　*vt.* 恢复,苏醒

e. g.　The fresh air soon revived him.

　　　　新鲜空气很快使他振作过来。

rural　/ˈrʊərəl/　*adj.* 乡村的,农村的

e. g.　The disease occurs most frequently in rural areas.

　　　　这种疾病多见于农村地区。

self-absorbed　/selfəbˈsɔːbd/　*adj.* 热衷于自己想法的,自恋的

e. g.　He's too self-absorbed to care about us.

　　　　他只顾自己,不关心我们。

showcase　/ˈʃəʊkeɪs/　*n.* (商店或博物馆等的)玻璃陈列柜

e. g.　The thieves smashed the showcase and stole the vase.

　　　　盗贼打碎了玻璃陈列柜并偷走了花瓶。

technical　/ˈteknɪkəl/　*adj.* 技术的;艺术的

e. g.　Your thesis wouldn't get across if you used too many technical terms in it.

　　　　如果你用了过多的专业术语,你的论文就不会被人理解。

tense　/tens/　*n.* 〈语〉(动词的)时态

e. g.　The tense used is decided by the subject.

　　　　所用的时态取决于主语。

theme　/θiːm/　*n.* 主题,主旨

e. g.　Waterfalls are from very early times a favourite theme for the painter.

　　　　从很早时候起,瀑布就是画家所喜爱的题材。

urbanization　/ˌɜːbənɪˈzeɪʃən/　*n.* 都市化

e. g.　Along with the rapid spread of urbanization has come the prolific growth of huge

　　　　slums and shantytowns.

　　　　在城市化迅速发展的同时,贫民区的数目也不断增长。

Phrases and Expressions

as much as possible 尽可能

e. g. I try to ward off fatigue by resting as much as possible.

为了防止疲劳，我尽可能多休息。

as regards 关于，至于

e. g. As regards the education of young children, Madame Montessori's methods seem to me full of wisdom.

关于幼儿的教育，在我看来，蒙台梭利夫人的方法是充满了智慧的。

as well 也，还有

e. g. This is true of management as well as of workers.

很多管理人员和工人都是这种情况。

be engaged in 从事于

e. g. He is engaged in the research into the packaging of a new product line.

他从事于新产品系列包装的研究。

concentrate on 专心于……，把……集中于

e. g. I must concentrate on my work now.

我现在必须集中精力工作。

drop in 顺便拜访

e. g. The Smiths dropped in on some old friends on their vacation trip to New York.

史密斯一家去纽约度假时顺道拜访了一些老朋友。

in accord with 与……一致，融合

e. g. Such statements are not in accord with sound international relations.

这种言论与良好的国际关系不协调。

lay out 陈设，展开；摆出

e. g. She continued to lay out her cards.

她继续摆牌。

rather than （要）……而不……，与其……倒不如……；而不是

e. g. A teacher must be able to manage by implied rather than explicit authority.

一个教师应是一个善于通过启发诱导，而不是粗暴地使用权威的管理者。

struggle for 为……而斗争

e. g. The man was caught up every day in the struggle for survival.

男人每天为生存而奋斗。

Within the four seas, all men are brothers 四海之内皆兄弟

e. g. I enjoy good health so I loyally abide by the ancient Chinese philosophy and this is within the four seas, all men are brothers.

我身体很好，只是遵循中国古代哲学而已：四海之内皆兄弟也。

参考译文

不同的眼睛看世博

1　参观上海世博有什么感受？每个人都会给您不同的答案。

2　**有意义的主题**

3　来自法国的马丁很认同这个主题，他说，"我认为'城市，让生活美好'这个主题很不错，它使我们想到要为更好的生活环境和自然环境而努力奋斗，环境是我关心的问题之一。为我们的子孙留下一个美丽的环境太重要了。"

4　台湾某杂志的主编黄晓石认为这个主题是中国一定要探讨的。"西方很久以前就完成了都市化这一过程，但是中国大量的农村人口意味着对于正在发展的城市还有许多需要完善的地方。这个过程对西方社会来说已经是过去时了，但对我们来说却是进行时。"他认为世博会让各国有机会相互交流，了解城市化进程给西方带来的各种问题，并防止这些问题在中国加剧。

5　各国的展馆主要展现未来人类的生活。"展馆都有同一个主题——环境保护和节约能耗。例如，所有的材料都能可循环再利用，许多展馆使用了手工制作的材料而不是石头和水泥，这极有可能是未来的趋势。"

6　**最喜欢的展馆**

7　简·杰菲克是来自德国的专业摄影师。2008年，他拍摄了仍在建的德国馆和瑞士馆。"要说国家馆中，我最喜欢中国馆和英国馆。他们都很简单，没有过多的技术支持。我也喜欢德国馆，但对于我来说科技性太强了。我还喜欢城市人馆、城市生命馆和地球城市馆这三个主题馆，他们解决了我们正面临的各种如水、大气环境等问题。其它展馆都缺少解决的办法，他们更关注娱乐性而不是实用研究。"

8　来自广东省的邓建伟从事建筑设计的工作。他认为建筑的形式应该和他们各自国家风格相一致。他对沙特阿拉伯馆特别感兴趣。它就像只"月亮船"，但这只巨大的"月亮船"的船首像个碗。内部4-D的屏幕也像个碗。"这种设计完美地体现了它的内部功能。"

9　已定居上海的台湾籍艺术家谢伦表示，他最喜欢智利馆。他还了解到如果可以从上海地面向下，挖过地心，那头便是智利的首都。"我们实际上和其它国家紧密相连。"他很赞成孔子"四海之内皆兄弟"的观点。

10　**大开眼界的事物**

11　谢伦还高度表扬了上海这座城市和中国对修复古建筑所做的努力，他说重工业的撤离和住宅区的改建都是巨大的工程，这不单单需要政府的参与。和很多台湾人一样，谢伦认为上海世博最大的功能就是教育中国人民。"对于一个国家来说，主办世博和奥运会都是很好的机会。东道主国家的人民将变得更开放，改变他们对外面世界的看法。这个世界如此之大但却融为一体，我们每个人不能再自满或者固执己见了。"

12　在香港工作的马克，因出差而顺道到了上海。他说，"建筑太神奇了，我感觉在一座座城市中穿梭，基础设施完善又先进。"他相信大都市，像迅速发展的上海，及传统的世界性大都市，如纽约、伦敦和墨西哥等等，都将成为未来世界的象征。

Exercises

I. Reading Comprehension

Section A

1. D 2. B 3. D 4. C 5. A

Section B

1. Martin thinks that the city means the living conditions and environment we live in, so if we want to have a good life, we should first have a good city with good environment.

2. Because he thinks that Expo allows countries to exchange their experiences so they can understand these problems and prevent them from becoming more acute.

3. Because Chile Pavilion tells us every country is actually close to each other, even though there is a long distance from the surface, so it is in accordance with the opinion of Confucius.

4. Because he thinks that through hosting the World Expo, Chinese people will be more open-minded, and refresh their ideas on the outside world, and will not self-satisfied and self-absorbed.

5. Because the World Expo is just the epitome of every city, and his visiting from one pavilion to another is just like the travel of a city within a city.

Section C

1. (Open-ended)

2. The theme for Shanghai Expo 2010 is "Better City, Better Life". This slogan combines traditional Chinese philosophy and Western utopian ideals for a development strategy based on a balance between rural and urban life. Better City, Better Life—in conjunction with the branding of Shanghai as a "City of Harmony" — strives to portray an identity where technology, science, economic development, human space and culture exist and thrive in harmony.

3. The 2010 Shanghai Expo can bring us some benefits, which can be concluded in 3Cs: Creation, Challenge and Chance. It is known to all that the World Expo had brought us many creations, such as mobile phone, car and electric light. So what new inventions and creations can 2010 Shanghai Expo bring us and how can they change our life? It remains to be seen. We may take advantage of it. The 2010 Shanghai Expo is a challenge to Shanghai. Millions of foreigners will come to Shanghai. How can we organize the best World Expo? Everything we do may matter and lay deep impression on those foreigners. If we perform well in the Expo, our country's status and fame will raise a lot. Besides, 2010 Shanghai Expo is also a great chance. Many countries had a rapid growth in economy after the World

Expo, and their GDP broke through a bottleneck. I think we can also enjoy the economy growth after the 2010 Shanghai World Expo, and many of our 1. 2 billion brothers will have a better life. In that case, 2010 Shanghai Expo will bring us far more benefits than we expected.

II. Vocabulary and Structure

Section A

1. D   2. C   3. A   4. C   5. B   6. B   7. A   8. C   9. D   10. A

Section B

1. It is true that at times the U. S. A. has experienced periods of <u>acute</u> unemployment as well as labor shortages.

   确实,在美国有时会发生严重的失业问题,有时出现劳动力紧缺的现象。

2. Many development strategies now give priority to agricultural and <u>rural</u> development.

   现在,许多发展战略都把农业和农村的发展放在优先地位。

3. We'll soon see how to <u>address</u> the issue of understanding users and their behaviors with products.

   下面我们立即就会谈到如何了解用户及其使用产品时的行为。

4. A true <u>professional</u> could knock my efforts into a cocked hat.

   遇上真正的行家我的工作就相形见绌了。

5. The biggest challenge we have now is how to <u>integrate</u> the development for our bright future with our efforts in relieving the people's hardship.

   目前所面临的最大挑战是如何将美好将来的发展,同解决市民当前的困苦结合起来。

6. The flip side of big discounts is that less money is available to improve academic programs and keep school <u>infrastructure</u> up to date.

   在学费上大打折扣的不利面是,用于改善教学项目和更新学校的基础设施的资金减少了。

7. That rose will <u>revive</u> if you water it.

   只要你浇水,那玫瑰就又会活过来。

8. It took a week for me to <u>refresh</u> myself after I came back from U. S. at last time.

   上次我从美国回来花了一周时间才把自己调整过来。

III. Word Building

1. The policeman ran after a (n) <u>pickpocket</u> and eventually caught him.

   警察跟踪追击一名扒手终于把他逮住了。

2. He's a(n) <u>double-dealer</u>. Don't believe him.

   他是一个两面派,不要相信他。

3. The modernization of traditional Chinese medicines will be taken as a(n) <u>breakthrough</u> point to promote the development of pharmaceutical and related industries.

传统中药的现代化将成为促进医药及相关产业发展的突破口。

4. Do you carry anything that'll remove a(n) <u>bloodstain</u> from a silk shirt?

你们有东西可以去除丝质衬衫上的血迹吗?

5. He overdosed on <u>sleeping-pills</u> and died.

他服用安眠药过量致死。

6. It was this pride, this illusion of independence which was the source of his <u>downfall</u>.

正是这种傲慢,这种独断独行的幻想,导致了他的垮台。

7. <u>Editor-in-chief</u> Steve Forbes said Beckham's move to Real Madrid had made him a bigger international star.

《福布斯》杂志主编史蒂夫·福布斯说,转会皇马使贝克汉姆成为更大牌的国际明星。

8. Without time to relax and have fun, kids can suffer stress just like adults, warn experts — who say as many as one in four youngsters have symptoms of <u>burnout</u>.

专家警告说,如果没有时间放松,没有娱乐,孩子会像大人一样感到有压力,据说每 4 个孩子中就有一个有过于疲劳的症状。

IV. Grammar Focus

1. It is a waste of time for us to argue with him.

2. It is hard for Mary with a secondary education to get a good job.

3. It is a surprise for them to find that television enjoys its greatest competitive advantage on information.

4. It is doubtful for him to finish the difficult task in such short time.

5. It is a great pleasure to meet friends from afar.

V. Translation

1. I think if you want to speak English well, <u>listen to English professional tapes as much as possible.</u>

我认为如果你想说好英语,一定要尽可能多地听专业的英语录音带。

2. <u>As regards the education of young children</u>, Madame Montessori's methods seem to me full of wisdom.

关于幼儿的教育,在我看来,蒙台梭利夫人的方法充满了智慧。

3. Man's great challenge at this moment is <u>to prevent his exit from this planet.</u>

人类当前遇到的最大挑战是防止自己从这个星球上消失。

4. I grabbed the boy by the arm, <u>scaring him half to death.</u>

我一把抓住男孩的手臂,把他吓得半死。

5. The chairman of the International Olympic Committee for the Disabled sent congratulatory telegrams to China, <u>speaking highly of the efforts of the Chinese government and people for the cause of disabled people.</u>

国际残奥会主席发来贺电,高度评价中国政府和中国人民为残疾人事业所作的努力。

VI. Writing

Sample

Congratulation on Graduation

Dear Jack,

Here is my heartfelt congratulation to you on your graduation from Beijing University.

I have good reasons to feel proud of you. I know the Degree of Master meant many years of assiduous study and hard work. Now you have come through with flying colors and high honors. I'm sure your success at this moment is the fore-runner of many others, because you never feel self-sufficient in your study.

I take pride in your achievements and avail myself of this opportunity to send my best wishes for your continued success.

Yours sincerely,

Wang Lin

Notes

A letter of congratulation should be written when you have heard some good news about your colleagues, your boss or your friends. A letter like this implies more than its literal meaning. It works to promote the relationship between you and your receivers. It should sound pleasant and encouraging. Besides, the letter should be specific, concise and timely.

 **Text B**   **Background**

The International Exhibitions Bureau is an inter-governmental organization created to supervise international exhibitions (also known as Expos or World's Fairs) under the jurisdiction of the *Convention Relating to International Exhibitions*. The BIE was established by the *Convention Relating to International Exhibitions*, signed in Paris on 22 November 1928, with the following goals: to oversee the calendar, the bidding, the selection and the organization of World Expositions; to establish a regulatory framework under which Expo organizers and participants may work together under the best conditions. Till now 157 member countries have adhered to the BIE Convention. The BIE regulates two types of expositions: Registered Exhibitions and Recognized Exhibitions.

New Words

amusement /əˈmjuːzmənt/ *n.* 娱乐,乐趣

    e. g.   They made no effort to hide their amusement whenever I produced a packet of sweets from my pocket.

              每当我从口袋里拿出一包糖果时,他们就毫不掩饰地灿烂微笑。

assume /əˈsjuːm/ *v.* 假定,假设,猜想

e. g. Let's assume it to be true.

让我们假定这是真的。

comprehensive /ˌkɒmprɪ'hensɪv/ *adj.* 广泛的,综合的,全面的

e. g. The reporter has made a comprehensive report.

记者已做了全面的报道。

coordinate /kəʊ'ɔːdɪneɪt/ *vt.* 使协调,调和

e. g. Many companies have run into serious troubles when trying to coordinate their sales and promotional efforts.

许多家公司在试图协调销售和促销活动时,遇到了不小的麻烦。

crystal /'krɪstl/ *adj.* 水晶的

e. g. He drank from a crystal wine glass.

他用水晶杯喝葡萄酒。

evolve /ɪ'vɒlv/ *v.* 演变,进化

e. g. I think it is impossible for apes to evolve into something humanlike.

我认为类人猿进化成和人类一样不太可能。

fascinating /'fæsɪneɪtɪŋ/ *adj.* 迷人的,有极大吸引力的

e. g. The TV program is absolutely fascinating, I can't tear my son away.

电视节目实在吸引人,我没法能把儿子拉走。

guarantee /ˌgærən'tiː/ *v.* 担保,保证

e. g. You promised us fuel, but can you guarantee its supply?

你答应给我们提供燃料,但能保证供应吗?

high-minded /'haɪ'maɪndɪd/ *adj.* 高尚的,高洁的

e. g. Such behavior is not consistent with her high-minded principles.

这样的行为与她情操高尚的原则是格格不入的。

outweigh /'aʊtweɪ/ *v.* 超过,大于

e. g. Her need to save money outweighs her desire to spend it on fun.

她省钱的需要比她花钱娱乐的愿望更重要。

overall /'əʊvərɔːl/ *adj.* 总体的,全面的,综合的

e. g. The management has decided to give an overall pay increase.

公司领导决定全面提薪。

participate /pɑː'tɪsɪpeɪt/ *v.* 参加,参与

e. g. It's my great hornor to participate with you in the game.

能和你一起参加比赛我感到很荣幸。

precedent /'presɪdənt/ *n.* 范例,先例

e. g. If he is allowed to do this, it will be a precedent for others.

如果允许他这么做了,就会为别人开先例。

reflect /rɪ'flekt/ *v.* 表达,反映

e. g. Does this decision reflect back your opinion on this matter?

这一决定是否体现你对此事的观点？

revenue /ˈrevɪnjuː/ *n.* 收入，财政收入，收益

   e.g. A government's revenue and expenditure should be balanced.

      政府的财政收入和支出要平衡。

skeptical /ˈskeptɪkəl/ *adj.* 怀疑的

   e.g. He is skeptical about everything.

      他对于一切事都持怀疑的态度。

tangible /ˈtændʒəbl/ *adj.* 明确的，实际的

   e.g. The policy has not yet brought any tangible benefits.

      这项政策还没有带来任何实质性的好处。

timetable /ˈtaɪmˌteɪbl/ *n.* 计划，时间表

   e.g. There are ten English classes listed in the timetable.

      课表上排有 10 节英语课。

unwittingly /ˌʌnˈwɪtɪŋlɪ/ *adv.* 不经意地，不知不觉地

   e.g. He unwittingly reveals his own temperament.

      他不知不觉地泄露了自己的性情。

Phrases and Expressions

as well as 也，又

   e.g. Obviously he is interested in music as well as (in) painting.

      显然他对音乐和绘画都有兴趣。

be regarded as 被认为是，被当做是

   e.g. This should be regarded as an important principle.

      这应该成为一条重要的原则。

be responsible for 为……负责，形成……的原因

   e.g. You'll be responsible for anything wrong.

      出了事唯你是问。

one after another 相继地，依次地

   e.g. The boys jumped into the pool one after another.

      孩子们相继地跳进游泳池里。

originate from 来自，源于

   e.g. The world's great religions originate from Asia.

      世界上的几大宗教起源于亚洲。

参考译文

世　博

1　如果说奥运会对于人类来说是最重要的综合性运动会的话，那起源于 1851 年的世界博览会就可能被认为是集世界经济、文化、科学和技术的"奥林匹克"盛会。世界博览会是由国际展览局协调管理的。国际展览局要负责对参加举办国家的调查，协调世界博览会的时间计划并确保世界博览会的水平。就像奥运会一样，举办国也要经过几轮的投票，选举出来。举办一场成功的博览会意味着一个系统性的工程管理，它对一个国家的综合国力提出了全面的检验。这需要充足的人力、物力和财力资源投入其中，还需要科学成就，科学管理和人员能力达到一定的水平。

2　第一届世博会是在 1851 年伦敦海德公园的水晶宫举行的，题目为"伟大的万国工业作品展"。之所以称呼成"伟大的博览会"是源于维多利亚女王的丈夫阿尔伯特亲王的想法，它是第一届国际产品展览会。就其本身来说，它影响着包括艺术设计、教育、国际贸易及相关产业，乃至旅游等社会方方面面的发展。同时，他也是许多其他国际展览会的范例。

3　在 1851 年的伦敦博览会上，高速的蒸汽牵引机、自动精纺机、高速汽轮船和起重机被展出。之后，新的事物出现在一届又一届的博览会上，令参观者的眼睛应接不暇：1853 年纽约世博会的电梯、1889 年巴黎世博会的埃菲尔铁塔、1904 年圣路易斯世博会的飞机、1939—1940 年纽约世博会的电影摄像机和电视机，以及 1970 年大阪世界博览会展出的美国宇航员从月球带回的月亮石。

4　因此，举办世界博览会的目的既是高尚的又是有商业效益的。它让人类能探索日常生活体验之外的世界——外界的文化、新的技术进步和新的发明。

5　世界博览会最大的吸引力是由参展国参与创造的国家馆。在 2000 年的汉诺威世博会上，参展国家建造他们自己的展馆，其各自的投资达到约 1 300 万元。如果考虑成本的话，政府有时也常常质疑它的参展，因为参展带来的利润也常被认为不会超过成本的投入，实际的好处很难去测量。然而，一项独立的研究表明 2000 年世博会上荷兰展馆花费成本大约 350 万欧元，而据估计其展馆为荷兰经济创造了大约 3 500 万欧元的潜在收益。2010 年的上海世博会，由 40 多个国家参与建造各自的展馆，是数量最多的一年，它吸引了 246 个国家和地区参展，来自国内外的游客达到 7 000 万。世博会的另一个主要功能是娱乐。随着人们的娱乐选择越来越多，世界博览会的娱乐区及其展馆一直处于发展变化中。

6　世界博览会激励和鼓舞着成千上万的来自世界各地的人们表达他们那个时代的希望和梦想，或许，不知不觉中，他们为我们展示了他们那个年代迷人的社会一瞥。

7　随着时代的改变，世界博览会也在适应时代而变。它们继续反映着他们所处时代的商业需求，同时，它们还将展示人们的理想、希望和抱负，尽管这些都处于不断发展变化中。

Exercises

I. Reading Comprehension
1. D   2. C   3. A   4. B   5. C

II. Vocabulary and Structure
1. B   2. D   3. A   4. C   5. D   6. A   7. B   8. C   9. D   10. A

III. Translation

1. Realizing his own limitations, he was skeptical about the chance of running for president of the Student Union.

   由于认识到自己的局限性,他怀疑自己是否有机会竞选学生会主席。

2. It was a concept originated from China, taking into account the fundamental interest of China as a nation and Chinese as a people.

   中国提出来的这个构想,以整个中国和全中华民族的根本利益为出发点。

3. We had intended to talk about work, but unwittingly started to talk about pop music.

   我们本来是要说工作的,但不知不觉就谈开了流行音乐。

4. As society and times change, so will cultural development.

   随着社会和时势的改变,文化也相应地在演变。

5. China possesses enormous quantities of coal and is rich in other minerals as well.

   中国拥有大量煤炭,其他的矿藏也很丰富。

Part V   Time for Fun

参 考 译 文

我 很 高 兴

一个周日学校的老师正在对学生讲让别人高兴的重要性。

"现在,孩子们,"她说:"你们当中有谁让别人高兴过?"

"我,老师,"一个小男孩说:"昨天我就使别人高兴过。"

"做得好。是谁呢?"

"我奶奶。"

"好孩子。现在告诉我们,你是怎样使你奶奶高兴的。"

"是这样的,老师。我昨天去看她,在她那儿呆了三个小时。然后我跟她说:'奶奶,我要回家了。'她说:'啊,我很高兴!'"

Unit 4

The Prediction of the Future

Part I   Teaching Objectives

* Listening & Speaking:

Help students to be familiar with the topic of talking about the prediction of the future and to memorize useful expressions.

* Words & Expressions:

Grasp some new words and expressions, such as *assure*, *allay*, *ponder erupt*, *look forward to*, *in response to*, *rely on*, *scared out of one's wits*, *sooner or later* and so on.

* Grammar:

How to write a sentence using *an attribute*.

* Writing:

Understand and write *a certificate*

Part II   Listening——Prediction

New Words

confuse   /kən'fjuːz/   *v.* 使困惑,把……弄糊涂

    e. g.   They asked so many questions that they confused me.

        他们问了许多问题,都把我弄糊涂了。

doctor   /'dɒktə/   *vt.* 对……做手脚,作弊

    e. g.   They doctored her fruit juice with vodka and she got drunk.

        他们在她喝的果汁里搀入了伏特加酒致使她酩酊大醉。

doomsday   /'duːmzdeɪ/   *n.* 世界末日

    e. g.   In fact, this is one of the best known doomsday prophecies.

事实上,这是最著名的世界末日预言之一。

extinct /ɪksˈtɪŋkt/ *adj.* 灭绝的,绝种的

e. g.　Dinosaurs have been extinct for millions of years.

恐龙绝种已有几百万年了。

fabulous /ˈfæbjʊləs/ *adj.* 极好的,绝妙的

e. g.　We had a fabulous time at the party.

我们在晚会上玩得很痛快。

immune /ɪˈmjuːn/ *adj.* 免疫的,有免疫力的;不受影响的

e. g.　I am immune from the disease, for I had it once.

我对这病有免疫力,因为我已得过一次了。

immunity /ɪˈmjuːnətɪ/ *n.* 免疫力

e. g.　Once you have had a cold you build up immunity to that particular virus.

你一旦患上感冒,你的身体就会产生对付那种病毒的免疫力。

Mayan /ˈmaɪən/ *n.* 玛雅人

e. g.　Originally inhabited by the Mayan people, Belize saw its first European settlers around 1638.

贝里斯原住民为马雅人,首批欧洲移民在一六三八年前后迁移于此。

moron /ˈmɔːrɒn/ *n.* 傻瓜

e. g.　They're a load of morons.

他们是一群笨蛋。

prophecy /ˈprɒfɪsɪ/ *n.* 预言

e. g.　No prophecy can be expected to go on all fours.

凡预言皆不能指望其完全应验。

remedy /ˈremɪdɪ/ *n.* 治疗方法

e. g.　This doctor often uses herbal remedies.

这个医生常用草药治病。

shuttle /ˈʃʌtl/ *n.* 航天飞机

e. g.　Because of the shuttle, space flight has become an international commercial enterprise.

随着航天飞机的出现,空间飞行已经成为一个国际性的以赢利为目的的事业。

vehicle /ˈviːɪkl/ *n.* 交通工具,车辆

e. g.　No vehicles are permitted into the park.

公园内禁止任何车辆进入。

Phrases and Expressions

doctor up　篡改,伪造

e. g.　He was accused of doctoring up the figures.

他被指控篡改数字。

hook up　扣住,以钩钩住

 e. g. You can hook up the dress at the back.

    你可以把女衫从背后扣住。

keep your nose out（**of**）　别管闲事

 e. g. I'd prefer you to keep your nose out of my business！

    我宁愿你别问我的事！

make sense　有道理,有意义,讲得通

 e. g. This sentence doesn't make sense.

    这个句子不通。

 One

 Listen to the CD and mark T for True or F for False according to the dialogue.

1. T 2. F 3. T 4. F 5. F

Script

 Woman：Do you believe in UFOs?

  Man：Sure. A UFO is just a space vehicle from another planet. If you think about it, our space shuttles are UFOs.

 Woman：I've never thought about it like that before.

  Man：I've seen photos of UFOs in America before, but they've all looked doctored up.

 Woman：Do you think that there's life on other planets?

  Man：I think there must be.

 Woman：Why is that?

  Man：I don't think it would make sense if we were the only beings in this whole world. The world is just far too big for that.

 Woman：Do you think that there's intelligent life trying to contact us?

  Man：No, but we're trying to contact them.

 Woman：I suppose you're right.

  Man：I think that countries are working hard to find a planet that we can live on in the future, so when global warming destroys this planet, humankind will not become extinct.

 Woman：Do you really think that global warming will destroy Earth some day?

  Man：There's a lot of evidence that suggest it will, but I don't think it's going to happen any time soon.

Dialogue **Two**

 Listen to the CD and answer the following questions with the information you hear.

1. Whose friend is a scientist??

The girl's friend is a scientist.

2. What is the scientist studying?

He is studying *2010: the prophecies of Mayan*.

3. Did the scientist win the Nobel Prize?

No, he didn't.

4. What is Jake jealous about?

Jake is jealous about the scientist whom the girl would be with rather than Jake.

5. Does Jake still like the girl?

Yes, he does.

Script

Jake: Hey, look at you now. You are just fabulous. I heard you hooked up a rich idiot.

Maggie: He is a real scientist, moron. But he has a luxurious car.

Jake: A stupid science man with a luxurious car. How ironic! So what is he studying now? Will he win the Nobel Prize this year, Mrs. Nobel?

Maggie: His subject now is *2012: The Prophecies of Mayan*. How does that sound to you?

Jake: The movie is really getting on my nerves. Thanks to my shake-proof shoes, I can still stand and sit here. Can he fly a plane?

Maggie: Haha, funny! I mean it. That's his job. Why are you here today? Can you just keep your nose out of my life? I have already moved on.

Jake: I am jealous. You look happier. And when it's the Doomsday, you are with him rather than me.

Maggie: Jake, you are a great guy. But we are over. So be it. You will be with a perfect woman on the judgment day.

Jake: I don't have enough time for that. I have to learn how to fly a plane. When your science man can't save you, I will be the hero.

Maggie: Make time, for God's sake. It's his job to worry about 2012, not yours. See? That's our problem, actually, yours. But you just keep ignoring.

Spot Dictation

---

1. she predicted that already came true

2. communicating with the spirits of dead people

3. she made some seriously crazy claims as well

4. World War III would start in November, 2012

5. If these predictions come true over the next few years

<h1 align="center">Part III   Speaking——Future Life</h1>

Useful Expressions About the Future

What do you want to do in the future?

I don't feel like daydreaming right now.

It's not daydreaming.

Our life is uncertain, and things change quickly.

I don't know what will happen tomorrow.

Do you think that we'll one day be able to travel to another planet for a vacation?

Hopefully one day, we'll live in an interplanetary society.

Do you believe in UFOs?

I think there must be.

I don't think it's going to happen any time soon.

It would be wonderful.

Few people know where next discoveries will be made.

In the future, that could be possible.

When it's the Apocalypse, I stay with you.

You mean something's going to happen to the clover.

Global catastrophe will take place that will affect life on the entire planet.

The end of the world will happen on December 21, 2012.

Pair Work

Sample

Tom: Do you know well about space?

Kelly: No, we actually know relatively little about space and the cosmos.

Tom: Do you think that we'll one day be able to travel to another planet for a vacation?

Kelly: I suppose we could actually live on a planet outside of the Milky Way.

Tom: Do you think we'll ever get to meet an alien from the outer space?

Kelly: I hope not. I think they would be a threat to those of us that lived on Earth.

Tom: you're so old-fashioned. That's what people used to think about people from another country!

Tom: Point taken. Hopefully one day, we'll live in an interplanetary society.

Role-play

Sample

Peter: If we live in the next 100 years.

Nancy: Why do you think so?

Peter: Because I am longing for the future, it must be very beautiful.

Nancy: But the future is difficult to predict, perhaps it would be very bad.

 Peter: I don't think so; I think that science and technology must be very rich.

Nancy: Maybe, and what's your to-be future?

 Peter: I think there will still be intelligent robots in the future.

Nancy: Just like the science fiction movies?

 Peter: Yes, and it can help us do a lot of things.

Nancy: But then man will eventually be produced for robot, and lose their own labor ability.

 Peter: No, I think people will have special forms of exercise.

Nancy: Well, if so maybe people will live longer.

 Peter: Yes, they are likely to an alien living.

Nancy: Perhaps Mars is a good choice.

 Peter: Yes.

Nancy: Well, anyway, you want to say that all of the future is to develop into the direction of good.

 Peter: Yeah, but it will also have something bad.

Nancy: All have to be verified in the future.

Part IV   Reading

Text A   Background

1. The National Aeronautics and Space Administration (NASA) is an Executive Branch agency of the United States government, responsible for the nation's civilian space program and aeronautics and aerospace research. Since February 2006, NASA's self-described mission statement is to "pioneer the future in space exploration, scientific discovery and aeronautics research."

2. The European Organization for Nuclear Research, known as CERN, is the world's largest particle physics laboratory, established in 1954. The organization has twenty European member states, and is the workplace of approximately 2,600 full-time employees, as well as some 7,931 scientists and engineers representing 580 universities and research facilities and 80 nationalities. CERN's main function is to provide the particle accelerators and other infrastructure needed for high-energy physics research. Numerous experiments have been constructed at CERN by international collaborations to make use of them. It is also the birthplace of the World Wide Web.

3. YouTube is a video-sharing website on which users can upload, share, and view videos, created by three former Paypal employees in February, 2005. The company uses Adobe

Flash Video technology to display a wide variety of user-generated video content, including movie clips, TV clips, and music videos, as well as amateur content such as video blogging and short original videos. Most of the content on YouTube has been uploaded by individuals, although media corporations including CBS, BBC, Vevo and other organizations offer some of their material via the site, as part of the YouTube partnership program.

4. *Sky & Telescope* (S&T) is a monthly American magazine covering all aspects of amateur astronomy. The articles are intended for the informed lay reader and include detailed discussions of current discoveries, frequently participated by scientists. The magazine is illustrated in full color, with both amateur and professional photography of celestial sights, as well as tables and charts of upcoming celestial events. The magazine played an important role in the dissemination of knowledge about telescope making.

New Words

aeronautics /ˌeərəˈnɔːtɪks/　*n.* 航空(学)

　　e. g.　Aeronautics enables us to overcome great distances.
　　　　　航空学使我们能征服远距离。

align /əˈlaɪn/　*vt.* 使成一线,排整齐

　　e. g.　Align the ruler and the middle of the paper.
　　　　　使尺子与纸张的中部成一条直线。

allay /əˈleɪ/　*v.* 减轻,缓和

　　e. g.　They are trying to allay public fears about the spread of the disease.
　　　　　他们正竭力减轻公众对这种疾病传播的恐惧。

apocalypse /əˈpɒkəlɪps/　*n.* (尤指世界末日的)启示

　　e. g.　The famous 14th Century French prophet Nostrademus had predicted that the Apocalypse would come in July 1999.
　　　　　14 世纪法国著名的预言家诺查丹玛斯曾预言人类末日将在公元 1999 年 7 月来临。

assure /əˈʃʊə/　*v.* 使相信,使确信

　　e. g.　Nothing will assure permanent happiness to me.
　　　　　没有什么能保证我永久的幸福。

astronomy /əsˈtrɒnəmɪ/　*n.* 天文学

　　e. g.　Mathematics is connected with astronomy.
　　　　　数学与天文学有联系。

blowout /ˈbləʊˈaʊt/　*n.* 美餐,盛宴,大型社交活动;(车胎)爆裂,喷出

　　e. g.　He had a blowout and crashed his car.
　　　　　他的车胎爆裂,汽车撞坏了。

blue-ribbon /ˈbluːˈrɪbən/　*adj.* 头等的,第一流的

　　e. g.　Many buyers compete for the blue-ribbon goods.

许多买主争购第一流的货物。

disastrous /dɪˈzɑːstrəs/ *adj.* 灾难性的；极坏的，悲惨的

   e.g. Carelessness in driving often results in disastrous accidents.

       驾驶不慎常带来不幸的意外。

erupt /ɪˈrʌpt/ *vi.* （火山）爆发；（岩浆，烟等）喷出

   e.g. An active volcano may erupt at any time.

       活火山随时可能喷发。

folly /ˈfɒlɪ/ *n.* 蠢笨；愚蠢的行为、思想或做法

   e.g. He has given up youthful follies.

       他不再做年轻人的荒唐事了。

habitually /həˈbɪtjʊəl/ *adv.* 习惯地，惯常地

   e.g. Do you habitually use display screen equipment as a significant part of your job?

       你工作中经常使用屏幕显示设备吗？

magnetic /mæɡˈnetɪk/ *adj.* 有磁性的

   e.g. The iron has lost its magnetic force.

       这块铁已失去了磁力。

mortgage /ˈmɔːɡɪdʒ/ *n.* 抵押贷款

   e.g. The bank refused to accept any mortgage on land.

       银行拒绝接受任何土地抵押。

ponder /ˈpɒndə/ *v.* 考虑，深思熟虑

   e.g. We pondered whether to tell him.

       我们考虑是否要告诉他。

rogue /rəʊɡ/ *adj.* 行为失常的，暴力的

   e.g. He carefully drew a bead on the rogue elephant and shot it dead.

       他用枪仔细瞄准一头凶猛而离群的野象，开枪把它打死了。

speculation /ˌspekjʊˈleɪʃən/ *n.* 思考，思索；猜测，推测

   e.g. He was dropped from the team amid speculation that he was seriously ill.

       在一片以为他得了重病的猜测中，他被队里除名了。

sunspot /ˈsʌnspɒt/ *n.* 太阳黑子

   e.g. This is an intriguing theory that droughts tie in with the sunspot.

       这是一个关于干旱与太阳黑子活动周期有关的令人感到有趣的理论。

variation /ˌveərɪˈeɪʃən/ *n.* 变化，变异

   e.g. Prices are subject to variation.

       价格可以变动。

volcano /vɒlˈkeɪnəʊ/ *n.* 火山

   e.g. The eruption of a volcano is spontaneous.

       火山的爆发是自发的。

wit /wɪt/ *n.* 风趣；心智，才智

e. g.   He is a boy of quick wits.

他是一个机敏的孩子。

Phrases and Expressions

in response to   对……做出反应

e. g.   The quick recovery was truly in response to medication.

这次迅速康复确实是对药物治疗的反应。

look forward to   期望, 盼望

e. g.   We look forward to the return of spring.

我们期待着春天的到来。

put somebody to sleep   终止某人的生命

e. g.   Oh, I had to put my dog to sleep. He suffered too much from his sickness.

我只好让我的狗安息, 它饱受太多的病痛的折磨!

rely on   依赖, 依靠

e. g.   Don't rely on going abroad for our holiday—we may not be able to afford it.

不要指望去国外度假, 我们可能负担不起费用。

be scared out of one's wits   吓得要死

e. g.   I was scared out of my wits at the thought of having to make a speech.

我一想到要去演讲就吓得要死。

sooner or later   迟早

e. g.   If you drive like that, sooner or later you'll have an accident.

你如果那样开车, 迟早会出事的。

to begin with   以……开始, 从……开始

e. g.   You are wrong about the facts to begin with.

首先你把事实都没弄对。

参 考 译 文

末日来了? 或不在 2012 年到来

1 美国国家航空航天局上周表示, 世界并未走向末日, 至少短时间内不会。欧洲核子研究中心去年也曾发表过同样的声明, 我想这对我们当中那些动不动就心神不宁的人来说是个好消息。这类世界一流的科学权威机构双双向我们保证: 万事皆安。这种事你多久赶上过一回?

2   从另一方说, 如果你正盼着用还房贷的钱去休假来最后享受一番, 这么做有点令人郁闷。

3   欧洲核子研究中心的声明试图消除人们对新建成的大型强子对撞机在实验时将产生一个黑洞, 进而吞噬整个地球的恐慌。美国国家航空航天局在其官网上发了几次消息, 并在 YouTube 上发了视频, 就是为了回应人们对世界将在 2012 年 12 月 21 日终结的担心。

4 然而,这只是世界毁灭的一个版本而已。其他的版本还有名为 Nibiru 的行星撞向地球或者地球磁场翻转等灾难。

5 "大多数关于 2012 年的断言都来自某种臆想,异想天开的伪科学,对天文学的无知,或者一定程度的类似《活死人之夜》的妄想,"洛杉矶里菲斯天文台主任、古天文学专家埃德·克虏伯在 11 月号的《天空和望远镜》杂志上撰文如是写道。但戴维·莫里森认为,这种趋势太过火了,莫里森是英国国家航空航天局位于加利福尼亚莫非特基地埃姆斯研究中心的一位天文学家。就是他代表航天局在 YouTube 上发布相关视频的。莫里森博士说,他曾一天收到大约 20 封信和电子邮件,有的来自遥远的印度,都是些被吓得魂不附体的人发来的。莫里森举例说,在一封电子邮件里,一名妇女正在犹豫是否应该杀死她的女儿和尚未出生的孩子,然后自杀。在另外一封信中,一名女子正在考虑是否让她的狗安乐死,以避免在 2012 年遭劫。

6 大多数科学家说,如果你要担心,就去担心全球气候变化,飘忽不定的小行星或者核战争吧。但如果你担忧关于古代预言的各种猜测,莫里森博士和其他一些学者认为你应该了解以下几点:

7 首先,天文学家一致认为,太阳和银河系中心点在天空中连成一线没什么特别,这种事情每年的 12 月份都会发生,没什么自然后果。而且太阳和银河系中心点即使在 2012 年也不会精确地连成一线。

8 其次,即便真的有另外一颗行星正向我们撞来,那么我们每个人现在都应该能看到了。至于那些猛烈的太阳风暴,天文学家们接着说,在 2013 年之前不会发生下一个太阳黑子的大爆发期,而且强度也相对较弱。

9 实际上,地质学上的灾变预言或许更令人信服。加利福尼亚此前曾发生过大地震,今后也可能还会有。这些地震可能像电影中演的那样摧毁洛杉矶。黄石国家公园里的火山可能迟早会带着灾难性的自然威力再次喷发。我们和我们拥有的一切实际上非常脆弱,都只是地球的匆匆过客。但即使是这样的话,"迟早"也意味着有数亿年的时间,其间会有大量的前兆。

10 因此,还是接着还房贷吧。

Exercises

I. Reading Comprehension
Section A
1. C 2. D 3. A 4. B 5. C

Section B
1. It refers that there are many different versions of doomsday's coming, namely the world will end on Dec, 2012.

2. Most of claim relies on wishful thinking, wild unscientific folly, ignorance of astronomy and a level of paranoia of "Night of the Living Dead".

3. First, we should know that there is nothing special about the Sun and the Galactic center aligning in the sky, and the Sun and the Galactic center will not exactly coincide in 2012; secondly, the next sunspot maximum will not happen until 2013, and will be on mild side; thirdly, we should know that geological apocalypse might happen.

4. Because geological apocalypse have ever happened, and would happen again.

5. Because, compared with this cataclysmic force, human's power and ability are too limited; and compared with the history of the Earth, human's is too short.

Section C

1. Maybe doomsday is coming in the future, but its happening world be in hundreds of years, so we needn't worry about it.

2. Of course, I will not believe it. If it does happen, there must be some signs that can be detected by humans.

3. Because the Earth we live on has been damaged by our human, and the situation we live in is getting worse; we should care about our Earth.

II. Vocabulary and Structure
Section A
1. B 2. D 3. A 4. C 5. B 6. A 7. B 8. D 9. C 10. D

Section B

1. Lest anyone should think it strange, let me <u>assure</u> you that it is quite true.
我向你们保证那是真事，以免有人觉得奇怪。

2. Nearby, there may be a number of racks on which <u>magnetic</u> tapes and discs are stored.
附近可能有许多机架，这里存放着磁带和磁盘。

3. The wisdom of Chinese people will <u>erupt</u> like a volcano.
中国人的智慧就会像火山一样释放出来。

4. This is the <u>blue-ribbon</u> event of the season for the company.
这是公司这一季中最重要的事情。

5. It is worthwhile to <u>ponder</u> the reasons to copy the famous brand.
认真思考一下仿冒知名品牌的原因是有价值的。

6. Even when times were bad, there was always enough money for a good <u>blowout</u> at Christmas.
即使是在艰难的岁月，人们也有足够钱在圣诞节时吃上丰盛的一餐。

7. She said she was able to <u>allay</u> his fears and received her father's support.
她说她最终会打消父亲的忧虑，并得到了他的支持。

8. Her investment had <u>disastrous</u> consequences: she lost everything she owned.
她的投资结果很惨，血本无归。

III. Word Building

1. He is in a state of deep <u>depression</u> on account of his failure to pass the examination.
   他因考试不及格深感沮丧。

2. Tom showed sound <u>judgement</u> on deciding not to invest in the project.
   汤姆决定不对那项工程投资，这说明他的判断力很强。

3. A final <u>consideration</u>, especially in the case of business products, is the cultural differences between organizations in which the users are employed.
   最后要考虑一点，尤其在商业产品中是用户所在组织之间的文化差异。

4. He is under a <u>commitment</u> to finish the task by May 1.
   他应允五月一日以前完成这项工作。

5. Cruises on the Thames in London have become an annual <u>attraction</u>.
   在伦敦泰晤士河上的巡航已成为一年一度的引人注目的事。

6. He extended an <u>invitation</u> to the evening party to the entire class.
   他向全班同学发出邀请，参加晚会。

7. Because of my heavy cold, I wonder if I can postpone my <u>appointment</u> till some other time.
   由于我得了重感冒，不知是否可以把我的约会时间缓延几天。

8. Until 1300 the Arab <u>civilization</u> was dynamic and its learning became widespread.
   阿拉伯文明直到 1300 年还充满活力，它的学术传播四方。

IV. Grammar Focus

1. Is there anyone in your department whose father is a painter?

2. I left my keys at home, which was a pretty silly thing to do.

3. The bookstore where his sister works is the largest one in Taiyuan, Shanxi Province.

4. He will always remember the day when his mother returned from America.

5. I couldn't tell you who it was that revealed the secret.

V. Translation

1. We're <u>prepared to meet your claim for the loss</u> according to the contract.
   我们准备按合同赔偿贵方的损失。

2. For people <u>who relied on agriculture for their living</u>, this was a serious matter.
   对于靠务农为生的人来说，这是个很大的缺陷。

3. <u>Adults would be scared out of their wits</u> by some of the films on television as well as children.
   成年人也会被电视上的有些电影吓个半死，更不用说孩子了。

4. We have adopted a serial of safe measures <u>for assuring that the meeting can be held successfully</u>.
   为了保证会议顺利进行，我们已经采取了一系列安全措施。

5. If one is without hope, <u>one has nothing to look forward to in life</u>.
   如果一个人心中没有希望，他的人生中就没有什么东西值得期待。

VI. Writing

Sample

Graduation Certificate

This is to certify that Zhang Hui, male, born on May 2, 1988, was a student of computer application major from the Department of Computer Science & Engineering and, having completed the four years' courses from September, 2006 to July, 2010 and fulfilled all the requirements prescribed by the Department, graduated from Nanjing University in July, 2010.

(Signature)

Nanjing University

July, 2010

Notes

A certificate is any official document that affirms some facts. When writing a certificate, always make sure you include accurate information. A certificate includes three parts:

    a. Heading: "Certificate of Educational Background", "Graduation Certificate" or "Health Certificate". It may also have a headline.

    b. Text: it is the body, usually beginning with "This is to certify that..."

    c. Signature and Date

 **Text B**   **Background**

1. Julius Sextus

Sextus Julius Africanus (c. 160—c. 240) was a Christian traveler and historian of the late 2nd and early 3rd century AD. He is important, chiefly because of his influence on Eusebius, on all the later writers of Church history among the Fathers, and on the whole Greek school of chroniclers.

2. Arthur C. Clark

Sir Arthur Charles Clarke, (16 December 1917—19 March 2008) was a British science fiction author, inventor and futurist most famous for the novel *2001: A Space Odyssey*, written in parallel with the script for the eponymous film, co-written with film-director Stanley Kubrick, and as a host and commentator in the British television series Mysterious World. For many years, Robert A. Heinlein, Isaac Asimov, and Arthur C. Clarke were known as the "Big Three" of science fiction.

3. *Wireless World*

Wireless World was the pre-eminent British magazine for radio and electronics enthusiasts. It was one of the very few "informal" journals which were tolerated as a professional expense. It was the first journal written especially for wireless communication and circulated largely among engineers and operators. It also aimed at home constructors, publishing articles on building radio receivers.

4. *The View from Serendip*

The Collected Stories of Arthur C. Clarke, first published in 2001, is a collection of almost every science fiction story, shorter than novel in length that Arthur C. Clarke has ever published: with 114 in all arranged in order of publication, *Travel by Wire*! in 1937 through to *Improving the Neighborhood* in 1999. The story *Improving the Neighborhood* has the distinction of being the first fiction published in the journal *Nature*. The titles *Venture to the Moon* and *The Other Side of the Sky* are not stories but the series titles for groups of six interconnected stories, each story with its own title. This collection is missing the story *When the Twerms Came* which appears in his other collections, *More Than One Universe* and *The View from Serendip*. This edition contains a foreword by Clarke written in 2000, where he speculates on the science fiction genre in relation to the concept of short stories. Furthermore, many of the stories have a short introduction about its publication history or its literary nature.

New Words

confound /kən'faʊnd/ *v.* 证明……有错

    e.g. He is trying his best to confound the argument of his opponent.
        他正尽力证明他对手的观点是错误的。

dislocate /'dɪsləʊkeɪt/ *v.* 使(交通、事务等)混乱

    e.g. The traffic was badly dislocated by the heavy fall of snow.
        大雪使得交通非常混乱。

draw /drɔː/ *v.* 移动,来临

    e.g. The National Day is drawing closer.
        国庆节快到了。

echo /'ekəʊ/ *v.* 随声附和,重复 *n.* 回声,共鸣

    e.g. I should like to echo the words of the previous speaker.
        我想重复前面一位发言者的话。

entrepreneur /ˌɒntrəprə'nɜː/ *n.* 创业者,企业家

    e.g. The entrepreneur takes business risks in the hope of making a profit.
        企业家为追求利润而冒险。

fiction /'fɪkʃən/ *n.* 小说

    e.g. He prefers light fictions to serious novels.
        比起严肃小说来,他更为喜欢轻松的小说。

frustrating /frʌ'streɪtɪŋ/ *adj.* 令人沮丧的,令人挫败的

    e.g. It was a demeaning and ultimately frustrating experience.
        那是一次有失颜面并且令人沮丧至极的经历。

geostationary /ˌdʒiːəʊ'steɪʃənərɪ/ *adj.* 与地球位置相对不变的

    e.g. We can set a satellite in geostationary orbit to watch the movement of the Earth.

我们可以在与地球位置相对不变的轨道上运行一颗卫星来监测地球的运动。

gloomy /ˈɡluːmɪ/ *adj.* 令人沮丧的；前景暗淡的

    e. g.   Chances of getting the job were slim, so the young man felt gloomy about the future.

             得到这份工作的机会很小，所以这位青年人感到前途渺茫。

ingenuity /ˌɪndʒɪˈnjuː(ː)ɪtɪ/ *n.* 独创力

    e. g.   The boy showed ingenuity in making toys.

             那个小男孩做玩具很有创造力。

innovation /ˌɪnəʊˈveɪʃən/ *n.* 新发明，新方法；改革，创新

    e. g.   Farmers are introducing innovations to increase the productivity.

             农民们正引进提高生产力的新方法。

jetpack /ˈdʒetpæk/ *n.* 喷气飞行器

    e. g.   This is a new type of jetpack.

             这是一种新型的喷气飞行器。

limb /lɪm/ *n.* 肢，臂，膀，翅膀；大树枝，主枝

    e. g.   He was very tall with long limbs.

             他个儿很高，四肢很长。

magnetically /mæɡˈnetɪklɪ/ *adv.* 有磁力地，有魅力地

    e. g.   Foreign friends were magnetically By Chinese flower arrangement on a handsome model.

             外国友人被造型美观的中国插花深深吸引住了。

optimism /ˈɒptɪmɪzəm/ *n.* 乐观，乐观主义

    e. g.   Optimism made him alive through the hard days.

             乐观主义使他在艰难的岁月里活了下来。

patent /ˈpeɪtənt/ *n.* 专利，专利权

    e. g.   The patent runs out in three years' time.

             这项专利期限为三年。

permanent /ˈpɜːmənənt/ *adj.* 永久的，固定的，稳定的

    e. g.   He is one of our permanent employees.

             他是我们的终身雇员之一。

recall /rɪˈkɔːl/ *v.* 唤回，召回

    e. g.   I can't recall where he lives.

             我想不起他住哪里了。

sufficiently /səˈfɪʃəntlɪ/ *adv.* 充足地，足够地

    e. g.   The function of the stomach is to digest food sufficiently to enable it to pass into the intestine.

             胃的功能是充分消化食物，以便让其进入肠道。

underestimate /ˌʌndərˈestɪmeɪt/ *v.* 对……低估，轻视

e. g.   I underestimate the distance, and am exhausted.

没想到这么远，我可累坏了。

venture   /ˈventʃə/   *v.* 冒险

e. g.   Nothing ventured, nothing gained.

不入虎穴，焉得虎子。

Phrases and Expressions

benefit from   从……中获益

e. g.   He thought he would benefit from going to school.

他认为上学对他有好处。

go out on the limb   冒险

e. g.   You're on the right track and you can make money if you are willing to go out on the limb.

你处在正道上，如果愿意冒险就有机会获得收入。

long since   从前，很久以前

e. g.   He has long since been recognized as a great playwright.

他早就被公认为伟大的剧作家了。

on the other hand   另一方面来说

e. g.   Most software, on the other hand, doesn't know or care who is using it.

另一方面，大多数软件不知道或不关心是谁在使用它。

print off   复印，印刷

e. g.   How many copies do you want to be printed off?

你想付印多少份？

参 考 译 文

科技预言大都落空

1   这是一个预言流行的季节，因此我也要勇敢地对"信息时代"作出一个预测：绝大多数关于接下来一年的科技预言都不会成为现实。我们对科技创新如何孕育而生了解得越多，就越知道技术进步的道路不会笔直。

2   公元 10 年，古罗马工程师萨莱乌斯·弗朗提努曾说道："科学发明已经达到了极限，我看不到进一步突破的希望。"后来，这个悲观言论得到过很多人的共鸣，其中包括美国专利局委员查理斯·杜尔，他在 1899 年说："所有可以发明的东西都已经被发明出来了。"

3   值得反思的是，尤其是在生活黯淡的年份，比如快要结束的这一年，上面这些预言其实完全说反了：我们发明得越多，就会有更多的发明。知识是会自己成长的。

4   一些最差劲科技预言证明：当谈到科技进步时，我们要乐观才对。这些差劲的预言包括比尔·盖茨在 1981 年说"个人电脑的内存需要将不会超过 637kb，因此 640kb 对任何人来说都应该足够了"。英国企业家艾伦·苏格爵士在 2005 年说"明年圣诞节的时候，

iPod 就已经死翘翘了。"

5   有时候,科技预言没有应验是因为过于乐观——比如我们现在还没有乘坐喷射飞行器去旅行——但更多时候,预言失灵是因为我们低估了发明家的能力。

6   科幻作家亚瑟·克拉克曾揭示过"三大预测定律",反映出他对科技进步的乐观态度:定律一:如果一个年高德劭的杰出科学家认为一件事情有可能发生,他几乎总是正确的;当他认为什么事情不可能发生,那他很可能是错的。定律二:发现可能的极限的唯一办法是探索极限以外不可能的东西。定律三:任何非常先进的技术,初看都与魔法无异。预测未来的技术发展非常难,但克拉克是个例外。在 1945 年的《无线电世界》杂志上,他提议将一系列卫星发射到地球同步轨道上,从而形成一个全球通讯网络。在 1977 年发表的科幻小说《塞伦迪普景观》中,克拉克预言了互联网的出现:"在家里就能通过简单的计算机输入键盘和电视显示器立刻进入全球所有的大图书馆……需要永久保存阅读的资料可以通过一种复制机器马上打印出来——或以磁性记录方式保存在家庭存储系统之中。"在同一本书中,克拉克还预言了电子邮件和在线新闻的出现。

7   随着新一年的到来,企业家和技术专家正想尽办法征服科技预言。或者正如计算机科学家艾伦·凯所说:"预测未来的最佳方式就是创造未来。"一年前,人们一定很难预测到社交网站会成为新的大众媒体,谷歌(Google)会成为一种手机品牌。当几乎每个行业都被日新月异的变化搞得支离破碎时,技术进步也会让人感觉摸不着头脑。但从另一方面来说,我们都受益于这些技术进步,其中包括消费者所能获得的无穷无尽的选择权。

Exercises

I. Reading Comprehension
1. D   2. A   3. B   4. C   5. D

II. Vocabulary and Structure
1. C   2. D   3. B   4. A   5. C   6. B   7. C   8. D   9. A   10. C

III. Translation

1. Although the military training was really hard, it strengthened my will <u>and I've benefited a lot from it.</u>
尽管军训的确艰苦,但磨练了意志,我从中受益很大。

2. I hope you can tell me <u>why you always have to echo his opinions like that.</u>
我希望你能告诉我为什么你总是那样附和他的意见?

3. Some leaders have wisely noticed that <u>the best way to learn about the outside world is to engage with it.</u>
一些领导人已经明智地注意到,了解世界的最好办法就是接触世界。

4. If he might do as he likes, <u>he would make a lot of troubles.</u>
如果他想干什么就干什么的话,他会弄出许多麻烦来。

5. The longer you stay on the island, <u>the greater are your chances of finding the treasures.</u>
你在岛上逗留的时间越长,找到宝藏的可能性就越大。

Part V   Time for Fun

参 考 译 文

是 他 的 错

比利和波比都是小男孩。他们是兄弟,两人经常打架。上个星期六,他们的妈妈对他们说:"我现在要做午饭了。去,到花园去玩吧,别淘气。""好的,妈妈。"两个男孩回答,然后他们就出去了。

他们在花园里玩了半个小时,然后比利跑进了厨房。"妈妈,波比打碎了艾伦太太家的窗玻璃。"艾伦太太是他们的邻居。"他是个坏孩子,"他的妈妈说,"他是怎么把玻璃打碎的?"比利回答:"我朝他扔了一块石子,他赶紧蹲下。"

Part I Teaching Objectives

* Listening & Speaking:

Help students to be familiar with the topic —*fashion* and to memorize useful expressions.

* Words & Expressions:

Grasp some new words and expressions, such as *cumulative*, *prestigious*, *controversial*, *tally*, *prestigious*, *tally*, *boost*, *surge*, *to be bound to*, *dress up*, *amount to*, *hit upon* and so on.

* Grammar:

Learn to use the inversion structure with *so* or *neither*.

* Writing:

Understand and write *a poster*.

Part II Listening——Changes in Fashion

New Words

addiction /əˈdɪkʃən/ *n.* 沉溺,癖好,瘾

    e. g.   He stole money from his parents to feed his addiction.

            他从父母那儿偷钱以满足自己的嗜好。

budget /ˈbʌdʒɪt/ *n.* 预算

    e. g.   The work was finished on time and within budget.

            工作按时完成且未超出预算。

conference /ˈkɒnfərəns/ *n.* 会议

    e. g.   Nearly all the members attended the conference.

几乎全体成员都出席了这次会议。

couture /kuːˈtjʊə/ *n.* 高级时装

    e. g.   We would like to receive additional information about your haute couture Autumn collection.

          希望贵方提供秋季系列女装的进一步资料。

doyen /ˈdɔɪən/ *n.* 老资格,老前辈,首席

    e. g.   This is the doyen of the French Department.

          这是法语系的老前辈。

enthusiast /ɪnˈθjuːzɪæst/ *n.* 爱好者,热衷者

    e. g.   A group of enthusiasts have undertaken the reconstruction of a steam locomotive.

          一群火车迷已担负起重造蒸汽机车的任务。

fashionable /ˈfæʃənəbl/ *adj.* 流行的,时髦的

    e. g.   We ate at a new, fashionable restaurant.

          我们在一家新开张的时尚餐馆吃饭。

frenzy /ˈfrenzɪ/ *n.* 极度的激动

    e. g.   She pleaded with them in a frenzy to release her son.

          她发疯似地祈求他们释放他的儿子。

handstand /ˈhændstænd/ *n.* 倒立

    e. g.   Bonnie was showing off to her friends, doing handstands on the grass.

          邦尼向朋友们炫耀,在草地上拿大顶。

obsession /əbˈseʃən/ *n.* 使人痴迷的人(或物);痴迷,着魔

    e. g.   With him, gambling is an obsession.

          对于他来说,赌博是无法摆脱的。

receptive /rɪˈseptɪv/ *adj.* (对新的思想等)善于接受的

    e. g.   He is not very receptive to my suggestions.

          他不太接受我的建议。

stiff /stɪf/ *adj.* 僵硬的,不灵活的

    e. g.   The old man's joints are stiff.

          那个老人的关节不灵活了。

yoga /ˈjəʊgə/ *n.* 瑜伽,瑜伽修行法

    e. g.   He was deeply interested in meditation, the East, and yoga.

          他对默想、东方、以及瑜珈深感兴趣。

Phrases and Expressions

carry through   帮助渡过难关

    e. g.   Their faith and courage carried them through.

          他们的信心和勇气使他们渡过了难关。

go in for   参加;喜欢,爱好

e. g. This is not a hobby you should go in for unless you have plenty of money.

这不是非有不可的爱好,除非你有大量的钱。

Which events is he going in for at the Olympics?

他将在奥运上参加什么项目?

warm up 作准备活动

e. g. Have you all warmed up your instruments?

你们都做好演奏的准备了吗?

Dialogue One

Listen to the CD and mark T for True or F for False according to the dialogue.

1. F 2. T 3. T 4. F 5. T

Script

Woman: Do you think I am still fashionable in this dress?

Man: I think so. Green is still fashionable at the moment.

Woman: This style came out last year, though. I like the dress, but I'm not sure whether last year's fashions will be the same this year.

Man: I think this kind of dress will stay in fashion for a few more years. People don't change fashions every year. It would be too expensive.

Women: Yes. Only the top designer try to tell people to change fashion every year, but only rich people can do it.

Man: There are some real fashion victims who just have to keep totally up-to-date with expensive clothes.

Women: I wish I could be one of those people, but my budget simply doesn't stretch that far. I have to limit the amount of money I spend on clothes, otherwise I would go on a shopping frenzy.

Man: I know what you mean. The situation will be worse if you marry your boyfriend and have children. Then you'll have even less money to spend on fashionable clothes!

Dialogue Two

Listen to the CD and answer the following questions with the information you hear.

1. What is the man warming up for?

   He is warming up for yoga.

2. What does the man feel after warming up for yoga?

   It's marvelous and funny.

3. According to the woman's opinion, most yoga enthusiasts are women, aren't they?

   Yes, most yoga enthusiasts are women.

4. What's wrong with the man's back?

The man's back is too stiff so he couldn't sleep on his stomach anymore.

5. Does the man become stronger and more flexible?

Yes, he does.

Script

- -

Tina: You are always keeping up the changes in fashion. I heard now you are warming up for yoga. How is it?

Joe: Marvelous! It's fun. And I especially enjoy the handstands.

Tina: But to the best of my knowledge, most enthusiasts are women.

Joe: Yes, that's true. At the beginning, mainly women go in for it, but as its popularity grows, men are becoming more receptive to the idea. As a boy, I liked to stand on my head.

Tina: Why don't you have a go?

Joe: My back is so stiff that I couldn't sleep on my stomach anymore.

Tina: It can not be something easy to start, right?

Joe: Sure, the first classes were tough, but I stuck with it. The first main effect I noticed is that I'd feel very relaxed after class. I become stronger, more flexible and my posture has improved.

Tina: You must be used to it now.

Joe: Exactly.

Spot Dictation

- -

1. when he first started in the business

2. It is impossible to change the fashion every year

3. they are not making fashion for tomorrow

4. like trying to walk on the moon

5. around the world from couture clothing to alarm clocks

Part III   Speaking——*Fashionable Clothes*

Useful Expressions About Fashion

I don't have many designer clothes.

These sunglasses are very fashionable right now.

She is very well-dressed.

Mary always has many trendy clothes.

I don't care for brand-name clothing.

Those two always have matching clothing.

That suit makes you look very trendy.

It's hard for very shirt or very tall people to remain fashionable.

If I had more money, I would dress more stylishly.

Does this shirt match with the pants?

She always looks so elegant.

The color is very fashionable right now.

Pair Work
Sample

Nancy: Wow, I love those jeans! Are they designer jeans?

Kelly: I guess. My mother just gave them to me.

Nancy: Let me see. These are really expensive jeans!

Kelly: But I don't really like designer clothes, I think the money could be spent in a much better way. Do you have a lot of brand-name clothes?

Nancy: I wouldn't wear anything that isn't a brand name.

Kelly: Really? You must spend a lot of money on clothes then.

Nancy: I do, because I think people treat you differently when you have brand-name clothes.

Kelly: Do you think that's true?

Nancy: Sure. You can notice that people are looking at you as you walk down the street in those jeans.

Kelly: I don't believe. I think buying designer clothes is a complete waste of money, especially when you can not afford it.

Nancy: To each their own, I guess.

Role-play
Sample

Fred: What do you think of this coat? Do you think it suits me?

Dina: Sure. Why don't you try it on? The fitting room is over there.

Fred: It's just the right size, a perfect fit! Have you seen anything you like?

Dina: What about this sweater. I'm thinking about buying one, and this style is fashionable for autumn now.

Fred: It looks too big for you, but I like the color and the material is of good quality. Is it on sale?

Dina: Yes, it's half price. It's supposed to be too large, that's the fashion.

Fred: I might get one, too, but in a different color. I prefer blue to yellow.

Dina: There. It looks great, don't you think? I'm going to get some jeans as well. Look at this one, it's cool, isn't it?

Fred: Yes, it's really smart. You really have an eye for fashion.

Part IV   Reading

 **Text A**   **Background**

1. Tea Party

The Tea Party is an American populist political movement, which is generally recognized as conservative and libertaria, and has sponsored protests and supported political candidates since 2009. It endorses reduced government spending, opposition to taxation in varying degrees, reduction of the national debt and federal budget deficit, and adherence to an orginalist interpretation of *the United States Constitution*. The Tea Party's most noted national figures include Republic politicians such as Dick Armey and Ssrah Palin. As of 2010, the Tea Party is not a national political party, but has endorsed Republican candidates.

2. Abraham Lincoln

Abraham Lincoln (February 12, 1809 — April 15, 1865) served as the 16th President of the Unites States from March 1861 until his assasination in April 1865. He successfully led the country through its greatest constitutional, military and moral crisis—the American Civil War—by preserving the Union by force while ending slavery and promoting economic modernization.

3. Sarah Palin

Sarah Louise Palin is an American politician, author, speaker, and political news commentator who was the youngest person and the first woman elected Governor of Alaska. Chosen by Republican Party presidential candidate John McCain in August 2008 to be his running mate in that year's presidental election, she was the first Alaskan on the national ticket of a major party, as well as the first female vice-presidential nominee of the Republican Party.

4. *Harvard Business Review*

Harvard Business Review is a general management magazine published since 1922 by Harvard Business School Publishing. A monthly research-based magazine written for business practitioners, it claims a high ranking business readership among academics, executives, and management consultants.

5. Michelle Obama

Michelle LaVaughn Robinson Obama is the wife of the 44th and incumbent President of the United States, Barack Obama, and is the first African-American First Lady of the United States. Throughout 2007 and 2008, she helped campaign for her husband's presidential bid and delivered a keynote address at the 2008 Democratic National Convention. As the wife of a Senator, and later the First Lady, she has become a fashion icon and role model for women, and a notable advocate for poverty awareness and healthy eating.

6. *Huffington Post*

The Huffington Post is a proggressive American news website and content aggregating blog founded by Arianna Huffington, Kenneth Lerer, and Jonah Peretti, featuring various news sources and columnists. The site offers coverage of politics, media, business, entertainment, living, style, the green movement, world news, and comedy, and has news, blogs, and original content.

7. Nancy Pelosi

Nancy Patricia D'Alesandro Pelosi is an American politician who is the current Minority Leader of the United States House of Representatives. Pelosi served as the 60th Speaker of the United States House of Representatives from January 4, 2007 to January 3, 2011. She was the first woman to hold the office and the highest-ranking female politician in American history.

8. Kirsten Gillibrand

Kirsten Elizabeth Rutnik Gillibrand is the junior United States Senator from New York and a member of the Democratic Party. Prior to being appointed to the Senate by New York Governor David Paterson in 2009, she was elected twice to the House of Representives, representing New York's 20th congressional district.

9. John Boehner

John Andrew Boehner is the 61st and current Speaker of the House of Representatives United States. As Speaker, Boehner is second in line to the presidency of the United States following the Vice President.

10. Hillary Clinton

Hillary Diane Rodham Clinton is the 67th United States Secretary of State, serving in the administration of President Barack Obama. She was a United States Senator for New York from 2001 to 2009. As the wife of the 42nd President of the United States, Bill Clinton, she was the First Lady of the United States from 1993 to 2001. As Secretary of State, Clinton became the first former First Lady to serve in a president's cabinet.

New Words

alongside /əˈlɒŋsaɪd/ *prep.* 与……一起,与……同时

　　e.g. It's a pleasure to work alongside such men.

　　　　与这样的人一起工作是一件乐事。

boost /buːst/ *n.* 增加,推起 *v.* 向上推起,增加,提升

　　e.g. This has given share prices a big boost.

　　　　这大大拉升了股价。

　　　　The rocket boosts the astronaut into space.

　　　　火箭把宇航员送入太空。

candidate /ˈkændɪdət/ *n.* 候选人,申请求职者

　　e.g. He interviews many candidates for jobs.

　　　　他面试过很多求职者。

celebrity /sɪˈlebrətɪ/ *n.* （尤指娱乐界的）名流,名人;名声,名誉

    e. g.   Lots of celebrities were at the film premiere.

            许多名人出席了电影的首映式。

controversial /ˌkɒntrəˈvɜːʃəl/ *adj.* 有争议的,引起争议的

    e. g.   We don't like talking about this controversial topic.

            我们不愿谈论这个有争议的话题。

cumulative /ˈkjuːmjʊlətɪv/ *adj.* 累积的

    e. g.   This drug has a cumulative effect.

            这种药有渐增的效力。

currently /ˈkʌrəntlɪ/ *adv.* 当前,目前,眼下

    e. g.   She is currently studying at the Liverpool University.

            她目前正在利物浦大学学习。

drawling /drɔːlɪŋ/ *adj.* 慢吞吞的,有气无力的

    e. g.   She had a sweet voice, sometimes rapid and sometimes drawling in her throat.

            她声音甜润,时而口若悬河,时而拖声拖气。

endorsement /ɪnˈdɔːsmənt/ *n.* （通常为名人在广告中对某一产品的）宣传,吹嘘;支持,赞同

    e. g.   He also has endorsement deal worth at least ＄20 million.

            另外他还有至少2千万美元的广告合同。

feminise /ˈfemɪnɪs/ *v.* 有女性风度,（使）女性化

    e. g.   This kind of dress feminises her.

            这种裙子让她更有女人味了。

metaphorically /ˌmetəˈfɒrɪkəlɪ/ *adv.* 隐喻般地,含有隐喻意义地

    e. g.   Metaphorically speaking, the people are like water and the leaders at various levels are like swimmers who must stay in the water and swim with the current, not against it.

            打个比喻,人民就象水一样,各级领导者,就象游水的一样,你不要离开水,你要顺水,不要逆水。

poll /pəʊl/ *n.* 投票选举

    e. g.   The result of the poll won't be known until midnight.

            选举结果要到午夜才能揭晓。

pollster /ˈpəʊlstə/ *n.* 民意调查专家

    e. g.   A brilliant pollster will steer his candidate to the centre but will not try to turn an election victory into a White House empire.

            出色的民调专家引导自己助选的总统候选人走向中间路线,但不会试图利用胜选构建白宫帝国。

premise /ˈpremɪs/ *n.* 假定,前提

    e. g.   These are the major and minor premises on which the conclusion is based.

这是这个结论所依据的前提。

prestigious /presˈtiːdʒəs/ *adj.* 受尊敬的,有声望的,有威信的

e. g. Her first novel won a prestigious literary prize.

她的第一部小说就获得了一个颇具声望的文学奖。

retail /ˈriːteɪl/ *n.* 零售

e. g. The retail dealer buys at wholesale and sells at retail.

零售商批发购进货物,以零售价卖出。

return /rɪˈtɜːn/ *n.* 利润,受益

e. g. These shares have brought in good returns.

这些股票带来很好的收益。

sartorial /sɑːˈtɔːrɪəl/ *adj.* 服装的,缝纫的

e. g. John has never been known for his sartorial elegance.

约翰从来没有因为衣着讲究而出名。

sartorially /sɑːˈtɔːrɪəlɪ/ *adv.* 服装地,缝纫地

e. g. Her mother, an excellent designer, sartorially influences her eyes for beauty.

作为一名优秀的服装设计师,她的母亲从服装方面影响着她的审美眼光。

surge /sɜːdʒ/ *n.* (数量的)急剧上升,激增 *v.* 急剧上升,飞涨,激增

e. g. For a moment Peter felt a surge of sympathy for the older man.

一刹那间彼得对这位老头油然产生了一种怜悯心。

tally /ˈtælɪ/ *v.* (使)符合,(使)吻合

e. g. Your figures don't tally with mine.

你的数字和我的不符。

upcoming /ˈʌpˌkʌmɪŋ/ *adj.* 即将到来的,即将发生的

e. g. We shall be attending the upcoming concert.

我们要去听即将上演的音乐会。

stylish /ˈstaɪlɪʃ/ *adj.* 时髦的,新潮的

e. g. He's a stylish dresser.

他是个穿着很时髦的人。

wig /wɪɡ/ *n.* 假发;法官帽

e. g. The actress wore a black wig over her blond hair.

那个女演员戴一顶黑色假发罩住自己的金黄色头发。

Phrases and Expressions

as a result of 由于……的结果

e. g. He was injured as a result of boiler explosion.

他因锅炉爆炸而受伤。

be bound to 很有可能,肯定会

e. g. Find a girl just like your mother then she's bound to like her.

找个像你母亲那样的,这样你母亲一定会喜欢她。

by contrast 相比之下

    e. g.   By contrast, he was much cleverer.

            相比之下,他要机灵得多。

dress up 穿上特殊的服装;打扮,梳理

    e. g.   They all dressed up to take part in the New Year's party.

            他们都穿上盛装,去参加除夕晚会。

            She was dressed up as a lady of high society.

            她把自己打扮成一位贵妇人。

in the end 最后,最终

    e. g.   In the end, the Japanese agreed to change the machinery.

            结果,日本人只好同意更换机器。

tally with 与……相符合,与……一致

    e. g.   The goods we have received do not tally with the sample on which we ordered.

            我们收到的货物与我们定购的样品不符合。

vote for 投票赞成

    e. g.   Twelve men voted for the action and three against it.

            12 人投票赞成这个行动,3 人反对。

参 考 译 文

美国政客影响时尚

1 美国人正进行中期选举投票,到了周三,华盛顿的政治版图可能会呈现另一副模样——并非只是隐喻性的,而是实实在在的。如果最终选举结果正如民意专家所预测的那样:许多老面孔议员竞选连任失败,一些新面孔议员胜利进驻国会山,那必定会在时尚界产生连带效应。

2 我在此讨论的并非是古怪的"茶党"成员着装会不会象林肯那样一本正经。我谈论的也不是莎拉·佩林的装束在万圣节时销量大增。我所谈论的是这样的事实:政客们越来越多地成为时尚的引领者。一旦他们出现权力更替,时尚风格也会应声而变。

3 一项由纽约大学大卫·叶马克教授领衔进行的研究,结果刊登在《哈佛商业评论》上,在跟踪了米歇尔·奥巴马从 2008 年到 2009 年间在公开场合的服饰穿着后,研究团队得出结论:米歇尔为时装公司以及相关零售商创造了超过 27 亿美元的累积额外收益——市场正常销售之外的收益。

4 同时,在奥巴马对中国进行国事访问期间,他身穿 Weatherproof 牌夹克外套站在长城上的形象见诸媒体后,该品牌公司马上做出决定,向 200 位国会议员免费赠送类似夹克,因为根据该公司总裁弗雷迪·史托麦克的说法,在对时尚风格的影响程度上,如今任何好莱坞明星和模特都无法与这些声名显赫、有时还颇具争议的国会政客们相提并论。这与叶马克教授的研究结果相吻合:米歇尔·奥巴马的装束给该品牌带来了 2.3% 的额外销售收益,

而名人代言的品牌平均下来只能带来 0.5% 的额外收益。

　　5　毋庸置疑,尝到甜头的 Weatherproof 公司决定对"政治人物是否能有效引领时尚"的说法进行检测,于是就在《赫芬顿邮报》上对网友进行了调查:"11 月中期的选举将如何深刻影响时尚?"

　　6　在 3168 份网友回复中,只有 45.3% 的网友认为政客的政策比其着装更重要,38% 的网友说他们更倾向于把票投给穿着讲究的候选人。当被问及哪些女政客着装最"潮"时,南希·佩洛茜位居第一,参议员柯尔斯顿·吉利布兰德位居第七,莎拉·佩林位居第八。这个结果让人很感兴趣,因为这三位女士都将在即将进行的选战中在众目睽睽之下披挂上阵。

　　7　我们不妨来举个例子,本次选战后,佩洛茜的众议院议长的宝座很可能由共和党议员约翰·博纳接任。众所周知,博纳本人在穿着方面也很有眼光,虽然他可能更倾向于穿《广告狂人》风格的正装而非佩洛茜所青睐的阿玛尼品牌。所以,女衫裤套装的影响力可能会渐渐淡出,而《广告狂人》中唐·德雷珀式装束的销量会扶摇直上。此外还有正争取竞选连任的参议员吉利·布兰德,目前著名摄影师诺曼·简·罗伊为她拍摄了专门的特写,刊登在 11 月出版的美国版 Vogue 杂志上。然而,不管佩林最终能否竞选成功,都可能会对时尚界产生巨大影响。据叶马克教授的研究:有些销售商反馈,当初佩林在被选为约翰·麦凯恩的竞选搭档后,佩林式的假发和她所戴的川崎和男无框眼镜的销量激增。

　　8　但是,如今的影响可能还不止于此。这些女性政客展示的形象不同于佩洛茜与希拉里·克林顿(她位列最具时尚影响力女性政客第三名)等时尚引领者所展示的,佩洛茜与希拉里(她俩都是民主党人)穿的是女性化的职业男装。而与此相反,共和党的女政客们清一色地把头发焗成了青棕色,身穿亮色的裙装与长统靴。你可以想象她们拉长腔调说"女人就该像个女人样"以及发表"为何政府应该要大瘦身"的演讲时的样子。

　　9　如果她们中的任何人获胜,那就等着看上世纪 50 年代那种仿男式女衬衣以及电动滚筒的销量大增吧。

Exercises

I. Reading Comprehension

Section A

1. C　2. B　3. C　4. A　5. C

Section B

1. Yes, he does.

2. He looked at Michelle Obama's public appearances from 2008 to 2009, and accounted how much she get returns for fashion and retail companies associated with the clothes she wore.

3. Weatherproof President Freddie Stollmack.

4. Michelle Obama's appearance in a brand was associated with a 2.3 percent rise in returns for the brand, while the announcement of a new celebrity endorsement only resulted in a 0.5

percent average gain.

5. Because they are the Republican female politicians who are all brown hair, bright skirt suits and boots, and they need to wash machine to wash their bright skirt.

Section C

1. Fashion is for a currently popular style or practice, especially in clothing, foot wear or accessories. Fashion refers to anything that is alongside the current trend in both look and the dress-up of a person.

2. Open-ended

3. I agree with what Coco Chanel said: Fashion is not something that exists in dresses only. Fashion is in the sky, in the street; fashion has to do with ideas, the way we live, and what is happening.

II. Vocabulary and Structure

Section A

1. B   2. A   3. D   4. C   5. A   6. C   7. B   8. A   9. B   10. C

Section B

1. The company <u>returns</u> over the last three years have been spectacular.
   这个公司过去三年的收入很可观。

2. She had a sweet voice, sometimes rapid and sometimes <u>drawling</u> in her throat.
   她声音甜润,时而口若悬河,时而拖声拖气。

3. Food intake does not produce any significant <u>variation</u> of heat production throughout the day.
   食物摄取量对全天产热量并不引起任何显著的变化。

4. He haunted famous men, hoping to get <u>celebrity</u> for him.
   他常跟踪名人,希望借此出名。

5. His criticisms of my book <u>tally</u> closely with yours.
   他对我这本书的批评跟你的批评非常吻合。

6. Four years later, Julian's music won him a scholarship to a <u>prestigious</u> school.
   4 年后,朱利安的音乐才能为他赢得了一笔就读一所名校的奖学金。

7. There are some ways to build and <u>boost</u> children's self-motivation in a way that will be as beneficial to you as to them.
   然而,有一些办法可以发展和促进孩子的自我激励意识,它对父母和孩子都有益。

8. In recent years, economic growth has become a <u>controversial</u> goal.
   这些年来,经济增长成了一个有争议的目标。

III. Word Building

1. He promised to <u>abstain</u> from smoking and profanity as long as he remained a member.
   他答应戒烟,一日当着会员,一日不破戒。

2. The police caught the man who tried to abduct the boy for ransom.

警察抓住了那个企图拐走这男孩以便勒索赎金的家伙。

3. The abaxial surface of a leaf is the underside or side facing away from the stem.

叶子的远轴表面就是背离叶梗底部或旁边的部位。

4. Whether Edward would abdicate in favor of his brother became the question of the hour.

爱德华是否会放弃王位而支持他的兄弟成了当前的热门话题。

5. We do not think such an abnormal phenomenon will last long.

我们认为这样的反常现象不会持续很久。

6. He had been obliged to offer an abject apology to his boss for his impertinence.

他不得不低声下气，为他的傲慢举动向他的老板请罪。

7. Will the world market absorb production in excess of domestic needs at profitable prices?

世界市场能否以有利的价格吸收入国内需求以外的剩余产量呢？

8. Abortion can be very harmful to a girl, both physically and mentally.

堕胎对少女的身体和心理都可能造成很大危害。

IV. Grammar Focus

1. As the French love their wine, so do the English love their beer.

2. She never again appeared in the city, neither have I since that day either seen or heard anything concerning her.

3. Achievements have a dual character and so have mistakes.

4. The weather was unusually variable and so were tempers.

5. We did not think it suitable to disturb them at their feast, neither did they take much notice of us.

V. Translation

1. Things are bound to be difficult; you should prepare yourself as well as possible.

事情一定挺麻烦，你该多做些准备。

2. Its image has improved. Our own people have seen this, and so have people in other countries.

我们国家的形象变了，国内的人民看清了这一点，其他国家的人民也看清了这一点。

3. As a result of many such diligent studies, our present knowledge of the oceans has accumulated.

因为做了许多这类的艰苦研究，我们现有的海洋知识才得以积累起来。

4. The man whom you met yesterday and whose name often appears in the newspaper is a famous designer.

你昨天遇见的其名字常在报纸上出现的那个人是一位著名的服装设计师。

5. We are supposed to dress up as movie characters for the party, what a novel idea!

我们在晚会上要装扮得像电影中的角色，这是一个多么新奇的主意啊！

VI. Writing

Sample

POSTER

Friendly Basketball Match

All Are Welcome

Tuesday, April 1.

In order to celebrate the Youth Day, the Students' Union of our college will hold a friendly basketball match between English Department and Law Department on the basketball court on Saturday, 4 pm, April 5, 2010.

The College Students' Union

Notes

A poster is a sign posted in a public place as an advertisement. It is a special type of presentation. The following are some guidelines for writing a post. Firstly, the title of an effective poster should quickly orient the audience. Secondly, the poster should quickly orient the audience to the subject and purpose. Thirdly, the specific section such as the results should be easy to locate on the poster. Last, you should design the individual section of a poster so that they can be quickly read.

Text B   **Background**

1. Dunhill

Alfred Dunhill, Ltd. is a British-based company, specializing in men's luxury leather goods, writing implements, lighters, timepieces, fragrances and clothing. Dunhill has built a series of retail emporiums for men.

2. Missoni

Missoni is an Italian fashion house based in Varese. It is famous for its unique knitwear, made from a variety of fabrics in colourful patterns. The company was founded by Ottavio ("Tai") and Rosita Missoni in 1953. Missoni knitwear is known for its multitude of patterns such as stripes, geometrics and abstract florals, in a kaleidoscope of colours. They are also known for the liberal use of many different fabrics such as wool, cotton, linen, rayon and silk.

3. Krizia

Krizia is a manufacturer and designer of handbags and clothes, founded by Mariuccia Mandelli in 1950 in Bergamo, Italy.

4. Gucci

The House of Gucci, better known simply as Gucci is an Italian fashion and leather goods label, part of the Gucci Group, which is owned by French company Pinault-Printemps-Redoute (PPR). Gucci was founded by Guccio Gucci in Florence in 1921.

5. Savile Row

Savile Row is a shopping street in Mayfair, central London, famous for its traditional men's bespoke tailoring. The term "bespoke" is understood to have originated in Savile Row when cloth for a suit was said to "be spoken for" by individual customers. The short street is termed as "the golden mile of tailoring", where customers have included Winston Churchill, Lord Nelson and Napoleon III. Savile Row runs parallel to Regent Street between Conduit Street at the northern end and Vigo Street at the southern. Linking roads include Burlington Place, Clifford Street and Burlington Gardens.

New Words

accessible /æk'sesəbl/ *adj.* 可接近的,易进入的;容易取得的

 e. g. Medicine should not be kept where it is accessible to children.
   药物不应放在容易被小孩拿到的地方。

accommodate /ə'kɒmədeɪt/ *v.* 容纳,提供空间

 e. g. Are there enough shelves to accommodate all our books?
   有足够的书架容纳我们所有的书吗?

alternative /ɔːl'tɜːnətɪv/ *n.* 可供选择的事物;替换物 *adj.* 两者择一的,供选择的

 e. g. We have the alternative plans of having a picnic or taking a boat trip.
   我们在去野餐或者去乘船旅游两个计划中只能选一个。

awkwardly /'ɔːkwədlɪ/ *adv.* 不雅观地;笨拙地,无技巧地

 e. g. He walked awkwardly and gingerly around outside his hut without the crutches.
   他没有拄双拐,笨拙地、小心翼翼地在木屋外面走了一圈。

bellow /bɪ'ləʊ/ *n.* 吼叫 *v.* 发出吼叫声;大叫

 e. g. We could hear he was bellowing commands to his troops.
   我们听见他正向他的兵士大声发布命令。

catwalk /'kætwɔːk/ *n.* (时装表演时模特儿走的)伸展台;狭窄过道

 e. g. There are 4 models on the catwalk now.
   现在有4个模特儿在伸展台上作时装表演。

concede /kən'siːd/ *v.* 承认

 e. g. I conceded that I had made a mistake.
   我承认我犯了一个错误。

conservative /kən'sɜːvətɪv/ *adj.* 保守的,守旧的

 e. g. The professor's a radical in politics but a conservative dresser.
   教授在政治上是激进派,但衣着却很守旧。

detachable /dɪ'tætʃəbl/ *adj.* 可分开的,可拆开的

 e. g. The handle is detachable from the bag.
   手柄可以从包上取下来。

fake /feɪk/ *adj.* 假的,冒充的

e. g.　These are fake diamonds.

　　　　这些是假钻石。

fashionist /ˈfæʃəˌnɪst/　*n.* 倡导时尚者

e. g.　As a fashionist, she thinks that she must wear high-fashion clothes and use the most fashionable goods.

　　　　作为一名时尚的倡导者, 她认为自己必须穿最时尚的衣服, 用最时尚的东西。

flap /flæp/　*n.* (附于某物的)扁平下垂物, 封盖, 口盖, 袋盖

e. g.　I licked the flap of the envelope and sealed it.

　　　　我舔了舔信封盖口, 把它封好。

gilet /gɪˈleɪ/　*n.* 马甲, 背心

e. g.　Have you seen the new gilet at Altman's?

　　　　你看到奥尔特曼公司的新款马甲了吗?

masculine /ˈmɑːskjʊlɪn/　*adj.* 男子汉的, 像男人的

e. g.　She has a rather masculine voice.

　　　　她的声音有点男性化。

murse /mɜːs/　*n.* 男士钱包

e. g.　The murse is a purse especially for man.

　　　　男士钱包是专为男士使用的。

ongoing /ˈɒnˌgəʊɪŋ/　*adj.* 继续进行的, 不断发展的

e. g.　The issues raised in the report relate directly to Age Concern's ongoing work in this area.

　　　　报告中提出的问题与"关心老人"组织在这方面正在做的工作有直接的关系。

reassure /ˌriːəˈʃʊə/　*v.* 使……安心, 恢复信心, 打消……的疑虑

e. g.　The police reassured her about the child's safety.

　　　　警察让她放心, 她的孩子很安全。

rectangular /rekˈtæŋgjʊlə/　*adj.* 长方形的, 矩形的

e. g.　He put a rectangular box on the table.

　　　　他把一个长方形的箱子放在桌子上。

resort /rɪˈzɔːt/　*v.* 求助于某事物

e. g.　One has sometimes to resort to these little devices.

　　　　人们有时还得依靠这些小玩意儿。

safari /səˈfɑːrɪ/　*n.* (狩猎)旅行

e. g.　When we go on safari we like to cook on an open fire.

　　　　我们远行狩猎时, 喜欢露天生火做饭。

soar /sɔː/　*v.* 急升, 猛增

e. g.　The temperature soared to 86℃.

　　　　温度猛增到摄氏 86 度。

staple /ˈsteɪpl/　*n.* 支柱产品, 主要产品; 主要部分

e. g.   Cotton is the staple of the area.

棉花是这个地区的主要农作物。

stitch   /stɪtʃ/   v. 缝,缝补,缝合

e. g.   I don't know anything about this, but my colleague can help you.

我对这事一无所知,但我的同时可以帮你。

surreal   /səˈrɪəl/   adj. 超现实的

e. g.   Meeting you here like this is positively surreal!

像这样与你在此相逢真好比一场梦!

temptation   /tempˈteɪʃən/   n. 诱惑

e. g.   The purse on the table was a strong temptation to the poor child.

桌上的钱包对那个穷孩子是一个强烈的诱惑。

Phrases and Expressions

amount to   意味着;共计

e. g.   His words amounted to a threat.

他的话实际上是威胁。

distinguish from   与……区别开来

e. g.   Elephants are distinguished from other animals by their long noses.

大象以其长长的鼻子显示出与其他动物的不同。

focus on   致力于

e. g.   He focused his mind on his lessons.

他把心思集中在功课上。

hit upon   偶然发现

e. g.   Finally, he hit upon a good idea which could be applied to such a case.

最后他忽然想到一个可以适用于这种情况的好主意。

say goodbye/hello to   向……告别/问好

e. g.   Please say hello to Mr. Downes for me when you see him.

见到道森先生,请代我向他问好。

参 考 译 文

你的外套有几个口袋?

1   随着时尚继续前行,告别伦敦迎来米兰,应该注意到,不仅 T 形台上的女装看上去大不相同,大街上的男装也风格相异。虽然纽约和伦敦最早接受时尚的超级潮人手中拎的也算得上手提包(被奇怪地称作"男士钱包"或男士手提包的皮质信封状小包),登喜路创意总监卡洛斯·德弗赖塔斯表示,其实还有"另一种选择"。

2   在保持男装阳刚气概的战斗中,在男士钱包上的激烈竞争以口袋的形式出现——通

常为矩形,有时带有翻盖。事实上,登喜路本季一款茄克外套的销售火爆:黑色、剪裁考究、风格保守、外面设计有 4 个大大的口袋,更不用说可脱卸的内胆马甲衬上还有 5 个口袋。"口袋太多了,"德弗赖塔斯承认,"我尽量不把它们都装满,但这很难做到,特别是在旅行时。"

3　旅行的增加,航班上复杂的行李携带规则确实刺激了对口袋数量多于平均水平的物品的需求,同样增加的还有被认为必不可少的个人日常用品的数量,例如钥匙、钱包、手机、黑莓和 iPod。因此,设计师将前所未有的精力集中在口袋上面,为不同物品设计了形状不同、深浅不一的口袋。

4　登喜路不是将多口袋作为主题的唯一品牌;近几季,军装裤、狩猎外套、战地外套和渔夫马甲回归,而米索尼、朗万和古姿等品牌也推出了注重口袋的其它款式。

5　设计师约翰·罗查表示,"口袋实用,而且是区分男装和女装的一种标志——男人拎着小包看上去实在太过阴柔了,"本季他推出的正装外套上风箱式的口袋大得足以容纳一个人的所有家当。"当然最近有些设计师有点夸张过度——你真的需要 4 个以上的口袋吗?或是专门为手机准备一个口袋?但是我认为在深度心理层面上,男人对口袋有种依恋。即便口袋空着,也能带来某种安全感。最简单的理由是,把手插在口袋里也很不错。"

6　尽管如此,萨维尔街的设计师表示,说服定制客户不要为了适应日常随身品的需要而在西装衬里上缝制五六个口袋越来越难,即便多些口袋往往会毁掉一套西装的线条。当然,保持轮廓优雅是女装一直注意避免设计口袋的一个原因,往往采用假口袋这种最超现实的设计细节。

7　在制衣工人偶然想出在衣物上缝制方便使用的扁平袋子之前,过去的男士和女士都习惯于携带被称为"口袋"的小型手袋。这些手袋往往绣工精美,挂在男士的皮带和女士的衬衣上。由于中产阶级人数增长,以及露在外面的"口袋"容易对小偷产生诱惑,口袋开始被缝制在外套内侧。到了 19 世纪早期,口袋又开始出现在裤装、背心和短上衣上。

8　军队对男装一直有影响,而在历史上,需要功能型服装的探险家、飞行家和摩托车手往往是男性,这使得口袋成为一种男性特征。把口袋装满东西以至于破坏了衣服的线条是多数女人想都不会想的事,而对男人来说,口袋就是为了装东西而存在的——这就是为什么他们常常最后会糟蹋了那一身西装。

Exercises

I. Reading Comprehension

1. D　2. D　3. B　4. A　5. C

II. Vocabulary and Structure

1. C　2. B　3. A　4. D　5. C　6. D　7. C　8. A　9. B　10. D

III. Translation

1. I got fed up with <u>doing what amounts to little more than high school chemistry experiment.</u>

我真受够了做些和高中化学实验差不了多少的事情。

2. Ecology may play a big role <u>in the battle to keep the world's wild animals alive.</u>

生态学在为维护世界野生动物生存斗争中可能会起重大作用。

3. <u>As he said goodbye to her abroad</u>, mother kept a firm hold on her son's hands.

儿子向母亲告别到国外去时,母亲紧紧地拉住他的双手。

4. When prices rise so fast and pay remains the same, <u>it gets increasingly difficult to live within one's means.</u>

物价飞涨而工资仍旧不变,量入为出地过日子真是越来越难了。

5. A man adores a woman out of love, <u>while a woman loves a man out of adoration.</u>

男人因为爱而崇拜一个女人,女人因为崇拜而爱一个男人。

Part V   Time for Fun

参 考 译 文

新 生 儿

泰勒夫妇有一个七岁的男孩,名叫帕特。现在泰勒太太正怀着第二胎。帕特在别人家看见过婴儿,他不太喜欢他们,所以他对自己家里也将有一个婴儿的消息不是很高兴。

一天晚上,泰勒夫妇正在为这个婴儿的降生计划做安排。泰勒先生说:"有了婴儿,我们的房子就太小,不够住了。"帕特恰好在这个时候走进屋,他问:"你们在说什么?"他的母亲回答说:"我们在说我们现在得搬家,因为婴儿就要诞生了。""那没用,"帕特绝望地说。"他会跟我们到那儿去的。"

Unit 6

Internet of Things

Part I   Teaching Objectives

* Listening & Speaking:

Help the students to be familiar with the topic—*how to express yourself when talking about the Internet of Things and its applications in the life* and memorize useful expressions.

* Words & Expressions:

Study some new words and expressions, such as *monitor*, *ecosystem*, *consume*, *sustainable*, *renewable*, *artificial*, *function*, *thrive*, *generate*, *update*, *in the pipeline*, *wander off*, *at short notice* and so on.

* Grammar:

Learn to use the structure of *not only... but also....*

* Writing:

Understand and write *a letter of job application*.

Part II   Listening——*Internet-based Objects*

New Words

consumer /kənˈsjuːmə/ *n.* 消费者，顾客

　　e.g.　The price increases were passed on by the firm to the consumers.
　　　　　公司把上涨的费用转嫁到了顾客身上。

ease /ˈiːz/ *v.* （使）减轻，舒缓；（使）安心，宽慰

　　e.g.　The news that her child was safe eased her mind.
　　　　　孩子平安的消息使她放心了。

ecosystem /ˈiːkəʊˌsɪstəm/ *n.* 生态系统，生态环境

e. g.　We all have an interest in maintaining the integrity of the ecosystem.

维持生态系统的完整是我们共同的利益。

ingredient　/ɪnˈɡriːdɪənt/　*n.* （烹调的）原料；要素，因素

e. g.　What are the ingredients of the cake?

这个蛋糕是用什么原料做成的?

investment　/ɪnˈvestmənt/　*n.* 投资；（时间、精力的）投入

e. g.　They made an investment in heavy industry.

他们投资于重工业。

monitor　/ˈmɒnɪtə/　*v.* 监视，监测；密切注视

e. g.　They were monitoring the air to collect evidence of bomb explosions.

他们正在监测空气以收集炸弹爆炸的证据。

notify　/ˈnəʊtɪfaɪ/　*v.* 通知，告知

e. g.　When my guest arrives, please notify me.

我的客人到的时候，请通知我。

occupant　/ˈɒkjʊpənt/　*n.* （房屋等的）居住者，占有人

e. g.　The previous occupants had left the house in a terrible mess.

以前的住户搬走后，留下了一屋子的狼藉。

recipe　/ˈresɪpɪ/　*n.* 烹饪方法；食谱；处方

e. g.　Do you know the recipe for chicken soup?

你是否知道做鸡汤的方法?

RFID　*abbr.*　射频识别（Radio Frequency Identification）

track　/træk/　*v.* 追踪；循着（痕迹、线索等）探索

e. g.　The police use dogs to track the criminal.

警察用警犬来追踪罪犯。

Dialogue One

Listen to the CD and mark T for True or F for False according to the dialogue.

1. F　2. F　3. T　4. F　5. T

Script

Jane：Hey, Bob, what are you reading?

Bob：It's a computer magazine.

Jane：Is there anything new?

Bob：Yeah, I think so. Do you know the Internet of Things?

Jane：No, I don't. What's that, a new technology?

Bob：Sort of. It is a network of Internet-based objects.

Jane：What? I don't understand.

Bob：Simply speaking, real world objects, such as fridges, lights and toasters, are connected to the Internet.

Jane: So what?

Bob: And then, with the web services, you can interact with these objects.

Jane: Does that mean you can control the lights at home through the Internet when you are at work?

Bob: Right. You can even do that by your smartphone.

Jane: Wow. That's really amazing!

 Two

Listen to the CD and answer the following questions with the information you hear.

1. What is Mike doing these days?
   He is working on a smart house system recently.
2. What is the smart house system?
   It is a system that can sense the activities of the occupant.
3. Why does Mike design such a system?
   Because more and more old people are living alone now.
4. Is the system designed for children?
   No, it is for the old people.
5. How does the system work?
   It can share all kinds of information with homeowners.

Script

Kate: Hey, Mike, long time no see!

Mike: Hi, Kate. I'm working on a smart house system recently.

Kate: What's that, the smart thing?

Mike: It's a house system that can sense if an occupant catches a fever or makes a fall.

Kate: What's the system for? Why do you design such a system?

Mike: You know, there is a growing population of elderly people, and statistics show that more and more of them are going to live alone at home.

Kate: So the system is for the old people?

Mike: Yes. It can share all kinds of helpful information with homeowners, such as a strain on electricity, or even a strain on the heart.

Kate: That's a really great idea! Hopefully this will be able to ease some worries and possibly save people's lives.

Spot Dictation

1. might be the most famous smart home to date

281

2. lights come on ahead of you and fade behind you

3. as will whatever you're watching on television

4. all available on demand

5. When two different chips enter the same room

Part III Speaking——*The Applications in Life*

Useful Expressions About the Internet of Things (IoT)

IoT is still in its infancy.

IoT displays real time streams of news and information.

IoT will be a great platform for people to get news live from their laptops and mobile phones.

IoT is only practical when you have a critical mass of devices and a cloud infrastructure.

There's a lot of infrastructure work that needs to be done first.

With IoT, the physical world itself is becoming a type of information system.

In IoT, sensors and actuators embedded in physical objects are linked through wired and wireless networks, often using the same Internet Protocol (IP) that connects the Internet.

The introduction of IP technologies has sparked a revolution in communication between objects.

IP communications bring about further changes in the way we monitor and manage our homes.

Real-time information delivery is fast emerging.

It can place sensors to transmit data that can then be analyzed in real time.

The personal computing devices will become super smart drawing on the intelligence of IoT.

It presents us with many opportunities to do new and interesting things.

All the devices and appliances in a smart home can communicate with each other and with the owner.

A smart home probably sounds like a nightmare to those people not comfortable with computers.

The barrier at the present time is the absence of regulatory requirements or guidance documents.

Pair Work

Sample

Salesperson: May I help you, sir?

　Customer: I would like to buy a fridge. Do you have any recommendation?

Salesperson: Did you hear of the Internet fridge, sir?

Customer: No. What's that?

Salesperson: It is probably the most often-quoted example of what the Internet of Things will enable.

Customer: How it works?

Salesperson: The refrigerator can monitor the food inside it and notify you when you're low on milk.

Customer: Oh, really?

Salesperson: Yes, sir. It can also monitor all of the best food websites, gathering recipes for your dinners and adding the ingredients automatically to your shopping list.

Customer: OK, that's good.

Salesperson: Indeed the fridge helps you take care of your health, because it knows what kinds of food you like to eat, and which food is good for you.

Customer: That sounds attracting. I'll take one.

Role-play

Sample

Betty: Honey, here is today's newspaper.

Jack: Thank you, sweetheart.

Betty: Is there something interesting?

Jack: Let me see. Yeah. Here they are. A new report on airport satisfaction points to opportunities for more sensors.

Betty: And?

Jack: Sensors are used to track interactions between prisoners and guards.

Betty: It's happening now.

Jack: And a hospital will use sensors to alert staff of the medical histories of patients.

Betty: Indeed, good news.

Jack: The growth of the Internet of Things brings online sensor data to create a foundation for innovation.

Betty: Does that mean it has great potentials?

Jack: Yes, I guess so. But now it isn't suitable for the initial investment.

Betty: Why?

Jack: Because a great number of ecosystems are incomplete.

Part IV   Reading

Text A   Background

Internet of Things is a new revolution of the Internet. The Internet of Things, also known as the Internet of Objects, refers to the networked interconnection of everyday objects. It is described as a self-configuring wireless network of sensors whose purpose would be to interconnect all things. The technologies include sensors, RFID and smartphone standards.

RFID (Radio Frequency Identification) is a technology that uses communication through the radio waves to exchange data between a reader and an electronic tag attached to an object, for the purpose of identification and tracking.

RFID tags are smarter than the widely known barcodes, which makes RFID easier to use and more efficient than barcodes. RFID is a key enabler of the future Internet of Things (IoT) and it has a great economical potential.

If all objects of daily life were equipped with radio tags, they could be identified and inventoried by computers. The next generation of Internet applications using Internet Protocol Version 6 (IPv6) would be able to communicate with devices attached to virtually all human-made objects because of the extremely large address space of IPv6. This system would therefore be able to identify any kind of objects.

Objects make themselves recognizable and they get intelligence thanks to the fact that they can communicate information about themselves and they can access information that has been aggregated by other things. Alarm clocks go off early if there is traffic; plants communicate to the sprinkler system when it is time for them to be watered; running shoes communicate time, speed, and distance so that their wearers can compete in real time with people on the other side of the world; medicine containers tell your family members if you forget to take the medicine. All objects can get an active role thanks to their connection to the Internet.

New Words

anaerobic /ˌæneəˈrəʊbɪk/   *adj.* 厌氧的
    e. g.   The process of anaerobic digestion consists of three steps.
           厌氧消化包括三个步骤。

appearance /əˈpɪərəns/   *n.* 外观,外貌;出现
    e. g.   She is a young woman of good appearance.
           她是一位年轻貌美的女子。

artificial /ˌɑːtɪˈfɪʃəl/   *adj.* 人造的,人工的
    e. g.   The new dam will form a large artificial lake behind it.

新筑的水坝将会在其背后形成一个人工湖。

benign /bɪˈnaɪn/ *adj.* 友善的，温和的；有益的

    e. g. Martha is a benign old lady.

        玛莎是个仁慈的老妇人。

by-product /ˈbaɪˌprɒdʌkt/ *n.* 副产品；副作用

    e. g. Poverty is a by-product of greed.

        贫穷是贪婪的一个副产品。

consume /kənˈsjuːm/ *v.* 消耗，消费，耗尽

    e. g. We consume energy when we move.

        我们运动的时候要消耗能量。

distil /dɪsˈtɪl/ *v.* 蒸馏；从……提取，提炼

    e. g. Gasoline is distilled from crude oil.

        汽油是从原油中提炼出来的。

divert /daɪˈvɜːt/ *v.* 改变用途；使转移，转向

    e. g. We can divert water from a river into the fields.

        我们可以把水从河里引入田间。

enzyme /ˈenzaɪm/ *n.* 酶

    e. g. It is said that washing powders containing enzymes remove stains more efficiently.

        据说加酶洗衣粉除污更有效。

ferment /fəˈment/ *v.* （使）发酵

    e. g. When wine is fermented, it gives off gas.

        当酒发酵时，它会释放出气体。

filter /ˈfɪltə/ *v.* 透过，过滤，滤出

    e. g. Filter out all the dirt before using the water.

        在用水之前先将其中所有污物滤去。

flush /flʌʃ/ *v.* 冲刷，清除；（使）脸红

    e. g. Please flush these test tubes.

        请把这些试管冲洗一下。

function /ˈfʌŋkʃən/ *v.* （器官等）发挥机能；（机器等）运行

    e. g. The machine will not function properly if it is not well-oiled.

        机器如果不上好油，就不会正常地运转。

generate /ˈdʒenəreɪt/ *v.* 生成，产生；引起，导致

    e. g. This new boiler generates more heat than the old one.

        这个新锅炉产生的热量比旧的多。

guzzle /gʌzl/ *v.* 大吃大喝

    e. g. He's been guzzling beer all evening.

        整个晚上他都在狂饮啤酒。

humidity /hjuːˈmɪdɪtɪ/ *n.* （空气中的）湿度，湿气

e. g. It's difficult to work because of the humidity.
由于空气湿度很大,工作很难进行。

irrigation /ˌɪrɪˈɡeɪʃən/ *n.* 灌溉

e. g. Irrigation is important for farming.
灌溉对农业是非常重要的。

microbe /ˈmaɪkrəʊb/ *n.* 微生物

e. g. The probe is sensitive enough to detect the presence of a single microbe.
这个探针的灵敏度很高,足以测出任何微生物的存在。

pollutant /pəˈluːtənt/ *n.* 污染物质(尤指工业废物)

e. g. Pollutants are constantly being released into the atmosphere.
污染物质正在不断地被排放到大气中去。

renewable /rɪˈnjuː(ː)əbəl/ *adj.* 可再生的

e. g. The village obtains all its energy from renewable sources.
这个村子完全从可再生资源中获取所需的能源。

sensor /ˈsensə/ *n.* 传感器

e. g. There are more than 2 000 sensors here.
这里装有两千多个传感器。

sustainable /səsˈteɪnəbl/ *adj.* 可持续的;合理利用的

e. g. The strategy of sustainable development should be adopted.
我们应采取可持续发展的战略。

thrive /θraɪv/ *v.* 兴旺,繁荣;蓬勃发展

e. g. A business cannot thrive without good management.
生意兴隆离不开好的管理。

Phrases and Expressions

be applied to 适用于,应用于

e. g. This rule can not be applied to every case.
这条规则并不是在每种情况下都能适用的。

in the pipeline 在准备中;在进行中

e. g. Important changes are already in the pipeline.
重大的变革已在酝酿之中。

knock out 使不能使用;毁坏;击倒;淘汰

e. g. The telephone communications were knocked out by the storm.
风暴使电话通讯中断了。

on average 平均

e. g. On average we receive five letters each day.
我们平均每天收到五封信。

wander off 迷失,离开正确方向

e. g. How could they just let her wander off alone like this?

他们怎么能让她这样独自一人乱逛呢?

参 考 译 文

有"大脑"的绿色城市

1   假如现代的城市是一种生物的话,那它们就是凶猛的巨兽——每年它们要消耗的自然资源占到全球资源消耗的75%。

2   如今,一种更友善的"城市生物"即将登场。就像生物体一样,它也有一个"大脑"——中央电脑,通过它来控制管理从用水到能源消耗等所有问题。

3   **大脑和神经系统**

4   同其它可持续发展城市一样,这座城市将拥有自己的水处理系统和能源再生系统。它将拥有自己的人造神经系统来控制水的使用和能源消耗。

5   每座建筑物内的传感器会对房屋居住情况、温度、湿度和能源消耗进行监测。这些信息连同城市的发电量,还有用水及所产生的废物等信息一并传输给中央"大脑"。

6   城市数据中心将处理系统传感器收集到的所有信息。为防止数据中心出现问题而使得整个城市的控制系统崩溃,每座建筑还将拥有足够的数据处理能力来进行独立运作。

7   中央"大脑"随后便可利用这些信息控制管理城市的方方面面。例如,如果传感器显示一座建筑物的储水箱水位低,系统就可以从水量有盈余的另一座建筑物调水来补充。

8   **眼睛和耳朵**

9   如果有小孩走失,他的父母则可以求助于城市的"眼睛":连接到系统软件的摄像头网络。

10   这套应用软件能帮助家长找到如在购物中心走失的孩子。软件首先会核实申请人是否有权利获得相应信息——比如走失儿童的父亲——然后根据父母描述的儿童衣着和相貌搜寻监控录像,寻找走失儿童。

11   这套软件还能通过传声器听辨声音。例如,人们能从办公楼会议室中的与会者讲话时的一些关键词判定会议主题。系统随后可以通过这一功能为公司从内部或者外部找到潜在的合作伙伴。

12   **肾脏**

13   一座城市总耗水量中,仅有3%是用于饮用和煮饭。所以这座城市的建筑物都将尽可能多地循环使用水源。

14   厨房用水可以被收集起来冲洗马桶。同样,雨水会被收集到建筑物"由植物覆盖的绿色屋顶"上的水箱中,然后通过植物滤掉雨水中的污染物。此外,城市中央公园的一系列污水贮留池将利用芦苇、竹子及其它植物来过滤废水,使其成为适合于用作灌溉的"生活污水"。

15   **胃**

16 平均来讲,现在的城市只能将垃圾总量的5%回收或者用于能源再生。而对于该城市来说,这个数字将可以达到80%,并因此通过垃圾的回收处理而获得繁荣发展。

17 人类的排泄物及有机废物将被用来发电。这些废物将被投入到一个厌氧消化池,池中加入酶以促进微生物分解这些废物。分解产生的化学物质经过发酵和蒸馏转化成生物燃料,为城市的汽车提供动力或者被用来发电。与此同时,这一过程中还能产生一些副产品,其中的氨基酸和维生素 B12 可以出售给药厂。

18 目前,各种各样的生态城市都在建设或者规划中。而这座城市所使用的科技手段也同样能应用于改造现在的传统城市。这将是一个伟大的目标,但这个项目的成功与否要等人们入住之后才能判定。

Exercises

I. Reading Comprehension

Section A

1. D 2. C 3. D 4. D 5. C

Section B

1. The sensors in every building compose the artificial nervous system of the city.

2. They can measure occupancy, temperature, humidity and energy use, and send the information to the central computer.

3. The rainwater can be collected by tanks on the plant-covered roofs of buildings.

4. Because the trash can be recycled for energy production.

5. No, various eco-cities are in the pipeline right now.

Section C

1. Frankly speaking, I don't know much about it. I think sensors are indispensable, as they can monitor objects in the life and send the information to the Internet. Then, the objects can be controlled as long as one can get access to the Internet.

2. If all objects in the world were connected to the Internet, daily life on our planet could undergo a great transformation. As they can communicate information about themselves and share it with the people, all objects can play an active role in the life.

3. It could be used in the business world. With such a network of the sensors, I guess it could greatly reduce the chances of a company running out of stock or wasting products, since all involved parties would know exactly which products are required and consumed.

II. Vocabulary and Structure

Section A

1. B 2. B 3. C 4. B 5. A 6. D 7. B 8. A 9. D 10. B

Section B

1. We should try to <u>recycle</u> all our waste paper.
   我们应该把所有废纸回收再利用。

2. An increase in crime is one of the <u>by-products</u> of unemployment.
   犯罪率增加是失业问题造成的恶果之一。

3. The oil is one-off <u>non-renewable</u> resource.
   石油是一次性的不可再生资源。

4. The new <u>biofuel</u> can be made directly from corn and soybeans.
   这种新型的生物燃料能够直接由玉米和大豆制造出来。

5. Few plants or animals <u>thrive</u> in the desert.
   几乎没有植物或动物能在沙漠中很好地生长。

6. Water is the core of a healthy <u>ecosystem</u>.
   水是维持生态系统良性循环的根本。

7. Mary is a smart young lady who would be an excellent <u>co-operator</u> for you.
   玛丽是一位聪颖的年青女士,她能成为你称心如意的合作伙伴。

8. The results will be very useful to monitor the percentage of <u>pollutants</u> in the air.
   研究结果对于监测空气中污染物含量比例是很有帮助的。

III. Word Building

1. The water <u>shortage</u> has affected everyone on the island.
   水源的短缺已经影响到了岛上的每一个人。

2. In calculating profit, retailers must allow for <u>breakage</u> and spoilage.
   计算利润时,零售商们必须考虑到破碎和损坏情况。

3. The news of their <u>marriage</u> was not made public until three months later.
   他们结婚的消息三个月后才公开。

4. What is the <u>postage</u> for an air letter?
   寄一封航空信的邮费是多少?

5. The fish should be kept in cold <u>storage</u>.
   那些鱼应冷藏起来。

6. What is the <u>percentage</u> of oxygen in air?
   空气中所含的氧气比例是多少?

7. She was brought up in an <u>orphanage</u> after her parents died.
   她的父母去世后, 她是在孤儿院里被抚养大的。

8. The hundreds of hours of <u>footage</u> showed how and why the couples fight.
   几百个小时的连续录相表明了这对夫妻是如何和为何打架的。

IV. Grammar Focus

1. The artificial flowers are not only beautiful, but also practical.

2. The beggar is not only thirty, but also hungry.

3. This lecture is not only interesting, but also helpful.

4. Mr. Wang can speak not only English, but also French.

5. The little boy can not only swim, but also skate.

V. Translation

1. The hot topic in technology in recent years <u>has always been the emergence of Internet of Things</u>.

   近几年科技领域的热门话题，一直都是物联网技术的出现。

2. <u>Data storage and processing power on the industrial scale</u> makes it possible to unleash supercomputing power on everyday tasks.

   已成为产业化规模的数据存储及处理能力使超级计算能力可以被用于日常工作中。

3. Billions of intelligent personal devices, such as smart phones, <u>are capable of plugging into the centralized computing resource</u> via the Internet.

   数十亿台智能个人设备，如智能手机，能够通过互联网接入这一集中化计算资源。

4. <u>Science could be revolutionized</u>, as researchers gain access to previously unimaginable amounts of data.

   科学领域可能会发生彻底的变革，因为研究人员能够获取之前难以想象的巨量数据。

5. It is predicted that so much information and processing power available at very low cost will <u>produce new breakthroughs in different fields.</u>

   据估计，以非常低的成本获得如此多的信息与处理能力将在不同的领域带来新的突破。

VI. Writing

Sample

A Letter of Job Application

Mar. 10 th, 2011

Dear Mr. Byron,

  I am writing in response to your advertisement for recruiting a software programmer in yesterday's China Daily. I hope I can take the job.

  I am a graduate student majored in computer science. The main reason for my confidence in this post lies in both my extensive academic training in software programming, and my work experience in the relevant industry which has further polished my abilities. Moreover, I also possess better interactive personal skills and teamwork spirit. Please find more details in my enclosed resume.

  Thank you for your time, and I would greatly appreciate it if you could grant me an interview.

Yours sincerely,

Li Ming

Notes

  When writing an application letter you should include:

First Paragraph: Why you are writing — mention the job you are applying for and where you get the information.

Middle Paragraph(s): What you have to offer the employer — mention why your skills and experience would be a good fit for the job.

Last Paragraph: Say thank you to the hiring manager for considering you and note how you will follow up.

Some supporting documents may be required when applying for a job. Supporting documents may include a resume, a transcript, portfolios, certifications, letters of recommendation, and other supporting documentation as specified in the job posting.

Useful Expressions for Job Applications:

In reply to your ad in today's newspaper, I respectfully offer my services for the position.

Replying to your ad in the newspaper, I wish to apply for the position in your esteemed firm.

I have been in the office of the XX Trading Co. Ltd., where I have been an accountant.

I have been employed for the last two years by the XX Co. Ltd., for the clerical work in an office.

I have acquired the knowledge of English, mathematics and elementary business practice.

At school I won a scholarship and the first prize in a speech contest.

I request an interview, and assure you that I will do my best to give you satisfaction.

I hope that you will be kind enough to consider my application favorably.

You will find enclosed copies of two letters of recommendation.

Enclosed please find a resume and a photo.

 **Text B**   **Background**

A smart house is a house that has highly advanced automatic systems for lighting, temperature control, multi-media, security, window and door operations, and many other functions.

A smart house appears "intelligent" because its computer systems can monitor so many aspects of daily living. For example, the refrigerator may be able to invent its contents, suggest menus, recommend healthy alternatives, and order groceries. The smart house systems might even take care of cleaning the cat's litter box and watering the plants.

The idea of a smart house may sound like something out of Hollywood. A 1999 movie titled *Smart House* presents the comical antics of an American family that wins a "house of the future" with a robot maid who causes havoc. Other films show a sci-fi vision of smart house technology that seems improbable.

However, smart house technology is real and it's becoming increasingly sophisticated. Coded signals are sent through the house's wiring to switches and outlets that are programmed to operate appliances and electronic devices in every part of the house. House automation can be especially useful for elderly and disabled persons who wish to live independently.

The smart home networking environment allows computers, appliances and devices to share and exchange data on a local area network (LAN). These individual home networks can be connected to a wide area network (WAN) for remote data exchange as well as communication functions. Many companies offer a series of smart house devices that operate in the BA/HA (Building Automation/Home Automation) category, acting as go-between devices that link in-home networks with WAN networks. The emergence of wireless and high-speed networking technologies is fueling the growth of this industry with more services being added and costs continuing to fall.

New Words

appliance /əˈplaɪəns/ *n.* 器具;(家用)电器
 e. g. Dish washer is one of the appliances.
   洗碗机是家用电器的一种。

capacity /kəˈpæsɪtɪ/ *n.* 容量;生产能力;生产量
 e. g. Power capacity expansion slows down from 2008.
   发电量的提升速度从 2008 年开始放缓。

conceive /kənˈsiːv/ *v.* 想出(主意、计划等);构想
 e. g. I conceived that there must be some difficulties.
   我料想到一定有些困难。

cottage /ˈkɒtɪdʒ/ *n.* 小屋,村舍
 e. g. We live in a humble cottage.
   我们住在一所简陋的小屋里。

device /dɪˈvaɪs/ *n.* 装置,设备;手段,策略
 e. g. A computer is a device for processing information.
   电脑就是一个用来处理信息的机器。

epic /ˈepɪk/ *n.* 史诗;惊人的壮举
 e. g. Mending the car became something of an epic.
   修理汽车竟然也算是了不起的事。

glow /gləʊ/ *v.* 燃烧;发出暗淡的光;脸红
 e. g. A cigarette glowed in the dark.
   黑暗中有支香烟散发着暗红的光芒。

grid /grɪd/ *n.* 系统网络;输电网
 e. g. Power can be fed from wind generators into the electricity grid system.
   电力可以从风力发电机流入输电网。

install /ɪnˈstɔːl/ *v.* 安装;安置
 e. g. Yesterday he installed a telephone in my house.
   昨天,他给我家安装了一个电话。

investigate /ɪnˈvestɪɡeɪt/ *v.* 调查;审查;研究

    e.g. The police are investigating the murder.

        警察在调查那起凶杀案件。

peak /piːk/ *n.* 最高点,最高水平;高峰

    e.g. He's at the peak of his career.

        他正处于事业的巅峰。

proposal /prəˈpəuzəl/ *n.* 提议;建议;求婚

    e.g. They presented concrete proposals for improvement.

        他们提出了具体的改进建议。

quarterly /ˈkwɔːtəlɪ/ *adj.* 一年四次的,每季的

    e.g. It is a quarterly magazine.

        这是一份按季出版的杂志。

remote /rɪˈməut/ *adj.* 远离的,遥远的;偏僻的

    e.g. At night I like to look at the remote stars in the clear sky.

        晚上我喜欢观看晴朗的夜空中遥远的星星。

trivial /ˈtrɪvɪəl/ *adj.* 琐碎的;平常的,普通的

    e.g. At first, the problem seemed to be trivial.

        起初,这个问题似乎并不重要。

update /ˈʌpdeɪt/ *v.* 更新;向……提供最新信息

    e.g. The TV updated a news story on the bad storm coming to our area.

        电视就我们地区即将来临的暴风雨作了最新报道。

Phrases and Expressions

at short notice 立即,仓促

    e.g. He found it difficult to get a hotel room at short notice.

        要在这么短的时间里找到一个房间,对他来说也太难了。

be aware of 知道,意识到

    e.g. He doesn't seem to be aware of the problem.

        他好像没有意识到这个问题。

leave on 让……燃着,让……开着

    e.g. It's expensive to leave the electric stove on all day.

        整天开着电炉太浪费钱了。

take a toll on 夺去,造成损失

    e.g. Researches show a pessimistic outlook can take a huge toll on your health.

        调查显示,悲观厌世会大大损害你的身体健康。

Proper Names

Ridley Scott　里德利·斯科特(英国著名导演)

New Exploration College English

Stanford Clark　斯坦福·克拉克

Twitter　推特网(国外的一个提供社交网络及微博客服务的网站)

British Science Festival　英国科学节(在英国,每年九月份举办一次面向各个年龄层、各个群体的科普活动)

参 考 译 文

能上网的智能房屋

1　想象一下那将会是一个什么样的情景:玻璃窗可以自动清洗干净;房屋周围的阳光像涓涓细流在五彩的颜料中流淌,能随着你的心意而自动变换颜色;又或者是收到文本信息后,一组圣诞麋鹿彩灯便会自动闪亮。

2　也许最好的情景是,每个季度都可以从电力公司收到一张支票,因为你的房屋的发电量要比耗电量多。难道这是里德利·斯科特最新的史诗般作品中的场景吗?

3　不,上述这些想法都源自于一个探究人工智能技术如何被应用于家庭中的研究项目。昨晚,工程师斯坦福·克拉克在英国科学节上发表讲话,描述了他在自己的16世纪茅屋安装传感器的事。这些传感器能告诉他房屋的所有信息,从用了多少水,到窗户是否开着等等。

4　房屋中共装有大约24个无线传感器以监控温度和水电使用情况,并将这些信息传至中央服务器。服务器根据这些信息作出智能决定,管理房屋内的各种设施。克拉克还在书房安装了一个灯泡,当房屋的耗电量达到最大值时,就发出红光警告。

5　说得更具体些,当克拉克辛勤工作了一天回家时,服务器能确保院子里的喷泉打开以迎接主人。如果服务器通过识别主人口袋里的手机感应到主人进了屋,一个显示屏将会向他致以问候。它甚至还能准备好暖和的浴巾,供主人健身后淋浴使用。

6　然而,这些技术的主要目的是减少房屋的耗电量。接入网络中每种设备的选用都取决于其能耗使用率。去年,克拉克使中央服务器能自动通过Twitter网及时告诉他家里的水电使用的情况,不管他在世界上哪个地方。

7　每消耗5英镑的电能,房屋里安装的各种蜂鸣器就会发出鸣叫声,并且以同样的方式监测水的使用。因此,家人们能更好地意识到让高耗能家电一直开着的后果,从此开始更有效地安排电能的使用,从而使家庭的电费减少大约三分之一左右。

8　然而,所有这些仅仅是开始。克拉克设想在全国范围内建立一个半感应的"智能电网",从厨房里的冰箱到远山上的风能发电机都能监控。他认为,将能源链条从生产到消耗的每一环节连结在一起,能使我们更有效地利用能源。目前,高耗能电器的使用耗费了电网大量的能源。

9　能够自动监测和管理家庭用电的智能电网可随时为人们提供额外电能,比如说,关掉电冰箱或者甚至可以向电动车"借"电,以供人们看电视后烧水泡茶。这样不仅终端用户的电费减少了,而且生产等量电能所消耗的化石燃料也少得多。

10　所有这些建议都是智能星球倡议的一部分,旨在让我们思考如何获得和消耗能源——这是在减少碳排放量的努力中我们全人类将必须认真思考的问题。

294

Exercises

I. Reading Comprehension

1. D 2. D 3. B 4. D 5. C

II. Vocabulary and Structure

1. C 2. D 3. B 4. D 5. A 6. B 7. B 8. A 9. A 10. B

III. Translation

1. Imagine <u>receiving a quarterly check from the electricity company</u>, because your house is producing more power than it is consuming.

   设想一下每个季度你都会从电力公司收到一张支票,因为你的房屋的发电量要比耗电量多。

2. <u>In the event that someone were to fall</u>, the smart house system would immediately monitor the pulse to see if the person has gone into shock.

   假如有人摔了一跤,智能家居系统将会立刻监测他的脉搏,以观察他是否休克。

3. Smart home appliances <u>can share all kinds of helpful information with homeowners</u>.

   各种智能家用电器能与房主一起分享各种有用的信息。

4. Data from the smart appliances can be securely transmitted to the home network and <u>accessed by authorized users</u>.

   智能家用电器监测到的数据可以安全地传输到家庭网络上,供授权用户访问。

5. The intention of designing the smart house system is <u>not to invade privacy</u>, but to help the elderly people who are living alone.

   设计智能家居系统的目的不是为了侵犯隐私,而是为了帮助那些独自生活的老人。

Part V Time for Fun

参 考 译 文

大 脑 袋

"所有的孩子都拿我开玩笑," 小男孩哭着跟妈妈说:"他们说我长了一个大脑袋。"

"别听他们的",他妈妈安慰说:"你的脑袋长得很漂亮。好了,别哭了,去商店买 10 磅土豆来。"

"购物袋在哪?"

"我现在没有购物袋,你就用你的帽子吧。"

Unit 7

3-D Technology

Part I Teaching Objectives

* **Listening & Speaking:**

Help the students to be familiar with the topic—*how to express yourself when talking about the application of 3-D technology in movies & TV* and memorize useful expressions.

* **Words & Expressions:**

Study some new words and expressions, such as *episode*, *brew*, *unveil*, *anticipate*, *dimension*, *upgrade*, *privilege*, *forefront*, *entice*, *induce*, *perspective*, *unfamiliar*, *adjust*, *on the horizon*, *strive for*, *anything but* and so on.

* **Grammar:**

Learn to use the structure of *whereas*.

* **Writing:**

Understand and write *a letter of resignation*.

Part II Listening——3-D Films

New Words

amusing /əˈmjuːzɪŋ/ *adj.* 有趣的,逗人笑的
    e. g. He told amusing jokes after dinner.
           他在饭后讲了几则令人捧腹的笑话。

angle /ˈæŋgl/ *n.* 角度;观点,立场
    e. g. They discussed the matter from all conceivable angles.
           他们从各种角度讨论了那件事。

digital /ˈdɪdʒɪtl/ *adj.* 数字式的,数码的

e. g.   There's a digital watch on the table.

桌子上有一块数字手表。

launch   /lɔːntʃ/   *v.* 上市，发行；发动；发射

  e. g.   They launched an aggressive election campaign.

他们发起了一场大张旗鼓的竞选活动。

manufacturer   /ˌmænjʊˈfæktʃərə/   *n.* 制造商，生产商

  e. g.   She designs for a coat manufacturer.

她为一家外衣制造厂设计图样。

perception   /pəˈsepʃən/   *n.* 感知（能力）；觉察（力）

  e. g.   He is a man of acute perception.

他是一个感觉敏锐的人。

Drugs can change your perception of reality.

毒品能够改变你对现实的感知。

project   /ˈprɒdʒekt/   *v.* 投射；发射；投影；规划

  e. g.   I had no screen, so I projected the slides onto the white wall.

我没有幕布，所以我把幻灯片投射到白墙上。

ridiculous   /rɪˈdɪkjʊləs/   *adj.* 可笑的，荒谬的

  e. g.   It's the most ridiculous thing I've ever heard in my life.

这是我有生以来听到的最为荒唐可笑的事。

spectacle   /ˈspektəkl/   *n.* 壮观的场面或景象

  e. g.   The spectacle greatly excited us at the time.

当时那场面令我们十分激动。

Phrases and Expressions

around the corner   迫在眉睫的；即将到来；在拐角处

  e. g.   Victory is just around the corner.

胜利就在眼前。

be scheduled to   安排、计划做某事；排定时间

  e. g.   The meeting is tentatively scheduled to be held on Tuesday.

这个会议暂定于星期二举行。

 One

Listen to the CD and mark T for True or F for False according to the dialogue.

1. F   2. F   3. F   4. T   5. T

Script

David：Hey, sweetie, come and look at this news.

  Alice：I'm coming.

David: James Cameron's *Avatar* is proving the most successful 3-D movie ever made.

Alice: Wow! It says the box office has topped over a billion.

David: Now, the 3-D technology is suddenly everywhere. This year, around 7 out of 10 movies will be made in 3-D.

Alice: It seems you are right. So what's the difference?

David: Digital technology. Instead of using film, digital camera project images from a computer's hard drive.

Alice: Why would so many films ride the 3-D wave?

David: It transforms cinema-goers' experience. I think it is also the future of television.

Alice: It is only a matter of time before the technology reaches TV, I guess.

David: Yeah, TV manufacturers are ready to launch 3-D channels.

 Two

Listen to the CD and answer the following questions with the information you hear.

1. Why does Ellen want to read magazines?

   She reads magazines to refresh the mind.

2. How does Alex think of the 3-D movie?

   He thinks it is the greatest innovation in film.

3. What is the advantage of the 3-D movie?

   It creates a richer and more engaging experience.

4. What are the side effects of the 3-D movie?

   The side effects are headaches, blurred vision, and unnatural eye movements.

5. Is there any solution?

   No, there is no clear way right now.

Script

Ellen: Hi, Alex. Do you have any magazines? I'd like to refresh my mind.

Alex: OK, there are some movie magazines. Here you are.

Ellen: Thank you, man. Are you a movie lover?

Alex: Of course, I am.

Ellen: So, you know the 3-D movies, the new trend.

Alex: Yes. It is the greatest innovation in film since color film, I think.

Ellen: Wow.

Alex: 3-D creates a richer and more engaging experience than 2-D flat image. I think it will become the new standard and become more popular.

Ellen: But do you notice that many movie-goers report the discomfort after watching 3-D movies?

Alex: Yeah, I know. It indeed has some unwanted side effects. Many viewers complain that 3-D films give them headaches, blurred vision, and unnatural eye movements.

Ellen: Any solution?

Alex: No, up to now, there is no proven way.

Spot Dictation

----

1. the technology is older than your great grandfather
2. in the late 19th and the early 20th centuries
3. to display their movies in three dimensions
4. broadcast films on two separate screens
5. merging the two images and creating the illusion of 3-D

Part III   Speaking——3-D Movies and TV

Useful Expressions About the 3-D Movies & TV

3-D technology has come a long way.

3-D is even making its way into our living rooms already.

3-D TV is quickly growing in popularity.

New technologies are paving the way for 3-D TVs.

More and more 3-D TVs and kits are being developed and released to the public.

In today's age of technology and entertainment, 3-D is acquiring a groundbreaking status.

Almost all 3-D movies released in past years have been a hit at box office.

It does leave you feelings like you've just seen a spectacle.

It can cause unnatural eye movements that induce strain, headaches and sickness.

It would just take some post-production video rendering and a pair of stereoscopic glasses.

It will probably be the technology that doesn't require glasses coming through.

It might be cool to see action moves come at you and animated characters jump out of the screen.

It shows the outstanding creativity of imagination in the production of 3-D movies.

3-D movies acquire large popularity and are a hit in almost every theatre.

3 - D movies require intricate designing, good creative skills and above all good understandings.

3-D movies are all about imagining things and then picturing them onto screen with a storyline.

Pair Work

Sample

Allen: Hi, what's that in your hand?

Belle: A poster of *Avatar*.

Allen: Oh, so you already see that movie?

Belle: Yes, I went to see the 3-D *Avatar* last night.

Allen: How do you feel, the 3-D movie?

Belle: I think the 3-D quality is really good.

Allen: Really? I haven't seen that before.

Belle: The ticket price is a little bit ridiculous, but it does leave you feelings like you've just seen a spectacle.

Allen: Fine, forget that. Are you free tomorrow?

Belle: Let me check the schedule. Yeah, I am free tomorrow night. What?

Allen: I'd like to go to see the 3-D movie *Clash of the Titans*. Would you like to go with me?

Belle: Surely, I will.

Allen: Alright, see you tomorrow.

Belle: See you.

Role-play

Sample

Daughter: Daddy, I have finished my homework.

Father: Well done, my little girl.

Daughter: Can I watch the cartoons on 3-D TV?

Father: No, you can not, sweetie.

Daughter: Not even for a while?

Father: No, not even for a while.

Daughter: Why can't I watch it? It is really amusing.

Father: You are still too young, baby. The doctor says that it can cause unnatural eye movements that induce strain, headaches and sickness.

Daughter: Really? Why is that?

Father: Because normally we see things at a different angle that creates the perception of depth.

Daughter: Er...

Father: But the illusion that you see in 3-D TV is not processed in the same way.

Daughter: And that would harm my eyes?

Father: Yes, baby.

Daughter: OK, I'll go out and have some fun.

Part IV Reading

Text A   **Background**

1. 3-D

Generally speaking, 3-D refers to something having three dimensions: width, length, and depth. In computers, 3-D describes an image that provides the perception of depth. When 3-D images are made interactive, users would feel involved with the scene. The experience is called virtual reality.

2. 3-D TV

3-D has become the buzz word in the entertainment world, especially after the phenomenal success of *Avatar*. The buzz has now been carried over to the home entertainment world with major television set manufacturers announcing the production of 3-D television sets.

A 3-D TV is a television set that employs techniques of 3-D presentation, such as stereoscopic capture, multi-view capture, or 2-D-plus-depth, and a 3-D display—a special viewing device to project a television program into a realistic three-dimensional field.

3. 3-D TV Technology

While many are excited about the arrival of a new revolution in television viewing, they are not so clear about what 3-D TV technology is all about.

First of all, let us look at how it's possible to view moving pictures on television in 3-D. It's actually our two eyes that help us make 3-D vision possible. The two sets of images that our eyes capture from the cinema or TV screen are sent to our brains which piece them together to form a single 3-D image.

3-D cinema and TV take advantage of this potential of the eyes by offering slightly differing images to the left eye and the right eye. When this happens there's the simulation of 3-D images we are used to viewing in the real world. Essentially, the brain is tricked into thinking that it's actually looking at a three dimensional image.

4. 3-D TV Equipment

But then you may not be quite sure what equipment is needed to make 3-D TV view a reality. Among the equipments you would need are a 3-D TV set, a set-top box from a satellite television station that broadcasts 3-D content, a 3-D Blue-ray player and a pair of 3-D glasses.

New Words

align /əˈlaɪn/   *v.* 使成一线;使一致

    e. g. Could you align this table with those ones?

            你能把这张桌子同那些桌子排成一行吗?

anticipate /æn'tɪsɪpeɪt/ *v.* 期望;预见,预计(并做准备)

    e. g. I anticipate deriving much instruction from the lecture.

          我期望从演讲中获得很多指导。

brew /bruː/ *v.* 调制,酿造;酝酿,图谋

    e. g. It looks as if a storm is brewing.

          看样子一场暴风雨即将来临。

dimension /dɪ'menʃən/ *n.* 尺寸,度量;维度

    e. g. Length is one dimension, and breadth is another.

          长是一种度量,宽又是另一种度量。

entice /entaɪs/ *v.* 诱使,引诱

    e. g. Nothing will entice the children from television.

          没有任何东西能把孩子们从电视机前引开。

episode /'epɪsəʊd/ *n.* (人生的)一段经历;(小说的)片段;(电视的)一集

    e. g. The first episode goes out next Friday evening at 8:00 pm.

          下星期五晚上8时播出第一集。

equivalent /ɪ'kwɪvələnt/ *adj.* 相等的,相当的;等量的

    e. g. Changing her job like that is equivalent to firing her.

          那样调换她的工作等于是解雇她。

ESPN *abbr.* 娱乐体育节目电视网(Entertainment and Sports Programming Network)

flimsy /'flɪmzɪ/ *adj.* 不结实的;易损坏的

    e. g. The storm flattened the flimsy wooden huts that the villagers lived in.

          风暴将村民们居住的脆弱的木屋夷为平地。

forefront /fɔːfrʌnt/ *n.* 最前列,最前部

    e. g. The new product took the company to the forefront of the computer software market.

          新产品使得该公司在计算机软件市场处于领先地位。

full-fledged /'fʊl'fledʒd/ *adj.* 成熟的;羽毛生齐的

    e. g. The book was a full-fledged study of American history.

          这是本很完备的美国历史书。

gimmick /'gɪmɪk/ *n.* 花招,诡计,骗人的玩意儿

    e. g. It is only a new gimmick to encourage people to go to the cinema.

          那只不过是鼓动大众去看电影的新噱头。

HD *abbr.* 高清晰度(High Definition)

hurdle /'hɜːdl/ *n.* 跳栏;障碍;难关

    e. g. In starting a new company, many hurdles must be crossed.

          刚开办一个公司时,必须克服许多障碍。

immerse /ɪ'mɜːs/ *v.* 使沉浸于;深陷于

    e. g. He immersed himself totally in his work.

          他埋头于工作中。

LCD *abbr.* 液晶显示屏(Liquid Crystal Display)

mean /miːn/ *adj.* 吝啬的;自私的;卑鄙的

e.g. Her husband is rather mean over money matters.

她的丈夫在金钱方面非常小气。

NBA *abbr.* 美国职业篮球联赛(National Basketball Association)

plasma /ˈplæzmə/ *n.* 等离子体

e.g. Why do you want a 42-inch Plasma Television?

你为什么想要一台 42 英寸等离子电视呢?

privilege /ˈprɪvɪlɪdʒ/ *n.* 特权,特别待遇;特殊荣幸

e.g. He never abuses his privilege.

他从不滥用特权。

surpass /sɜːˈpɑːs/ *v.* 超过,优于,多于

e.g. The beauty of the scenery surpassed my expectation.

该处风景之秀丽超出我的预料。

turf /tɜːf/ *n.* 地盘;势力范围

e.g. Turf wars are inevitable when two departments are merged.

两个部门合并时总免不了争夺权限。

unveil /ˌʌnˈveɪl/ *v.* 除去面纱(或覆盖物);揭幕;揭露

e.g. He has promised to unveil a new plan this week.

他承诺要在这周公布新计划。

upgrade /ˌʌpˈgreɪd/ *v.* 升级;提高,改进

e.g. Why not upgrade your operating system?

你怎么不升级操作系统呢?

Phrases and Expressions

be bound to 一定会,必然

e.g. Your effort is bound to be successful.

你的努力一定会成功的。

be dying to 渴望,迫不及待地

e.g. I'm dying to be with you again.

我热切盼望着再次回到你们身边。

in the infancy 处于萌芽状态,在初期

e.g. The industry was still in its infancy.

这一产业当时仍处于发展初期。

on the horizon 即将来临的

e.g. The economic revival might be on the horizon.

经济的复苏似乎近在眼前了。

strive for 为……奋斗,争取

e. g. We must strive for further increase in production.
　　　我们必须为进一步发展生产而努力。

Proper Names

Ralph Kramden	拉尔夫·卡拉门登
Jackie Gleason	杰克·格里森
James Cameron	詹姆斯·卡梅隆(著名电影导演,擅长拍摄动作片以及科幻电影。目前电影票房史上最卖座的两部电影《泰坦尼克号》和《阿凡达》都是他执导的作品)
John Taylor	约翰·泰勒
Riddhi Patel	瑞迪希·帕特尔
World Cup	世界杯(足球赛)
Super Bowl	超级碗(美国国家橄榄球联盟的年度冠军赛)
The Honeymooners	《蜜月伴侣》(电影)
Avatar	《阿凡达》(电影)

参考译文

电视开始步入三维时代

1　拉尔夫·卡拉门登终于可以买一台电视机了。

2　那是半个多世纪以前,在1955年上映的电影《蜜月伴侣》中有这样的一幕:由杰克·格里森饰演的卡拉门登是一位吝啬的公交车司机,他告诉妻子,之所以没买电视机,是因为"我在等待3-D电视机"。

3　现在,这种等待即将结束。随着电视制造商开始推出3-D电视机,有线电视节目运营商也急于为它们开通新频道,一场关于3-D电视市场份额的争夺战已蓄势待发。

4　然而,很多人对此持怀疑态度。因为他们不相信消费者会立刻将液晶电视和等离子电视从墙上取下来换掉。此外,这种起价在2 000美元左右的3-D电视机甚至比目前市场上最高端的平板电视的价格还要高。除此以外消费者为了看这种电视还得购买特殊的眼镜——护目镜。

5　但是,电视节目运营商和技术公司都认为,消费者将会立刻爱上3-D电视。在某种程度上说,它可能是电影《阿凡达》带来的效果;3-D电影极大地提高了电影的票房收入。詹姆斯·卡梅隆的《阿凡达》上映不久就突破了惊人的20亿美元票房大关,因此许多公司现在已经下定决心要把同样效果的体验带入到人们的起居室中。

6　对于即将到来的3-D浪潮,美国娱乐体育节目网表示,他们将会在一个全新的网络上以3-D模式播放世界杯足球比赛和全美职业篮球联赛。主要的电视生产商也都表示,他们将于明年共同开通一个3-D娱乐频道。

7　"众星联手将把2010年变成3-D之年,"一家电视生产商的副总裁约翰·泰勒如是说。尽管3-D电视现在刚处于起步阶段,但一旦它的羽翼日渐丰满,能提供大量的电视节目供人们观看——很多人正在为此而付出努力——那将会成为消费者真正的引爆点。

8　到那时,问题就转变成了那些刚刚花了大价钱升级到高清电视机的消费者是否依然因非常想观看3-D电视而再度花钱。分析师瑞迪希·帕特尔说:"我认为这个国家90%的男人都极其渴望自己能融入到超级碗的比赛中。"

9　但是,对于大多数消费者来说,3-D电视仍然很遥远。多家媒体公司正试图投身于这一新兴技术的前沿,正如他们10年前领军高清电视那样。

10　借助大量的高清节目和便宜得足够吸引中产阶级消费者的价格,高清电视用了10年时间才成为娱乐主流的一部分。分析师们预测3-D电视也会经历同样的艰苦历程。

11　当然,这种技术也可能会完全失败。

12　几十年来,3-D都是B级电影(水平不高的影片),时而也是电视上的花哨噱头——戴着脆玻璃纸造的质量低下的眼镜来观看——但新技术已经大大地抹掉了这种印象。即将问世的新技术可以让人们在不戴特殊眼镜的情况下就可以观看3-D画面,但也存在严重的局限性,如观看者必须在一定的距离外观看。

13　事实上,3-D电视大范围推广仍然存在大量的障碍,比如说,缺乏生产设备和统一的3-D传输标准。但是支持者们声称:3-D必将得到重视,因为消费者和生产商一直在为最大限度地贴近现实生活而努力。

Exercises

I. Reading Comprehension

Section A

1. D　2. B　3. D　4. C　5. A

Section B

1. They are brewing a 3-D television turf war.

2. Many people are skeptical about that.

3. It takes HD television about a decade to become a part of the entertainment mainstream.

4. It is around $2 000 for a 3-D set at the beginning.

5. Because consumers and producers are always striving for what looks closest to real life.

Section C

1. I don't know much about the technology. I just know it has been applied to the movie production. There are many movies released in 3-D in recent years, and a lot of people are attracted to watch them.

2. Yes, I do. It is said that the 3-D movie does leave you wonderful feelings. I think it's cool to see actors jump out of the screen.

3. I think it is bound to gain a lot of publicity, as many TV manufacturers are launching types

of 3-D TV into the market. The future is unimaginable.

II. Vocabulary and Structure

Section A

1. B   2. B   3. B   4. A   5. A   6. D   7. D   8. A   9. D   10. A

Section B

1. We are looking forward to their visit with eager <u>anticipation</u>.
   我们热切地期待着他们的来访。

2. If you can not <u>upgrade</u> your media player, it is because your Internet Explorer is too old.
   如果你不能升级媒体播放器,那是因为网络浏览器的版本太旧了。

3. The <u>enticements</u> of the big city lured her away from her home.
   大城市的种种诱惑吸引了她离家出走。

4. Silence is sometimes <u>equivalent</u> to agreement.
   沉默有时等于同意。

5. With her speed, Cage cut out all her competitors in the <u>hurdle</u> race.
   凯奇在跨栏赛跑中速度很快,击败了其他的所有选手。

6. These professors always <u>immerse</u> themselves in their subjects.
   这些教授一直埋头研究他们的课题。

7. She owns the house <u>jointly</u> with her husband.
   她和丈夫共同拥有这所房子。

8. How do you <u>entertain</u> yourself after work?
   你如何消磨工作之余的时间?

III. Word Building

1. The fishermen were <u>forewarned</u> of the oncoming storm.
   渔民预先得到了暴风雨来临的警告。

2. They are the most precious cultural legacy our <u>forefathers</u> left.
   它们是我们祖先留下来的最宝贵的文化遗产。

3. It was hot in the studio, and drops of sweat stood on her <u>forehead</u>.
   工作室里很热,她的额头渗出了汗珠。

4. No one can <u>foresee</u> what will happen in the future.
   谁也无法预见到将来会发生什么事。

5. Now scientists can <u>forecast</u> the weather accurately.
   现在科学家们能准确地预报天气。

6. His team is at the <u>forefront</u> of scientific research into viruses.
   他的小组处在病毒研究领域的最前沿。

7. This book has a <u>foreword</u> by the President.
   这本书有一篇总统作的序言。

8. Every disaster gives a <u>foretaste</u> of death.

每一个灾难都让我们预先尝到了死亡的的滋味。

IV. Grammar Focus

1. Wise men love truth, whereas fools shun it.

2. Some people like coffee, whereas others like tea.

3. Tom is very diligent, whereas his brother is quite lazy.

4. Modesty helps one go forward, whereas conceit makes one lag behind.

5. I think he meant what he said, whereas you believe it was a joke.

V. Translation

1. With 3-D TV to take over the entertainment world, <u>it is bound to become part of our style experience</u>.

随着3-D电视逐渐成为娱乐界的主流,它注定会成为我们时尚体验的一部分。

2. We should expect that the use of 3-D technology <u>will make its way into the normal household</u>.

我们应该期待3-D技术能够进入到普通百姓的家庭中。

3. New technologies and adaptations of old technologies <u>pave the way for the 3-D TV.</u>

新技术的出现以及旧技术的改进为3-D电视的到来铺平了道路。

4. The cable programmers have not confirmed <u>an exact launch date for its 3-D channel.</u>

电视节目运营商尚未确定3-D电视节目频道上市的准确日期。

5. If you've been fascinated with the latest 3-D movie <u>and want to reproduce that experience at home</u>, a 3-D TV would be the way to go.

如果你非常喜欢最近上映的3-D电影,并且想把这种体验复制到家中,那3-D电视将是你的选择。

VI. Writing

Sample

A Letter of Resignation

Mar. 10th, 2011

Dear Mr. Wang,

I am writing to notify you that I am resigning from my position as Customer Service Manager with XXX Company. My last day of employment will be April 1st.

Thank you for the opportunities for professional and personal development that you have provided me during the last five years. I have enjoyed working for the company and appreciate the support that you and my dear colleagues have provided to me.

I wish you and the company the best of success in the future. If I can assist with the transition, please do let me know.

Yours sincerely,

Li Ming

Notes

When writing a resignation letter, it's important to keep your resignation letter as simple, brief and focused as possible. It should also be positive. Once you have made the decision to move on, there's no point in criticizing your employer or your job.

First Paragraph: Your letter should state you are resigning and when your resignation is effective.

Middle Paragraph(s): The next section of your resignation letter should thank your employer for the opportunities you have had during your employment with the company.

Final Paragraph: Conclude your resignation letter by offering to assist with the transition.

Regardless of why you are resigning or how you feel about it, if you mention why you are leaving, make sure that you do not include anything negative or disparaging about the company, your supervisor, your co-workers or your subordinates.

This letter will be included in your employment file and could be shared with potential future employers. Therefore, it should be professional and polite.

Useful Expressions for Resignation Letter:

I am writing to inform you of my resignation, effective on July 15.

I write to tender my resignation. My last day of employment will be June 16.

By this letter I am resigning my position as Quality Engineer, effective immediately.

My experience at XXX Company has been both educational and rewarding.

I appreciate the opportunity to work and learn at XXX Company.

I want to thank you for the wonderful experience I had with XXX Company.

I wish you and company the best of luck and future success.

Text B   **Background**

1. 3-D Film

A 3-D (three-dimensional) film or S3-D (stereoscopic 3-D) film is a motion picture that enhances the illusion of depth perception. Derived from stereoscopic photography, a regular motion picture camera system is used to record the images as seen from two perspectives (or computer-generated imagery generates the two perspectives in post-production), and special projection hardware and/or eyewear are used to provide the illusion of depth when viewing the film.

3-D films have existed in some forms since the 1950s, but had been largely relegated to a niche in the motion picture industry because of the costly hardware and processes required to produce and display a 3-D film, and the lack of a standardized format for all segments of the entertainment business. Nonetheless, 3-D films were prominently featured in the 1950s in

American cinema, and later experienced a worldwide resurgence in the 1980s and the 1990s driven by IMAX high-end theaters and Disney-themed venues. 3-D films became more and more successful throughout the 2000s, culminating in the unprecedented success of 3-D presentations of *Avatar* in December, 2009 and January, 2010.

2. Possible Side Effects and Other Health Risks

Be aware of the possible side effects of watching 3-D movies & TV. Particularly at risk are young children, the elderly, those under the influence of alcohol and the pregnant women.

If you experience any of the following symptoms, immediately stop watching 3-D pictures and go consulting a medical specialist: (1) altered vision; (2) lightheadedness; (3) dizziness; (4) involuntary movements such as eye or muscle twitching; (5) confusion; (6) nausea; (7) loss of awareness; (8) convulsions; (9) cramps; and/or (10) disorientation.

Viewing in 3-D mode may also cause motion sickness, perceptual after effects, eye strain and decreased postural stability. It is recommended that viewers take frequent breaks to lessen the likelihood of these effects.

DO NOT watch 3-D if you are in bad physical condition, namely, you need sleep or have been drinking alcohol.

DO NOT use the 3-D Active Glasses for any purpose other than viewing 3-D television. Wearing the glasses for any other purpose (like general spectacles, sunglasses, protective goggles, etc.) may physically harm you or weaken your eyesight.

DO NOT place your television near open stairwells, cables, balconies or other objects that may cause you to injure yourself, as viewing in 3-D mode may cause disorientation for some viewers.

New Words

adjust /əˈdʒʌst/ *v.* 适应；调整，校正

    e. g.   If fate does not adjust itself to you, adjust yourself to fate.

            命运不能迁就你时，要学会迁就命运。

appetite /ˈæpɪtaɪt/ *n.* 胃口，食欲；强烈欲望

    e. g.   Proper exercises give us a good appetite.

            适度运动能增加人的食欲。

comparable /ˈkɒmpərəbl/ *adj.* 同类的，相当的，可比较的

    e. g.   Your achievements are comparable with the best.

            你们的成就可比得上最好的。

convincing /kənˈvɪnsɪŋ/ *adj.* 令人相信的，有说服力的

    e. g.   This argument seems convincing, but is easily overturned.

            这个论点好像令人信服，但很容易就被推翻了。

distraction /dɪsˈtrækʃən/ *n.* 分散注意力的事，分心

    e. g.   There are too many distractions here to work properly.

这里叫人分心的事太多,无法好好工作。

executive /ɪɡˈzekjʊtɪv/ *n.* 行政领导,领导层

e.g. The executives have been making decisions about the future of the company.

领导层一直在研究公司未来的决策。

hit /hɪt/ *n.* 成功而风行一时的事物

e.g. It is a hit song.

这是一首风行一时的歌曲。

hysterical /hɪsˈterɪkəlɪ/ *adj.* 情绪异常激动的,歇斯底里般的

e.g. His hysterical laughter made everybody stunned.

他那歇斯底里的笑声使所有的人不知所措。

illusion /ɪˈluːʒən/ *n.* 错觉,幻想,错误观念

e.g. The Sun appears to go round the Earth, but it's an illusion.

太阳看起来好像绕着地球转,但这只是个错觉。

imbalance /ɪmˈbæləns/ *n.* 不平衡,不均衡,失调

e.g. Medical experts say this disorder is caused by an imbalance in brain chemicals.

医学专家说这种紊乱是由于大脑中的化学物质失衡造成的。

induce /ɪnˈdjuːs/ *v.* 引诱,劝导,导致

e.g. Her illness was induced by overwork.

她的病是操劳过度引起的。

ophthalmologist /ɒfˌθælmɒlədʒɪst/ *n.* 眼科专家,眼科医师

e.g. You should let an ophthalmologist examine your eyes problem as soon as possible.

你应该尽快让眼科医师检查你的眼睛问题。

perspective /pə(ː)ˈspektɪv/ *n.* 远景;透视;观点,想法

e.g. You can get a perspective of the whole city from here.

从这里你可以看到城市的全景。

premium /ˈpriːmjəm/ *n.* 额外费用,附加费

e.g. You have to pay a premium for express delivery.

寄快速投递你得付额外费用。

propel /prəˈpel/ *v.* 推进,推动,驱使,迫使

e.g. To take responsibility will propel you forward to your greater good.

承担责任能推动你不断前进,创造更美好的前程。

savior /ˈseɪvjə/ *n.* 救助者,救星

e.g. They regarded him as the savior of their country.

他们把他看成国家的救星。

speck /spek/ *n.* 斑点,污点,微粒

e.g. I've got a speck of dirt on my shirt.

我的衬衫上有一点污垢。

stumble /ˈstʌmbl/ *v.* 绊脚,蹒跚而行

e.g.   It is a good horse that never stumbles, and a good wife that never grumbles.

好马无失闪,好妻无怨言。

unfamiliar   /ˌʌnfəˈmɪljə/   *adj.* 不熟悉的;不常见的;陌生的

e.g.   He can quickly adjust to the unfamiliar environment.

他能很快适应陌生的环境。

Phrases and Expressions

a slew of   许多,大量

e.g.   On that night, a slew of stars dazzled the audience with their performances.

那天晚上,众多明星用他们的表演让观众们看花了眼。

a string of   一串的,一系列,一批

e.g.   The basketball team had a string of victory last season.

这个篮球队在上一个赛季中赢得了一连串的胜利。

anything but   绝对不,根本不

e.g.   The problem is anything but easy.

这个问题绝不容易。

be opposed to   反对,不赞成

e.g.   She is opposed to your going abroad.

她非常不赞成你出国。

bet on   为某事打赌,下赌注

e.g.   Let's bet on the football match.

我们打赌看这场足球赛谁赢。

under normal circumstances   在正常情况下

e.g.   Under normal circumstances people tend to blink less frequently while at a computer.

一般情况下,人们在电脑前会减少眨眼频率。

Proper Names

Hollywood	好莱坞(世界著名的电影城市)
Lawrence of Arabia	托马斯·爱德华·劳伦斯(也称阿拉伯的劳伦斯,因在 1916 年至 1918 年的阿拉伯大起义中作为英国联络官的角色而出名。)
Reuters	路透社(世界前三大多媒体新闻通讯社之一)
Dr. Michael	迈克尔医生
Dr. Deborah	黛博拉医生
Jackass	《蠢蛋搞怪秀》(电影)
Step Up	《舞出我人生》(电影)
Casablanca	《卡萨布兰卡》(电影)
Consumer Reports	《消费者报告》(美国著名消费决策杂志)

参考译文

3-D 电影未来的忧虑

1   3-D 技术曾被奉为电影行业的伟大救世主,但自从该技术令《阿凡达》创下破纪录的 27.3 亿美元票房后,外界正愈发担心,好莱坞正使这一有利可图的新模式陷入危险中。

2   3-D 技术不仅为好莱坞赚了个盆满钵满,而且产生了许多轰动一时的效应。当年位居票房排行榜前三的电影全部都是 3-D 影片,然而这才是序幕。人们极其期待的 3-D 电影《蠢蛋搞怪秀》很可能会引发一阵盲目的观看热潮。但是,最近一些 3-D 电影的票房却遭遇滑铁卢,例如,3-D 电影《舞出我人生》的票房都不及同系列前两部的 2-D 影片。

3   好莱坞的制片公司之所以钟爱 3-D 电影,是因为到目前为止,消费者一直愿意花高价观看此类电影。但由于 3-D 电影票价高出同类 2-D 电影票价的 50% 以上,分析人士对消费者能否保持住对 3-D 电影的热情提出质疑,特别是在影片情节糟糕的情况下。

4   3-D 电影是一种空间的浪费。当你在观看 2-D 电影时,只要你深深关注电影的情节,电影的画面就已经是三维立体的了,因为你已经深陷其中。当你看见"阿拉伯的劳伦斯"骑在马背上,横穿荒芜人烟的沙漠,从一个小小的黑点渐渐一点点的变大,慢慢地朝你走来,你是否会想,"看他从地平线那端走来,走地多么的缓慢啊!"我们的思想通过透视法则对远景画面进行整体解读,就已经制造出立体的画面。而通过人工制造的幻象使画面缺乏说服力。

5   3-D 电影对于观影体验毫无影响。试着回想一下这辈子你所体会到的深刻最印象的观影经历,那些经历需要 3-D 技术的帮助吗?一部伟大的电影作品会充分发挥我们的想象力。电影《卡萨布兰卡》如果以 3-D 的方式播放,你能体会到什么感受呢?

6   3-D 电影会让观众分散注意力。有些 3-D 电影仅仅是两个分开的视觉平面相互交错,从而产生立体的效果,其实它们本身还是 2-D 电影。在 2-D 电影中,导演经常会采用焦点的变化将观众的注意力引向故事情节的前景或背景。而 3-D 技术本身似乎在表明场景的纵深立体感就应该是人们关注的焦点,从而使导演失去了吸引观众注意力的一种技术手段。

7   3-D 电影会导致部分观众产生头痛感。当 3-D 电影刚刚开始发行上市的时候,路透社采访了两位资深的眼科专家。迈克尔医生说,在生活中,我们身边一些人的眼睛有着非常微小的差别,比如说,眼部肌肉不均衡。在正常的情况下,大脑可以将这些微小的差别自然地调整好。但 3-D 电影给人以不同以往的视觉体验,这种体验会迫使人脑产生很大的精神压力,故而使这类人极易产生头痛感。

8   黛博拉医生说,在正常的情况下,人的双眼会从两个略微不同的角度观察事物,经过大脑的加工处理,产生立体感。而 3-D 电影中的立体画面产生的方式与平时人们眼睛与大脑相互调节产生立体画面的方式并不相同。一篇刚发表在《消费者报告》杂志上的文章指出,15% 的观众在观看 3-D 电影的时候感觉头痛和眼睛疲劳。

9   这一娱乐活动的未来可能会越来越追求立体效果,但是对相当大的一部分观众来说,观看 3-D 电影绝非是一种愉悦的体验。他们并非是反对将 3-D 电影作为其发展的一种选择,他们所反对的是好莱坞将 3-D 电影常态化,使其成为一种大众的制片方式。电影公司市场部主管们的看法是对的,观众是乐意获得一种家中无法得到的视觉体验。但是,他们的赌注却下错了方向。

Exercises

I. Reading Comprehension

1. B 2. B 3. B 4. D 5. D

II. Vocabulary and Structure

1. B 2. B 3. C 4. C 5. A 6. A 7. D 8. C 9. B 10. C

III. Translation

1. 3-D technology is taken as the great savior of the film industry.

   3-D 技术被人们认为是电影行业的伟大救世主。

2. Hollywood studios favor 3-D because consumers have so far been willing to pay a premium to see the films.

   好莱坞的制片公司钟爱 3-D 电影,是因为到目前为止,消费者一直愿意花高价钱观看此类电影。

3. The new released movies in 3-D may induce a wave of hysterical blindness.

   新发行的 3-D 电影将会引发一阵盲目的观看热潮。

4. Analysts have expressed doubts about whether consumers' appetite for the 3-D movie can be sustained.

   分析师们对于消费者能否保持住对 3-D 电影的热情提出质疑。

5. For a significant number of viewers, watching a 3-D movie will be anything but a pleasurable experience.

   对于大多数的观众来说,观看 3-D 电影绝非是一种愉悦的体验。

Part V   Time for Fun

参 考 译 文

我知道上帝是谁了!

一个男孩问他的母亲:"妈妈,上帝是男人还是女人?"

妈妈想了一会儿说:"宝贝,上帝是男人也是女人。"

男孩有些疑惑,于是他继续问道:"那上帝是白人还是黑人?"

妈妈回答说:"上帝既是白人也是黑人。"

男孩仍然很好奇,又问道:"妈妈,那上帝是同性恋还是异性恋呢?"

妈妈有些担忧的回答道:"上帝既是同性恋也是异性恋。"

过了一会儿,男孩以为自己终于找到了答案,兴奋地说:"难道上帝是迈克尔·杰克逊!"

Unit 8

Sportsmanship

Part I   Teaching Objectives

* **Listening & Speaking:**

Help the students to be familiar with the topic — *sportsmanship* and memorize useful expressions.

* **Words & Expressions:**

Study some new words and expressions, such as *celebrity*, *ennoble*, *fealty*, *flare*, *hoist*, *huddle*, *humble*, *indulge*, *pitch*, *recall*, *resounding*, *rival*, *romp*, *thrive*, *toss*, *wink*, *hand down*, *indulge in*, *reflect on* and so on.

* **Grammar:**

Learn to use the structure of *as though*.

* **Writing:**

Understand and write *a letter of apology*.

Part II   Listening——*Favorite Sportsman*

New Words

anniversary /ˌænɪˈvɜːsərɪ/ *n.* 周年纪念, 周年纪念日

    e. g. Today is my parents' 30th wedding anniversary.

        今天是我父母结婚 30 周年纪念日。

charity /ˈtʃærɪtɪ/ *n.* 慈善团体, 慈善事业

    e. g. These homeless children received some money and clothes from some charities.

        这些无家可归的孩子收到了来自一些慈善机构的钱和衣物。

elect /ɪˈlekt/ *v.* (进行)选举, 推举

e. g. Then the congress elected its presidium.

然后代表大会选出主席团。

We elected him (to be) monitor.

我们选他当班长。

exhibit /ɪgˈzɪbɪt/ *v.* 表现,呈现,展现

e. g. He exhibited a spirit of liberality and reasonableness in the game.

他在比赛中表现出了心胸宽大和通情达理的气魄。

generous /ˈdʒenərəs/ *adj.* 慷慨的,大方的,宽宏大量的,宽厚的

e. g. He is a generous contributor.

他是位慷慨的捐助者。

It was generous of you to forgive me.

你原谅我的过错真是宽宏大量。

influential /ˌɪnfluˈenʃəl/ *adj.* 有很大影响的,有权势的,有支配力的

e. g. He is a very influential man in the government.

他在政府中是个很有影响的人物。

The fact is influential in reaching a decision.

这一因素对做出决定是有影响的。

prone /prəʊn/ *adj.* 俯卧的

e. g. The police found him in a prone position with a knife in his back.

警方发现他俯卧着,背上有一把刀。

rifle /ˈraɪfl/ *n.* 步枪

e. g. They have a few rifles. 他们有几支步枪。

target /ˈtɑːgɪt/ *n.* (射击的)靶子

e. g. The arrow missed the target.

箭未中靶。

vanish /ˈvænɪʃ/ *v.* 消失,突然不见,(莫名其妙地)突然消失

e. g. With a wave of his hand, the magician made the rabbit vanish.

魔术师手一挥,兔子便不见了。

The smile vanished from her face. 笑容从她脸上消失了。

worship /ˈwɜːʃɪp/ *v.* 崇拜,尊崇

e. g. A miser worships money.

守财奴崇拜金钱。

Phrases and Expressions

take the initiative in 主动做……

e. g. He is shy and does not take the initiative in making acquaintances.

他很腼腆,不去主动交友。

One

Listen to the CD and mark T for True or F for False according to the dialogue.

1. T 2. F 3. T 4. F 5. T

Lily: Have you ever heard of Matthew Emmons?

Adam: Yes, of course. He is a great shooter, but he didn't win the gold medal in the prone position event at the 2004 Summer Olympic. However, then it was also him who fired at the wrong target in the men's 50m rifle three-position target event to gift the gold medal to China's Jia Zhanbo.

Lily: Yes, but as we all know, he also only won the silver medal in the men's 50m rifle three-position in the 2008 Summer Olympic.

Adam: You're right. I have watched that game on TV. I remembered that his 3.3 point lead vanished when he posted a 4.4 on his final shot.

Lily: What a pity! He had missed two chances to be the champion.

Adam: Yes, it seems that God has played a joke on him. However, we can see the sportsmanship he exhibited in the game. He took the initiative in coming up to congratulate on the winner instead of complaining.

Lily: Well, I think it is very generous for him to do that, and every player should learn from him.

Adam: I agree with you.

Two

Listen to the CD and answer the following questions with the information you hear.

1. Why does the man like Messi?
   Because he thinks Messi is confident.

2. Which basketball team does the woman like best?
   Huston Rockets.

3. According to the man, what kind of ceremony has been held in 2009?
   The Awards Ceremony of the 60th Anniversary for Sports in China.

4. What has happened to Yao Ming at the ceremony held in 2009?
   Yao Ming was elected to be the most influential sportsman.

5. What does the woman think about Yao Ming?
   He thinks that Yao Ming lets us know more about NBA and he deserves the award issued to him in the ceremony.

Alice: What's your favorite sport?

Michael: I like football. I really enjoy watching the Football League on TV.

Alice: Which football team do you support?

Michael: I support F. C. Barcelona.

Alice: Who's your favorite player?

Michael: Messi at F. C. Barcelona, because he is very confident. What about you? What's your favorite sport?

Alice: I'm a true basketball fan.

Michael: Which team do you like best?

Alice: I'm really fond of the Houston Rockets right now, and I worship Yao Ming very much.

Michael: Oh, really? Then do you know The Awards Ceremony of the 60th Anniversary for Sports in China held in 2009?

Alice: Yes, My idol Yao Ming was elected to be the most influential sportsman.

Michael: He is one of the most influential players in the world sports.

Alice: Yeah, he lets us know more about NBA.

Michael: He also throws himself into charity work and public service besides basketball and becomes the most famous sports celebrity.

Alice: Yeah, he is well deserved.

1. a component of morality in sport

2. respect for others including team members, opponents, and officials

3. helping an opponent up or shaking hands with each other after a match

4. a team's calling timeouts to run up the score on an opponent

5. an enduring and relatively stable characteristic or disposition

Part III Speaking——*Spirit of the Games*

Useful Expressions About Sportsmanship

We can see the sportsmanship he exhibited in the game.

He took the initiative in coming up to congratulate on the winner.

It is very generous for him to do that.

Every player should learn from him.

What's your favorite sport?

Which football team do you support?

Which team do you like best?

He is well deserved.

Pair Work

Sample

> **Leo:** What a pity! I had to go to a wedding yesterday so I haven't watched the final of 110m hurdles.
>
> **Jane:** Well, flying man Liu Xiang won undoubtedly.
>
> **Leo:** Wow, if I am correct, it is the third gold medal he won in the national games.
>
> **Jane:** Yes, he won the grand slam.
>
> **Leo:** Did he slow down after clearing all hurdles as what he did in heat?
>
> **Jane:** No, his competitors like Ji Wei and Shi Dongpeng gave him some pressure. So in order to assure his first place he could not slow down obviously.
>
> **Leo:** Did he perform his best state?
>
> **Jane:** I think not. He said he just took a conservative policy in the national games. The game was more like a practice to him.
>
> **Leo:** He never let people down. We all know the return of the king!
>
> **Jane:** Let's wait and see his better and better performance!

Role-play

Sample

> **Dean:** Celia, do you know what is the Olympic Spirit?
>
> **Celia:** Is it mutual understanding, friendship, unity and fair play?
>
> **Dean:** Yes, it is. But, as I know there exists some negative effects brought by athletic sports. Stimulant, bribery and miscarriage of justice always puzzle the Olympic Spirit all the time.
>
> **Celia:** Yes, to some degree, they abused the gold medal and made the competition unfair.
>
> **Dean:** Therefore, someone compares those stimulants as a "cancer", "something underworld" or "the hacker of the sports community".
>
> **Celia:** It can't be more visualized! I hope it can give back pure Olympics to human beings.

Part IV   Reading

 **Text A**   **Background**

1. Thanksgiving Day

Thanksgiving Day is a harvest festival celebrated primarily in the United States and Canada. Traditionally, it has been a time to give thanks for a bountiful harvest. While there was an underlying religious element in the original celebration, Thanksgiving today is primarily

identified as a secular holiday.

Currently, in Canada, Thanksgiving Day is celebrated on the second Monday of October and in the United States, it is celebrated on the fourth Thursday of November. Thanksgiving Day in Canada falls on the same day as Columbus Day in the United States.

2. American Football

American football, known in the United States as football, is a sport played between two teams of eleven. The objective of the game is to score points by advancing the ball into the opposing team's end zone. The ball can be advanced by running with it or throwing it to a teammate. Points can be scored by carrying the ball over the opponent's goal line, catching a pass thrown over that goal line, kicking the ball through the opponent's goal posts or tackling an opposing ball carrier in his own end zone.

The sport is also played in Europe, Japan and Mexico. The International Federation of American Football acts as an international governing body for the sport. American football is closely related to Canadian football but with some differences in rules and the field.

3. Football Rules

Field and Players

American football is played on a field 360 by 160 feet (120.0 by 53.3 yards; 109.7 by 48.8 meters). The longer boundary lines are *sidelines*, while the shorter boundary lines are *end lines*. Sidelines and end lines are out of bounds. Near each end of the field is a *goal line*; they are 100 yards (91.4 m) apart. A scoring area called an *end zone* extends 10 yards (9.1 m) beyond each goal line to each end line.

Start of Halves

Similarly to association football, the game begins with a coin toss to determine which team will kick off to begin the game and which goal each team will defend. The team that wins the coin toss has three options: They may choose whether to kick or receive the opening kickoff. Or they may choose which goal to defend. They may choose to defer the first choice to the other team and have first choice to start the second half.

Game Duration

A standard football game consists of four 15-minute quarters, (12-minute quarters in high-school football and often shorter at lower levels) with a 12-minute half-time intermission after the second quarter.

Advancing the Ball

Advancing the ball in American football resembles the six-tackle rule and the play-the-ball in rugby league. The team that takes possession of the ball (the offense) has four attempts, called downs, in which to advance the ball at least 10 yards (9.1 m) toward their opponent's (the defense's) end zone. When the offense succeeds in gaining at least 10 yards, it gets a first down, meaning the team starts a new set of four downs to gain yet another 10 yards or to score. If the offense fails to gain a first down (10 yards) after four downs, the other team gets possession of the ball at the point where the fourth down ended, beginning with their first down to advance the ball in the opposite direction.

Scoring

A team scores points by the following plays:

A touchdown (TD) is worth 6 points.

After a touchdown, the scoring team attempts a try (which is also analogous to the conversion in rugby).

A field goal (FG) is worth 3 points, and it is scored by kicking the ball through the goalposts defended by the opposition.

A safety, worth 2 points, is scored by the opposing team when the team in possession at the end of a down is responsible for the ball becoming dead behind its own goal line.

Kickoffs and Free Kicks

Each half begins with a kickoff. Teams also kick off after scoring touchdowns and field goals.

After safeties, the team that gave up the points must free kick the ball to the other team from its own 20 yard line.

Penalties

Fouls (a type of rule violation) are punished with penalties against the offending team. Most penalties result in moving the football towards the offending team's end zone. If the penalty would move the ball more than half the distance towards the offender's end zone, the penalty becomes half the distance to the goal instead of its normal value.

Most penalties result in replaying the down. Some defensive penalties give the offense an automatic first down. Conversely, some offensive penalties result in loss of a down (loss of the right to repeat the down).

American Football Positions

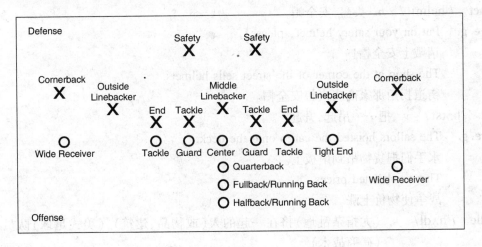

New Words

adroitly /əˈdrɔɪtlɪ/ *adv.* 熟练地，敏捷地

e. g.　She has not used chopsticks adroitly.

　　　　她用筷子还不熟练。

burly　/ˈbɜːlɪ/　*adj.* （指人）魁梧的，健壮的

e. g.　a burly policeman

　　　　魁梧的警察

celebrity　/sɪˈlebrətɪ/　*n.* 名声，名誉，名人，名流

e. g.　She said social class in America was largely decided by celebrity.

　　　　她说在美国社会阶层主要由名声决定。

　　　　Lots of celebrities were at the film premiere.

　　　　许多名人出席了电影的首映式。

ennoble　/ɪˈnəʊbl/　*v.* 使崇高，使高贵

e. g.　In a strange way she seemed ennobled by the grief she had experienced.

　　　　她因历经艰辛而似乎出奇地备受敬重。

fealty　/ˈfiːəltɪ/　*n.* 忠诚

e. g.　He swore fealty to the king.

　　　　他宣誓效忠国王。

flare　/flɛə/　*v.* （使）闪耀，（使）闪亮，（使）照耀，（使）燃烧

e. g.　The torch flares in the darkness.

　　　　火炬在黑暗中闪光。

　　　　Her flared her scarf to catch my eye.

　　　　她炫示她的围巾以引我注目。

halfback　/ˈhaːfˈbæk/　*n.* 中卫

e. g.　The star halfback hauled down the pass for a touchdown.

　　　　那位明星中卫接住远传球触地得分。

helmet　/ˈhelmɪt/　*n.* 头盔，安全帽

e. g.　Put on your safety helmet, please!

　　　　请戴上安全帽!

　　　　The shop at the corner of the street sells helmets.

　　　　街道拐角那家商店出售安全帽。

hoist　/hɔɪst/　*v.* 把……吊起，升起

e. g.　The sailors hoisted the cargo onto the deck.

　　　　水手们把货物吊到甲板上。

　　　　The war hoisted prices.

　　　　战争使物价上涨。

huddle　/ˈhʌdl/　*n.* （尤指杂乱地）挤在一起的人（或物品、建筑），（美式足球）队员靠拢
　　　　　　　（磋商战术）

e. g.　People stood around in huddles.

　　　　人们三五成群地到处聚集着。

　　　　The track led them to a huddle of barns and outbuildings.

那条路把他们带到一片杂乱拥挤的谷仓和库房。

The practice concluded with a team huddle and the players broke off to separate hoops to shoot free throws.

球队合练结束后,球员分开开始练罚球。

humble /ˈhʌmbl/ *adj.* 谦逊的,谦虚的

e.g. In my humble opinion, he will win the election.

依我拙见,他将在选举中获胜。

indulge /ɪnˈdʌldʒ/ *v.* 使(自己)沉溺于,满足(自己的欲望等)

e.g. He would indulge her every dream.

他会尽量满足她的每一个奇思妙想。

locker room /ˈlɒkəˌrʊm/ *n.* 衣帽间,休息室

e.g. Can you go in the locker room before and after games?

在赛前或者赛后你是否能进入球员休息室?

pitch /pɪtʃ/ *v.* 投,掷,扔

e.g. He was pitching the ball. 他正在投球。

quarterback /ˈkwɔːtəbæk/ *n.* (美式足球)(指挥进攻的)四分卫,枢纽前卫

e.g. The coach said he wasn't worried about any position except quarterback; that was where the shoe pinches.

教练员说除四分卫的位置以外,他不担心其他别的位置;四分卫的位置是困难所在。

recall /rɪˈkɔːl/ *v.* 回忆起,回想

e.g. As you may recall, he was in the army then.

你可能记得当时他正在从军。

John recalled attending school with Mary.

约翰回想起同玛丽一起上学的情景。

I recalled that he had mentioned the problem once.

我回忆起他曾经有一次提到过这个问题。

resounding /rɪˈzaʊndɪŋ/ *adj.* 鸣响的,回响的,回荡的,响亮的

e.g. a resounding clash of cymbals.

钹撞击出的响亮的共鸣

The astronaut was welcomed with joyous and resounding acclaim.

人们欢声雷动地迎接那位宇航员。

rival /ˈraɪvəl/ *n.* 竞争对手,敌手

e.g. He beat his rival.

他击败了他的竞争对手。

romp /rɒmp/ *n./v.* (尤指在赛跑或竞选等中)轻易获胜

e.g. The Queen's horse romped home in the first race.

女王的马在第一场比赛中轻松胜出。

The Democratic Party romped to victory in the recent elections.

民主党在最近几次选举中轻而易举地获胜。

tackler /ˈtæklə/ *n.* 抢球的队员,擒抱的队员

e.g. He is renowned as a fearless tackler.

他是一位勇于拼抢而出名的队员。

thrive /θraɪv/ *v.* 兴盛,兴隆,长得健壮

e.g. A business cannot thrive without good management.

商业兴旺离不开好的管理。

Few plants or animals thrive in the desert.

极少数植物或动物能在沙漠中苗壮成长。

thud /θʌd/ *n.* 重击声,砰的一声

e.g. The encyclopedia fell to the floor with a thud.

那本百科全书砰的一声掉在地上。

toss /tɒs/ *n./v.* (轻轻或漫不经心地)扔,抛,掷

e.g. The decision depended on the toss of a coin.

那项决定是靠掷硬币的方法做出的。

Let's toss to see who pays it.

让我们来掷钱币决定谁付账吧。

He was tossing the ball.

他正在投球。

touchdown /ˈtʌtʃdaʊn/ *n.* 触地得分

e.g. Jeremy scored three touchtowns.

杰罗姆三次触地得分。

wink /wɪŋk/ *v.* 眨眼,使眼色

e.g. Uncle John winked at me across the table.

约翰叔叔隔着桌子向我眨眼。

Phrases and Expressions

hand down 把……传递下来,遗留;流传,传下

e.g. Will you please hand down that book from the shelf?

请你把书架上那本书拿下来好吗?

Our fathers handed down these customs to us.

我们的父辈把这些习俗传给了我们。

indulge in 任凭自己沉溺于……

e.g. We indulged in an expensive supper after the concert.

音乐会后我们尽情地享受了一顿昂贵的晚餐。

I no longer indulged (myself) in smoking.

我不再抽烟了。

on hand 在场;在手边,在附近

e. g. Mr. Blake's secretary is always on hand when he appears in public.

布雷先生在公开场合露面时,他的秘书总在场。

reflect on 仔细想,回忆

e. g. I often reflect on my schooldays.

我经常回忆起我上学的日子。

take out 清除,除掉

e. g. There's a nasty mark on the tablecloth, and I don't think the usual washing powder will take it out.

桌布上有一块污迹,我想用普通洗衣粉是洗不掉的。

参 考 译 文

谦虚的橄榄球英雄

比利不仅仅是一名体育明星,他给人留下了终身难忘的印象。

1　体育需要运动员能把运动变得崇高,能够塑造体育道德和正确价值观并能在名誉上赋予实质内容。我想起一名运动员,他将一种运动道德和价值观传递给了我。我永远不会忘记他打的最后一场比赛。

2　那是 1949 年秋的感恩节,天气很冷,还刮着风。我正匆匆赶往山上的老球场,去看我所在社区的费城东瀑布队和同城对手弗兰克福德队的俱乐部橄榄球比赛。到现场看比赛的观众很多,可能有 300 到 350 人。

3　在 20 世纪三四十年代,橄榄球俱乐部在全国大城市的各个社区兴盛起来,但没有哪座城市的橄榄球俱乐部像费城这么火爆——该城居民都狂热地忠于各自社区的球队。这里,橄榄球运动把社区的居民联合了起来,让他们团结一心,艰固而永远地团结在一起。

4　我那时 8 岁,被幸运地选定在球员们从更衣室走到赛场一路上替比利拿头盔。比利是东瀑布队的明星前卫,是我们社区的一个传奇人物。

5　比赛快开始的时候,比利到我这儿来拿他的头盔。"谢谢。"他边说边"啪"地一下把头盔扣在头上,然后冲我眨了下眼睛,又说:"今天我会努力为你攻下一个达阵。"我感觉自己仿佛置身于天堂。根据橄榄球队员的标准,比利个头不算大,只有 5 英尺 8 英寸高,体重 155 英镑,但他动作流畅,可以如流水般从阻截队员的臂弯中穿过。

6　离比赛开始只有几分钟了,所有人都兴奋起来。东瀑布队掷硬币赢了,选择让对方开球。第一节比赛中,比利接到一个传球,一冲进二线,他就敏捷地绕过了一名后卫,之后,从远处看就像个俾格米人的他穿过了球门线——冲球 72 码轻松达阵。我的小心脏像个叮叮当当的锡罐一样怦怦直跳。比利得分后没恣意炫耀——没有疯狂地手舞足蹈,也没有和队友相互击掌欢呼。他只是把橄榄球递给了裁判——就像递一块面包一样。

7　第二节比赛已经进行了好一会儿,这时比利在右侧底线附近接到一记横传球。弗兰克福德队一名身材粗壮的大个子前锋搞小动作,挥肘击打他的面部——当时的头盔没有现今的这种防护面罩。比利面朝地栽倒在沙地赛场,但他马上站了起来,朝东瀑布队的边线走去。

8　"我们要报复他。"一名队友说到。比利摇了摇头,然后戴上头盔,跑进了正碰头商

讨的队友们中间。

9　下一次进攻中,当东瀑布队的四分卫将球传给比利时,我的脉搏加速了。弗兰克福德队那名身材粗壮的大个子前锋又一次准备将比利打出局,但这一次比利将身体压低成一个炮弹的形状,惊人地迅猛加速,一直撞向那名大个子前锋,那前锋砰地一声重重倒地。比利也摔倒了——但他已冲到了前场,距球门25码的位置。

10　在第三节比赛接近尾声的时候,弗兰克福德俱乐部队转守为攻得了分,以14:13领先。比赛还剩三分钟的时候,东瀑布俱乐部队在自己这方38码线的位置拿到了球。东瀑布队球员们碰头商议战术的时候,我声嘶力竭地喊道:"把球给比利!"

11　比利接到队员手递手传球,快速直向前冲,冲破了行进路线上每一位阻截队员的防守,然后突进到二线——我紧张地摒住了呼吸。比利像脚下踩着风火轮似地一路跑到了门线。

12　达阵得分! 赢了!

13　枪响时,比利的队友们将比利举起来,扛在他们的肩上,把他一路抬到了更衣室。我跟在他们后面。路上,比利随手将他的头盔抛给了我,我接住了。"它是你的了。"他说。

14　今天,每当我回想起那场比赛时,我就想到了今天的体育偶像们。拿他们和过去那些杰出的运动员相比,如今能够成为小孩子心中真正的体育偶像的人太少了,而这也限制了孩子们的希望和梦想。

15　我那时是幸运的,因为我有比利,他就是我的老爸。

Exercises

I. Reading Comprehension
Section A
1. C　2. D　3. A　4. B　5. C

Section B
1. The integrity and values of a sport.
2. Football helps unite and hold the neighborhood together.
3. Billy lowered his body into the shape of a cannonball, picked up amazing speed and exploded into the big, burly lineman.
4. They hoisted him on their shoulders and carried him to the locker room.
5. Because he thought Billy was a real hero and handed down the integrity and values of a sport to him.

Section C
1. Sportsmanship can typically be regarded as a component of morality in sport. Every sportsman should have sportsmanship. When defeated, he should greet his opponent and congratulate him. If he can't, no one will care to be his opponent because he lacks the basic decorum and the spirit of being a good sportsman. A true sportsman has a generous heart,

admits his loss and does not act with vexation. Learning to have sportsmanship is very important. It doesn't always matter whether one wins or not. What's even more important than results is what you have learned from each competition.

2. I have ever seen a football match on the spot. When the match finished, the players of the defeated team often exhibit poor sportsmanship. Shouting loudly and tossing the ball heavily, they cursed the referee for his unfair judging that led to their failure. I think this behavior is so awful that it will bring negative effect on the audiences. For example, it will let them down and they will think they are unworthy of being respected and worshipped. What's more, sometimes it will also arouse the collision between the fans. Therefore, as a model, the players should be responsible for their behaviors and can be generous enough to accept the result.

3. My favorite sports star is Ronaldo, who is a retired Brazilian football player and who last played for Corinthians. He is widely considered by experts and fans as one of the greatest players of all time. Although he was born in a poor suburban area in Rio de Janeiro, he began playing football in the street. He retired on 14 February 2011. He cited pain and hypothyroidism as the reason for his premature retirement. Even though he had been tortured all the time by his pains, he continued his devotion to football. Although sometimes there were some negative reports about him, I still love and support him because I think the spirit of insisting on the pursuit of one's dream and being diligent as a sportsman have shown us what is the most precious. Meanwhile, the perfect teamwork he has conducted with his teammates is also what we should learn from in this competitive society. He has revealed sportsmanship vividly in my mind. Therefore, I worship him very much.

II. Vocabulary and Structure
Section A
1. A   2. C   3. A   4. B   5. D   6. C   7. C   8. B   9. D   10. B

Section B
1. When the villagers were asked if they wanted the factory to be built, the answer was a resounding yes.
当村民被问及这个工厂是否要建,回答是响亮的"要建"。

2. The fireman hoisted the boy up onto his shoulder.
消防队员把那男孩举到自己的肩上。

3. He piloted the car adroitly through the traffic.
他熟练地驾车穿过来往的车辆。

4. A business will not thrive without good management.
没有良好的经营管理,事业就不会兴旺发达。

5. Knowledge makes humble while ignorance makes proud.
博学使人谦逊,无知使人骄傲。

6. She used to be an obscure novelist but now she is a celebrity.
他以前是位名不见经传的小说家,但现在却是个名人了。

7. The fire flared up as I put more logs on it.
我加上了几块木柴,火顿时旺了起来。

8. The small courtesies sweeten life; the greater ennoble it.
有点礼貌使生活愉快,多点礼貌使生活高尚。

III. Word Building

1. For the revolutionary cause, the fine sons and daughters of the Chinese nation fought and sacrificed their lives, one stepping into the breach as another fell.
中华民族的优秀儿女为革命事业奋斗牺牲,前仆后继。

2. Scientists tell us these notions are groundless.
科学家告诉我们这些想法都是毫无根据的。

3. The committee brushed off his enquiries with meaningless promises.
委员会用毫无意义的许诺来搪塞他的要求。

4. Elementary education should be available to all children.
所有的儿童都应当接受初等教育。

5. For once, she dropped her customary reserve and became quite lively.
这次,她一反平时的沉默寡言,表现得很活跃.

6. Before the recent political scandal, her reputation had been stainless.
在最近的政治丑闻之前,她的名声是洁白无瑕的。

7. The reactionary regime was thrown down by an armed uprising.
那个反动政权被一次武装起义推翻了。

8. She sat motionless, waiting for their decision.
她坐在那里一动不动,等候他们的决定。

IV. Grammar Focus

1. He speaks English as though he were an American.
2. He looked at me as though I were mad.
3. Mary loves the boy so much as though he were her own son.
4. He shrugged off my criticism as though it were beneath his notice.
5. He likes to talk big as though he were a very important person.

V. Translation

1. We indulged in an expensive supper after the concert.
音乐会后,我们尽情享受了一顿昂贵的晚宴。

2. I need time to reflect on your suggestions.
我需要时间来考虑你的建议。

3. Our fathers handed down these customs to us.

我们的父辈把这些习俗传给了我们。

4. As for her, she felt as though Ralph were a member of her family.
至于她来说,她觉得拉尔夫仿佛是她的一位亲人。

5. Solids expand and contract just as liquids and gases do.
固体也像液体和气体那样,能膨胀和收缩。

VI. Writing
Sample

City, State, Zip Code
Phone Number
Email Address
April, 2 nd, 2011
Dear Prof. Patent,

I am writing this letter to express my regret. I feel terribly sorry for missing the deadline of the book report that you assigned last week, due to a sudden illness falling upon me a few days ago. For the past few days I have been in hospital with a continuous fever, which has thus prevented me from any academic activity. I hereby submit the doctor's note.

I would be very much obliged if you could grant me another week for the task, as my health is turning better.

Please allow me to say sorry again. I want to let you know how regretful I am feeling now. Hope you can understand my situation and accept my apology.

Enclosure doctor's note

Yours faithfully,

Ling Feng

Notes

An apology letter shows that you are sorry and that you value your relationship with the other party. The sooner an apology letter is written and sent out, the better it is for the relationship. Depending on the nature of the letter, it can either be written in a friendly or a business letter format.

Friendly/Personal Apology Letter

If this is a personal letter, you should start the letter by saying that you are sorry to the recipient. Next you should admit your fault and take responsibility for your actions. Next you should ask if there is any way that you can do to help out the situation. Then you should let the recipient know that you won't let the situation happen again. To end the letter you should apologize again. a personal apology letter should be sincere.

Formal/Business Apology Letter

If this is a business letter, you should start the letter by saying you are sorry to the recipient. Next you should give an explanation as to what went wrong. Then you should try to rectify the problem. To end the letter you should apologize again.

This sort of letter has to be short and concise. The tone used should be positive and soft. The letter has to be written immediately after the mistake is committed. The letter should not talk about how the error happened, but how you are going to rectify the error, what steps you are taking to repair the damage done and how those measures will not lead to further problems. The letter should have your plan of action. The language should not be dramatic but clear and the message has to be understood easily by the reader.

Personal Apology Letter Template:

Your Address Information:

Your Address

Your City, State, Zip Code

Your Phone Number

Your Email Address

Date

Salutation:

Dear First Name,

First Paragraph:

    The first paragraph of your letter should state what you are apologizing for, give as much detail about the situation as possible and take full responsibility.

Middle Paragraph:

    Explain your role in the situation and ask for forgiveness. Don't blame the other person when you offer your apology. Promise that it won't happen again.

Final Paragraph:

    Ask that they give you another chance to prove yourself. Apologize again and say you will call or meet them as to apologize in person.

Complimentary Close:

Lovingly yours,

Signature:

Handwritten Signature

Typed Name

Useful Sentences:

I am writing this letter to express my regret...

I am writing to apologize for...

I would like to give you my apology for...

I am very sorry to say that...

I must apologize about (not) doing...

Please accept my sincere apology for...

I am writing to say sorry for. . .

I am terribly sorry, but. . .

Once again, I am sorry for any inconvenience caused.

Please allow me to say sorry again.

Hope you can accept my apologies and understand my situation.

I sincerely hope that you will be able to think in my position and accept my apologies.

I want to let you know how regretful I am feeling now.

I am sorry that I can't. . . and wish you could understand my situation.

 **Text B**　　　　　　　　**Background**

Baseball

    Baseball is a bat-and-ball sport played between two teams of nine players each. The goal is to score runs by hitting a thrown ball with a bat and touching a series of four bases arranged at the corners of a ninety-foot square, or diamond. Players on one team (the batting team) take turns hitting against the pitcher of the other team (the fielding team), which tries to stop them from scoring runs by getting hitters out in any of several ways. A player on the batting team can stop at any of the bases and later advance via a teammate's hit or other means. The teams switch between batting and fielding whenever the fielding team records three outs. One turn at bat for each team constitutes an inning and nine innings make up a professional game. The team with the most runs at the end of the game wins.

Rules and Gameplay

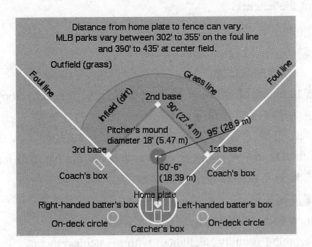

    A game is played between two teams, each composed of nine players, that take turns playing offense (batting or hitting) and defense (fielding or pitching). A pair of turns, one at bat and one in the field, by each team constitutes an inning.

    A game consists of nine innings. One team—customarily the visiting team—bats in the top, or first half, of every inning. The other team — customarily the home team — bats in the bottom, or second half, of every inning.

The goal of the game is to score more points (runs) than the other team. The players on the team at bat attempt to score runs by circling or completing a tour of the four bases set at the corners of the square-shaped baseball diamond. A player bats at home plate and must proceed counterclockwise to first base, second base, third base, and back home in order to score a run. The team in the field attempts both to prevent runs from scoring and to record outs, which remove opposing players from offensive action until their turn in their team's batting order comes up again. When three outs are recorded, the teams switch roles for the next half-inning. If the score of the game is tied after nine innings, extra innings are played to resolve the contest. Children's games are often scheduled for fewer than nine innings.

There are three basic tools of baseball: the ball, the bat, and the glove or mitt. Protective helmets are also standard equipment for all batters.

At the beginning of each half-inning, the nine players on the fielding team arrange themselves around the field. One of them, the pitcher, stands on the pitcher's mound. The pitcher begins the pitching delivery with one foot on the rubber, pushing off it to gain velocity when throwing toward home plate. Another player, the catcher, squats on the far side of home plate, facing the pitcher. The rest of the team faces home plate, typically arranged as four infielders — who set up along or within a few yards outside the imaginary lines between first, second, and third base — and three outfielders. In the standard arrangement, there is a first baseman positioned several steps to the left of first base, a second baseman to the right of second base, a shortstop to the left of second base, and a third baseman to the right of third base. The basic outfield positions are left fielder, center fielder, and right fielder. A neutral umpire sets up behind the catcher.

New Words

batboy /ˈbætbɔɪ/ *n.* 棒球队球童

    e. g. Although he is unable to be a pitcher, he can be a good batboy.

            虽然他成为不了一名投球手,但是他可以做一名好球童。

clobber /ˈklɒbə/ *v.* 狠揍,(不停)猛打,彻底击败

    e. g. It seems that Jimmy is going to clobber John in the baseball match.

            看起来吉米是要在棒球赛中痛扁约翰了。

grin /grɪn/ *v.* 露齿而笑

    e. g. She grinned with delight. 她高兴地咧开嘴笑。

            He was grinning proudly, delighted with his achievements.

            他为自己的成就感到高兴,自豪地咧着嘴笑。

handle /ˈhændl/ *v.* 处理,应付,对待

    e. g. He refused to allow his secretary to handle confidential letters.

            他不让秘书处理机密信件。

Do you know how to handle the machine?

你知道怎样操作这台机器吗?

inning /ˈɪnɪŋ/ *n.* 一局

e.g. In a baseball match, there are usually nine innings. 棒球比赛通常进行九局。

locomotive /ˈləʊkəˌməʊtɪv/ *adj.* 移动的,有移动力的,产生运动的

e.g. locomotive power 移动力

pitcher's mound /ˈpɪtʃəsmaʊnd/ *n.* 投球区

e.g. You're a catcher, so do not stand in the pitcher's mound.

你是一个接球手,所以不要站在投手区。

punch /pʌntʃ/ *v.* 用拳猛击

e.g. He punched the man on the head.

他一拳狠狠地打在那个男人的头上。

retrieve /rɪˈtriːv/ *v.* 寻回,找回,恢复,挽回,扭转颓势

e.g. Yesterday I retrieved the bag I left in the train.

昨天我取回了遗留在火车上的包。

He did his best to retrieve the situation, amidst some laughter.

他在哄笑中尽力挽回尴尬的局面。

shrimp /ʃrɪmp/ *n.* 虾,小虾,矮小的人

e.g. Shrimps are a popular type of seafood.

小虾是比较普遍的一种海味。

He's a shrimp.

他是个矮子。

slide /slaɪd/ *v.* 滑动,滑行

e.g. She slid along the ice.

她沿着冰面滑行。

snarl /snɑːl/ *v.* 龇牙低吼,咆哮着说,气急败坏地说

e.g. The dog snarled at me.

这狗对我低吼。

She snarled abuse at anyone who happened to walk past.

谁碰巧走过,她就冲谁叫骂。

stamp /ˈstæmp/ *v.* 重重地踩在(地面)上等,跺

e.g. He stamped in anger.

他气得直跺脚。

strike zone /ˈstraɪkzəʊn/ *n.* (击球的)好球部位

e.g. Although it was not in the strike zone, he pounded the ball.

虽然不在好球范围内,但他还是击打了球。

swing /swɪŋ/ *v.* (使)摇摆,(使)摇荡,(使)旋转

e.g. The monkey was swinging in the tree.

猴子在树上荡来荡去。

He was swinging his arms.

他在摇摆手臂。

He swung the axe and with one blow split open the door.

他挥动着斧子一下就把门劈开了。

tackle /ˈtækl/ *v.* 抢球，抢断，抢截，铲断

    e. g. Foul tackle from behind. 背后抢截犯规。

tie /taɪ/ *v.* 与……成平局

    e. g. We were tied in the last 3 minutes. 在最后三分钟我们打成了平局。

trophy /ˈtrəʊfɪ/ *n.* （为竞赛获胜者颁发的）奖品，奖杯，纪念品，战利品

    e. g. The cup is a cherished trophy of the company.

        那只奖杯是该公司很珍惜的奖品。

        He hung the lion's head as a trophy.

        他把那狮子头挂起来作为狩猎纪念品。

Phrases and Expressions

at bat   轮到击球

    e. g. Pete is on deck, waiting his turn at bat.

        彼特准备就绪，正在等着轮到他击球。

be big at heart   心胸开阔

    e. g. He's someone who is big at heat, so he will forgive you.

        他是一个心胸开阔的人，他会原谅你的。

cut it out   停止，住手（口）

    e. g. Cut it out. Stop being so mushy!

        够了，别那么肉麻！

reach out   （使）伸出

    e. g. He reached out and took my arm.

        他伸出手来扶住我的胳膊。

        A tree reaches out its branches towards the light.

        树枝向阳光处伸展。

strike out   用力打，猛烈攻击

    e. g. The man lost his temper and struck out wildly.

        那人因发怒而大打出手。

take advantage of   利用

    e. g. They took advantage of the hotel's facilities.

        他们充分利用旅馆的设备。

try out   试用，试验，选拔

    e. g. We won't be able to tell what skills the man has until we try him out.

        要等试用一个时期以后，我们才能知道这人有什么专长。

Scientists tried out thousands of chemicals before they found the right one.

科学家们试验了数千种的化学药品才找到一种合适的。

wipe out　了结,彻底摧毁,消灭

e. g.　This last payment will wipe out your debt to me.

这最后一笔付款将了结你欠我的债务。

We are always ready to wipe out any enemy who dares to attack.

我们时刻准备着消灭一切胆敢来犯之敌。

参 考 译 文

心 胸 开 阔

1　我最好的朋友拉里特别矮小。我们上五年级时,拉里矮小得跟一年级生一样。虽然他身材矮小,但他有开阔的心胸。此外,他思维敏锐。所有认识拉里的孩子都很喜欢他。

2　拉里酷爱运动,可有些运动项目他参加不了,比如橄榄球。对方球员在阻截时,一下子就可以抱住他并把他彻底摔倒。不过有一项运动似乎是为他而设的——棒球。他是我们的明星队员。在球场上,他的接球和投球就跟我们最高大的队员一样。

3　我记得他第一次来到我们少年棒球联合会球队试打时的情景。教练瞅了他一眼,摇了摇头。"我很抱歉,不行,我们需要身高体壮的球员。听我说,球童我们倒需要!"拉里只是咧嘴一笑,说道:"给我一次机会试试。要是你还认为我球技差的话,那我就给你当个最好的球童!"教练用尊敬的目光看着他,递给他一根球棒,说道:"好吧,一言为定。"

4　每次他都会被保送上第一垒,而教练明白如何利用这一优势。当他看到拉里的腿能跑多么快和他处理球有多么好后,他弯身拍了拍拉里的背说道:"队里有你我感到骄傲。"

5　那个赛季我们连胜。昨天是我们最后一场比赛。在争夺冠军上,我们和慧星队积分相同。他们的投手马特·克伦肖是个从没喜欢过拉里的刻薄男孩——可能就是因为他从没能使拉里三击不中而出局。

6　我们设法不让慧星队在第九局的前半局占到优势。轮到我们上场击球时,两队平局。当马特经过我们队的队员替补席走向投球区的时候,他对拉里吼叫道:"你干吗不回去跟你的白雪公主呆在一起?"

7　我听到他说这话,就跳了起来,准备给他一拳。这时,拉里走到我们中间。"别这样!"他嚷嚷说,把我从马特身边推开。"我能为我自己干架。"

8　马特看上去像是要狠揍拉里一顿,可我的朋友伸出一只手说道:"咱们赛棒球,行吗?我知道你想要你们队赢,想必投球给我这样的一只小虾米够难的。"

9　"你的意思是说你是个孬种。你连挥棒击球的机会都没有!"马特说完就大步走向投球区,拉里慢慢放下了伸出的手。

10　轮到拉里上场击球时,我们已经有两人出局。垒上没有人,教练告诉拉里像往常一样等着被保送上垒。拉里坚持等了三个坏球,对方再投出一个坏球他就能走上一垒了。

11　后来,出于某种原因——或许因为马特管他叫"孬种"——拉里举棒准备击打下一个投球。来球根本不在好球部位,可他却举棒击打,他的击球又准又狠。我们听到响亮的"啪"的一声,看见球从外场上方飞过。对方不得不去追球,而拉里的腿开始启动,就好似火车头轮子,越跑越快,踏了二垒和三垒,径直向本垒奔去。慧星队终于捡到球,把它扔给接球手。接球手接到球时,拉里已经在他身下安全滑垒了。

12　这局我们赢了,比赛就此结束,我们是冠军。被授予冠军奖杯后,我们把它给了拉里,并且轮流把他架在肩膀上绕场一周。

13　经过马特时,我正架着他。他说:"把我放下一会儿。"他走向马特,再次伸出早些时候马特曾拒绝去握的手。

14　"比赛很精彩,"拉里说道,"你们几乎胜出了……"

15　马特看着拉里,似乎看了很长一段时间,不过最后他还是握了拉里的手。

16　"你可能是个小虾米,"马特说,"可你决不是孬种。你们该赢。"

17　随后我和拉里跑回到队里,我们全队去了比萨饼店庆祝胜利。我的确为有拉里这样的朋友感到骄傲。正像我说的,他确实心胸开阔。

Exercises

I. Reading Comprehension

1. D　2. A　3. B　4. D　5. C

II. Vocabulary and Structure

1. A　2. C　3. B　4. D　5. B　6. D　7. A　8. D　9. A　10. C

III. Translation

1. We, busy city dwellers, often fail to take advantage of our many opportunities for cultural enjoyment.
   我们这些忙碌的城市居民常常不能利用机会享受文化。

2. By collecting clothing we all tried to reach out to those affected by the earthquake.
   我们大家都努力收集衣物支援遭受地震灾害的人们。

3. We are determined to wipe out any enemy who dares invasion.
   我们决心消灭一切敢于来犯之敌。

4. We should try out all the equipments before setting up the experiment.
   实验前,我们应检验所有的设备。

5. In a recent article she strikes out at her critics.
   她最近写了一篇文章对批评她的人给与猛烈回击。

Part V   Time for Fun

参考译文

第一次乘飞机

约翰逊先生从前未乘过飞机,他读过许多关于飞行事故的报道。所以,有一天一位朋友邀请他乘自己的小飞机飞行时,约翰逊先生非常担心,不敢接受。不过,由于朋友不断保证说飞行是很安全的,约翰逊先生终于被说服了,登上了飞机。

他的朋友启动引擎开始在机场跑道上滑行。约翰逊先生听说飞行中最危险的是起飞与降落,所以他吓得紧闭双眼。

过了一两分钟,他睁开双眼朝窗外望去,接着对朋友说道:"看下面那些人,他们看起来就象蚂蚁一样小,是不是?"

"那些就是蚂蚁",他的朋友答道,"我们还在地面上。"

Unit 9

Attitude

Part I   Teaching Objectives

* **Listening & Speaking:**

  Help the students to be familiar with the topic—*attitude* and memorize useful expressions.

* **Words & Expressions:**

  Study some new words and expressions, such as *adversity*, *bear*, *confront*, *deflate*, *extraordinary*, *flaw*, *inspiring*, *optimistic*, *repulse*, *resent*, *uplifting*, *be born with*, *deprive of*, *free from*, *in return*, *warts and all* and so on.

* **Grammar:**

  Learn to use the structure of *just as*.

* **Writing:**

  Understand and write *a letter of advice*.

Part II   Listening——*Attitudes to Life*

New Words

adjust   /əˈdʒʌst/   *v.* （改变……以）适应，调整，校正

  e. g.   The man adjusted very precisely.

  那个人调得很准。

optimistic   /ˌɒptɪˈmɪstɪk/   *adj.* 乐观的

  e. g.   He is an optimistic young fellow.

  他是位乐观的年轻人。

  She is not optimistic about the outcome.

  她对结果并不乐观。

transfer   /trænsˈfɜː/   *v.* 转移，迁移

e. g. The company has transferred to an eastern location.

这家公司已搬到东部某地。

I intend to transfer the property to my son.

我想把这笔财产转给我儿子。

Phrases and Expressions

be not all roses 并非十全十美,未必完全安逸

e. g. Life is not all roses, and it has ups and downs.

人生并非十全十美,也有盛衰沉浮。

rack one's brains 绞尽脑汁

e. g. He had to rack his brains to solve that complicated problem.

他不得不绞尽脑汁去解决那个复杂问题。

Dialogue One

Listen to the CD and mark T for True or F for False according to the dialogue.

1. T 2. F 3. F 4. F 5. T

Script

Jack: Sometimes I'm really tired of this kind of life. People are always competing with one another. It seems there's no true love among people nowadays.

Cathy: To some extent you're right. Competition is everywhere and it is tough. We have to compete with others in order to survive. But that does not mean love has gone.

Jack: Oh? I really doubt it. Can't you see people rack their brains trying to defeat their opponents? It's so cruel.

Cathy: Actually, competition is not as frightening as you see it. No competition, no progress. Come on, just have a right attitude towards it.

Jack: I don't know if I can be more optimistic a little bit. Anyway, I'll have a try.

Cathy: Don't feel that way. You can't always be the best one. The most important thing is that you've made progress.

Jack: Maybe I need some time to adjust myself.

Cathy: Sure. It does take time.

Dialogue Two

Listen to the CD and answer the following questions with the information you hear.

1. Why was the woman late for work?

   Because the traffic was really bad.

2. What did the woman's boss do when she was late for work?

   Her boss yelled at her.

3. Did the woman remember to save everything when she tried to transfer them into the disk?

No, she totally forgot it.

4. Did the woman believe that there was the bright side just then?

No, she didn't.

5. According to the dialogue, what did the man suggest the woman to do if she couldn't redo it?

Just choose to learn something from the mistakes that have been made.

Script

Danny: How's work today?

Tina: It's been a crazy day today. First, I was one hour late. You know, the traffic is really bad. Then I got yelled by my boss.

Danny: Oh, man.

Tina: That's not all. After that, I sat down, working on my computer. when I tried to transfer everything into the disk, I found my disk was broken.

Danny: You forgot to save it?

Tina: I totally forgot. The goddamn disk was broken. I just lost a whole-day's work. It's like I've been working like a mad man and I got nothing finally.

Danny: Buddy, it's not the end of the world. There are always two sides to everything. Try to look on the bright side. Everything will be good.

Tina: If there were the bright side.

Danny: Calm down. They are already mistakes. If you can not redo them, just choose to learn something from them.

Tina: I just made a promise that I shall never stay up late again.

Danny: That's it. See, that's the bright side of mistakes. You can always learn something from them.

Tina: I see your point, buddy, but I...

Danny: There's no such thing as ifs or buts. What happens is you're talking to your friend and he's trying to be a real friend. You didn't lose your job anyway.

Tina: All right, thanks. I feel much better now.

Spot Dictation

1. give us the inspiration needed during those turbulent times in our life

2. it may be the single most effective way to increase happiness

3. 25% higher on life satisfaction afterwards

4. are happier and more peaceful

5. Gratitude is one powerful emotion

Part III   Speaking——*Positive Encouragement*

Useful Expressions About Attitude

No competition, no progress.

You can't always be the best one.

The most important thing is that you've made progress.

It's not the end of the world.

There are always two sides to everything.

Try to look on the bright side.

Everything will be good.

We all make mistakes, and that is life.

Life is not all roses.

Attitude is everything.

Pair Work

Sample

Bob: Charlotte, did you have your super?

Charlotte: No, I don't want eat anything.

Bob: Why? Don't you feel well?

Charlotte: I'm down in spirits.

Bob: What's up?

Charlotte: My manager jumped on me for my mistake today.

Bob: You must not feel depressed about such a trivial thing.

Charlotte: I think I'm too clumsy. I can do nothing well.

Bob: You'd better shape up if you want to get the job done.

Charlotte: But I have doubt to myself.

Bob: Cheer up! Don't let me down. We all make mistakes, and that is life.

Role-play

Sample

Allen: Did you hear about what happened to Mike?

Jennifer: Yeah, how could I not? He just had a kidney transplant.

Allen: He said he has to quit his job, and his wife...

Jennifer: Yeah... even his wife left him.

Allen: I know life is not all roses, but still, that's just too much. Do you think he will pull through?

Jennifer: Well, I think he will.

Allen: Yes, it is said that he is the kind of guy who never says die.

Jennifer: Certainly. He's now trying his best to look for a new job.

Allen: Good. As we all know, attitude is everything. I'm sure he can get it through.

Jennifer: You're right and good luck to him.

Part IV   Reading

Text A   **Background**

1. Ed and Deb Shapiro

They are the authors of sixteen books on personal development, meditation and social action, many of which are published in over seventeen languages; and they have led meditation retreats and personal development programs worldwide for over 25 years. They are corporate consultants and personal coaches, working with CEO's and senior management. They have hosted their own TV series, CHILL OUT, which was rated the most popular show on Channel Health TV in London.

Together they have been deeply inspired by HH the Dalai Lama, who has even written a personal foreword for the new book. They began teaching together in 1988 after being empowered and encouraged by their teachers.

They have been featured on Oprah. com, in *The Sunday Times*, *The Evening Standard*, *The Daily Mail*, *Variety*, *OK Magazine*, *Hello Magazine Celebrity Health Special*, and on New Dimensions Radio.

2. Nick Vujicic

Born in 1982 in Melbourne, Australia, without any medical explanation or warning, Nicholas Vujicic (pronounced Voy-a-chich) came into the world with neither arms nor legs.

Throughout his childhood Nick dealt not only with the typical challenges of school and adolescence such as bullying and self-esteem issues; he also struggled with depression and loneliness as he questioned why he was different to all the other kids surrounding him; why he was the one born without arms and legs. As Nick grew up he learned to deal with his disability and started to be able to do more and more things on his own.

After school Nick went on with further study and obtained a double bachelor degree majoring in accounting and financial planning. By the age of 19, Nick had started to fulfill his dream of encouraging others by sharing his story through motivational speaking.

In 2005, Nick was nominated for the "Young Australian of the Year" Award, which is a large honor in Australia.

Nick shares with his audiences the importance of vision and dreaming big. Using his own experiences in worldwide outreach as examples, he challenges others to examine their perspective and look beyond their circumstances. He shares his view of ceasing to see obstacles as problems, but instead begin to see them as opportunities to grow and reach out to others. He stresses the importance of how attitude can be the most powerful tool we have at our disposal, and illustrates how the choices we make can have a profound effect on our lives and the lives of those around us. Nick shows through his own life that the major keys in fulfilling our biggest dreams are persistence and choosing to embrace failure as a learning experience, rather than allowing the guilt and fear of failure to paralyze us. According to Nick, the victory over his struggles throughout his journey, as well as his passion for life can be credited to his faith, his family, his friends and the many people he's encountered during his life who have encouraged him along the way.

New Words

acceptance /əkˈseptəns/ *n.* 接受,认可,赞成,赞同
  e. g. We have the pleasure to ask your acceptance of our presents.
    恭请接受我们的礼物。
    The new laws gained widespread acceptance.
    新法令受到广泛赞同。

adversity /ədˈvɜːsətɪ/ *n.* 不幸,灾祸,逆境
  e. g. As fire tries gold, so does adversity try virtue.
    烈火炼真金,逆境见美德。
    A well-prepared mind hopes in adversity and fears in prosperity.
    有充分准备的人,在逆境中充满希望,在顺境中不忘担忧。

altitude /ˈæltɪtjuːd/ *n.* 高度,海拔
  e. g. The plane flew at an altitude of 20 000 feet.
    这架飞机在两万英尺的高空飞行。

awe /ɔː/ *n.* 敬畏,惊惧,惊叹
  e. g. The sight filled us with awe.
    这景色让我们大为惊叹。

awkward /ˈɔːkwəd/ *adj.* 不优美的,难看的,令人尴尬的,使人难堪的
  e. g. She is an awkward girl.
    她是一个笨手笨脚的女孩。
    John is so shy and awkward that everyone notices him.
    约翰如此害羞狼狈,以至于大家都注意到了他。

bear /beə/ *v.* 成功地经受,经受住,经得住,经得起(考验等),耐得住
  e. g. Her claim can bear close examination.
    她的要求经得起仔细检查。

confront /kənˈfrʌnt/ *v.* 面对,对抗,与(某人)对峙
  e. g. A soldier has to confront danger.
    士兵须面对危险。

deflate /dɪˈfleɪt/ *v.* 缩小,挫败锐气,使泄气

e. g.　I was quite deflated by her lack of interest in my suggestions.
　　　　他对我的建议兴趣不大,令我感到十分气馁。

extraordinary　/ɪksˈtrɔːdɪnərɪ/　*adj.* 意想不到的,令人惊奇的,不平常的,不一般的,非凡的

e. g.　It's extraordinary that he managed to sleep through the party.
　　　　真想不到他竟然从聚会开始一直睡到结束。
　　　　She was a truly extraordinary woman.
　　　　他是位非常杰出的女性。

eye-opening　/ˈaɪˈəʊpənɪŋ/　*adj.* 很有启发的,使瞠目吃惊的

e. g.　It is eye-opening to put theories that we have learnt from textbooks into practice.
　　　　将书中所学到的理论应用于实践是很有启发意义的。
　　　　It made them feel eye-opening that the wanted man had been arrested in just one hour.
　　　　通缉犯于一小时之内被捕获,这使他们惊讶得目瞪口呆。

flaw　/flɔː/　*n.* 缺点,瑕疵,缺陷

e. g.　The flaw in this stamp makes it less valuable.
　　　　这张邮票因为有点缺陷,不那么值钱。

inspiring　/inˈspaɪərɪŋ/　*adj.* 鼓舞人的,激励的,启发灵感的,使人感兴趣的

e. g.　His inaugural speech was very inspiring.
　　　　他的就职演说很鼓动人心。

inspire　/ɪnˈspaɪə/　*v.* 鼓舞,激励,赋予某人灵感,启迪

e. g.　His speech inspired the crowd.
　　　　他的演说鼓舞了群众。
　　　　You inspired me by playing the piano so beautifully.
　　　　你弹奏的优美的钢琴曲激发了我的灵感。

ultimately　/ˈʌltɪmɪtlɪ/　*adv.* 最后,最终

e. g.　Ultimately, the war had to end; it cost too much in both lives and dollars.
　　　　由于人员伤亡过重和花费过多,战争最终不得不终止。

unhampered　/unˈhæmpərɪd/　*adj.* 无妨碍的,无阻碍的

e. g.　A correct solution of this problem is one of the factors for the unhampered development of guerrilla warfare.
　　　　这个问题的正确解决,是游击战争顺利发展的条件之一。

uplifting　/ʌpˈlɪftɪŋ/　*adj.* 令人振奋的,使人开心的

e. g.　an uplifting experience 振奋人心的经验
　　　　a suitably uplifting ending for the film
　　　　该影片有一个恰到好处、鼓舞人心的结局

repulse　/rɪˈpʌls/　*v.* 击退,驳斥,拒绝

e. g.　The charge was repulsed.
　　　　冲锋被击退了。
　　　　At the first brush, the enemy was repulsed.

敌人在第一次交火时就被击退了。

resent /rɪˈzent/　*v.* 对……感到愤怒

e.g.　He resented his friend's remark.

　　　　他怨恨他朋友所说的话。

resentment /rɪˈzentmənt/　*n.* 愤恨,不满,怨恨

e.g.　Don't let your resentment build up.

　　　　别让你的怨恨郁积起来。

　　　　A greater cause for resentment is the discrepancy in pay.

　　　　导致愤怒的更主要原因是报酬上的差异。

skipper /ˈskɪpə/　*v.* 担任船长,球队队长等

e.g.　He was skippering a small boat with his kids in the park then.

　　　　他那时正和他的孩子们在公园里划小船。

yardstick /ˈjɑːdstɪk/　*n.* 比较或衡量的标准,尺度

e.g.　The new test provides a yardstick against which to measure children's learning.

　　　　新的测试提供了一个标准去检测儿童的学习。

Phrases and Expressions

at times　有时,间或

e.g.　His language is a bit vulgar at times.

　　　　他说话有时有点粗俗。

be born with　天赋的,生而具有的

e.g.　He was born with no arms and we should try our best to help him.

　　　　他生来就没有胳膊,所以我们应该尽力帮助他。

be worthy of　值得的,应得的

e.g.　There occurred nothing that was worthy of being mentioned.

　　　　没有值得一提的事发生。

come near to　接近

e.g.　Such actions come near to treason.

　　　　这种行为近乎叛国。

deprive of　剥夺某人的……

e.g.　They deprived the criminal of political rights for all his life.

　　　　他们剥夺那罪犯的终身政治权利。

　　　　These misfortunes almost deprived him of his reason.

　　　　这些不幸的事几乎使他丧失了理智。

free sb from　把某人摆脱或脱离……,使某人解放出来

e.g.　Try to free yourself from all prejudices.

　　　　尽量消除一切偏见。

in return　作为报答,反过来

e. g. We should help those who are in trouble, without asking for rewards in return.

我们应该不求回报地帮助那些有困难的人们。

warts and all 不隐瞒缺点,不遮丑

e. g. You agreed to marry me, warts and all!

是你同意和我结婚的,我又没掩饰缺陷.

参 考 译 文

态度如何决定人生

1　杯子里有半杯水,你认为它是半杯空还是半杯满？不管度过了多么糟糕的一天、一个月或一年,要改变境遇,保持积极态度是关键。埃得·夏皮罗和德布·夏皮罗诠释了在人生道路上如何接受自己的身份和现状,感激所拥有的幸福。

2　我们都听说过一些奇人,他们克服了生命中的巨大苦难。没人会说生活容易,然而决定其挑战精彩度的可能常常是自己的态度。我们刚看了尼克·武伊契奇积极向上、令人感动的录像。这位现年25岁的非凡人物出生时没有四肢,靠一小片木板走路,但他现在可开车、打高尔夫、钓鱼、划船,两眼炯炯有神,笑容非常灿烂。他给孩子和成人讲述自己鼓舞人心的故事,把他们感动得流泪,并彻底改变了他们。尼克曾在超过15个国家演讲,听众逾200万。

3　尼可克服了我们大多数人永远不可能经历的磨难,看过他的经历,我们心存敬畏,并敢于直面一些想法和时刻,如我们认为自己不足、没用,甚至无能,或者我们感到自己太笨、太胖、太矮或太高。我们时常把自己的一些小问题看得太大,以至很容易受其支配。生命中发生的一切你并非都能选择,但你能选择如何应对:害怕或喜爱、发怒或接受。你不能控制风向,但可调整风帆。

4　像尼克这样的人能鼓励你坦然接受自己的现状,明白自己虽然有缺点,但实际上很优秀。他的乐观和真诚让人倍感亲切,他对自己的一切都认可。我们需要从一个顽强抗争过的人那里亲耳听到这一切后才敢相信,才茅塞顿开。但当你真正认识到生活是赐福,不管有多艰难,你都会尊重这种抗争。

5　我们许多人一遭遇失意挫折,便对上天心生怒火与怨恨,又哭又叫。上帝为什么这样对我？失去健康,错过提升,丢掉工作,这些事情难以承受,可能更难以理解。但我们不能用人的思维去度量神圣的天意,我们眼中的坏事很可能最终是好事。

6　生活的要求有时看似非常艰难,但我们不应怨天尤人。上帝从不会只索取而不赐予。失忆与困难往往就是上帝为我们打造更美好未来的工具。

7　人生绝不是一条笔直顺畅的通道,我们可以轻松前行。它是一座有无数岔路的迷宫。在穿过它时,我们必须找寻自己的路,可能会迷路,也可能会走进死胡同。但只要有信心,上帝总会为我们打开一扇门,他或许不是我们想象的那扇门,但最终一定会证明这扇门不错。

8　有时你容易怨恨生活给予你的一切,会盯着那些没得到或做不了的,这会让你失望沮丧。相反,应该关注你所拥有的、你所能做的,并且对此心怀感激。如果你认为不可能,那就不可能;如果你认为可能,那就肯定可能！正如尼可所言:"要认为自己不够好或一无是处,这不符合事实。态度决定高度。"

Exercises

I. Reading Comprehension

Section A

1. C 2. B 3. D 4. B 5. A

Section B

1. From a video about him.

2. Someone like Nick can inspire you to accept yourself just as you are, warts and all, and to see that despite the flaws, you are actually beautiful.

3. We shouldn't raise a cry of anger and resentment against heaven and measure Divine Providence by the yardstick of human mentality.

4. Life is no straight and easy corridor along which we travel free and unhampered, but a maze of passages, through which we must seek our way, now lost and confused, now checked in a blind alley.

5. Your altitude is about the height to which you can grow. We all have the potential to reach tremendous height. However, many of us won't even reach half that potential. Your altitude is fueled by your attitude. The manner in which you approach any situation is crucial to the results that you ultimately achieve. If you can maintain a positive attitude, you will always be able to find the positive side in almost any situations.

Section C

1. Life is full of challenges, whereas life is also full of opportunities. Sometimes you will be stuck in various setbacks, which will make you depressed and frustrated. However, setbacks sometimes may not be so bad and it may also imply some chances. We have got to realize that the closed door can be a blessing sometimes. If you get terminated from your job, maybe it indicates new opportunities. Therefore, be grateful for the many times that God has closed doors to us just to open them in the most unexpected places. All in all, attitude is everything.

2. No one can be avoided from encountering setbacks in our lives. However, what we will do in setbacks can determine definitely whether we can do better in the future or not. Our attitude determines our mindset, which is the foundation on which our responses sit. The attitude we choose to have will determine how effective we are. The way that we approach our lives and our outlooks for the future are the fuel for a positive attitude. Without a positive attitude, it will be hard for us to imagine a better tomorrow. Therefore, when in setbacks, believe in choice, believe in possibilities and believe in the future to maintain a positive attitude.

3. Zhang Haidi became a paraplegic at the age of 5, following four operations that removed

tumors in her spine. She has overcome a lot of difficulties in the following years. She believes that disabled people should acquire knowledge and skills according to their characteristics, for living and for society. She started to learn English 20 years ago. She published a bilingual book *Beautiful English*. She also translated some western literature works into Chinese and introduced the art of living with her husband who is not disabled. She is regarded as China's Helen Keller or China's Pavel Korchagin. Since the early 1980s, she has been a heroine for the Chinese youth to learn from, especially the disabled persons.

II. Vocabulary and Structure
Section A
1. B 2. A 3. C 4. D 5. D 6. B 7. A 8. D 9. C 10. A

Section B
1. When confronted with the evidence of her guilt, she confessed.
   她面对罪证供认不讳。

2. We are pleased that our son showed fight; previously he had allowed the other boys to <u>dominate</u> him.
   我们很高兴儿子表现出了反抗精神,以往他总是任别的孩子支配他。

3. Their critics seem to <u>resent</u> them because they have a flair for self-promotion.
   批评者似乎对他们很气愤,因为他们在自我标榜上很有天分。

4. The unforgettable sarcasm that can <u>deflate</u> a candidacy is the worst nightmare of any presidential hopeful.
   那些难以忘记的讽刺挖苦,对于任何有可能成为总统的人,都是一场噩梦。

5. The audience was carried away by his <u>inspiring</u> speech.
   他鼓舞人心的发言使听众听入了神。

6. At the meeting his plan met with universal <u>acceptance</u>.
   在会上,他的计划得到了普遍接受。

7. If you do not drive carefully, I shall be obliged to <u>deprive you of</u> your licence.
   如果您不谨慎驾驶,我将不得不吊销您的驾照。

8. <u>Ultimately</u>, the war had to end, because it cost too much in both lives and dollars.
   由于人员伤亡过重和花费过多,战争最终不得不终止。

IV. Word Building
1. There was an <u>abundance</u> of good food at the party.
   宴会上有丰盛的食物。

2. The rightful heir should obtain his rightful <u>inheritance</u>.
   合法的继承人应获得其合法的继承权。

3. He could not account for his <u>absence</u> from school.
   他无法说清楚为什么旷课。

4. He is a person who is true to his words, and you can place complete <u>reliance</u> on his promise.

他是一个恪守承诺的人,你可以充分信赖他的许诺。

5. Showing no fear, he answered the questions with <u>confidence</u>.

他毫无畏惧地,很有把握地回答了那个问题。

6. The play is full of <u>references</u> to the political events of those days.

剧本涉及当时的许多政治事件。

7. He showed remarkable <u>endurance</u> throughout his illness.

他生病期间表现出非凡的忍耐力。

8. When it comes to learning, <u>diligence</u> is indispensable.

说到学习,勤奋是必不可少的。

IV. Grammar Focus

1. The electric current cannot go through an insulator, just as water cannot go through iron.

2. Air supports a balloon just as water does a ship.

3. Just as water has its pressure, the electric current has its voltage.

4. Absence can diminish little passion and increase great one, just as the wind can blow out a candle and fan a fire.

5. Just as it is important to find the right pulse for a piece of music, you must find the right rhythm to live your life.

V. Translation

1. It is generally believed that <u>education can free people from poverty</u>.

人们普遍认为教育能使人摆脱贫穷。

2. We are not in a position to accept your claim as we cannot <u>bear the responsibility for the unforeseen circumstances.</u>

对于贵方的索赔我们不能接受,因我们不能对无法预测的情况承担责任。

3. I <u>bought him a drink in return for</u> his help with my computer repair.

我请他喝酒以酬谢他帮我修电脑。

4. We decided to <u>buy an old country cottage, warts and all.</u>

我们决定毫不遮丑地买下一幢乡村旧别墅。

5. <u>No matter how hard the work was</u>, no complaint ever passed her lips.

不论工作多艰巨,她从来没有怨言。

VI. Writing

Sample

Dear John,

  You have asked me for my advice with regard to whether you should study history or computer science at university. I will try making some conductive suggestions here.

  In my humble opinion, university is the preparation for your career. You should consider studying a subject which will best equip you to earn a living. Computer science offers more job opportunities than history. We are now in a high-tech age. So it would be necessary for everyone to be equipped with computer skills merely to earn a living in a foreseeable future!

Of course, you don't have to devote all your university time to studying computers. I would recommend that you continue reading history in your spare time. In that way, you will find your leisure hours are enriched when you are preparing yourself for a worthwhile career in computer science.

I hope you will find these suggestions useful and I would be ready to discuss this matter with you in further details. Whatever you decide to do, good luck with your studies!

Yours sincerely,

Ling Yu

Notes

A letter of advice is to provide information or advice. Its writing can be a difficult, yet rewarding experience. It is a unique opportunity to share your wisdom with someone you care about. When a friend, a family member, or a work colleague approaches you for suggestion, be careful and considerate in your response. Your comments are likely to be taken quite seriously, so if you don't feel confident, you should politely decline your friend's request.

Some tips for writing a letter of advice are provided as follows.

Respond quickly to the request for advice. Take time to think your answer carefully. Let the person know that you care about him/her and the situation by sending your letter as quickly as possible.

Keep the tone respectful. No matter how you may feel personally about the subject you are asked to give advice on or the person who asked for it, keep the tone respectful, helpful and congenial.

Avoid direct or implied criticism.

If you cannot give advice, express your regret. Suggest that someone else would be in a better position to offer such advice. Avoid Personad comments or expressions unless they are complimentary. If the topic is a sensitive one, measure your approach carefully.

Language. Strong language may discourage your reader. Make your advice simple and to the point.

Give personal advice only when asked. Remember that personal advice should be given only when someone has sincerely asked for it. Even then it must be done with caution and sensibility.

If someone takes your advice, maintain a tone of appreciation without any hint of condescension or feelings of superiority. Emphasize the reader's strengths, rather than the value of your advice.

When you are the one seeking advice, turn to the people you can rely on. They should be trusted and be willing to keep your request confidential.

Show gratitude with a nice letter. When someone responds to your request for advice, whether you ultimately take the advice or not, it is always a good idea to write a thank-you letter or a letter of appreciation.

If you take the advice or the suggestion, give appropriate recognition. If you did not take it, you may wish to keep the advice letter at hand for future reference in case you should change your mind.

Some Sentence Structures in Writing a Letter of Advice:

I am writing in reply to...

I would like to suggest that...

I am writing with my suggestion about...

I am writing to express my views concerning...

You have asked me for my advice with regard to... and I will try to make some suggestions.

I feel that it would be beneficial if...

I would like to suggest that...

I would recommend that...

If I were you, I would...

You may consider doing...

It would seem to me that you could...

As you may agree that...

I hope you will find these suggestions/proposals/recommendations helpful/practical/useful.

I wish you take my suggestion into account.

I would be very happy to see improvements in this regard.

I would be ready to discuss this matter in further details.

Text B   Background

Gratitude is considered to be a familiar concept to us. We were taught to say "please" and "thank you," in quite an early age. We learned about grace and gratitude through religious scripture, or through the celebration of Thanksgiving. We live in a fairly abundant society where most people have their basic needs met and live a comfortable life style. Why then is being grateful not so easy? This is because true gratitude is not a scripted or obligatory emotional experience. Being simply polite is not the same as gratitude.

We live a society that emphasizes materialism and individuality, and we are encouraged to have more and be the best. By comparing ourselves to others and focusing on what we lack, we experience an attitude of greed and envy, and it will become increasingly more difficult to experience gratitude. Gratitude is a skill that we need to learn. We're not born with understanding and knowing how to be grateful, appreciative and thankful. If you weren't taught to say "thank you" and appreciate what you have as a child, there is still time to turn around your thinking, and there is a good reason to do so.

What is gratitude?

Science shows that that people who keep a gratitude journal or a list of what they're thankful for report having more energy, improved mood, more life satisfaction, and are more supportive to others.

It helps us focus on the good things we have, instead of on what we lack.

It promotes positive social interactions and makes it more likely we'll help others.

It helps us cope with difficulties and overcome traumatic experiences.

It helps us focus on the positive and access positive memories.

How to increase gratitude?

There are many ways to begin making gratitude a habit in your life. Research has revealed that gratitude can be enhanced by writing a letter of gratitude to someone you need to thank and then by personally delivering it to them.

If this is a little too outgoing, you can also count your blessings everyday by writing a list of what you're thankful for and the positive things that happened to you throughout the day.

Meditation can also help to cultivate an attitude of gratitude by taking time to focus on the people who have helped and offered you support in your life.

Telling someone they did a good job or saying thank you offers some feelings of appreciation.

Focusing on what we have and what's going well aren't easy. However, sometimes the key to getting through distress and misfortune is to find value amidst the chaos. We need to find something we're grateful for.

By making gratitude a habit in your life you will begin to see the impact it has on your overall level of positivity.

New Words

clutch /klʌtʃ/ *v.* 抓住,紧紧抓住

 e. g. The mother clutched her baby in her arms.
    母亲紧紧地把婴儿抱在怀里。

composure /kɒmˈpəʊzə/ *n.* 镇静,沉着

 e. g. Throughout the crisis he retained his composure.
    危机期间,他始终保持镇定。
    He wondered at her composure in such a crisis.
    他很惊讶,在这样的危机中,她竟泰然自若。

elaborate /ɪˈlæbərɪt/ *v.* 详尽说明

 e. g. You understand the situation; I needn't elaborate any further.
    你对情况是了解的,我不必再进一步详谈了。

etch /etʃ/ *v.* (感情)明显地表露在(脸上),(脸上)明显流露出(感情),铭刻在心里/记忆里/脑海里

    e. g.   Anthea's face was etched with horror.

            安西娅的脸上流露出恐惧。

            Tiredness and despair were etched into his face.

            疲乏与失望刻在他的脸上。

gratitude /ˈgrætɪtjuːd/ *n.* 感激,感谢

    e. g.   Her eyes were immediately filled with gratitude.

            她的眼里立刻充满了感激之情。

grave /greɪv/ *adj.* (指情况)严重的,严肃的,庄重的

    e. g.   This heavy rain could have grave consequences.

            这场大雨会造成严重后果。

            The situation was grave.

            情况是严重的。

            He looks terribly grave.

            他脸色很严肃。

mission /ˈmɪʃən/ *n.* 使命,任务,天职

    e. g.   The minister was sent to Spain on mission.

            这位部长奉命前往西班牙。

pen /pen/ *v.* 围来,关进围栏(指牲畜等)

    e. g.   pen up the chickens for the night.

            把鸡关进鸡棚过夜。

            She feels pent in by her life as a housewife.

            她觉得做家庭主妇很受束缚。

semi-conscious /semiˈkɒnʃəs/ *adj.* 半意识状态的

    e. g.   The state between sleeping and waking is semi-conscious.

            半睡半醒是一种半意识状态。

sniffle /ˈsnɪfl/ *v.* 抽鼻子,抽噎

    e. g.   I wish you wouldn't keep sniffling.

            但愿你别总抽鼻子就好了。

            I have been sniffling for weeks.

            我伤风鼻塞了好几个星期。

            The child stopped crying, but kept on sniffling.

            那个小孩子不哭了,但仍在抽噎。

summon /ˈsʌmən/ *v.* 传唤,召集,传讯(出庭)

    e. g.   The general summoned all his officers.

            将军把所有的军官召集到一起。

            He was summoned as a witness by the court.

            她被法庭传唤作证。

trickle /ˈtrɪkl/ *n.* 滴,淌,细流

    e. g.   A trickle of blood ran down his neck.

             血自他的颈部一滴滴地流下。

testimonial /ˌtestɪˈməʊnjəl/ *n.* 感谢信

    e. g.   I'm here writing this testimonial to thank you for the help.

             在此写封感谢信,谢谢你的帮助。

unsolicited /ˌʌnsəˈlɪsɪtɪd/ *adj.* 未被恳求的,主动提供的

    e. g.   An anonymous person, to whom I shall eternally be in debt, mailed me an unsolicited copy.

             那是一个匿名人主动邮寄给我的一个副本,我永远欠这个人一份情。

Phrases and Expressions

be grateful for 感谢(感激)……,对……心存感激

    e. g.   We should be grateful for your trial order.

             如承试订货,不胜感激。

by this time 到现在

    e. g.   By this time, he was hopelessly pickled.

             到这时他已经烂醉如泥了。

commit to 对……作出承诺,承担义务,担负责任,使(自己)致力于……

    e. g.   I must go. I have committed myself to the club tonight and the members are expecting me.

             我得走了,我已经答应今晚去俱乐部,会员们正等着我呢。

             He has committed himself to the cause of education.

             他已决心献身教育事业。

             A thinking person must commit himself to working for peace.

             一个有头脑的人必须致力于为和平而工作。

fight back 强忍住,抵抗,反击

    e. g.   It was difficult for her to fight back her tears.

             她很难忍住不流泪。

             The aggressors were fiercely fought back.

             侵略者遭到猛烈的抵抗。

pass on 去世

    e. g.   He passed on in his sleep.

             他在睡眠中死去。

pull up 把……拉过〔起来〕

    e. g.   Pull your chair up to the table.

             把你的椅子挪近桌子。

             Please pull up a chair and join the conversation.

             去拿把椅子坐过来一起聊天。

参考译文

感激的态度

1 中午时分,我接到电话得知祖父病危,情况急剧恶化。我的家人不知道他还能活多久,白天亲朋好友陆陆续续去探望他,从本质上来说是在告别。

2 我知道我必须去医院告诉他我是多么爱他。谁知道他还有多少时间?在驱车前往医院的路上,我想象着在还没来得及告诉他他对我有多么重要时,他就离我而去。我强忍着不让眼泪流出,希望在见到他时保持镇静。

3 到达医院后,我赶紧寻找他的病房。护士离开房间后,我走到祖父的床前。我发现他已处于半昏迷状态,被各种仪器包围着,身上还插着许多管子。我跪下来,轻声地对他说:"你好,爷爷。"

4 还是感到有些不好意思说出口,但我决定在离开他之前一定要让他知道。我拉过一把椅子,开始跟他说话。我询问他的情况时,他告诉我:"我会好起来的。"尽管我们都清楚那不是实话。然后他微笑着问我过得怎么样。

5 爷爷想知道我的情况,这让我感到受到特殊关爱,但我清楚我来这里不是来跟他谈我的近况的。我有使命在身,我已作出决定要向他表达我的感激之情。我鼓起勇气,握住他的手。他从我脸上的表情推测我有要紧的话要和他说。

6 我靠近他,说道:"爷爷,我有话要对你说。"此时泪水滚滚流下我的脸颊。不是涓涓细流,而是像决堤一样。这些年来集聚在心而未向他表露的爱,此时一泻千里。

7 我深吸了一口气,努力重新镇静下来。这时,我们四目相交。你知道人们说过眼睛是灵魂的窗户吧?我们通过眼神相互倾述,在这短短的数秒中,情感的交流远远胜过语言。在抽泣中,我大声说道:"爷爷,我只是想让你知道我是多么爱你。我希望你已经知道,但我还是想要确定一下。"

8 爷爷咧嘴笑了,说:"我知道。谢谢你告诉我。"他进一步说道:"我在这个星球上所拥有的一切就是我的家人和我对他们的爱。如果我有什么需要你做的,那便是要你善待家人,善待你的母亲、你的父亲、还有你的兄弟。这就是我要你做的。"我一个劲地点头,许诺我一定会的。我们俩转过头,注意到护士进来了。

9 她告诉我探视时间已经结束,她需要做些检查。我紧紧握住我爷爷的手,给了他一个温暖的拥抱,对他所有的爱在我全身的血管中涌流。我知道这很有可能是最后一次见到他了。我走出他的房间,然后又停了下来。我必须再看他最后一眼。我转过身,看见他微笑着向我挥手告别。爷爷依然在微笑,尽管病入膏肓,他依然快乐。这一形象永远地铭刻在我的记忆里。

10 那天我所领悟到的改变了我的一生。

11 从那以后,我开始向人们表达我是多么地爱他们、关心他们、尊重他们。我主动给我所接触的人(比如,我的美发师、我的金融顾问、我的健身教练)写热情洋溢的感谢信。我每周进城一次给那些无家可归的人端上免费的披萨饼。每天早晨我醒来后的第一件事就是开一张单子,一一写下我应对之心存感激的一切。

12　因为我们实在难以知道我们所关爱的人能在我们的生活中停留多久,所以我为自己写下了一条座右铭:"感激的态度"。

Exercises

I. Reading Comprehension

1. C　2. B　3. A　4. D　5. B

II. Vocabulary and Structure

1. A　2. D　3. B　4. C　5. D　6. C　7. D　8. A　9. B　10. C

III. Translation

1. The thought came to him that maybe the enemy had fled the city.

   他突然想起可能敌人已经逃出城了。

2. He has decided to commit himself to the cause of education.

   他已决心献身教育事业。

3. To her amazement, her son was grateful for her willingness to call and offered an apology of his own.

   让她吃惊的是,儿子对她主动打来电话很是感激,并承认了自己的过错。

4. Please pull up a chair and join the conversation.

   请拿把椅子过来一起聊天。

5. On such an occasion, it was difficult for her to fight back her tears.

   在这种场合下她很难强忍住泪水。

Part V　Time for Fun

参 考 译 文

我老婆的照片

　　一个生意人走进一家酒馆,在吧台坐下,点了一杯加冰的双料马提尼。喝完,那生意人往自己衬衣的口袋里瞥了一眼,然后又让服务员把杯子满上。

　　喝完,生意人又往自己衬衣的口袋里瞥了一眼,然后又让服务生帮他把杯子满上。

　　这时酒馆的服务生说话了,"呃,老兄,我整个晚上给你倒马提尼都没有问题,但你得告诉我,你为什么在点下一杯酒前都要往自己衬衣的口袋里偷偷看那么一眼。"

　　生意人回答,"我看的是我老婆的一张照片。如果照片上的人开始变得好看起来,那就说明我喝得差不多了,该回家了。"

10 Unit

Family Affection

Part I Teaching Objectives

* Listening & Speaking:

Help the students to be familiar with the topic — *family affection* and memorize useful expressions.

* Words & Expressions:

Study some new words and expressions, such as *balk*, *bristle*, *critical*, *detention*, *glum*, *halting*, *pound*, *retreat*, *smash*, *swell*, *wane*, *wince*, *back up*, *come clean with*, *patch up*, *set out to*, *stumble over* and so on.

* Grammar:

Learn to use the structure of *even though*.

* Writing:

Understand and write *a note for leave*.

Part II Listening——Family Affection

New Words

publication /ˌpʌblɪˈkeɪʃən/ *n.* 发行,出版

   e. g. This book is ready for publication.

        这本书已准备好,随时可以出版。

schoolmaster /ˈskuːlˌmɑːstə/ *n.* 教师,校长

   e. g. His teaching career began as a village schoolmaster.

        他的教师生涯是从一名乡村小学教师开始的。

        The schoolmaster pushed out the teacher.

校长开除了这位老师。

treat /triːt/ *n.* 宴请,款待,请客

    e. g. She was cooking fish as a treat.

            她正在煮鱼来款待客人。

Phrases and Expressions

in a way 在某种程度上

    e. g. In a way, I'm glad you made that mistake, for it will serve as a warning to you.

            在某种程度上说,你犯那个错误我倒感到高兴,因为它可以对你敲警钟。

lay a foundation for 为……奠定基础

    e. g. We have to lay a solid foundation for industry.

            我们必须为工业打下一个坚实的基础。

 One

Listen to the CD and mark T for True or F for False according to the dialogue.

1. F 2. T 3. F 4. T 5. T

Script

Jim: Mom, Happy Mother's Day! Here's my card.

Mom: What a surprise! Thanks, Jim. It's beautiful.

Jim: Thank you for your love and care over the years. I appreciate it, ma.

Mom: This is the best card I've ever received.

Jim: Mom, what can I do for you today?

Mom: Nothing, son. I'm already very happy.

Jim: How about dinner tonight? My treat.

Mom: Actually, I prefer we eat at home. We'll have more time to catch up that way.

Jim: I'm sorry I haven't dropped in that much these past few years. Business has kept me too busy. I apologize.

Mom: Oh, don't mention it. I'm proud of you.

Jim: Thanks, ma. I love you so much.

Mom: I love you, too.

 Two

Listen to the CD and answer the following questions with the information you hear.

1. For what was the man congratulating the woman?

   For the publication of her new book.

2. Why did the woman hate her parents when she was young?

   Because they always told her to do what she really didn't want to do.

3. How did the woman feel when seeing the peers playing happily?

She felt gloomy.

4. According to the woman, does she still hate her parents now?

No, she doesn't.

5. What does the man think the woman should do now?

She should show her gratitude for her parents.

Script

John: Lisa, congratulations to you for the publication of your new book.

Lisa: Thank you.

John: What do you think is the key factor to your success?

Lisa: Well, the only thing I want to tell you is to do as your parents say, because they will never wanna hurt you.

John: Really?

Lisa: Well, you know, when I was young, I hated my parents so much because they always told me to do what I really don't wanna do, just like reading, playing the piano, running, etc.

John: How did you feel then?

Lisa: I felt so gloomy when I saw my peers playing happily with each other. However, today I become a writer, and in a way, I'm sure that it is my parents who have laid a foundation for me as a writer.

John: Yes, I see. I also think that you should show your gratitude for your parents now.

Lisa: Of course, I couldn't agree with you anymore. We always say that a good mother is worth a hundred schoolmasters.

Spot Dictation

1. to hug and kiss her babies a lot

2. warmth, understanding, happiness, generosity and forgiveness are the most crucial

3. regards touch as an essential ingredient to the growth of a child just as diet and exercise

4. Expression of affection benefits the giver as much as the receiver

5. the affection is expressed towards those who are worried, depressed and insecure

Part III　Speaking——*Parents' Devotion*

Useful Expressions About Family Affection

Thank you for your love and care over the years.

I appreciate it.

This is the best. . . I've ever received.

I'm already very happy.

I'm sorry I haven't dropped in that much these past few years.

Oh, don't mention it.

I'm proud of you.

I love you so much.

Do as your parents say, because they will never wanna hurt you.

A good mother is worth a hundred schoolmasters

I couldn't agree with you anymore.

Take care of yourself at college.

I hope you will study hard at college.

Concentrate on your studies.

Don't worry about us.

I will try my best.

Good luck to you.

Pair Work

Sample

Wife: I don't want you to be worried, but our son has some bad habits now. He says painful words everyday.

Husband: What words? Can you tell me?

Wife: He says "kick mommy, beat mommy, don't want mommy" very quickly if I do something that he doesn't like. You know, if I wash his face or change his clothes, things will happen like that.

Husband: Honey, I don't know what to tell you. Of course Tony is a young child. But do not underestimate his ability to learn and reason.

Wife: Yes, but sometimes he is just not reasonable.

Husband: I suggest you treat him with patience, affection and respect. If he needs to do something, like going to bed, or being washed, etc., please guide or help him to get it done, and lead him with gentleness.

Wife: It's easy to say, but I will try.

Husband: Motivate Tony to cooperate by rewarding his good behavior. Do not emphasize punishment for bad moods. Do not threaten him with punishment if he resists the behaviors you desire.

Wife: I know my parents sometimes threaten to punish him. But this doesn't work. Instead he picks up another bad habit.

Role-play

Sample

A: Daisy, you were also a mother of young kids. So, can you tell me what you did when your kids didn't behave very well?

B: I know Mark is your only child. You may do it differently from what I did. Sometimes I would tap their hands when they made troubles.

A: I do it, too. You know, sometimes when we eat, my child would pull a dish towards him and grab it with his hands and eat. He does it very often. I really get mad. I can't help spank him sometimes.

B: And what does your wife do?

A: My wife criticizes me when I do that. She says that I can't change a child's behavior by using force. She is learning what I am doing now.

B: But spoiling a child is not going to do him good either! You've got to have patience with him and teach him. It's not easy, I know. It's hard.

A: Yeah. I'm still learning how to control his behavior and my temper. My child is almost two years old, and I've learnt the "distraction" technique when he cries for something.

Part IV   Reading

 **Text A**   **Background**

1. Henry Miller

Henry Valentine Miller (December 26, 1891—June 7, 1980) is an American novelist and painter. He is known for breaking with existing literary forms and developing a new sort of "novel" that is a mixture of novel, autobiography, social criticism, philosophical reflection, surrealist free association and mysticism, and one that is always distinct about and expressive of the real life. His most characteristic works of this kind are *Tropic of Cancer*, *Tropic of Capricorn* and *Black Spring*. He also writes travel memoirs and essays of literary criticism and analysis.

2. Tropic of Cancer

Tropic of Cancer is a novel by Henry Miller, first published in 1934 by the Obelisk Press in Paris, France. Its publication in 1961 in the United States by Grove Press led to an obscenity trial that was one of several that tested American laws on pornography in the 1960s.

While famous for its frank and often graphic depictions of sex, the book is also widely regarded as an important masterpiece of the 20th century literature. In 1998, the Modern Library ranked *Tropic of Cancer* 50th on its list of the 100 best English-language novels of the 20th century. Time magazine included the novel in its TIME 100 Best English-language Novels from 1923 to 2005. The novel included a preface credited to Anaïs Nin (although allegedly penned by Miller himself).

The book was distributed by Frances Steloff at her Gotham Book Mart, in defiance of censorship pressures.

3. Youth for Christ

Youth for Christ (YFC) is the name of a number of previously unaffiliated evangelical Protestant religious campaigns which led to the creation of Youth for Christ International in 1946.

Youth for Christ is a worldwide Christian movement working with young people around the globe. Motivated by their faith in Jesus Christ, they share the good news of God with young people.

Youth for Christ is made up of tens of thousands of indigenous people in over 100 nations, each seeking to spread God's message of hope to the young people of their nation.

What do Youth for Christ programs look like? It's like asking what the weather is like in a large country. It all depends on where you are. Youth for Christ uniquely reaches young people in ways that are relevant to them in the context of their culture and life circumstances.

New Words

balk /bɔːk/ *v.* 畏缩不前,犹豫

> **e. g.** I wanted to buy the dress, but I balked at the high price.
> 我本想买这件连衣裙,但一看价钱太高就犹豫了。

bristle /ˈbrɪsl/ *v.* (毛发等)竖起,发怒,被激怒,怒发冲冠

> **e. g.** The dog's hair bristled when the visitors came to the door.
> 当来访者走近大门时,那条狗的毛都竖起来了。
> They bristled at his denigrating description of their activities.
> 听到他在污蔑他们的活动,他们都怒发冲冠。

critical /ˈkrɪtɪkəl/ *adj.* 评论的,鉴定的,批评的

> **e. g.** We must inherit in a critical way.
> 我们要以批判的方式继承。

detention /dɪˈtenʃən/ *n.* 滞留,留堂

> **e. g.** Will you give me after school detention?
> 放学后你留我堂吗?

glum /glʌm/ *adj.* 阴郁的,阴沉的

> **e. g.** She laughed at his glum face.
> 她嘲笑他闷闷不乐的脸。

halting /ˈhɔːltɪŋ/ *adj.* 踌躇的,迟疑不决的

> **e. g.** She always speaks in a halting way.
> 她经常说话吞吞吐吐。

hypothetical /ˌhaɪpəʊˈθetɪkəl/ *adj.* 假设的,假定的,爱猜想的

> **e. g.** This is a purely hypothetical situation.

这纯粹是一种假设的情景。

pinch /pɪntʃ/ *v.* 捏,掐,夹,拧

    e. g.   The mother pinched her baby black and blue.

            这位母亲将她的孩子掐得青一块紫一块的。

pound /paʊnd/ *v.* 连续重击,连续敲打

    e. g.   The boxer pounded his opponent.

            那拳击运动员猛击对手。

            The waves were pounding on the shore.

            惊涛拍岸。

prod /prɒd/ *v.* 刺激,促使

    e. g.   My father have to prod me to do my homework.

            我父亲只得督促我做家庭作业。

retreat /rɪˈtriːt/ *v.* 撤退,退却

    e. g.   Our soldiers force the enemy to retreat.

            我们的战士迫使敌人后退。

smash /smæʃ/ *v.* 打碎,粉碎

    e. g.   The cup fell and smashed.

            杯子落下来摔碎了。

            The key was lost, so we had to smash the door open.

            钥匙丢了,所以我们只得将门砸开。

swollen /ˈswəʊlən/ *adj.* 膨胀的,肿起的,浮肿的

    e. g.   Her thin hands were twisted by swollen knuckles.

            她那双纤手因肿大的指关节而变了形。

tap /tæp/ *v.* 轻打,轻敲

    e. g.   This music sets your feet tapping.

            这音乐能使你的双脚不由自主地跟着打拍子。

tie-dyed /ˈtaɪdɪd/ *adj.* 扎染,将衣服打结后再染

    e. g.   Behind me, a kid in a tie-dyed sweatshirt tried to shove a potted plant onto the conveyor belt.

            在我身后,一个穿扎染汗衫的小孩挤着我把花盆放在传送带上。

wane /weɪn/ *v.* 变小,亏缺,呈下弦

    e. g.   The moon was waning, and in such a waning light, it is very difficult to see the enemy.

            月亮渐亏,而在这如此暗弱的光下,很难看见敌人。

wince /wɪns/ *v.* 退缩,赶紧避开,畏缩

    e. g.   He winced inwardly at her harsh tone.

            她那严厉的语气令他胆寒。

            He winces at the memory of that experience.

            他一回想起那番经历就畏缩起来。

windowsill /ˈwɪndəʊˌsɪl/ *n.* 窗台,窗沿

    e. g. The bird hopped up onto the windowsill, looking for crumbs.

        鸟儿跳上了窗台寻找面包屑。

    e. g. He speaks in a halting voice.

        他说话吞吞吐吐。

Phrases and Expressions

back up   堵塞

    e. g. The accident backed up traffic.

        事故使交通堵塞。

come clean with   全盘招供

    e. g. We believe he knows what she did, but he has not come clean with the international community.

        我们相信他知道她究竟做了什么,但他还没有向国际社会说清楚。

in advance   预先,提前

    e. g. There is no reason that you shouldn't tell them in advance when you are going.

        你没理由不事先告诉他们你打算要走。

patch up   修补,包扎,弥补

    e. g. All the worn-out clothes have been nearly patched up.

        所有的破旧衣服都快补好了。

        They have tried to patch up their differences.

        他们已经设法弥合了他们的分歧。

set out to   开始

    e. g. The government has set out to make many needed reforms.

        政府开始进行许多必要的改革。

stumble over   结结巴巴地说

    e. g. When reading a list of words quickly, he stumbled over such words.

        当快速阅读一大串单词的时候,他结结巴巴地说这样的单词。

参 考 译 文

月亮破了,爸爸能补

    1 3 岁时,我指着亏缺的月亮说:"月亮碎了,但爸爸能补好它。"每当家里的化粪池堵塞了,窗沿的漆被山谷的烈日晒得翻了卷,父亲总能解决这些问题。直到多年后,我已不再相信父亲能补圆月亮,我的母亲仍乐于重复我天真的话语。

    2 孩提时代,我总是等着爸爸从葡萄园归来,然后跟着他进到他的作坊,里面堆满了锯子、焊工面罩和大大小小分类堆放的钉子。我长大了,不好和哥哥再住同一个房间,爸爸将木桩打入土中,度量新地基。当时,我上二年级,带着小学生特有的热情和技巧帮爸爸扩建

房间。

3 我被锤子砸到了手指,父亲教我用拇指与食指捏住钉子,轻敲钉帽,直到钉子自己能立直。那年夏天的生日,我得到一个金质小盒子,我把爸爸的照片剪成心形放在里面,挂在项链上。

4 升入初中后,我开始用较为挑剔的目光看父亲。每晚全家祈祷时,爸爸会大声朗读《圣经》中的段落,我注意到他念得断断续续,有时还结巴。如果他在我朋友面前说"甭",我会直皱眉头。

5 离家上大学后,起初,我每月回家探望父母,后来逐渐少回家了。我迫切希望用自己正在汲取的新思想来增补父亲仅有十年级的教育水平。当我问道假如我与一名黑人男子结婚会怎样,他面露犹豫之色,我对他的种族歧视大为恼怒。我的教授布置了亨利·米勒的《北回归线》作为课堂讨论内容,父亲在教堂签署了请愿书,请求禁止这位教授教学。几个月间,我的父母变得好像两位远亲,我认识他们,却一点也不了解他们。

6 之后的两年,我转离了父亲的轨道,愈行愈远。我脱下格子棉布裙,从陆海军百货商店买来喇叭裤,搭配扎染吊带衫。我再也不发青年基督团的传单了,而是开始与一个发表过作品的诗人男子在学生活动中心喝咖啡。我们在课堂上眉目传情,给彼此讲笑话。我迫不及待地渴望与他在一起,尽管我知道他已有家室。

7 每次回家时,我为对父母隐瞒了这段罪恶的爱情而紧张不安。常常编造借口,不等周末过完就匆匆返校。当我紧张得心脏好似要跳出胸膛时,我意识到自己必须向父母坦白了。

8 "我有件事要告诉你们,"我说道,喉咙深处发紧,泪水正涌上来。"我爱上了一个人……他是已婚男人,"我哽咽着说道。

9 房间里静得吓人,我能听到鸟在未结果实的桑树上叽叽喳喳地叫。我看着爸爸,他的指关节因为操持农活而肿胀开裂,指尖粘着黑色机油。他默默地走进作坊,我没有跟着。

10 一周后,打开公寓信箱时,我认出一个信封上写有父亲的字迹。在我的记忆里,我从未收到过父亲的信。每年十二月,母亲不得不提前好几个星期就督促他给他的战友们写圣诞贺辞,最后,他拿着信纸动笔了,如同被留堂的学生般闷闷不乐。

11 我双手颤抖地打开信封。

12 "亲爱的珍,我不善言辞。"爸爸在信里写道,他说希望我快乐,祈祷上帝赐予我智慧与指引。

13 "我只知道,恋爱理应是你一生中最幸福的时光,可是你看上去是那么悲伤。"

14 我的眼前涌现出父亲努力写这封信时的场景,他在用笔修补我破粹的心。信末的字如小鱼般透过我的泪水。

15 "那么,我应该很快就能收到你的回信吧。非常非常爱你的爸爸。"

Exercises

I. Reading Comprehension

Section A

1. C   2. A   3. C   4. B   5. D

Section B

1. The author thought her father to be the one who could solve all the problems.

2. Because she loved and worshipped her father very much.

3. No, he didn't.

4. They shared glances in class and laughed at each other's jokes. She couldn't wait to be with him, even though she knew he had a wife.

5. He wanted to show how much he loved her and wanted her to be happy.

Section C

1. Although the father is not good at expressing himself, the love he gave the author is great. The only thing that he wanted his daughter is happiness. He could understand what was actually on his daughter's mind.

2. The author thought her parents couldn't understand her very well and that they seemed to have bias against her marriage to a black man, from which she thought she couldn't communicate very smoothly with her parents any longer.

3. When I was in junior school, I had the habit of writing diaries. Unfortunately, my Mom always wanted to peek at my diaries. One day, I discovered that she had opened my diary book, so I walked towards her and had a talk with her. Mom apologized to me for her behavior, and told me the reason why she did so was that she cared about me so much that she was worried about my study. I promised to communicate with her in the following days about what were on my mind to release her anxiety. I knew that she did everything for my sake. From then, we came to an agreement that she would keep a certain privacy for me and I would talk with her in time.

II. Vocabulary and Structure
Section A
1. B   2. B   3. A   4. D   5. A   6. B   7. A   8. C   9. D   10. C

Section B

1. Her poor <u>delivery</u> spoilt an otherwise good speech.
她的演讲在各方面都很好,却因表达技巧差而功亏一篑。

2. The lock was rusty, so we had to <u>smash</u> the door open.
锁锈住了,我们得把门砸开。

3. I <u>supplement</u> my grant by working in the evenings.
我除享受助学金外,还打夜工以增加收入。

4. The book contains a fascinating <u>portrait</u> of life at the court of Henry VIII.
该书生动地描写了亨利八世的宫廷生活。

5. Large numbers of prisoners have been carted off to unknown places of <u>detention</u>.
大量的囚犯被运送到不知名的地点囚禁起来。

6. She is a fairly good worker, but she needs prodding occasionally.
   她干起活来倒是相当不错,不过有时需要加以督促。

7. His parents balked at the cost of the guitar he wanted.
   他想要那把吉他,但他父母看到价格却踌躇起来。

8. His face was swollen up with toothache.
   他的脸因牙痛而肿了起来。

V. Word Building

1. She's old enough to have the freedom to do as she likes.
   她已成年了,有权做她喜欢做的事。

2. In the crash he suffered severe injuries to he head and arms.
   在事故中他头部和双臂受了重伤。

3. In answer to your recent inquiry, the book you mentioned is not in stock.
   您近日询问的书暂时无货,谨此奉复。

4. After the old king died, his son ruled over the kingdom.
   老国王死后,他儿子统治这个王国。

5. During the Norman Conquest, British officialdom took on French as their official language.
   诺曼人征服英国期间,英国官场采用法语作为官方语言。

6. His police mug-shot was seen in every paper in the world. His stardom looked to be all over.
   他在警署拍摄的嫌疑犯照片登上了世界各地的报纸,他的星运看似到此结束。

7. Jealousy can make you totally oblivious to the good things you have.
   嫉妒常使你对本身具有的优点全然不知。

8. She showed complete mastery in her handling of the discussion.
   她处理这种辩论表现得应付自如。

IV. Grammar Focus

1. He works enthusiastically as ever, even though he has retired from the leading post.

2. He's the best teacher, even though he has the least experience.

3. I held my peace, even though I wanted to tell her exactly what I thought.

4. Jack was not defeated by life, even though he is a blind person.

5. Even though I am a magnanimous person, I can't stand your behavior.

V. Translation

1. The man suspected of killing the little girl come clean after he had been questioned for a long time.
   经过长时间的审讯,这个杀小姑娘的嫌疑犯招供了。

2. The judge has issued an injunction to ban the magazines from publishing the pictures.
   法官颁发命令,禁止杂志刊登这些照片。

3. Even though he is a casual worker, he works a normal work weekly.

尽管他是一个临时工,每周也做满正常工作时间。

4. Will you help me to <u>hand out the materials for the lecture</u>?

你可以帮我分发演讲材料吗?

5. There is no reason that you <u>shouldn't tell them in advance when you are going</u>.

你没理由不事先告诉他们你何时要走。

VI. Writing

Sample

A Note for Leave

April 2nd

Dear Mr. Robert,

I'm terribly sorry that I shall be unable to attend your English class tomorrow. I would like to know if I could ask for a leave of absence.

As you may know, the summer holiday is coming and we are busy these days with hunting for a company to serve as an intern in the holiday. Fortunately, I have got an interview opportunity offered by a famous company which I have been eager to enter. However, unfortunately, they scheduled the interview tomorrow. I cherish this opportunity so much that I don't want to miss it. Therefore, I'm here to ask for a leave. Meanwhile, I am sure that I will try my best to ask my classmates for notes to catch the missed lessons when I come back, and I promise I will finish the homework on time.

I hope you can approve my leave. Thanks a lot.

Yours sincerely,

Li Lei

Notes

A note for leave has four parts, Date, Salutation, Body and Signature.

Date: The date is the time when the note is written. It is in the upper right corner of the note.

Salutation: This usually begins with Dear XXX. The blank is for the name of the person you are writing to. There is a comma behind the person's name.

Body: The body includes the reasons, and the time that you want to ask for leave. If there is a certificate, it is better to mention it and enclose it with your note.

Signature: The signature tells who writes the note. It is in the lower right corner of the note.

Some Sentence Structures We May Use When Writing a Note for Leave:

1. I'm sorry I can't... today because....

2. I'm writing to ask for a leave of... days.

3. Please excuse my absence from... today.

4. Because of this I would very much like to have a leave... days beginning on...

5. I'm writing to let you know I shall not be able to... because of....

6. I shall be very much obliged if you grant me my request.

7. I hope that my request will be given due consideration.

8. I want to ask for... days leave from... to...

9. I hope you can approve my leave.

 **Text B**　　　　　　　**Background**

Valentine's Day

Saint Valentine's Day, commonly shortened to Valentine's Day, is an annual commemoration held on February 14 to celebrate love and affection between intimate companions.

The day is named after one early Christian martyr named Saint Valentine, and was established by Pope Gelasius I in 496 A. D. It was deleted from the Roman calendar of saints in 1969 by Pope Paul VI. It is traditionally a day on which lovers express their love to each other by presenting flowers, offering confectionery or sending greeting cards (known as "valentines"). The day first became associated with romantic love in the circle of Geoffrey Chaucer in the High Middle Ages, when the tradition of courtly love flourished.

Modern Valentine's Day symbols include the heart-shaped outline, doves, and the figure of the winged Cupid. Since the 19th century, handwritten valentines have given way to mass-produced greeting cards.

New Words

adore　/əˈdɔː/　v. 崇拜,热爱,爱慕(某人);非常喜欢
  e. g.　They adored her as a living goddess.
    他们把她当作活女神崇拜。

assortment　/əˈsɔːtmənt/　n. 分类,各种各样
  e. g.　This shop has a good assortment of goods to choose from.
    该店各色货物俱全,任君选择。
    She was wearing an odd assortment of clothes.
    她穿着奇装异服。

bubble　/ˈbʌbl/　v. (情感等)激动,充溢,变得生气(或兴致)勃勃
  e. g.　She was bubbling over with happiness and enthusiasm.
    她洋溢着喜悦和兴奋。

confine　/kənˈfaɪn/　n. 界限,范围
  e. g.　Beyond the confines of human knowledge　超出人类知识的范围
    Within the confines of family life　在家庭生活的范围内

conversion /kən'vɜ:ʃən/ *n.* 变换,转化

    e. g.   He underwent quite a conversion.

            他彻底变了。

dismissal /dɪs'mɪsəl/ *n.* 遣(解)散,开除,解雇

    e. g.   The dismissal of five workmen caused a strike.

            开除五个工人引起了罢工。

exclaim /ɪks'kleɪm/ *v.* (由于强烈的情感或痛苦而)呼喊,惊叫,大声说

    e. g.   She exclaimed in astonishment at the size of the bill.

            她看到帐单上的数目吓得叫起来。

            He exclaimed that it was untrue.

            他大声说那不是真的。

frosted /'frɒstɪd/ *adj.* 被霜覆盖的

    e. g.   a frosted bread   覆有糖霜的面包

giggle /'gɪgl/ *n.* 咯咯的笑,傻笑

    e. g.   Her nervous giggles annoyed me.

            她神经质的傻笑把我惹火了。

hum /hʌm/ *v.* 发出嗡嗡声,哼唱

    e. g.   The bees were humming in the garden.

            蜜蜂在花园里嗡嗡地叫。

            She is humming a folk song that I never heard before.

            她在哼一首我以前从未听过的民歌。

nestle /'nesl/ *v.* 抱,安置

    e. g.   She nestled the baby in her arms.

            她把孩子抱在怀里。

peek /pi:k/ *v.* 很快地看,偷看,窥视

    e. g.   She peeked over the top of her menu.

            她从菜单上往外偷看。

pliable /'plaɪəbl/ *adj.* 易弯的,柔韧的,易受影响的

    e. g.   Cane is pliable when wet.

            藤条潮湿时易弯曲。

punitive /'pju:nɪtɪv/ *adj.* 处罚的,惩罚性的

    e. g.   They took punitive measures against the whole gang.

            他们对整帮人采取惩罚性措施。

reign /reɪn/ *v.* 统治,支配,盛行,占优势

    e. g.   He reign over a small kingdom.

            他统治着一个小国。

slot /slɒt/ *n.* 缝,狭槽

    e. g.   Put a coin in the slot.

将硬币放入投币口。

torrent /ˈtɒrənt/ *n.* 爆发,迸发,连续不断

 e. g. He was answered with a torrent of oaths.

    他所得到的回报是一连串的咒骂声。

trigger /ˈtrɪɡə/ *v.* 引发,引起

 e. g. The incident triggered an armed clash.

    这起事件触发了一场武装冲突。

wilt /wɪlt/ *v.* (使)凋谢,枯萎

 e. g. The flowers wilted in the hot sun.

    花在烈日下枯萎了。

    You will adore this film.

    你将十分喜欢这部电影。

Phrases and Expressions

a torrent of 大量的,一连串的

 e. g. The news unlocked a torrent of emotion.

    这个消息引发了一股情感的狂潮。

all the way 一路上,一直,完全

 e. g. We can go all the way by motorboat.

    我们可以一路上乘摩托艇去。

    He stays all the way in the game.

    他自始至终参加比赛。

    I'm with you all the way.

    我完全同意并支持你。

compare with (把……)与……相比,比得上,可与……相比

 e. g. How does your new house compare with your old one?

    你的新房子和你的旧房子比起来怎样?

    Cast iron cannot compare with steel in strength.

    铸铁在强度方面比不上钢。

devote to 致力于……

 e. g. He devotes himself to his sick wife.

    他专心照顾着他生病的妻子。

    He has always devoted himself to his music.

    他一直致力于音乐。

    A true artist is devoted to his work.

    真正的艺术家献身于他的工作。

take note of 注意,留意

 e. g. The committee has taken note of objections.

委员会已注意到反对意见。

there is no mention of 未提及

e. g.　There is no mention of the new product in the press.
新闻界没有提到这项新产品。

within the confines of 在……(范围)之内

e. g.　This question was discussed within the confines of the group.
这个问题在小组范围内进行了酝酿。

参 考 译 文

父 爱 宝 盒

1　在我还是个小女孩时,有一次因为做家庭作业,我在一个盒子里发现了爱。一个星期五晚餐时,我激动得难以自制,兴致勃勃地宣布了一个消息:"老师说下周一我们得带一个盒子到学校,用来装情人节卡片。必须是一个特别的盒子,装饰得漂漂亮亮的。"

2　母亲说:"到时候再说吧。"然后她就继续吃饭了。

3　如花儿缺水而凋谢,我的情绪一落千丈。"到时候再说吧"是什么意思?我必须得有个盒子,否则将收不到情人节卡片,那样的话,我的二年级情人节就将是场灾难。或许他们并不那么爱我,连帮我做个盒子都不肯。

4　星期六一整天,我都在忧心忡忡的等待中度过,但是根本没有人提及情人节盒子。星期日,我更加不安,然而我知道询问此事可能激怒我的父母,他们或许会大声斥责我。一整天我都在焦虑地盯着他们的一举一动。那是 1947 年,我们的家规是,子女的要求只能提出一次,否则将会受到惩罚。

5　星期日的傍晚时分,父亲把我叫到我家狭小的厨房里。餐桌上堆着了各种装饰材料:白色绉纹纸、红色美术纸、从母亲的针线筐里跳出来的零碎蕾丝和缎带。一个空鞋盒放在纸堆上面。父亲说:"咱们开始做盒子吧。"听到这话,我顿时全身都轻松下来了。

6　接下来的一个小时里,父亲把那个空鞋盒变成了一个我永远不会忘记的情人节卡片盒。他用绉纹纸包裹起丑陋的硬纸板,然后把柔韧的纸弄破,粘在中间,再在盒盖上割开一个狭长的孔,并饰以更多的白色绉纹纸。接下来,在所有我觉得合适地方贴上红心。父亲边做边哼歌,我跪在椅子上,见证这个鞋盒的魔术变身,并在父亲需要时把胶水递给他。完工后,父亲双眼闪闪发光,瘦削的脸上绽开一抹笑容:"你觉得怎么样?"

7　我回以一个拥抱,并说:"谢谢爸爸。"

8　其实我的心里乐开了花。这是父亲第一次为我投入如此长的时间。他的世界就是辛勤工作、供养家庭、宠爱母亲、管束子女,以及收听广播电台中的一切体育赛事。突然之间,我生活中一扇全新的门敞开了,我的父亲爱我。

9　星期一早晨,我要把这个漂亮的盒子带到学校,母亲找出一只棕色杂货袋来装它,以免中途损坏。如同呵护珍宝般,我把它捧在怀中,几乎感觉不到二月的严寒。我绝不会让这个美丽的情人节卡片盒遭到任何破坏。

10　老师在一个长而宽的窗台上清理出一块地方,用来在情人节到来前放置那些装饰过的盒子。我仔细看了看每个放上去的盒子,没有哪个能和我的相比。每瞥一眼我的情人节盒子,我都会感到父亲的爱意。我的心中骄傲无比。那只盒子时时闪耀着它独有的光辉。无疑,我是唯一看到那种光辉的人。

11　每天都有一些同学带情人节卡片来,塞进那些特别的盒子里。情人节联欢会那天,我们把各自的盒子拿到桌上,打开卡片。心形糖霜饼干、红色水果甜饮、情人节卡片、欢笑声充满教室,热闹的景象直到放学才结束。

12　我带着我的情人节卡片盒回家,心中满是自豪。这次我没把它藏在杂货袋里,而是捧出来让所有人欣赏。一位警察引导我们穿过一条喧闹的街道,我把盒子给他看。他拍拍我的头,高兴地大声称赞。我让每位路人都留意到我的盒子。我的父亲为我做了这个盒子,对我而言,它所饱含的父爱比里面所有的情人节卡片都重要。

13　自那以后,我再没有怀疑过父亲对我的爱。那个情人节卡片盒成为父爱的象征,这种爱意在此后几十年的情人节里一直延续着。这些年来,父亲还送过我其它礼物,但是没有哪件能超越我从那个空空的旧鞋盒里所感受到的温柔的爱。

Exercises

I. Reading Comprehension

1. A　2. B　3. D　4. C　5. A

II. Vocabulary and Structure

1. A　2. B　3. B　4. D　5. C　6. B　7. A　8. D　9. C　10. B

III. Translation

1. A series of police arrests triggered (off) the riots.
   警察的一系列逮捕行动激发了暴乱。

2. Compared with apartment hunting, my research work is a cinch.
   跟找房子相比,我的研究工作真算不上什么。

3. He rushed all the way to the station only to miss the train.
   他一路冲往车站,结果还是错过了火车。

4. This article is all about her, but there is no mention of her contributions.
   这是关于她的一篇文章,但是文中并未提及她的贡献。

5. Please take note of our signature, and regard no others as genuine.
   请记下我们的签名,其他签名均属无效。

Part V   Time for Fun

参 考 译 文

天堂里的两队男人

世上的每一个人死后都上了天堂。上帝说:"男人分成两队。一队是在世上控制女人的男人;另一队是被女人鞭打的男人。另外所有女子自成一队,跟着圣彼德去。"

队伍列好后,被女人鞭打的男人队伍有100英里长。而另一队在世上控制女人的男人仅有一人。神生气地说:"你们男人应该感到羞耻。我按照自己的形象创造了你们,而你们却被女子鞭打。看看,我唯一的儿子,站着使我骄傲。你们应该向他学习。告诉他们,儿子,你如何成为唯一站在这一队上的?"

这男子回答说:"我不知道,我太太叫我站在这的!"

郑 重 声 明

　　高等教育出版社依法对本书享有专有出版权。任何未经许可的复制、销售行为均违反《中华人民共和国著作权法》，其行为人将承担相应的民事责任和行政责任；构成犯罪的，将被依法追究刑事责任。为了维护市场秩序，保护读者的合法权益，避免读者误用盗版书造成不良后果，我社将配合行政执法部门和司法机关对违法犯罪的单位和个人进行严厉打击。社会各界人士如发现上述侵权行为，希望及时举报，本社将奖励举报有功人员。

反盗版举报电话　　(010)58581897　　58582371　　58581879
反盗版举报传真　　(010)82086060
反盗版举报邮箱　dd@hep.com.cn
通信地址　北京市西城区德外大街 4 号　高等教育出版社法务部
邮政编码　100120